Modernism and Morality

Also by Martin Halliwell

ROMANTIC SCIENCE AND THE EXPERIENCE OF SELF

Modernism and Morality
Ethical Devices in European and American Fiction

Martin Halliwell
Lecturer in English and American Studies
University of Leicester

© Martin Halliwell 2001

All rights reserved. No reproduction, copy or transmission of this publication may be made without written permission.

No paragraph of this publication may be reproduced, copied or transmitted save with written permission or in accordance with the provisions of the Copyright, Designs and Patents Act 1988, or under the terms of any licence permitting limited copying issued by the Copyright Licensing Agency, 90 Tottenham Court Road, London W1T 4LP.

Any person who does any unauthorised act in relation to this publication may be liable to criminal prosecution and civil claims for damages.

The author has asserted his right to be identified as the author of this work in accordance with the Copyright, Designs and Patents Act 1988.

First published 2001 by
PALGRAVE
Houndmills, Basingstoke, Hampshire RG21 6XS and
175 Fifth Avenue, New York, N. Y. 10010
Companies and representatives throughout the world

PALGRAVE is the new global academic imprint of
St. Martin's Press LLC Scholarly and Reference Division and
Palgrave Publishers Ltd (formerly Macmillan Press Ltd).

ISBN 0–333–91884–3

This book is printed on paper suitable for recycling and made from fully managed and sustained forest sources.

A catalogue record for this book is available from the British Library.

Library of Congress Cataloging-in-Publication Data
Halliwell, Martin.
    Modernism and morality : ethical devices in European and American fiction / Martin Halliwell.
       p. cm.
    Includes bibliographical references and index.
    ISBN 0–333–91884–3
      1. Literature, Modern—20th century—History and criticism.
    2. Literature and morals. I. Title.

PN771 .H219 2001
809.3'9353—dc21

2001024549

10 9 8 7 6 5 4 3 2 1
10 09 08 07 06 05 04 03 02 01

Printed and bound in Great Britain by
Antony Rowe Ltd, Chippenham, Wiltshire

For Laraine

'If a story seems moral, do not believe it.'
— Tim O'Brien, *The Things They Carried* (1990)

Contents

Acknowledgements	viii
Introduction: Modernity and the Crisis of Morals	1

Part I Naturalism and Decadence

1	Decadence, Naturalism and the Morality of Writing (Huysmans, Wilde, Norris, Wharton)	29
2	Books and Ruins: Abject Decadence in Gide and Mann	49

Part II Symbolic Centres of Modernism

3	Extremist Modernism: The Avant-Garde and the Limits of Art (Tzara, Huelsenbeck, Breton, Aragon)	69
4	Moral Regeneration and Moral Bankruptcy: Conrad, Faulkner and Idiocy	88

Part III Sexual and Cultural Difference

5	American Expatriate Fictions and the Ethics of Sexual Difference (Stein, Hemingway, Miller, Nin)	111
6	The Blind Impress of Modernity: Lorca, Kafka and New York	133

Part IV Modernist Trickery

7	The Modernist Picaresque: Moralists without Qualities (Musil, Hesse, Hurston, Roth)	157
8	Myths of the Magician: Klaus Mann, Thomas Mann and Nazi Germany	179
Conclusion: Liberating the Fear of Modernity		196
Notes		210
Bibliography		240
Index		257

Acknowledgements

I am indebted to colleagues and students (present and past) at the University of Leicester and De Montfort University for their support and stimulation during the formulation and writing of *Modernism and Morality*. I would particularly like to acknowledge the following for generously offering time, advice and banter: Clive Bloom, Nick Everett, Peter Faulkner, Paul Hegarty, Richard King, Andy Mousley, Judy Simons, Martin Stannard, Douglas Tallack, Imelda Whelehan and Nicholas Zurbrugg. Especial thanks go to my parents, family and Laraine for their love and for keeping my dark moods at bay. Thanks also to Erika Gaffney at Ashgate for granting me permission to include revised and extended versions of Chapters 2, 6 and 8, which originally appeared in the following form: 'Books and Ruins: Abject Decadence in Gide and Mann', *Romancing Decay*, ed. Michael St John (Ashgate, 1999); 'American Exile and Modernist Aesthetics in Kafka and Lorca', *Displaced Persons*, ed. Sharon Ouditt (Ashgate, 2001); '*Mephisto* and the Magician: Klaus Mann, Myth and Nazi Germany', *Metamorphosis*, ed. George Ferzoco *et al.* (Ashgate, 2001).

Introduction: Modernity and the Crisis of Morals

Published in 1891, Thomas Hardy's novel of tragic heroism, *Tess of the D'Urbervilles*, stylistically reflects the nineteenth-century mode of literary realism but also foreshadows some of the major moral concerns of early twentieth-century modernism. Hardy's narrator comments that although Tess's meagre education in rural Dorset does not equip her with the self-consciousness to articulate her thoughts, she nevertheless feels 'the ache of modernism'.[1] He declares that, without speaking in words of '*logy* and *ism*', she realises intuitively her condition and manages to express 'sensations which men and women have vaguely grasped for centuries'.[2] In this way, Tess is shown to tap into an ancient repository of intuitive thought, but also stands on the cusp of a new age of modernity. Her world is marked both by the kind of bleak continuity Shakespeare's Macbeth experiences as his doom approaches, 'numbers of tomorrows just all in a line [that] all seem very fierce and cruel', and the processes of technological change, represented in the novel by the garish new farm machinery.[3] The ache Tess feels, although she cannot theorise it fully, derives from the recognition that although technological change is a reality, even in the remote corners of Hardy's late nineteenth-century Dorset, it will not bring about a manifest improvement in her family's life. Indeed, social change not only denies Tess real opportunities for self-improvement (other than surrendering to the will of her male suitors), but also fails to offer a clear set of moral values that would help her to contend with such change.

The barely articulate 'ache of modernism' which nags throughout Hardy's novel, as much at the narrator as at Tess, is an ache that, at the beginning of the twenty-first century, has taken on the form of a painful bruise. A close analysis of the wounds inflicted on Tess by the forces of modernisation provides a model for inspecting the aches recurring in modernist writing from the 1890s to the late 1930s, before the social bruises of modernity had become fully manifest. This reading of *Tess* suggests that one way to approach modernism is to analyse the range of techniques adopted by modern protagonists in their attempts to change or improve their lives, whether it be through ritual, perversity, cunning, trickery, reciprocity, psychic transference or love. These devices may protect a character from the often debilitating forces of modernity, but they rarely offer a coherent philosophy; as Hardy argued, literature works best in offering 'impressions of the moment' and rarely indulges in 'the Whence and Wherefore of things ... as a consistent philosophy'.[4] However, such techniques do lend significance to an individual's struggles to transform the material, spiritual, aesthetic and moral conditions of life. Most studies of early twentieth-century writing reinforce the pessimistic vision of the modern world eroding at its edges. This book challenges such apocalyptic readings by arguing that literary modernism can also refresh our memories (as readers and critics) and bring us to a deeper understanding of some of the most exacting moral dilemmas of the twentieth century. As Michael Wood detected in the mid-1970s, we may all be 'positively arthritic with the ache of modernity', but 'it would be a form of rejuvenation to find out what the ache felt like when it was just beginning'.[5]

This book focuses on a set of concerns often touched upon by critics of modernism but rarely studied closely: namely, the engagement of modernist writers with questions of morality. Although many early European and American modernists made noisy attempts to break away from bourgeois moral values and the utilitarian ethic characteristic of Victorianism, questions of morality continued to impinge on their aesthetic concerns. Whether in the form of the internal morality of the *fin-de-siècle* aesthetes and their doctrine of *l'art pour l'art*, or in the 'artist as hero' novels of the early years of the twentieth century, a set of exacting moral problems are explored in ways which are often overlooked by critics. One problem in dealing with the interface between modernism and morality stems from the declarations of writers – from the early modernists Joris-Karl Huysmans and Marcel Proust, to Dada artists and the high modernism of James Joyce and Gertrude Stein – to deal only with art and thus escape the restrictions placed upon them by a fixed ethical agenda. However, as the posthumous publication of Thomas Mann's letters reveals about the oft-denied homoerotic concerns of his fiction, or the series of provocative poetic masks adopted by Ezra Pound, the aesthetic declarations of modernist writers can only be trusted to a degree. The primary responsibility of modernists may have been to art itself, but this belies a continued and, in many ways, a more intense interest in moral values than their seemingly more earnest literary predecessors. It is precisely in the realm of experiential morality, rather than the abstract sphere of ethics, that modernists attempted to discover a passage between personal value and social action. The fact that so many works explore the barriers – some psychic, some social – that prevent such a 'moral passage' (to use Kathryn Pyne Addelson's phrase) does not mean the writers wished to abandon its possibility by escaping into a private aesthetic world.[6] Indeed, the modernist writers discussed in the following chapters were aware that an individual's isolation is likely to intensify without the aid of practical devices with which to mobilise moral sensibility.

In this book I argue that many modern protagonists are troubled by the same ache that Tess feels: the sense that a moral position must be ventured, but accompanied by a simultaneous realisation of the impossibility of doing so. Such a dilemma is often couched in the terms of the artist's responsibility to him- or herself, or to the type of art he or she prioritises and practises. Often the questioning of the parameters of 'the real' indicates an intense dissatisfaction with social values and implies that new codes of living should be devised to challenge and supersede them. As Robert Musil's morally confused protagonist Ulrich realises towards the beginning of the unfinished epic *The Man Without Qualities* (*Mann ohne Eigenschaften*, Volume 1, 1930), by 1913 no one could 'quite distinguish between what was above and what was below, between what was moving forwards and what backwards'.[7] Even if no alternative code is articulated as a coherent philosophy, the vacillation between stasis and action serves to dramatise the moral problematic explored in much modernist literature.

This same moral problematic often motivates a set of epistemological questions that haunt the reading of modernism. The psychic dizziness experienced by many protagonists, from T. S. Eliot's Prufrock and Mann's Aschenbach to Musil's Ulrich and Zora Neale Hurston's Janie Crawford, is a feeling the reader also confronts when trying to make sense of modernist texts. The freedom that the modern world promises, but rarely delivers, is often expressed either in terms of a world without purpose or of the individual's inability to decide between possible choices. Similarly, the reader is faced with unruly or fragmentary texts, the interpretation of which often results in anxiety or the need to recoup meaning even though such meaning is strained and inadequate. Just as many modernist protagonists are fallen heroes left to make sense of a world full of semantic slippage, so the implied reader of modernist literature is also fallen. There may be no moral comfort in reading this way, or any salutary consolations in the sense that Alain de Botton describes in his televised book *The Consolations of Philosophy* (2000).[8] However, as the Introduction discusses, a number of critics and theorists have proposed recently that taking moral dilemmas seriously is an ethical action in itself, an understanding gestured towards by the modernists considered in subsequent chapters.

The half-expressed ache felt by Tess can, a century later, be symbolised as a painful bruise, almost as if in the current move towards economic and cultural globalisation we are replaying visibly some of the moral dilemmas posed by early twentieth-century technology, urbanism and social change. Indeed, as Mike Jay and Michael Neve argue, the turn of the twentieth century can be viewed as 'the true Millennium, and what we imagine to be our "modern" crisis little more than the aftershocks of the *fin-de-siècle* amplified and diffused by an increasingly overwhelming global media'.[9] Michael Wood parallels this idea by suggesting that over the last forty years we have continued to return to modernist writing 'with a dim or sometimes anxious curiosity about what it was like to be around when the twentieth century had played so few of its now familiar marked cards'.[10] Many of the cataclysms of the twentieth century – wars hot and cold, the Holocaust, ethnic cleansing, the revival of religious fundamentalism and environmental damage – have resulted from the inability to arrive at positive moral answers to domestic dilemmas, national disagreements and international conflict. The bruises of modernity are largely the result of imperial aspirations, instrumental reason and the effects of pluralistic intolerance on the lives of individuals and communities. Although the scars of total war may have healed to an extent, the social body continues to look moribund and core values discoloured, despite the political attempts of the West in the 1990s to implement a new moral agenda in its role as global peace keeper in the Middle East and the former Eastern Bloc countries. As Michael Ignatieff has argued, the rhetoric of universal rights is often a smoke screen for obscuring a fragmented world divided into privileged or protected 'zones of safety' in which liberal values can be preserved, and 'zones of danger' in which universal morality cannot prevail.[11] Just as modernity began as an age of hope and reached its apotheosis in the political melting pot of the 1930s and the ensuing war, Ignatieff argues that the post-Berlin Wall period began with the promise of material and moral improvement of life, only to end in 'perplexity'.[12] If the most convincing critiques of 'universal morality' now come from outside the West in the guise of postcolonial theory, it is productive to examine early twentieth-century writers in Europe and America as offering an internal critique of social and cultural values. Many modernist writers publishing in the early twentieth century were concerned with examining the causes of social contusion (before it had fully manifested itself as a bruise) by focusing on moral dilemmas experienced by the individual. The fact that the moral 'vices' to which the characters are prone and the ethical 'devices' with which they attempt to deal with these dilemmas often merge into one another suggests there is no refuge from the 'zones of danger' that Ignatieff describes.

The form of literary criticism outlined and practised in this book provides no panacea or curative remedy for healing these bruises; rather it offers a reappraisal of modernist literature in this postmillennial phase when moral concerns have been re-introduced into theoretical, cultural and political agendas. If, on the one hand, the bruises of modernity continue to cause distress, then, obversely, the manifestation of the bruise is also a sign of healing and reparation. Some interest groups have promoted a form of cultural amnesia in their ideologically motivated revision of twentieth-century history, usually centring on the Holocaust. However, a closer inspection of the aches and bruises may enable the critic to assess the damage caused by the impact of modernisation and work through a set of moral positions that could counter, or negotiate, such polemic. Modernist writers generally resist certain features of the industrialised world for their dehumanising and alienating potential and, although the final vision they offer may be one of retreat or death, an examination of the *process* of such dissolution reveals a series of engaged responses to modernity. Many characters only have a loose grasp on these ethical devices and rarely articulate fully their position. Even more thoughtful protagonists, such as Joyce's Stephen Dedalus only half-understand their condition; Stephen's motto of approaching life with 'silence, exile, and cunning' represents both a positive rejection of nationality, religion and language in *A Portrait of the Artist as a Young Man* (1916) and a negative inability to commit to any firm ethical principle in *Ulysses* (1922).[13] Nevertheless, as grand artificers, characters such as Joyce's Stephen provide a repertoire of responses (and the relatively safe cultural exchanges of Henry James, T. S. Eliot and W. H. Auden) set against a more experimental Continental modernism, the literary examples in this book are chosen for their cultural diversity and their focus on such themes as immorality, amorality, Otherness, and the problem of evil. The chapters are arranged in pairs to maximise the interconnections between different authors and conflicting modes of writing. The first chapter in each section addresses broad cultural movements – decadence and naturalism, the avant-garde, expatriate writing and the modernist picaresque – whereas the second chapter focuses more closely on a pair of representative texts. One of the central features of modernism is its international scope and the broad selection of writers discussed in the following chapters all emphasise the problems, as well as the possibilities, of transcending cultural boundaries in order to deal with more inclusive moral questions than those shaped by national conditions.

Although a coherent intellectual impulse can be discerned throughout the eight chapters, this is not a uniform tradition in which writers conform to a single set of underlying principles, and neither is it a straightforward unfolding of tradition where later writers move towards a better understanding of moral issues than their predecessors. The main danger of referring to a fixed and teleological tradition is that the critic ceases to question its constructed nature and merely accepts it as a given. As the title of Peter Nicholls's book *Modernisms* (1995) implies, the modernist tradition is more accurately conceived as pluralistic and diverse. Lines of influence and coherent cultural groupings can be obviously identified, but there is no one broad intellectual current that can be traced throughout modernism that neatly aligns writers with each other, unless it is what Nicholls describes as a general shift from 'representational' to 'transformative' art.[16] It is important to interrogate the differences, transformations and conflicts in a literary tradition, as much as the similarities between the belief-systems of its various exponents. Consequently, this book is structured in such a way as to indicate trends shared by writers from different cultural and national backgrounds (without ignoring specific cultural pressures that bear upon individual works), while also emphasising the points of conflict and tension between them. To facilitate this discussion, the chapters deploy a range of ideas drawn from moral and social theory, new historicism, poststructuralism, psychoanalysis, French feminism and postcolonial theory, emphasising the fluid relationship between fiction and theory rather than muting creativity with abstract models.

8 *Introduction*

Chapter 1 discusses the twin phenomena of decadence in late nineteenth-century European culture and naturalism in turn-of-the-century American culture (itself influenced by the European movement), a climate in which a range of writers emerged to subvert cherished nineteenth-century beliefs concerning social progress and the pedagogic value of art. The first part of this chapter focuses on Joris-Karl Huysmans's decadent handbook, *À Rebours* (*Against Nature*, 1884), but also considers Oscar Wilde's *The Picture of Dorian Gray* (1890) and Marcel Proust's essay 'On Reading' (1905) to characterise the decadent attitude to Victorian morality. The category of 'the perverse', deriving from Charles Baudelaire's reading of Edgar Allan Poe, provided decadent writers with a conceptual and experiential tool for problematising moral boundaries. The second half of the chapter moves on to discuss the naturalistic responses of Frank Norris and Edith Wharton to what they considered to be the moral inertia of American culture. While in many ways decadence and naturalism can be understood as cultural opposites, a comparative study of the movements as inflections of Romantic thought and assaults on Victorian moralism is vital for understanding the shifting agenda of early twentieth-century art. These ideas are developed in Chapter 2 in a discussion of two European decadent novellas: André Gide's *The Immoralist* (*L'Immoraliste*, 1902) and Thomas Mann's *Death in Venice* (*Der Tod in Venedig*, 1912). Metaphors of illness enable Gide and Mann to explore the downfall of their protagonists as they struggle against alien forces, while their decadent experiences correspond to Julia Kristeva's study of abjection in *Powers of Horror* (1982). The physical and spiritual demise of Mann's Aschenbach when he contracts cholera on a trip to Venice contrasts sharply with the consumptive protagonist Michel in Gide's novella. The characters transform themselves creatively in the face of disease, but they are beset with anxieties that impinge on their initially safe moral world-views to leave them in a state of abjection.

The second pair of chapters considers the symbolic centres of modernism in the years leading up to the First World War and the interwar period. Chapter 3 provides a perspective on extremist modernist literature: the avant-garde practice of Dadaist artists in Central Europe and the postwar metamorphosis of Dadaism into French Surrealism. If decadent writing flouted nineteenth-century moral standards, then the European avant-garde is often interpreted as embodying a nihilistic disregard for all forms of morality. However, both the Dadaists and the Paris Surrealists, under the contested leadership of André Breton, attempted to reinvent a moral trajectory to give shape to their multiform artistic experiments. Chapter 4 goes on to consider the complex role of the idiot figure in the major modernist work of Joseph Conrad and William Faulkner as a symbolic device for destabilising accepted literary and social frames of reference. In Conrad's novel of political intrigue, *The Secret Agent* (1907), the idiot figure embodies the ideals of Romantic innocence and natural morality that are obliterated in modern London, whereas in Faulkner's *The Sound and the Fury* (1929) idiocy is a symptom of the moral barrenness and spiritual vacuity of the post-Civil War American South.

The fifth and sixth chapters discuss transatlantic literary crosscurrents more directly, arguing that the experience of cultural transit and exile presented modernist writers with the opportunity to link moral issues with questions of cultural and sexual identity. Chapter 5 focuses on four American expatriate writers – Ernest Hemingway, Gertrude Stein, Henry Miller and Anaïs Nin – who chose Paris as their stimulus for exploring alternative gender identities to those endorsed by American Progressive values. This chapter proposes that exile, literary experimentalism and the aesthetics of pleasure are vital ingredients for considering questions of gender difference and the possibility of an open exchange between the sexes, and it draws parallels between the French feminist Luce Irigaray's theory of 'angelic ethics' and the modernist development of a primitive aesthetic for subverting the strict gender and moral dichotomies of the time. Chapter 6 develops this discussion of morality and urbanism by comparing the work of the Czech writer Franz Kafka and the Spanish poet and playwright Federico García Lorca, whose imaginative visions of America, particularly the optical experience of New York City, provide a perspective on their recognition of cultural and ethnic Otherness. Whereas Lorca's *Poet in New York* (*Poeta in Neuva York*, 1940) describes the poet's ambivalence to a city that is both exciting and demoralising, Kafka's *America* (*Amerika*, written in 1927) imagines New York from a European vantage point. Despite these differences, the emphasis on sight and visuality in Lorca and Kafka helps them to address issues of Otherness, as well as indicating the problems posed by crossing cultural boundaries.

The final two chapters deal with writers who expanded the parameters of modernism in the 1930s by focusing on the themes of trickery and transformation and raising questions about the legitimacy of particular forms of social action. Chapter 7 discusses modernist picaresque novels in which the modern *pícaro* is often portrayed as lacking moral quality or fibre. The reinvention of the traditional picaresque enabled writers as diverse as Herman Hesse and Robert Musil (in Europe) and Zora Neale Hurston and Henry Roth (in America) to explore the aesthetic possibilities and moral consequences of 'adventure' without resorting to realistic modes of description or nineteenth-century narrative forms. Chapter 8 deals with the ways in which Klaus Mann and Thomas Mann negotiate the troubled political climate of Germany in their respective fictions, *Mephisto* (1936) and 'Mario and the Magician' (1929). To deal with the rise of totalitarianism the writers drew from a vocabulary of stage performance and masquerade (with parallels to Bertolt Brecht and Walter Benjamin) as a way of tapping into the transformative dimension of myth.

The Conclusion develops the concerns of the eight chapters by discussing recent writers and theorists who have dealt with moral issues as they have arisen out of historical climate shifts, from the postwar ashes of a ruined Europe and the conspiratorial climate of Cold War America to the accelerated globalisation of the late twentieth century. For the former East German writer Christa Wolf and the American novelist Paul Auster, the bruises of modernity linger on and the process of social reparation is arduous. But, together with recent theorists and social commentators such as Michel Foucault, Jürgen Habermas, Zygmunt Bauman and Naomi Klein, they indicate a continued, almost compulsive, moral engagement with what they see as a world of diminished possibilities. In the Conclusion I argue that a certain strain of postwar writing, often labelled as postmodernist, actually develops the attempt by early modernists to forge moral passages while sustaining their effort to liberate the fear of modernity.[17]

The modernist rejection of moralism

Before discussing the ways in which modernist aesthetics diverged from dominant nineteenth-century moral principles, it is important to define three terms central to the following discussion: modernisation, modernity and modernism. First, 'modernisation' refers to the changes to technological processes driven by the development of capitalism and urbanism which made living in the early twentieth century markedly different from life prior to and in the nineteenth century. Industrial and social changes were sharply felt in Britain in the mid-nineteenth century with the formation of railways, the development of communication networks, the domestic use of electricity, and, later, the mass production of cars. As Steven Kern documents in *The Culture of Time and Space* (1983), technological changes radically altered spatial and temporal experience: machinery and labour-saving devices enabled activities to be accomplished more quickly and improvements in transport systems meant that regional boundaries could be traversed swiftly.[18] By the second quarter of the nineteenth century work in Britain was beginning to be centralised in urban offices and factories, in contrast to eighteenth-century home-based crafts (America and Germany were to experience the force of industrialisation slightly later in the century than Britain). Victorian novelists, such as Charles Dickens (in England), Honoré de Balzac (in France) and William Dean Howells (in America) were concerned with these social changes, but they remained secure in relatively stable moral belief-systems. Not until the late nineteenth and early twentieth century, in the wake of Darwinism and the impact of total war were these moral comforts literally blown away.

I will use 'modernity' to refer to the individual and collective *experience* of the modern world, particularly as it is embodied in ideas which represent a reaction to the social and economic processes of modernisation. These ideas swing between the extremes of willingly accepting the transformed environment and a rejection of all that has made the modern. Examples of these extremes are seen in the following two quotations: the first from Charles Baudelaire's essay 'The Painter of Modern Life' (1863), and the second from the German thinkers Theodor Adorno's and Max Horkheimer's *Dialectic of Enlightenment* (1944):

> And so, walking or quickening his pace, he goes his way, for ever in search. In search of what? We may rest assured that this man ... this solitary mortal endowed with an active imagination, always roaming the great desert of men, has a nobler aim than that of the pure idle, a more general aim, other than the fleeting pleasure of circumstance. He is looking for that indefinable something we may be allowed to call 'modernity', for want of a better term to express the idea in question ... Modernity is the transient, the fleeting, the contingent; it is one half of art, the other being the eternal and the immovable.[19]

> Nature ... is that which is to be comprehended mathematically; even what cannot be made to agree, indissolubility and irrationality, is converted by means of mathematical theorems. ... Thinking

objectifies itself to become an automatic, self-activating process; an impersonation of the machine that it produces itself so that ultimately the machine can replace it.[20]

The historical distance between these two expressions is crucial: Baudelaire's essay was written in Paris in 1863 when the excitement of modernity had yet to be weakened by the full effects of urbanisation and war. His lyrical description of the 'fleeting' nature of modernity contrasts sharply with Adorno's and Horkheimer's pessimistic description of an oppressive, highly rationalised and machine-run world, distressingly evident to these two exiled German intellectuals in the mid-twentieth century. Most modernist writers can be positioned somewhere between the two extremes of celebrating or bemoaning modernity and, although this book considers moral crosscurrents in modernism, it is important to address the cultural conditions experienced by the individual writers in order to ground an analysis of their work historically.

Finally, 'modernism' refers to the artistic medium through which the experience of modernity is expressed, whether in poetry, prose, film, painting, sculpture, or in other art forms. Modernism was not a movement, in the respect that all the artists pursued the same goals, although there were many (often conflicting) groupings and manifestos, especially in the optimistic years preceding the Great War. Instead, modernism should be understood as a collective term to describe a series of experimental artistic trends that revolted against the dominant art forms and belief-systems of the nineteenth century. As such, the modernist artist tried to reflect and contend with modernisation in an attempt to find new and more authentic ways of representing modernity. Many modernists were highly self-conscious about their reaction to what they saw as a sterile nineteenth-century sensibility and outmoded forms of writing, and they were intensely aware of their symbolic place in a new century. If the typical nineteenth-century writer was the intellectual descendent of Enlightenment moralists such as Samuel Johnson or Benjamin Franklin, who sought to instruct by example or by portraying an exemplary life, then the typical modernist rejects such a role for its implicit arrogance. Instead, modernist fiction is characterised by uncertainty and contradiction, with the narrator's voice sceptical or ironic and protagonists rarely worthy in the sense of deserving social respect or merit.

One of the most productive ways of demonstrating both the historical self-awareness that accompanied the experience of modernity and the modernist assault on moralism is to consider an early example: Fyodor Dostoevsky's proto-modernist manifesto, *Notes From Underground* (1864). Not only does Dostoevsky provide a prototype for the modernist protagonist, or anti-hero, in his figure of Underground Man, but he also attacks a number of nineteenth-century social and moral trends for their constriction of individual life. Many of Underground Man's complaints are directed at the Russian co-editors of the Leftist journal *Contemporary*, Nikolai Chernyshevsky and Nikolai Dobrolyubov, especially their rejection of idealism in favour of an anti-aesthetic and scientific materialism. Although it is important to do justice to the historical context of *Notes From Underground*, here I will consider Dostoevsky's manifesto chiefly as foreshadowing the spirit of European and, to a large extent, American modernism.

Chernyshevsky, the author of *What Is To Be Done?*, subtitled 'Tales About New People' (1863), viewed the reform of society as fundamentally a scientific problem, to be solved by adhering to a variant of the utilitarian theories championed in different forms by Jeremy Bentham and John Stuart Mill in England. As a philosophy of self-interest that provides the foundations for ensuring the 'common good' and 'mutual happiness', utilitarianism furnished Chernyshevsky with a purposeful moral and social creed. He argued that literature is merely a sensual pleasure and therefore manifestly inferior to a social reality demanding the manufacture of useful objects such as shoes. The main difference between Chernyshevsky and the British utilitarians is that the Russian defines his 'new people' as needing to be disciplined in their cold-blooded strength, whereas the liberal humanist tradition in Britain fits more easily with Mill's philosophy. Dostoevsky was concerned about Chernyshevsky's social programme for two reasons: first, the inner life of the artist was abandoned for a materialistic and rational belief-system and, second, art was marginalised in favour of a social ethic which purported to ensure the common good, but often served to promote self-interest. Dostoevsky explicitly attacks Chernyshevsky's rationalist and utilitarian dogma in *Notes From Underground* on political, aesthetic and moral grounds. It is important to distance the voice of the author from the first-person perspective of the Underground Man (in fact, the author's editorial voice emerges at the end of the narrative). However, Dostoevsky's letters indicate that he believed passionately that reason alone cannot create the conditions for moral behaviour; belief in the individual is required as a stabilising force. He viewed Chernyshevsky's 'new man' as a gross simplification of the psychologically complex and contradictory nature of human beings. In opposition to the strength of convictions characterised by these 'new people', Dostoevsky's Underground Man possesses a voice that wavers between aggression, equivocation, scepticism and irrationalism. Although his views are often inconsistent, Underground Man is able to justify the grounds for his argument: 'all spontaneous people, men of action, are active *because* they are stupid and limited ... they are more quickly and easily convinced than other people that they have found indisputable grounds for their action, and they are easy in their minds'.[21] Here, Underground Man speaks with the voice of someone who finds it difficult to give allegiance to any social programme. He rejects 'men of action' for too facilely assimilating dogma and for blindly accepting rationalism; worse than this, 'man is so partial to systems and abstract deduction that in order to justify his logic he is prepared to distort the truth intentionally'.[22] Underground Man claims that the only way to undermine this blind faith in social utility is to adopt the voice of the ambivalent critic, a forerunner of other modern protagonists: Chekhov's students, Eliot's Prufrock and Joyce's Stephen Dedalus.

The *psychomachia* experienced by Underground Man forces him to withdraw from social engagement in order to confront his doubt and uncertainty. For Chernyshevsky faith in reason entails an investment in determinism and with it the sacrifice of individual desires in the name of the greater social order. Underground Man rebels against Chernyshevsky's tone of certainty by affirming his individuality and constantly challenging the 'calming, morally decisive and final' stone wall, the laws of nature and mathematic formulae: 'I agree that two and two make four is an excellent thing; but to give everything its due, two and two make five is also a very fine thing.'[23] He balks against the 'essentially limited' view of the man of character by claiming that 'a man of the nineteenth century ought, indeed is morally bound, to be essentially without character', arguing that the traits of greatness discernible in those of superior character often mask a weak, immature or corrupted moral sensibility.[24]

For Dostoevsky, the tragedy of Underground Man is that of the educated individual divorced from a communal sense of rootedness in the world, leading to self-hatred and what the critic Jack Clayton calls 'moral masochism'.[25] The inability to affirm, or rediscover, these roots drives individuals underground to a withdrawn world of inner consciousness. One of the central dilemmas Dostoevsky pursues in *Notes From Underground* is that if the individual is to move out of the underground he must attempt to re-integrate himself with the world he despises and fears without renouncing personal integrity. The terms 'rediscover' and 're-integrate' paradoxically imply both a return to a prior condition *and* a meaningful future-oriented act. Underground Man worries that 'men of action' react blindly to their situation by relying on customary props: what is socially defined as 'the good' may actually prove a smoke screen behind which individual or group interest is advanced or justified. The valency of good and bad is thus thrown into radical doubt: 'What if it sometimes happens that a man's advantage not only may but must consist in desiring cases not what is good but what is bad for him? And if so, if such cases are even possible, the whole rule is utterly destroyed.'[26] But if moral actions cannot finally be 'calculated' or 'classified', then what constitutes the foundation of moral behaviour? Although Underground Man wrestles with this question he does not reach any firm ground: 'I am certain that underground people like me must be kept in check. Though we may be capable of sitting underground for forty years without saying a word, if we do come out into the world and burst out, we will talk and talk and talk.'[27] Underground Man is careful not to distort the moral framework to serve his own interests; nevertheless, there is a sense that so much 'talk' may serve to creatively disrupt the moral equilibrium of society.

Four years after the publication of *Notes From Underground*, Dostoevsky wrote a letter to his niece Sonechka Ivanova in which he reveals that his new novel (published as *The Idiot*, 1868) is an attempt to 'portray the *positively* good' man.[28] In many ways the resulting character, Myshkin, possesses diametrically opposite characteristics to Underground Man, about whom it is difficult to say anything univocally 'positive'. However, in the same letter Dostoevsky stresses the exacting nature of modernity by commenting that 'there is nothing more difficult in the world, and this is especially true today'.[29] Although Myshkin is portrayed as being innocent and morally purer than Underground Man, he has an evil alter ego in the shape of Rogozhin, whose presence complicates any stable moral schema that may otherwise exist. Indeed, the equivocal Underground Man and the split personality of Myshkin–Rogozhin in *The Idiot* together indicate the difficulty Dostoevsky experienced in giving unequivocal support to any set of moral beliefs. However, there is a sense in Dostoevsky's writing, and in the work of the modernist writers considered in this book, that an individual's struggle with moral questions in itself implies an active engagement with some of the central problems of

16 Introduction

modernity. Virtue defined in traditional terms as the practice of moral excellence or the Aristotelian sense of 'the good life' is rarely discernible in the lives of modernist protagonists. However, this does not mean that moral questions are abandoned for being either insoluble or twisted to justify any action. Following the lead of Underground Man, although they are rarely professional thinkers, modernist protagonists often display the moral aptitude to question general structures of belief *and* to scrutinise their own motives.

Modernism and morality

As I will argue in this book, many modernist writers used fiction to serve a similar function to Dostoevsky's rebellious riposte to Chernyshevsky's utilitarian programme. At the end of *Notes from Underground*, Underground Man claims: 'I have only carried to a logical conclusion in my life what you yourselves didn't dare take more than half-way; and you supposed your cowardice was common sense, and comforted yourselves with self-deception.'[30] The attempt to wrestle the ethical agenda away from advocates of socially legitimated morality can be examined through two related perspectives. First, Dostoevsky's renunciation of moral certainty is exemplary of the modernist stance; and, second, such a renunciation also involves a reappraisal of the parameters of what is considered to be 'reality'. The modernist preoccupation with time is again clearly evident in the sense that such reappraisal is both retrospective and projective: both encouraging reflection and promoting considered action. Reacting against nineteenth-century realism which portrayed social reality as relatively objective, modernist writers not only *re*-present reality from the perspective of individual experience (usually characterised as a state of flux), but many (especially late modernists such as Beckett and Nabokov) remained sceptical about whether 'reality' can be represented at all. As Underground Man states: 'we don't even know where "real life" is lived nowadays, or what it is, what name it goes by'.[31] Instead of being familiar and orderly, for modernist writers reality loses its stability.

The various strategies modernist writers deploy to reassess the status of reality have been documented by the literary critics Colin McCabe, Randall Stevenson and Peter Nicholls, among others.[32] What has been less substantially considered is the manner in which these strategies take on a certain moral valency that directs the writers towards prioritising some values and degrading or eliminating others. Modernist writing can be understood as a stage upon which moral problems are enacted at a slight remove from their direct application to life. However, such aesthetic staging does not imply an evasion of the moral realm in favour of a fictional playground full of caprice. On this model, rather than reality being a straitjacket it offers the protagonist the relative freedom to reshape the future in the face of debilitating forces. As Musil's 'man without qualities', Ulrich, reasons:

> if there is such a thing as a sense of reality – and no one will doubt that it has its *raison d'être* – then there must also be something that one can call a sense of possibility. Anyone possessing it does not say, for instance: Here this or that has happened, will happen, must happen. He uses his imagination and says: Here such and such might, should or ought to happen. And if he is told that something *is* the way it is, then he thinks: Well, it could probably just as easily be some other way. So the sense of possibility might be defined outright as the capacity to think how everything could 'just as easily' be, and to attach no more importance to what is than to what is not.[33]

This 'possibilitarian' reading of modernism (to use Ulrich's phrase) replaces a sense of stable reality with a 'web of haze, imaginings, fantasy and the subjunctive mood', in which the protagonist and, to a fuller extent, the reader can work through moral considerations without incurring direct social consequences in the public arena.[34] Although it is dangerous to generalise about the vast body of modernist literature, or to suggest an 'ideal' reading stance the reader may adopt, I will outline two broad, but related, perspectives that illuminate the moral problematic of modernism. The first perspective stems from the eighteenth-century thought of Immanuel Kant (clarified by Max Weber in the late nineteenth century), and the second concerns the reaction of Hungarian critic Georg Lukács to what he considers to be the modernist turning away from an engagement with political, moral and social concerns.

As Jürgen Habermas claims in his influential essay 'Modernity: An Incomplete Project' (1980), Weber (following Kant) argues that social transition into modernity necessitated the separation of three distinct spheres of substantive reason: the cognitive-instrumental, the moral-practical, and the aesthetic-expressive. Habermas states that the separation of the spheres resulted from a 'professionalisation' of the respective fields of inquiry: 'as a result, the distance grows between the from which the reader can learn. I do not wish to propose that reading modernist literature is a therapeutic experience, or that modernists were secret moralisers in the didactic or neo-classical sense of the term. Rather, modernist writing can guide the reader through a treacherous minefield of moral dilemmas in order that they might learn one or more of these devices; as the philosopher Colin McGinn argues in *Ethics, Evil and Fiction* (1997): 'the strength of an ethical idea lies in its applications, in how it *plays out*. In fiction, we can put an ethical idea through its paces, testing its ability to command our assent. We can also explore its alignments, limitations, repercussions.'[14] Because modernist writing is concerned with its own artifice and often lays bare its status as a constructed or 'told' story, it lends itself readily to considering what McGinn calls the 'embeddedness of the ethical in the fictional'.[15] This does not transform literary modernism into a pedagogic cultural movement, but shifts its conception away from the New Critical understanding of it as a retreat into 'the word' and as having no substantive social, moral or political content. In this sense, whether fictionalised as dreary continuity or rapid change, the dilemma of modernist writing (and of a certain way of reading it) is one in which moral questions are of paramount importance.

To explore these issues the book is divided into eight chapters that follow the Introduction, in which I construct a framework for considering modernist writing, to adapt Michael Ignatieff's terms, as both a zone of moral experimentalism and a zone of moral danger. The Introduction is split into three parts corresponding to the three layers of thought that contribute to this study: first, it offers a literary historical overview of the modernist break from the climate of nineteenth-century moralism; second, it considers the manner in which modernist writers attempted to devise moral patterns internal to their art; and, third, it discusses the ways in which the reader of modernist literature can develop a kind of moral criticism without resorting to outmoded forms of moralistic analysis. The following eight chapters interweave these three layers of thought by considering examples of European and American modernism from a historical perspective – from the 1890s to the late 1930s – and by offering a series of cultural crosscurrents that provide a transatlantic perspective on common moral problems. While the discussion focuses primarily on fictional prose, the examples I have chosen from poetry and drama suggest that the testing of moral parameters was not only the domain of modernist novelists. Rather than privileging any one national tradition, or accepting the model of an Anglo-American cultural alliance culture of the experts and that of the larger public'.³⁵ If Weber's argument is valid, then the gap between everyday life and those discourses patrolled by the language and terminology of experts had grown to significant proportions by the early twentieth century. Habermas claims that if this trend continues to intensify then the 'life-world' (values which are unique to the individual, even though certain of them are common to specific cultures or societies) 'will become more and more impoverished'.³⁶ Rather than ensuring the 'accumulation of specialised culture for the enrichment of everyday life', Habermas argues that the true spirit of eighteenth-century Enlightenment philosophy has been misdirected into the highly rationalised modern world, epitomised in the above quotation from Adorno's and Horkheimer's *Dialectic of Enlightenment* and described by Robert Musil as being 'that spirit from which ... poison-gases and fighter aircraft have been born'.³⁷ Although Habermas has been much criticised for the idealist subtext of terms such as 'life-world' and 'everyday communication', his argument that contemporary critics should 'try to hold on to the *intentions* of the Enlightenment, feeble as they may be' is laudable. The real consequence for modernist writers is that they avoid the specialised philosophical language of ethics (because it is not directly applicable to the experiences of most individuals) and search for an alternative 'fictional' language with which to engage with moral concerns. Colin McGinn expresses this opposition as a contrast between the abstract 'list of moral directives' (embodied in the Ten Commandments and the 'ethical prescriptions' of Enlightenment thought) and the literary parable 'in which concrete characters take part, equipped with intelligible motivations and personalities'.³⁸ If modernist writing corresponds with McGinn's definition of the literary parable, then it invites the reader to make 'an aesthetic evaluation as well as to teach [him or her] a moral lesson'.³⁹

Second, the Marxist thinker Georg Lukács is critical of modernism for its abandonment of the 'full process of life' and the 'extensive totality' of the social whole, which he locates in the work of writers such as Walter Scott, Leo Tolstoy and the early Thomas Mann.⁴⁰ He argues that a certain type of narrative order (which he calls 'epic' narrative) duplicates the inner structure of reality: in other words, when deployed in a 'correct' manner the mimetic use of language and the temporal projection of story replicate historical reality in uncomplicated ways. Lukács was unhappy with modernist art, especially forms of Expressionism, because he believed its disruptive strategies resisted narrative integration with the social whole. Only the epic novels of pre-industrial society (for him, before 1848) actually incorporate the integrated objective reality within a paradigmatic story. For example, in *The Meaning of Contemporary Realism* (1963), Lukács claims the modernist move away from realism involves a 'distortion' or misrepresentation of reality in favour of the idiosyncratic, and often pathological, world of the individual. On this view, common moral values are abandoned either for a nihilistic realm without value or a solipsistic life in which the individual reinterprets moral action solely on his or her own terms.

Lukács claims that 'literature must have a concept of the normal if it is to "place" distortion correctly': that is to say, the writer must have a firm sense of social norms and legitimate moral questions from which one can deviate.[41] However, his claim that modernist 'distortion becomes the normal condition of human existence; the proper study, the formative principle, of art and literature' relies too heavily on what is actually a set of artificial norms constructed after the historical fact. In other words, Lukács's claim that 'modernism must deprive literature of a sense of *perspective*' can be criticised for his retrospective projection of the 'true' perspective on to a pre-modern (that is, pre-capitalist) past that probably never existed as such. For this reason, Fredric Jameson criticises Lukács for indulging in nostalgia, causing him to mythologise the past as an integrated community.[42] Similarly, although not referring directly to Lukács, Jameson indicates that there was never, not even in classical Greek society (which Lukács praises for its 'integration'), an unproblematic relation between ideas, words and things. In other words, there has always been a gap between sign and referent, which is a distinction Lukács (and nineteenth-century realists) ignored and modernist writers, such as Joyce and Stein, sought to exploit. From a pro-modernist perspective, moral problems cannot be classified as either legitimate or illegitimate in reference to a set of universal standards (what Kant called his 'categorical imperative'); rather, moral valency is influenced by social and historical forces which are impossible to transcend.

One theory that draws together the views of Habermas and Lukács would assert that modernist writers should attempt to devise strategies in order to reunite the separate spheres of modernity (the word 'should' denoting a moral imperative), but without recourse to a set of either traditional or abstract moral standards. The problem with this conclusion is that if one refuses to rely on custom, tradition or habit to determine action, then within what frame of reference can value or the orientation of morality be defined? In order to address this question I will consider briefly the intellectual content of an important late modernist play: Eugene Ionesco's *Rhinoceros* (1959). A consideration of *Rhinoceros* provides a useful counterpoint to Dostoevsky's *Notes From Underground*, emphasising the continuities, as much as the differences, between two works written virtually a hundred years apart and in very different cultural and historical climates. Nevertheless, both works focus on the central character's resistance to manipulative social forces, while the performative nature of Ionesco's play develops Underground Man's dramatic monologue by stressing the significance of the moral *act*.

Rhinoceros is an absurdist play, dramatising the multiple transformations of the inhabitants of a French provincial town into rhinoceroses. The play does not provide any rational explanation for the transformations; rather, the prevailing dramatic tone indicates that the absurd world of *Rhinoceros* is governed by inexplicable and irrational principles. The opening act shows a meeting between the protagonist, Bérenger, and his friend Jean in a café. Jean is disdainful of Bérenger for his unkempt appearance, his drunkenness and his inability to conform to the standards of the town. In response to Bérenger's claim that 'I can't get used to it. I just can't get used to life', Jean states 'the superior man is the man who fulfils his duty'.[43] This definition of duty based on customary practice is one that the play challenges by focusing on Bérenger's resistance to the lure of conformity when his friends, including Jean, and work colleagues are transformed into rhinoceroses. As Ionesco comments in an essay written in response to critics of *Rhinoceros*: 'the aim of this play was to denounce, to expose, to show how an ideology gets transformed into idolatry, how it seeps into everything, how it reduces the masses to hysteria'.[44]

One of the most interesting aspects of the play is its criticism of all conventional moral standards for just perpetuating inclinations and habits dressed up in the guise of custom and tradition. All discourses of authority are subverted in the play: the character of the Logician emerges as a spokesperson for false reason (his philosophy is redundant and his syllogisms are erroneous, perhaps indicating the failure of specialised knowledge in an irrational world); the claims of science are burlesqued ('we'd be less thirsty, if they'd invent us some scientific clouds in the sky');[45] the boundaries between sanity and pathology are continually blurred; and moral standards are exposed as sham. During the scene in which Jean transforms physically and mentally into a rhinoceros, Bérenger, in a rare moment of lucidity, expresses his belief that humans can be differentiated from animals on moral grounds: 'we have our own moral standards which I consider incompatible with the standards of these animals'.[46] The rhinoceritic Jean responds energetically by bastardising Nietzsche's proposal to transvalue all moral values: 'Moral standards! I'm sick of moral standards! We need to go beyond moral standards!'[47] He expresses a fascistic desire to replace the individual's ability to engage with moral questions (relating to a shared world of others) with the natural law of 'primeval integrity' that, in the world of the play, marks a degeneration into the herd mentality of the rhinoceros.

It should be noted, however, that even this herd mentality, which Ionesco discusses in his essay 'Rhinocéros' (1961), is complicated in the illogical world of the play. At the end of Act Two Bérenger exclaims: 'A whole herd of them! And they always said the rhinoceros was a solitary animal! That's not true, that's a conception they'll have to revise!'[48] As such, the play explores meaning and language as much as it questions the basis of action that goes under the guise of morality. The last act of the play sees Daisy, to whom Bérenger declares his love, joining the rhinoceroses (although her transformation is only implied as she leaves the stage) and Bérenger is left alone to contemplate his enforced isolation. The boredom and ennui he feels at the beginning of the play develops into an active and engaged response – 'I feel responsible for everything that happens. I feel involved, I just can't be indifferent'[49] – and although, like Hardy's Tess, he can only intuit his condition to a large extent, he does succeed in giving voice to the kinds of moral dilemmas in a world without authentic value. Although Bérenger wavers at the end of the play when he begins to hear the rhinoceroses 'trumpet' as a 'charming' and beautiful song, he manages to resist the urge to conform and finishes in a moment of rebellious triumph: 'I'll put up a fight against the lot of them, the whole lot of them! I'm the last man left, and I'm staying that way until the end! I'm not capitulating!'[50]

Ionesco defended himself from the attacks of some critics who blamed him 'for denouncing evil without saying what good is'.[51] Furthermore, he states: 'I have been reproached for not letting Bérenger say what ideology inspired his resistance.'[52] His response to the critic Walter Kerr writing in the *New York Tribune*, for example, takes the form of a proposal to liberate the individual from convention in order that he or she can morally improvise in a world of confused values:

It seems to me absurd to ask a dramatist to produce a bible, a way to salvation, it is absurd to think for a whole world and give it some automatic philosophy: a playwright poses problems. People should think about them, when they are quiet and alone, and try and resolve them for themselves, without constraint; an unworkable solution one had found for oneself is infinitely more valuable than a ready-made ideology that stops men from thinking.[53]

This critical, but engaged, position epitomises the spirit of modernism, especially in the way that Ionesco refuses to replace conformism with another substantive template: 'A free man should pull himself out of vacuity on his own, by his own efforts and not by the efforts of other people.'[54] The performative morality that Ionesco dramatises in *Rhinoceros* and discusses more clearly in his essay describes what the German intellectual Hannah Arendt has called 'virtuosity'. For Arendt, virtuosity represents the 'excellence we attribute to the performing arts ... where the accomplishment lies in the performance itself and not in an end product which outlasts the activity that brought it into existence and becomes independent of it'.[55] As the last section of this Introduction discusses, this improvised virtuosity exemplifies the way in which modernist writers struggled with questions of morality and helps to establish an 'ethics of reading' that does not fall back into a customary moralistic position.

Reading morally/responsive reading

Arendt's emphasis on performative virtuosity provides a useful way of characterising the modernist engagement with moral questions, by emphasising the *act* of improvisation rather than the consequences. It also offers a way of moving between a discussion of the form and content of modernism and a particular technique of reading modernist literature. This last section of the Introduction deals with the central theoretical problem of how to read morally, especially in terms of developing a language in which to express the significance of moral issues for modernist writers. By synthesising the work of critics who have considered the relation between morality and reading, it is possible to rescue the bad name of 'moral criticism' deriving from the influential, yet theoretically fragile, work of the English literary critic F. R. Leavis. Until the late 1980s critical theorists attempted to dissociate modes of literary analysis from the kinds of ill-defined moral agenda that informed Leavis's criticism in the 1930s and after.

However, more recently thinkers such as J. Hillis Miller, Stanley Cavell, Simon Critchley, Ewa Ziarek and Robert Eaglestone have sought to reconsider the moral implications of what Miller calls the 'act' of reading by fusing the poststructuralist insights of Continental theory with the more analytic impulses of Anglo-American criticism.[56]

Leavis's mode of criticism carried a moralistic subtext that influenced his decision to privilege works of 'high seriousness' for offering a morally uplifting perspective on life, but without him needing to justify them as such. At the beginning of *The Great Tradition* (1948), Leavis claims that 'the best way to promote profitable discussion is to be as clear as possible with oneself about what one sees and judges'.[57] His two critical priorities are, first, that major novelists should 'change the possibilities of art for practitioners and readers' and, second, that their novels are 'significant in terms of the human awareness they promote; awareness of the possibilities of life'.[58] Although both priorities seem positive, the major weakness with his approach is that terms such as 'life' and 'experience' are dangerously undertheorised and his critical agenda remains nebulous. Furthermore, he fails to differentiate clearly between alternative world-views and conflicting beliefs held by writers and artists who fall outside *his* cultural parameters. Leavis's 'great tradition' of literature – Austen, George Eliot, Henry James and Conrad (although he also acknowledges Lawrence and T. S. Eliot) – is not only narrow and parochial (anglicising James and Conrad and ignoring the true internationalism of modernist writing) but, to a large extent, it excludes literature set itself against literary convention.

Although Leavis claims that his criticism is inclusive – 'the business of the literary critic is to attain a peculiar completeness of response' – his agenda is really very narrow.[59] This kind of critical study is actually circumscribed tightly by what Zygmunt Bauman calls 'a code of law that prescribes the correct behaviour "universally"'.[60] The real problem is that Leavisite criticism sets up false expectations for moral reading: namely, that there is an exemplary morality to which 'great' (or major) writers rise while others (minor writers) fall short. There may be some merit in Leavis's celebration of writers who enlarge the 'possibilities of life', but his obligation to define what kinds of possibilities are most valuable is unfulfilled. René Wellek argued that because Leavis failed manifestly to define his theoretical criteria – what Wellek calls 'your "norm" with which you measure every poet' – the foundations of his literary criticism are very weak.[61] However, it is possible to develop Leavis's critical lead without falling into the same theoretical (or anti-theoretical) trap. Indeed, it is his very lack of firm critical foundations that, paradoxically, provides the springboard for developing a different strain of moral criticism. In *Life in Fragments* (1995), Zygmunt Bauman suggests a manner by which the critic can avoid a narrow analytical perspective without renouncing moral questions entirely. Bauman calls the kind of moral practice based on firm foundations (firm because unexamined), such as those found in Leavisite criticism, an 'ethical code'. He contrasts an activity that adheres to ethical rules with a set of responses that he calls 'ethically unfounded morality'.[62] Bauman's distinction between ethical codes and postfoundational morality implies that it is possible to fashion a mode of reading which avoids the pitfalls of Leavisite criticism without needing to abandon the search for moral value. Serious consideration of 'ethically unfounded morality' may provide the individual with a bridge to act – even if such action is hesitant or uncertain – in a world in which there is no stable ground on which to stand. Instead of basing moral practice on clearly defined principles, Bauman claims that 'moral selves do not "discover" their ethical foundations, but ... build them up while they build themselves'.[63] In other words, moral practices are fashioned piecemeal out of a plethora of cultural and social codes, some of which are recognised as legitimate at any one time. Like Arendt's description of 'virtuosity', Bauman emphasises the need for improvisation in an insecure environment. Such a postfoundationalist position may provide an adequate description of late twentieth-century and early twenty-first-century life (under certain social and economic conditions), but also offers a way of reading a range of modernist writing written in response to cataclysmic social change and moral uncertainty.

One of the most important books dealing with questions of morality and reading is the American critic J. Hillis Miller's collection of essays, *The Ethics of Reading* (1987). Miller's work is inflected by the concerns of American deconstruction, the practitioners of which stress the ambiguity of language as much as the difficulties of the reader arriving at stable meaning. In his introduction, Miller claims that there is a 'necessary ethical moment in the act of reading' that some types of writing emphasise more than others.[64] He claims that moral reading results from the reader rising to the challenge of the imperative – 'I must' – in a close reading of the text. This does not mean necessarily that reading is always a serious cognitive activity; it is possible to respond emotionally or playfully to a text without renouncing moral questions. Miller calls this ethical moment an 'event' that can only be positioned within a narrative structure: 'without storytelling there is no theory of ethics'.[65] Such an emphasis on time (narrative) and activity (storytelling) indicates one of the reasons why modernist writing is particularly suited for encouraging this kind of moral response. In making this claim Miller shifts the context of ethical debate away from conventional philosophy (although he does analyse the philosophy of Kant and Paul de Man) and towards a consideration of discourses that mix conceptual and theoretical concerns with literary and narrative ones. Such heterogeneous discourses enable modernists to foreground the creative and improvisational aspects of fiction that, in turn, may encourage the reader to adopt the form of readerly 'virtuosity' theorised by Arendt. In this way, to deploy the phraseology of Stanley Cavell, 'responsive' or moral reading can be equated with 'responsible' reading.[66]

Cavell is another American critic who has done much to reorientate the focus of ethical debate towards the study of discourses that reflect on their own process of composition. Modernist literature exemplifies this notion of a self-reflexive and self-critical discourse: 'literature becoming its own theory – literature in effect becoming philosophy while contrariwise philosophy becomes literature'.[67] Like Miller, Cavell displays parallels with French deconstruction; as he writes in poetic refrain on the Romantic ideas of Henry David Thoreau: 'a deep reading is not one in which you sink away from the surface of words. Words already engulf us.'[68] Mirroring Jacques Derrida's view of language, Cavell attests that, instead of providing clarity and precision, language may reveal a lack of sense, or a sense that cannot be positioned within any stable frame of reference. Taking his metaphor from Thoreau's account of his retreat to Walden pond, Cavell sees 'deep reading' as a project 'in which you depart from a given word as from a point of origin; you go deep into the woods'.[69] As demonstrated by Dostoevsky's and Ionesco's protagonists, the probing of ideology and interpretation leads one away from securing a place in the world and towards the need to respond to experiential flux, moral uncertainty and dissemination of meaning. However, following the tradition of American pragmatism (exemplified in the thought of William James), Cavell argues that aesthetic interpretation can link personal value to social action by encouraging individuals to make moral decisions, 'acting beyond the self and making oneself intelligible to those beyond it'.[70]

Miller's discussion of the 'event' or 'act' of reading and Cavell's work on 'responsive' reading both lead towards a general (rather than specialised) language for thinking about the performative activity of reading, without falling back on an ethically-founded position. This general theory mirrors the current postfoundational interest in ethical action and corresponds to Colin McGinn's claim that the 'enormous background of tacit knowledge about human life' that comes into play while reading cannot be 'clearly codifiable into theoretical principles'.[71] In this way, moral reading would engage with the belief-system of the protagonist or narrator, but also reserve a critical space in which the reader can question the ideological and moral 'stage' upon which such engagement is set. McGinn claims that reading fiction is a 'safe, convenient, inconsequential' way of working through alternative responses.[72] However, the peril of being led down blind alleys or making wrong decisions (precisely because there are no unequivocally 'right' decisions), transforms modernist writing into 'a zone of danger' (Ignatieff) that requires from the reader an act of 'moral urgency' (Cavell).[73] Even if this kind of interpretation begins by renouncing firm moral foundations, the feelings of doubt and uncertainty that modernist literature tends to provoke – what Cavell calls 'a loss of self-knowledge; of being, so to speak, at a loss' – may provide the reader with the stimulus to engage in a moral act of responsive reading.[74]

Part I
Naturalism and Decadence

1
Decadence, Naturalism and the Morality of Writing

(Huysmans, Wilde, Norris, Wharton)

European and American modernism emerged as a transatlantic experimental trend out of a two-pronged backlash to the positivities of the nineteenth century. First, the decadent *fin-de-sièclisme* in Europe in the late 1880s and 1890s (largely absent in America with the industrial revolution still in its infancy) was a reaction to the rise of middle-class ideologies in the mid-nineteenth century and, second, naturalism (first in France and England and later in America) was both an extension and critique of the dominant mode of realist writing. While decadence with its *l'art pour l'art* slogans and naturalism with its 'writer as scientist' formula may appear to be cultural opposites, both movements reacted against the conventions of middle-class morality by questioning the limits of the human condition: for decadents, this meant a study of hedonistic life-styles characterised by artifice and masquerade and, for naturalists, an interrogation of the degradation brought on by poverty and sickness. Both embraced sensationalism as a way of captivating its (largely middle-class) readers, actively implementing them in the dilemmas faced either by decadent (mainly aristocratic) heroes or naturalistic (usually lower-class) characters.[1] In other words, the exponents of both trends rejected the social mimicry of mid-nineteenth-century realism in favour of literary modes that posed questions about what was commonly deemed to be natural or moral. Both emerged in the shadow of Darwin's assault on celestial design in the 1860s and 1870s and his explanation of human behaviour in terms of heredity and environmental conditioning, fused with the late-Romantic belief that contradiction and perversity are central human characteristics. Although figures such as Duc Jean Des Esseintes in Joris-Karl Huysmans's decadent manifesto *Against Nature* (*À Rebours*, 1884) and Lord Henry Wotton in Oscar Wilde's *The Picture of Dorian*

Gray (1890) heroically attempt to overcome the forces of determinism with the mercurial power of art, their aesthetics offer only temporary transcendence of their environment. Similarly, the murderous characters of Émile Zola's naturalistic *Thérèse Raquin* (1867) and the brutish, but hapless, protagonist of Frank Norris's story of San Francisco life, *McTeague* (1899), take their place amongst the social debris of the late nineteenth century as 'the human jetsam' of the world.[2]

The cultural confusion between 'degeneration', as a term of mental and bodily decline, and 'decadence', denoting the cultural rot of over-civilisation, was prevalent in the 1890s. This was aided largely by Max Nordau's popular, but spurious, book *Degeneration* (1892), in which any new cultural artefact potentially became a symptom of Nordau's diagnosis of the 'severe mental epidemic' prevalent in Western society.[3] While, as Richard Lehan argues, degeneration offers a 'biological' view of reality and decadence implies an 'aesthetic' perspective, the complex intertwining of these discourses characterise both naturalism and decadence as troubled attempts to break with the liberal consensus of nineteenth-century European and post-bellum American society.[4] The movements can be understood as jointly exemplifying the paradigm shift from the moral liberalism of the Victorian period to the moral experimentalism which had been emerging in France in the 1850s, but had taken on widespread appeal to writers by the late 1880s. Rather than considering decadent and naturalist writing as anti-moral, or immoral (as many contemporary critics argued), they can be seen to replace the neo-classical notion of moral instruction with the Romantic emphasis on the kind of moral sensibility that is incommensurate with social purpose. However, although both movements were highly critical of what their exponents deemed to be the complacent morality of middle-class liberalism, the characters are not cleansed entirely of the values they react against. In this way, there is a radical instability between the 'devices' deployed by the characters' efforts to free themselves from the social constraints to which they are subject and the 'vices' which delimit their rebellion and, in certain cases, paralyse them and thus prevent them from acting. If, as the following discussion suggests, one of the central features of the decadent sensibility is perversity, then often the characters are undermined by their duplicity and their own perverse logic. Similarly, naturalistic characters seem to exist beyond the moral law but usually end up demoralised either by their own actions or by the seemingly uncontrollable forces that govern their behaviour.

Decadence, Naturalism and Morality 31

All the authors discussed in this chapter – Baudelaire, Huysmans, Wilde, Marcel Proust, Zola, Norris and Edith Wharton – make interesting contextual statements about the priorities and purpose of their art, with their fiction becoming a test-ground, or, to recall Michael Ignatieff's phrase (discussed in the Introduction), a 'zone of danger' in which moral experimentalism is pitted against the intractable forces which beset it. Although decadent writers were, on the whole, more daring in their experimentalism than naturalists, there are interesting points of convergence, especially on the relation between perversity and demoralisation. The next chapter examines two late decadent texts that prefigure the aesthetics of high modernism, while this chapter considers representative examples of European decadence and American naturalism in order to demonstrate that, although the manner with which moral issues are dealt are different, the problems besetting the characters are remarkably similar.

The perversity of decadence: Baudelaire, Proust, Huysmans and Wilde

In Edgar Allan Poe's tale of gothic incongruity, 'The Imp of the Perverse' (1845), the narrator meditates on the inconsistencies that often arise in human behaviour between intention and performance: as Poe's narrator suggests, 'the speaker is aware that he displeases' even though 'he has every intention to please'.[5] The narrator ruminates that even though we may be eager to begin work immediately 'we put it off until tomorrow; and why? There is no answer, except we feel *perverse*', a condition in which the need to act is accompanied by an incomprehensible 'craving for delay' as one becomes immersed 'in a cloud of unnameable feeling'. For Poe, this 'unnameable feeling' rends the self in a form of modern *psychomachia*, pushing the individual into a state of 'sickness and dizziness, and horror'.[6] This spectre of perversity suffuses the work of the European decadent writers (of which Poe is a rare American exponent) as a manifestation of the central tension between, on the one hand, the dandy's heroic aloofness from everyday life and, on the other, his obsession with the corporeal human body as subject to age and decay. Just as Poe describes the human desire to reject 'the indefinite' (in favour of 'the definite') and 'shadow' (in favour of 'substance'), so these forces overwhelm the modern self in its search for clarity and enlightenment. Poe's meditation on perversity offers an allegory for understanding the relationship between decadence and morality: despite concerted efforts to rid themselves of the bourgeois constraints of Victorian morality, moral impulses continue to undermine the decadent protagonist's attempts to transvalue ethical codes. In this sense, Poe's 'unnameable' cloud, which both scares and delights, symbolises the way in which morality is both jettisoned and yet returns to obsess the *fin-de-siècle* European imagination. If, as Henry James argued, William Thackeray, George Eliot, Ivan Turgenev and George Sand as exponents of nineteenth-century realism all cared for 'moral questions' and were 'haunted by a moral ideal', then the decadents were often tortured by moral spectres which they could not banish.[7]

Charles Baudelaire provides the most direct route from Poe's tales of gothic perversity to the decadent expression of modern ennui, both as a French translator of Poe and as a close reader of his work.[8] Baudelaire was fascinated by the 'strange genius' of Poe, his 'indefinable seal of melancholy' and his exploration of characters so 'out of tune' with themselves that the tension between their 'nerves and mind' eventually tears them apart.[9] Baudelaire was particularly inspired by the strangeness of Poe's subject matter – a 'natural perversity that results in man's being constantly, and at one and the same time, homicidal and suicidal, murderer and executioner' – together with his 'energetic and deadly method' of composition and his disregard for contemporary American literary tastes.[10] In two essays, 'Edgar Allan Poe, His Life and Works' (1856) and 'Further Notes on Edgar Poe' (1857), Baudelaire depicts Poe as a writer who eschews common-sense morality (a self-congratulatory sense that 'we're all born good'); he refuses 'to be elbowed by the crowd' and is willing to run off 'to the extreme easterly point when the fireworks are being let off in the west'.[11] Baudelaire is scathing of the kind of 'counting-house morality' exemplified by Benjamin Franklin in eighteenth-century America (in which Franklin ticked off on a chart the particular moral duty he had practised that day) as a prime example of the kind of quantitative system of moral worth that had found a recent manifestation in British utilitarianism.[12]

For Baudelaire, like Poe, what passes for social morality often invests in 'the heresy of didacticism', instructing people about good conduct, but most often serving to normalise behaviour and to sanitise imaginative life.[13] Rather than promoting a quantitative notion of morality, Baudelaire adopts Poe's triad of mental faculties as outlined in 'The Poetic Principle' (1848) – 'pure intellect', 'taste' and 'moral sense' – and his vision of an untapped reservoir of morality ('a vast unexpended store of vital energy') into which the artist can step only by fusing aesthetic sensibility with critical intellect.[14] On this view, as P. E. Charvet discerns, morality is more akin to 'feeling' and 'pleasure' than a socially progressive model of morality, with literature suggestive of spiritual and moral life rather than providing a guide to ethical conduct.[15] This understanding may lead the aesthete away from the public sphere of morality into a private realm of art appreciation (the 'hard gem-like flame' of Walter Pater's Impressionist aesthetics), but Poe and Baudelaire suggest that the disregarding of social standards does not necessarily mean a complete repudiation of 'moral sense'. Before returning to Poe's description of perversity for understanding the ambivalence of decadent writers towards conventional morality – what Wilde calls the dandy's 'living protest against vulgarity and means-end living' – it is useful to consider two essays by Marcel Proust, 'John Ruskin' (1900, revised 1904) and 'On Reading' (1905) that exemplify the modernist rejection of Victorian social morality.[16]

Proust composed 'On Reading' (also published as 'Days of Reading') as an introduction to a French translation of John Ruskin's *Sesame and Lilies* (1864), but it also represents an indirect attack on Ruskin's views of reading and of morally edifying art. As one of three great thinkers of Victorian Britain (along with Thomas Carlyle and Matthew Arnold), Proust's essays offer critiques of Ruskin's social and political theories defined as moral sciences. In the earlier essay, Proust describes Ruskin's two great loves as Joseph Turner's landscape painting and books of moral improvement, both of which provided the Victorian thinker with a clear perspective on the natural state of being he believed was being eroded by modern mercantile culture. Although he attacked the roots of utilitarianism in *Unto This Last* (1862), Ruskin's emphasis on resources that provide strength (as opposed to the 'illth' of accumulation which drains vitality) oriented him towards urging his readers to acquire the moral provisions for public life. He recommends reading books which ennoble and educate readers, teaching them social morality (based on Christian ethics), wisdom and truth as contributing to the 'extension and ennobling of life'.[17] Ruskin is critical of artistic practices that privilege aesthetic beauty over religion or morality because they lead to indulgence and withdrawal from society; for him 'advancement in life' means 'becoming conspicuous' in public affairs.[18] Although beauty was a part of Ruskin's art appreciation it was secondary to moral learning, whereas, for Proust, 'a worshipper of Beauty is a man who, practising no other form of worship but his own, and acknowledging no other god but it, must spend his life in the enjoyment afforded by the voluptuous contemplation of works of art'.[19] Proust does not deny Ruskin's love of art but, rather than maintaining Kant's divisions between pure and practical reason, he was worried that art will be confused with moral duty and social responsibility. To this end, the chief difference between the two writers rests on their conceptions of truth: for Ruskin, truth is bound up with goodness and duty, whereas for Proust it derives from artistic sincerity.

Proust shared with Ruskin a form of religious reverence for art, but he did not let issues of conventional morality bar him from appreciating art for its own sake. Because, for Proust, art has a supreme value, in 'On Reading' he places enjoyment over moral conduct or practical use: 'for me my room derived its beauty precisely from those objects which were not there for my convenience, but seemed to have come there for their own pleasure'.[20] Paralleling Baudelaire's reading of Poe's 'heresy of didacticism', Proust accuses Ruskin of preferring artistic erudition as a form of idolatry which offers only superficial knowledge, rather than pursuing the sincere appreciation of art that provides intense personal pleasures and encourages the reader (or the viewer) to become his or her own creator. Proust follows Baudelaire in his claim that beauty is glimpsed only through fragments, rather than having an essence which can be grasped and represented fully in art: 'reading is on the threshold of the spiritual life; it can show us the way into it; it does not constitute it'.[21] His reverence for art is directed by the conviction that sincerity leads the writer/painter and the reader/viewer (with a conflation of these terms) into a spiritual world existing behind the veneer of the page or the surface of the canvas. This expression of inner morality, as for Baudelaire, stems from 'the depths of our spiritual life' and not from the pages of worthy books.[22] In other words, painting and writing should not instruct as would a teacher, but offer intimacy and friendship to spur the viewer and the reader in search of a reality that cannot be fully represented, but only gestured towards through symbols, textual elisions and diminishing perspectives.

Proust's description of the role of art is exemplary of both the decadent and, more broadly, the modernist relationship to nineteenth-century models of morality. Such a view may suggest that a retreat from the social world and a rejection of moral value is the only way that such an intimate and private relationship can be fostered. This could not justifiably be called an anti-moral view, although the knee-jerk reaction to the publication of Gustave Flaubert's *Madame Bovary* (1856) and Baudelaire's *Les Fleurs du mal*

(1857) may suggest this to be the case. Nevertheless, Proust's view of art is uncontaminated by the kind of perversity which Poe and Baudelaire describe as a crucial feature of the decadent sensibility: a perversity which may lead the reader (or artist) to the edge of the spiritual world, but also sends him (and for the decadent writer it was almost always a 'him') spiralling into a state of desolation and demoralisation. The authenticity of Proust's art is at odds with the emphasis on artifice explored by Huysmans and Wilde. As Jonathan Dollimore argues, 'the falsity and hollowness' which often accompanies the posturing of decadent writers 'are not just the opposite of the true and the wholesome' (and, one might add, the moral), 'but threaten to undermine' them.[23] In other words, decadent writing is characterised less by a linear move from socially-orientated morality to aesthetic sincerity (*à la* Proust) and more by a reluctant acknowledgment of the inseparability of art and corruption as, in Dollimore's words, 'a profoundly inimical, vitiating lack (of normality, or truth)'.[24] As this and the next chapter discuss, this notion of perversity inscribes an aesthetic in which the 'repressed or disavowed' becomes as important to understanding the moral sense of art, as that which the artist acknowledges and expresses.

Huysmans's *Against Nature* is often hailed as the definitive expression of the decadent sensibility, charting the tastes and tribulations of the aristocratic dandy Des Esseintes as he reacts against the 'idiotic sentimentality' and 'ruthless commercialism' of his age.[25] The prologue depicts the protagonist as the last of the Floressas des Esseintes family and describes the portraits of the patriarchal line hung in the family chateau as 'becoming progressively less manly' due to 'impoverished stock' and interbreeding.[26] Des Esseintes is portrayed as an isolated child. Both his parents die when he is still young and, like Proust, he spends hours reading and daydreaming, enjoying his 'fill of solitude', but without the familial comforts that the later writer enjoyed.[27] His isolation intensifies as he grows up, coming to despise and reject his contemporaries for being empty-minded, for being interested only in debauchery, or for displaying vacuous erudition. Women also tire (and even frighten) him, leaving him exhausted and close to impotence. He resolves to retreat to the deserted family chateau so as not to sully himself in the affairs of Parisian imbeciles, but to be near enough to the capital to 'strengthen him in his solitude'.[28] This parody of the conventional novel form, where the young man rises from troubled pubescence or obscurity to commanding social respect, marks *Against Nature* as a reactionary anti-novel (the novel form being respected only notionally), in which Des Esseintes rejects the lures of Paris for a life of aesthetic solitude with its own 'peculiar satisfactions – pleasures which were in a way heightened and intensified by the recollection of past afflictions and bygone troubles'.[29]

The subsequent chapters document Des Esseintes's interest in aesthetics, describing the decor and his belongings in the chateau (including an ornate copy of Poe's *The Narrative of Arthur Gordon Pym* (1838) and Gustave Moreau's iconic painting, *Salome*, 1876), his interest in decadent Latin, his outrageous jewelled tortoise and his love of flowers and perfumes. Like Proust's description of reading, these intimate pleasures take Des Esseintes to the edge of a spiritual life; his passion for illusion, artifice and imagination over 'monotonous' nature lead him into an aestheticised and counterfeit world in which social and moral issues are held at bay.[30] The expulsion of moral meaning is best illustrated by his fascination for the early Christian poet Commodian of Gaza, the content of whose 'moral maxims' interest Des Esseintes far less than the fact they are presented as acrostics 'full of everyday expressions and words robbed of their original meaning'.[31] However, although his personalised canon of literature and painting define him as an idiosyncratic art collector, his indulgences rarely satisfy him for any length of time. Duplicating the 'thirsty, ruthless passion' of Baudelaire's *Les Fleurs du mal*, he swings from 'splenetic boredom' to chasing 'dreams of the ideal', dreams which derive from sensuous intoxication rather than the pursuit of knowledge or reason.[32] As such, his life-style shuttles between hedonism and asceticism, when even his beloved accoutrements tire him. He prevaricates as to whether his bedchamber should be a place 'for sensual pleasure' or 'a setting for quiet meditation, a sort of oratory'. He even feels solidarity for other social pariahs 'persecuted by a vindictive society'; this kind of 'fellow-feeling' may be a fantasy on Des Esseintes's part, but it suggests an incipient morality emerging from the midst of his decadent lifestyle.[33]

The dynamic of uncertainty, which characterises Des Esseintes's move from 'spleen' to 'ideal' and back again, defines his revolt against social convention and is symptomatic of his decline into a restless mid-world in which nothing allays his anxiety. Late in the book, he turns to Poe's 'The Imp of the Perverse' as a study of the 'depressing influence of fear on the will' and an analysis of 'moral poison'.[34] Although Huysmans does not allow his character to work through the full implications of Poe's tale, the perversity of Poe's and Baudelaire's positions (in which action and negation co-exist) dramatises the double-bind in which Des Esseintes finds himself, as he creates his own aestheticised world but becomes exhausted and paralysed in the process. The permanent state of demoralisation he inhabits towards the end of the book may be due to his worsening nerves, but it is galvanised by the intoxicating world he has created for himself. If, in the positive sense of demoralisation, Des Esseintes manages to liberate himself 'from moral constraint' by rejecting the social and natural order (as Dollimore describes it), then he is also 'dispirited' by his own efforts and degenerates into a condition of mental and bodily exhaustion.[35] When a doctor advises him to give up his solitary existence and return to Paris to enjoy the company of others (a reversal of the popular rest cure for neurasthenia or nervous exhaustion), he is appalled at the thought of having to converse with those people he had so firmly rejected. He considers joining the Catholic Church as a means of re-entering society on his own terms, but he detects the fact that this institution is no less corrupt than others. On this note the novel ends with his prayer that God will take pity on him; opening 'the flood-gates myself, against my will' he cries 'my courage fails me, and my heart is sick within me!'[36] Here, courage and weakness dissolve into each other, as Des Esseintes experiences the paralysis he has so carefully avoided in becoming his own creator. At the end he fears that the decadence he criticises (the superficiality of Parisian society) and the decadent life-style he has adopted will collapse into each other, serving to confirm that perversity is both an integral and a prodigal feature of decadence.

Oscar Wilde's dialogue 'The Decay of Lying' (1889) echoes both Proust's revolt against convention in 'On Reading' and Des Esseintes's rejection of social value. The dialogue between Cyril, a lover of nature, and Vivian, an aesthete whose passion for artifice casts the 'curious crudities' of the natural world into stark relief, promotes aesthetics as a sphere of pure indulgence beyond the practicalities of morality.[37] Lying becomes a way of subverting the truth claims of doctrinaire morality, as Wilde constructs a playful fiction in which contraries can co-exist without negating each other. This world corresponds to what Nietzsche called an 'extra-moral' realm in which the lies of fiction-making are more meaningful than the illusions and dead metaphors used to define a solid sense of social reality. Dollimore interprets Wilde's deployment of perverse lying as a transgressive aesthetic act that helps to expose 'instabilities and contradictions within dominant structures'.[38] However, if Wilde's wit and artistic guile enable him to expose the groundlessness of social morality, by Dollimore's own logic his own perversity must contain traces of the dominant he seeks to disrupt. In this way, the decadent world rarely offers a stable critique of conventional value, but is contaminated by that which it seeks to disturb in its constant reconfiguring of social order. Wilde's *The Portrait of Dorian Gray* (often viewed as a retelling of *Against Nature*) presents a dark Poe-like world in which the didactic story demonstrating the failures of pride and hubris is twisted into a tale of perverted morality. Public reaction to the book can be gauged in the reviewer Charles Whibley's claim that:

> [it] were better unwritten ... it is false art – for its interest is medico-legal; it is false to human nature – for its hero is a devil; it is false to morality – for it is not made sufficiently clear that the writer does not prefer a course of unnatural iniquity to a life of cleanliness, health and sanity.[39]

If Whibley is looking for a clear moral, then he should have attended to the Preface to the novel which comprises a list of epigraphs outlining Wilde's own aesthetic views, most notably: 'There is no such thing as a moral or an immoral book. Books are well written, or badly written. That is all', and 'The moral life of man forms part of the subject-matter of the artist, but the morality of art consists in the perfect use of an imperfect medium.'[40] The first epigraph is clear enough (implying, by Wilde's own dictum, that 'the artist has to educate the public'[41]), but the second suggests that 'the morality of art' may encourage the artist to transcend 'the moral life of man', but he is constrained by the artistic medium itself as a flawed interface between the two realms. On this reading, Dorian Gray's portrait becomes a zone of 'in-betweenness' in which his fantasy life is refracted into a pictorial representation of his moral degradation. The search for the unfettered soul energises all the characters – Gray, Henry Wotton and the painter Basil Hallward – but also suggests that stirrings of morality continue to disturb the 'romance of art', a view substantiated by Wilde's admission to Arthur Conan Doyle that the novel has an 'inherent moral' that he wished to subordinate to 'the artistic and dramatic effect'.[42]

For much of the narrative the 'spoiling' of Dorian is hidden from public (but not the reader's) view in the form of the painting, but the denouement reveals that Dorian's aestheticised masquerade cannot overcome either his ageing body or his inner moral rectitude. He is filled with self-loathing after the death of the actress Sibyl (to whom he cannot relate beyond her stage persona), but he is too far immersed in a life of sensuality to turn back, later stabbing Hallward and disposing of his corpse. Wotton's philosophy that 'the aim of life is self-development ... to live out [one's] life fully and completely' initially inspires Dorian's insouciant narcissism, but actually foreshadows the despicable creature which he hides behind closed doors.[43] Wotton's advice that Dorian should follow his youthful caprice encourages him to fashion a decadent lifestyle but also, perversely, leads to the kind of vulgarity he is warned to avoid, as the picture begins to display this inner monstrosity. Dorian realises that one day the painting will mock him, but he does not yet know it will reflect the physical reality he has bargained to hide from public view. For these reasons Colin McGinn argues that Dorian becomes 'a walking illusion of virtue that the viewer cannot shake off, even when he knows the truth', suggesting that aesthetics ('illusion') and morality ('virtue') are intricately intertwined.[44] As such, Dorian should be understood symbolically as 'suspended between life and art' (between Wotton's conversation and Hallward's painting), existing neither in the realm of pure artistry nor in the realm of grounded morality, but shifting precariously between the two.[45] If the novel can be read as 'a plea for moral beauty', then Dorian's degradation, demoralisation and eventual demise suggest a dangerous and perverse mid-world in which the morality of art is denied.[46] The final insoluble question of who is the real Dorian mirrors the ambivalence at the close of *Against Nature*, when Des Esseintes is frozen between death from isolation or rejoining the society he so despises. It also implies that the precarious realm of moral aesthetics is one that neither protagonist has yet reached. However, neither text denies that this moral aesthetic realm is at least theoretically possible, to be glimpsed perhaps only in Baudelaire's poetic correspondences or the spiritual illumination of Proust's reading.

Naturalism and moral paralysis: Norris and Wharton

In his canonical study, *The American Novel and its Tradition* (1957), Richard Chase identifies two primary modes of American writing emerging in the nineteenth century: first, literary naturalism, characterised by the novelistic study of social conditions and focusing on the close relationship between human beings and their environment, and, second, the romance form, as a version of what Nathaniel

Hawthorne called the 'twice-told tale', existing at one remove from the everyday in the realm of imaginative fiction.[47] This polar view of American writing has persisted in separating the serious study of social values undertaken by realist and naturalist writers such as William Dean Howells and Frank Norris between the end of the Civil War and the early twentieth century, from the earlier Romantic enterprises of Hawthorne and Herman Melville as writers exploring the inner life of characters troubled by, but partly transcending, their environmental circumstances. On this orthodox view, while the morality of individuals at odds with their peers often provides the focus for writers of romances, naturalists concentrate on the constraints that prevent moral action within the social and legal systems of urban American. While Howells as a cultural propagandist was largely responsible for establishing this opposition in his argument that 'the romance and the novel are as distinct as the poem and the novel',[48] the modes of American fiction produced in the post-bellum period are more tightly woven than Howells attests. For example, over a thirty-year period Henry James worked with different modes of social realism, drawing as much from romance as from cool empirical observation. Younger naturalist writers, such as Norris, Stephen Crane and Theodore Dreiser, were more direct than James in the depiction of urban conditions and class conflict, but their explorations of the tensions between individuals and environment also contain discernible Romantic impulses. Although a study of American naturalism begins on a different tack from that of European decadence, its interest in the devaluation of life and the demoralisation of characters directly parallels the interests of decadent writers.

Frank Norris is particularly interesting as a writer usually identified as a literary naturalist, but developing a hybrid form of fiction in the 1890s and early 1900s between the literary poles that Howells identifies. Reacting forcibly against the 'New England school' of American writing, the Chicago-born Norris argued that the establishment of literary convention and 'blind adherence to established forms' would lead only to 'inertia' and the 'dry rot of national literature'.[49] Norris criticises Howells in his essay 'Zola as a Romantic Writer' (1896), particularly for his focus on 'small passions, restricted emotions' and 'crises involving cups of tea': a 'well behaved and ordinary and bourgeois' form of realism which does not upset any literary conventions or question any moral boundaries.[50] Rather than accepting the principles of the genteel literary tradition which tend to depict virtuous and respectable characters leading pious and industrious lives and for whom the author shows overt sympathy, Norris argued that it is the moral responsibility of the contemporary writer to rejuvenate polished and refined forms with the energy and 'vitality' of what he calls 'the "Nature" revival' in American literature.[51] He does not mean that new writers should didactically point out the faults of the conventional novel, or abandon the study of contemporary America for flights of romantic fancy, but that the careful construction of character, scene and narrative should not deaden the vibrancy of fiction writing. Norris was not interested in producing well-ordered fiction, but in exploring the 'complications of real life' that he argued are much 'stronger and more original than anything you can make up'.[52] In his description of the fiction writer as a 'mosaicist' (a precursor of the postmodern *bricoleur*) who combines different modes of experience in creative ways, Norris exemplifies James's notion of the selection principle as central to literary modernism.

Donald Pizer argues that this emphasis on 'life' and 'experience' epitomises Norris's 'primitivistic anti-intellectualism', especially in his view that fiction should prove 'practical and useful' in developing the reader's 'literary instincts'.[53] Norris hopes to achieve this educative goal by staging moral dilemmas for the reader to encounter alongside the characters on a fictional stage full of energy and emotion. This kind of staging may direct attention towards the exteriorised world of social realism, but his main interest was to explore the intersections between literary forms that Howells divided into strict categories: on this model, naturalism dialectically synthesises elements of realism and of romance. The strains of naturalism in Norris's major novels *McTeague* (1899), *The Octopus* (1901) and *The Pit* (1903) traverse various subjects – class conflicts in late nineteenth-century San Francisco, the effects of the Transcontinental Railroad on the American South West, and the working conditions of Chicago's wheat industry – but in each case he delves 'down deep into the red, living heart of things', rather than depicting only 'clothes and tissues and wrappings of flesh'.[54] For Norris, the true writer takes realism out of the parlour room and into the street, and fuses it with a Romantic impulse that is heedless of moral limits and of the distinction between what is fit and unfit for examination. In his most famous essay, 'The Responsibilities of the Novelist' (1902), he argues that the novel writer should have a commitment to his reading public in combating falseness with 'earnestness, with soberness, with a sense of his limitations' and with sincerity.[55] Norris is certainly a 'popular moralist' in his role of educator, but his interest in the possibilities of fiction led him beyond being a didactic writer or simply 'the instructor of public conscience'.[56] The major literary influence on Norris's reconsideration of the author's role was Émile Zola. The French naturalist's desire for 'exact and meticulous copying of real life' and 'analysis of the human mechanism' is post-Darwinian in its exploration of the 'hidden workings of the passions, the urge of instinct, and the derangement of the brain'.[57] In the Preface to the second edition of *Thérèse Raquin* (1868), Zola offers the most provocative statement of his naturalistic method, arguing that the writer's role is 'scientific' in its attention to detail and its focus on human 'temperaments', rather than emphasising 'character' in a nineteenth-century realist sense.[58] Zola declares his resistance to writing a Preface, but he was angered by the 'hostile and indignant reception' of *Thérèse Raquin* when it first appeared in 1867 (following in the wake of *Madame Bovary* and *Les Fleurs du mal*). He argues that this public response was simply a knee-jerk reaction to his story of adultery and murder among the Parisian poor, 'a handful of mud' flung in his face 'in the name of morality'.[59] Zola admits he does not know whether his novel is 'immoral' (Des Esseintes calls him a writer of 'moral stamina'), but he goes on to accuse the so-called moralists of finding 'filth' which he never intended to produce.[60] His defence is based on what he sees as the hollow self-righteousness of his critics as he attempts (like the decadent writers who followed him) to sketch out a literary *carte blanche* to explore human instincts and physiological drives whatever their moral consequences. Zola's self-defence is passionate, but Donald Pizer argues that naturalism is often held to be 'morally culpable because it appears to concentrate on the physical in man's nature and experience'.[61] Although Norris's statements on the responsibility and practical intent of novel writing are more earnest than Zola's declarations, they share what is often seen as a disdain for characters they portray as the hapless victims of circumstance, environment or inherited weaknesses. But this view simply elides the narrator of their stories with an authorial voice, rather than providing a more nuanced reading in which the narrative voice becomes as ambivalent and problematic as the cruel fictional world. As such, Norris argues that his and Zola's naturalism constitutes a literary mid-world between realism and Romanticism, between the literary commitment to document external reality accurately and the responsibility of the writer to explore the passions and desires of 'common people' wherever they may lead them.[62]

Norris's novel *McTeague* (1899) is particularly interesting for working through some of the moral implications of the naturalist project. Focusing on the adult life of McTeague, the witless and heavily-built son of an 'overworked drudge' and an alcoholic father who learns his trade from a travelling dentist, the novel depicts *fin-de-siècle* San Francisco as a melting-pot of ethnic diversity and class conflict.[63] The novel follows McTeague's courtship of Trina Sieppe, the daughter of a Swiss immigrant family. It focuses on their rise to bourgeois respectability and their demise into poverty, primarily because Trina's jealous ex-fiancé, Marcus Shouler, reports McTeague for practising dentistry without a college certificate, leading to the closing of his practice. The ensuing degradation might have been alleviated by Trina's unexpected windfall in the lottery, but her unwillingness to spend any money grows into an extravagant psychological mania, stripping their marital relationship of its humanity and turning the two into depraved animals. McTeague discovers Trina has been hoarding money but forcing them to live in poverty and in a rage strangles her, taking the money into the Californian desert where eventually he is tracked down by Marcus. After a struggle between the two, the final scene shows McTeague 'looking stupidly around him', handcuffed to the dead body of Marcus in the middle of Death Valley with a fortune in money, but without water or any chance of rescue.[64]

Like Zola's *Thérèse Raquin* and Wilde's *Dorian Gray*, *McTeague* was condemned by critics on publication for 'searching out the degraded side of humanity', for lacking in 'spiritual significance' and for having 'no moral, esthetical or artistic reason for being'.[65] Throughout the novel the narrator denies the characters any higher mental faculties and the ability to self-consciously respond to their condition. McTeague is described as being stupid and brutish; Trina's temperament is at the mercy of her nerves; and other characters, such as the miserly Jew Zerkow, rarely rise above the level of ethnic stereotypes. Although McTeague has little moral sense at the opening of the novel and he is comfortable in his indolence, he is industrious and displays signs of restraint. But, when he comes to operate on an anaesthetised Trina, 'suddenly the animal in the man stirred and woke; the evil instincts that in him were so close to the surface leaped to life, shouting and clamoring'.[66] Although he lacks good sense and intelligence, at this moment the narrator describes an 'unreasoned instinct of resistance ... a certain second self, another better McTeague rose with the brute ... The two were at grapples.' At this moment, the realistic description of the dental parlour shifts into a hyperbolic register, suggesting that 'the smudge of a foul ordure, the footprint of the monster' threatens Trina's passive innocence.[67] He kisses her once 'grossly, full on the mouth' and, although he then restrains himself, the 'brute' is described as being 'now at last alive, awake', a 'perverse vicious thing' born of 'hereditary evil'. Here, the narrator seems to adopt an omniscient perspective and condemns McTeague both for his former indolence and now for this vicious predatory instinct, but the text actually opens up questions – 'Why should it be? He did not desire it. Was he to blame?' – that create fissures in the narrative. On this view, the narrator is both deliberating in his description of McTeague's impulses, but uncertain about whether the dentist can be held accountable for his actions and uncomfortable about the moral status of these primitive instincts. As Stephen Crane's narrator comments in 'The Open Boat' (1897), 'viewed from a balcony, the whole thing would doubtlessly have been weirdly picturesque', but the uncertain moments of Norris's text unsettle the reader and prevent him or her having such a detached perspective.[68]

The perceptive narrator offers a counterpoint to McTeague's lack of reflexivity ('he never questioned himself, never looked for motives, never went to the bottom of things'), but the voice is not as consistently omniscient as its mid-nineteenth-century counterpart.[69] Similarly, although Trina begins the novel with a modicum of self-knowledge and she continues to have fleeting moments of insight, her growing obsession with money rapidly clouds rationality, her sense of demoralisation and instinct to hoard worsening at the expense of self-respect. As McTeague grows ever more hostile towards her, she submits to his physical assaults just as she succumbs to the seductive power of money, as an 'unwholesome love of submission, a strange, unnatural pleasure in yielding, in surrendering herself to the will of an irresistible, virile power'.[70] The narrator makes the reader aware of this erosion of selfhood and moralises with words such as 'unwholesome' and 'unnatural' as a condemnation of Trina's perversity. However, in these charged phrases the narrator seems to be playing with contemporary ethical and medical discourses rather than offering sincere expressions of repulsion. This manipulation of discourse is best expressed in the murder scene in which the reader sees McTeague attack Trina with 'his enormous fists, clenched till the knuckles whitened, raised in the air. Then it became abominable.'[71] Norris cut the full description of mutilation in the manuscript version for an oblique passage in which a nearby cat hears 'the sounds of stamping and struggling ... his eyes bulging like brass knobs'.[72] Rather than sparing the reader the murder scene for sentimental reasons, the narrator seems deliberately to defeat the reader's expectations, just as at other times he appears indignant and unknowing in order to confound the reader's moral prejudices. In this way, *McTeague* questions the limits of morality through its demoralised characters, rather than Norris affirming a normalised system of value judgements.

Edith Wharton is, in many ways, a very different naturalist writer from Frank Norris. She is part of the New England literary tradition against which Norris reacted, and her fiction often deals with the imprisoning mantle of the social elite in contrast to Norris's working-class subject matter. Like Henry James, Wharton is commonly classified as a realist writer (as well as a naturalist) for her detailed portrayal of social manners and the cultural conflict between European traditions and American self-belief, as exemplified in *The Age of Innocence* (1920), and her narrative voice is characterised by sharpness of wit and satirical gentility. Although she has been classified as an anti-modernist writer, reacting against mass urbanisation and the new economic order in favour of genteel values, Wharton deals with decadent themes in her work more explicitly than Norris (mainly due to her first-hand knowledge of European culture); but, like Norris, she chose to emphasise the style of writing as the defining factor for addressing the intricacies of the modern condition. In one of her late essays, 'Visibility in Fiction' (1929), she argues that style is crucial for unifying the form and content of fiction; not only does style lend the story the 'enduring semblance of vitality' but it is necessary for the creation of 'visible' characters.[73] She warns that making the characters too visible, as in the case of Dickens and Balzac (and, by extension, Norris in *McTeague*), leads to the reader identifying them solely by their 'physical and mental oddities'.[74] However, instead of ending up with pale, insipid characters, in her unpublished essay 'Fiction and Criticism' she states that 'the immoral writer is ... the writer who lacks imagination', the writer 'who handles a sombre or complex subject without power to vivify its raw material'.[75] As such, she aspires to the proto-modernist craft of Tolstoy and Flaubert of sustained visibility, by interweaving realistic physical descriptions with a subtle symbolic rendering of the emotional and moral complexities of characters.

One of Wharton's few literary forays into regional naturalism, her novella *Ethan Frome* (1911), compares well with *McTeague*, both in its description of stunted masculinity and its exploration of barely articulated morality. A project which Wharton began in French as a homage to Flaubert, the tale developed into a symbolic story of Ethan

Frome's imprisonment in a loveless marriage in the bleak New England village of Starkfield (later twinned with her novella *Summer*, 1917). Like Hardy's and Faulkner's semi-fictional landscapes, Starkfield is rooted in the reality of harsh New England winters, but also offers a psychological landscape in which the natural 'granite outcroppings' act as a barometer of the characters' frigidity and frustration.[76] In her Introduction to the 1922 edition of *Ethan Frome*, Wharton identifies the 'deep-rooted reticence and inarticulateness of the people I was trying to draw' as the novella's stylistic, psychological and moral focus, with the narrative rendering of the story being as important as the tale itself.[77] Told from the perspective of an outsider-narrator who goes to Starkfield to work, the story is pieced together 'bit by bit, from various people' with the conflicting tales being elided into a powerful drama of Ethan's vacillation between puritan duty to his wife, Zeena, and his romantic impulse to escape with his passionate cousin Mattie.[78] While Wharton, like Norris, could be accused of cultural snobbishness in her depiction of Ethan's 'frozen woe' (she was criticised for not being intimately acquainted with New England customs), she uses an ignorant narrator to place doubt in the reader's mind as to the fidelity of the story that is subsequently told.[79] The first few pages focus on the narrator's introduction to Starkfield and his curiosity about the maimed Ethan Frome (after the real-life events have taken place), with his 'bleak and unapproachable face' and 'shortened and warped' right side. But, rather than gleaning Ethan's tale from him straight, the narrator is forced to rely on rumour, gossip and 'innocuous anecdote' from peripheral characters whose testimony contains 'perceptible gaps'.[80] Interestingly, the lack of reliable information (for example, the old newspapers which circulate in Starkfield) is expressed in terms of the 'mental and moral' limits of these informants, as if their own world-views are not expansive enough to capture the drama of Ethan's life fully. As such, the narrator is impelled to work within these gaps and 'put together this vision of his story' from a series of inferences and guesses.[81] These narrative gaps mirror the textual fissures in *McTeague* by creating moments when, in J. Hillis Miller's words, the reader 'faces in two directions', caught between a responsive interpretation of the text and an ethical act of reading in which decision-making plays an important role.[82]

The central dilemma for Ethan, whether to remain in a loveless state of domestic attrition with his hypochondriac wife or to leave Starkfield with Mattie, cannot be easily resolved. If Ethan stayed with Zeena he would keep his marital pledge to her, enduring her ill-health, her false teeth and 'puckered throat' and stoically accepting winter as a permanent condition, whereas if he followed his 'desire for change and freedom' and Mattie's youthful exuberance by escaping to the West (even though the reader senses this is a fantasy) he would transform himself into a truly Romantic protagonist.[83] Even when Zeena becomes 'a mysterious alien presence, an evil energy secreted from the long years of silent brooding' there is a sense that Ethan is following a moral code by remaining with her. It is precisely because the novella wavers between naturalistic determinism and Romantic symbolism that the difficulties of this dilemma are brought to the fore.[84] As soon as Ethan is brought to the 'brink of eloquence' in his love for Mattie, Zeena's paralysing hold on him prevents him from acting on his impulse.[85] Just as the characters in Joyce's *Dubliners* (1914) feel paralysed within topographical and psychic boundaries, so Ethan's good sense quickly makes him 'a prisoner for life'.[86] His loss of moral fibre is best illustrated in Ethan's and Mattie's sledge ride, before she is to be sent away by Zeena. Here, Mattie becomes the dominant figure for the first time, when she suggests to Ethan that a fatal crash would free them from their exacting circumstances. While Ethan is complicit when faced with the 'hated vision of this house', he does not make a decision but silently acquiesces, as would a child.[87] The fact that the reader knows the sledge ride will lead not to blissful death but to the crippling of Ethan (and, we learn later, of Mattie too) lends this scene pathos, but his real 'tragedy of isolation' (as Wharton calls it) derives less from physical impairment and more from a loss of moral bearings and a demoralised surrendering to external forces, which after the accident dominate him to the point of living death.[88]

The use of unreliable narration allows Wharton some flexibility in dealing with her characters, prompting the reader to work through unresolved issues. However, due to 'the seriousness of [her] moral intention', Lionel Trilling has argued that she is ultimately 'responsible' for the suffering and 'dreadful fate' of her characters.[89] Because the story is a frozen and 'grim tableau' in which nothing happens, or nothing can happen given Ethan's insoluble moral dilemma, Trilling claims the reader can only 'endure' the telling of a tale that presents 'no moral issue at all'.[90] On this view, *Ethan Frome* (like *McTeague*) can be dismissed as just a literary exercise that fails to address real ethical issues such as social inequality or religious constraint. Although he is critical of Wharton's intentions, Trilling is interested nevertheless in the way the tale deals with 'moral inertia', illustrating that the '*not* making of moral decisions ... constitutes a large part of the moral life of humanity'.[91] While there are weaknesses in Trilling's argument – his interpretation relies too heavily on Wharton's Preface and he ignores her device of the outsider-narrator – the phrase 'moral paralysis' does identify the central theme which makes *Ethan Frome*, like *McTeague*, James's 'The Beast in the Jungle' (1903) and Eliot's 'The Love Song of J. Alfred Prufrock' (1915), such a powerful expression of modernity.

Just as Norris wished to avoid stasis and habitual modes of representation, both he and Wharton return to moral inertia as the central counterforce in the modern world, whether in the ethnic melting pot of San Francisco or the rural backwater of Starkfield. As Trilling argues, the 'morality of biology' – a habitual and barely conscious code of living – is usually imposed by 'brute circumstance' and is rarely viewed as moral conduct 'until we see it being broken'.[92] Rather than allowing Ethan the freedom of the moral philosopher who reasons his way out of domestic imprisonment or of the aesthete who valorises private notions of beauty, Wharton's tale deals with the morality of the 'dull daily world' in which the heroic posturings of the decadents seem as alien to the McTeagues and the Fromes as would the perversity of Baudelaire's spleen.[93] These two examples of the 'inertia of the will' exemplify the tangible and practical barriers which prevent certain individuals, in Proust's words, from 'descending into the deeper parts of the self where the true life of the mind begins' without being hampered by misgivings or crippled by doubt.[94] As this chapter has demonstrated, the condition of demoralisation is evident in the decadent work of Huysmans and Wilde just as much as in the naturalism of Norris and Wharton. These two major literary currents at the turn of the century mark a site of tension in modernism between the heroic preoccupations of aesthetes and the banal dilemmas of the barely worthy protagonists of naturalistic writing, a tension developed in the next chapter on late decadent writing.

2
Books and Ruins: Abject Decadence in Gide and Mann

Naturalism and decadence had virtually disappeared as cultural movements by the first decade of the twentieth century, but both lingered as strong impulses in a range of modernist work, from Joyce's *A Portrait of the Artist as a Young Man* (1916) to the high modernism of John Dos Passos's *Manhattan Transfer* (1925) and Arthur Schnitzler's *Dream Story* (*Traumnovelle*, 1926). In developing the themes of perversity and demoralisation from the last chapter, here I consider two late decadent novellas written by influential European writers – André Gide's *The Immoralist* (*L'immoraliste*, 1902) and Thomas Mann's *Death in Venice* (*Der Tod in Venedig*, 1912) – that portray characters propelled by decadent and naturalistic forces they find difficult to control. The novellas were written early in Gide's and Mann's respective careers, well before they began correspondence in early 1922 and met in May 1931. In the ensuing years they developed a respect for each other and by 1951, in a *New York Times* review of the American critic Albert Guerard's book *André Gide*, Mann declared his 'brotherly feelings' towards the French writer.[1] Despite their different cultural and linguistic backgrounds, Mann's feelings towards Gide, combining a mixture of friendship, respect, inspiration, rivalry and misunderstanding, makes for fruitful comparison of their artistic priorities and develops the modernist perspective on art and morality discussed in the last chapter. However, in *The Immoralist* and *Death in Venice* the writers arrive at very different conclusions concerning the heroism of their protagonists and, while the pairing of the two novellas seems natural, their views of decadence differ significantly.

In his *New York Times* review Mann praises Gide for his 'unending sense for harmony', applauding his 'prankishness', his 'tendency to hoax', his 'demonic unfaithfulness' and his 'delight in teasing' readers, whereas he is critical of Albert Guerard for making unsubstantiated judgements about the relative qualities of Gide's novels.[2] In commending Gide's major novel *The Counterfeiters* (*Les Faux-Monnayeurs*, 1925) over *The Immoralist*, Mann reflects his own tendency to favour the high modernist novel of stylistic trickery, most notably evident in his picaresque *Confessions of Felix Krull, Confidence Man* (*Bekenntnisse des Hochstaplers Felix Krull*, 1953). The mixture of realism, experimentation and 'new classicism' in Gide's mature work stimulated Guerard to call him 'a cautious radical and a daring conservative', whereas Mann lionised Gide's 'hobgoblinism' and 'intellectual restlessness' as features of his 'unending search for truth, and a readiness to suffer the solitude of freedom which could be called heroic'. However, Mann deems *The Immoralist* to be a work of 'faded originality', whose capacity to shock had faded fifty years on and whose title, inspired by Nietzsche and the *fin-de-siècle* decadents, 'smothers the content by sheer philosophical dead weight'.[3] This aversion may represent an intertwined anxiety of influence of which he was eager to rid himself: Nietzsche remained a major force in Mann's work and his biographer Anthony Heilbut argues that Gide taught him 'how to live' as well as write.[4]

Despite Mann's criticism of the decadent aspects of Gide's work, both authors use dialectic modes as a means for cultivating thematic 'extremes' in order to hold disparate elements of their fiction in 'precarious harmony'.[5] Michel in *The Immoralist* swings between the poles of hedonism and asceticism without being able to fully absorb them into a coherent lifestyle and Mann claims that *Death in Venice* was an attempt to find the kind of aesthetic 'equilibrium of sensuality and morality' that he believed had been 'perfected' in Goethe's *Elective Affinities* (*Die Wahlverwandtschaften*, 1809).[6] But, if Mann wished to distinguish his work from French decadence, then Gide was wary of German idealism: as Guerard notes, although Gide was attracted to Goethe's 'comprehensiveness and equilibrium', he was critical of the German's 'hatred of darkness'.[7] In this light, *The Immoralist* and its companion tale *Strait is the Gate* (*Le Porte étroite*, 1909) can be read as counterpoints that do not neutralise the dark elements in each other. It is precisely this narrative 'darkness' that makes Gide's tale more disturbing than Mann acknowledges and links it to the transgressive and perverse impulses of *fin-de-siècle* decadence.

Contrary to Mann's stated aims, even if 'precarious harmony' is achieved at the end of *Death in Venice*, Mann's criticism overlooks one of the major issues of *The Immoralist*, in which Gide's dark and reckless 'hobgoblinism' undermines the veneer of narrative order and moral certainty. In other words, Mann's preoccupation with harmony and balance is really a diversion, or a manner of sublimating, a darker undercurrent, which in part derives from the surrendering of artistic control and in part from the homoerotic content of Gide's tale. Although the French writer's sexual impulses were caught uncomfortably between what Mann calls 'unfettered puritanism' and cultivation of the self ('the self-preservation of a natural drive that deviates from the so-called "natural"'), Gide's homosexuality is more apparent than in the work of his German counterpart.[8] Indeed, Mann famously pronounced that 'homoeroticism' is only incidental in *Death In Venice*; instead he claimed 'passion as confusion and a stripping of dignity was really the subject of my tale'.[9] In many respects, Mann's emphasis on equilibrium is symptomatic of his concern about the moral ambivalence of decadent writers. His early work, including *Death in Venice*, can be read as his struggle to preserve heroism from the chaos of modernity, but it also emphasises his uncertainty about the status of the modern writer. For example, at the end of his story 'Tonio Kröger' (1903), the artist-figure stands uncomfortably between two worlds: the bourgeois and the decadent. He feels 'at home in neither' but as he gazes into 'an unborn, unembodied world that demands to be ordered and shaped' he senses both 'extraordinary possibilities' and 'extraordinary dangers'.[10]

Mann's attempt to resurrect heroic freedom corresponds to what the French theorist Julia Kristeva in *Powers of Horror* (*Pouvoirs de l'horreur*, 1980) calls the attempt to preserve the 'clean and proper' body: that is, a moral and virtuous form from which the messy aspects of corporeality have been purged. In terms of the last chapter, this represents an attempt to transvalue moral matter into a purified aesthetic realm. 'Abjection' is an appropriate term for dealing with the self-obsessed and, at times, self-repressed characters of Michel and Aschenbach, especially as Kristeva claims that it 'is a precondition of narcissism'.[11] This chapter uses Kristeva's theory of abjection for discussing the way in which Mann and Gide explored the interface between art and morality and for indicating how Mann's misreading of *The Immoralist* is based on his narrow understanding of decadence. While both novellas are concerned with what Michel describes as his obsession with 'books and ruins', only *The Immoralist* explores the ruins of modernity in a life-affirming way by rescuing morality from its very negation.[12] As such, the theme of abjection can be located in the two tales where decadent sensibilities and moral concerns meet, intersect and are thrown into conflict, in order to contest the modernist myth that aesthetic harmony is recoupable from those very qualities that Mann most admires in Gide's work: his prodigality, 'demonic unfaithfulness' and 'hobgoblinism'.

Death in Venice can be interpreted as a strong misreading of *The Immoralist* in working through a similar kaleidoscope of impulses, but with a different set of consequences. Mann exaggerates certain decadent aspects at the expense of others, particularly the sense of place and a fascination with the trappings of a decadent life-style over and above Gide's exploration of textual and psychic limits. Gide cultivates an open narrative in *The Immoralist*: the story is structured through a series of framing devices (the authorial preface, the letter to the Prime Minister and the scene of Michel's tale); it is told as a fragment of Michel's life after an absence of three years; there are gaps and omissions in his story; and the reader quickly realises he is an untrustworthy narrator. These techniques appear as signs of authorial control, but the contradictory impulses of potency and uncertainty embedded in Michel's tale eventually destabilise the narrative frame which ostensibly contains it. This argument is substantiated by Gide's prefatory comments that the book is neither 'an indictment' nor 'an apology', but rather an exploration of the European decadent temperament.[13] As such, G. Norman Laidlaw characterises him as an 'openminded' writer who is able to see 'several sides of the question at once – the *dédoublement* (dissociation or double perspective) that can be expressed ... in paradox, ambiguity, or the open question'.[14] Gide's narrative techniques can be contrasted to the closure of *Death in Venice* when Aschenbach dies of cholera on a Venice beach. Indeed, despite the narrator's ironic tone and critical distance from the protagonist, the story follows a downward spiral in which the reader is forewarned (even in the title) of Aschenbach's heroic death. The issue of heroism, what Baudelaire called the dandy's 'last flicker of heroism in decadent ages',[15] serves to divide the two writers: Michel's heroism is burlesqued and undermined by his own actions, whereas Aschenbach's dignity is preserved despite his moral and corporeal demise. By the end of *The Immoralist* (after his wife Marceline's death) Michel is able to acknowledge his own abjection, whereas Aschenbach continues to deny himself even to the last. The narrative modes of the two novellas are crucial for creating these effects: the first-person narrative of Michel is presented as a confession (with the framing sections acting as critical commentaries on it), whereas the third-person narrative in *Death in Venice* (together with the ironic tone of the narrator) distances the reader from a sympathetic engagement with Aschenbach. Because Aschenbach does not, or cannot, face his own abjection, his death vision of Tadzio walking Eros-like into the Adriatic sea, with 'floating hair out there in the sea, in the wind, in front of the nebulous vastness', represents what Kristeva calls an 'eroticization of abjection', or 'an attempt at stopping the hemorrhage' of modernity, rather than developing Michel's role of the 'borderlander' at the end of *The Immoralist* on the threshold of change.[16]

In other words, if *Death in Venice* is a tale about death (physical and moral), then *The Immoralist* is a story about moral dying in which the protagonist continues to dwell in the crevice between life and death as a kind of Foucauldian limit experience. Crucially, as this chapter argues, this is not a heroic limit experience as Baudelaire and the earlier decadent writers would claim. Informing Jonathan Dollimore's work on sexual dissidence (discussed in Chapter 1), in *The Use of Pleasure* (*L'Usage des plaisirs*, 1984) Michel Foucault theorises the idea of 'thinking the limit' as both an intellectual engagement with the liminal and an experience of living up to and transgressing the limit. In this vein, Foucault writes that 'philosophical activity ... does not exist in place of legitimating what one already knows, [but] in undertaking to know how, and up to what limit, it would be possible to think differently'.[17] Michel pays a heavy price for living the limit (the death of his wife) but he continues to do so at the close of the novel, whereas Aschenbach is debilitated and eventually consumed by his desire. This is not to valorise Michel and denigrate Aschenbach as moral protagonists (in many ways Michel is the more despicable of the two), but to indicate that, although on the surface *Death in Venice* is explicitly about abjection – one of Aschenbach's best known books is entitled *Ein Elender* (*A Study in Abjection*) and he hovers between misery and ecstatic spasms – it is *The Immoralist* which explores the indeterminate and unassimilable aspects of abjection as a central feature of the European decadent sensibility. In short, *Death in Venice* only deals with abjection as a surface issue, whereas Michel in *The Immoralist* enacts an abject life.

Two versions of late decadence

The two novellas offer a number of remarkable comparisons, but here I will discuss four themes – travel, doublings, homosexuality and illness – which bear explicitly on Aschenbach's and Michel's abjection as their experience of ontological, moral and aesthetic instability. This chapter discusses Kristeva's theory of abjection to support the argument that all these themes involve the contemplation, and potential transgression, of borders and limits (some of them spatial, some psychic and some corporeal). However, as I have suggested, only Gide portrays abjection as a positive condition, whereas Mann depicts decadence as directly leading to abject paralysis and moral inertia. This is particularly evident in the respective endings: *The Immoralist* offers an alternative to heroic decadence as Michel finally acknowledges abjection in himself after Marceline's death, whereas Aschenbach is 'attacked by waves of dizziness' and becomes overwhelmed by an 'increasing sense of dread' which renders him lifeless, with only the diminishing vision of Tadzio as consolation.[18] However, the complex interplay of similarities in, and contrasts between, the two novellas makes a comparative study of them fruitful and suggests that Mann's brotherly feelings towards Gide are not entirely imaginary (especially as Gide was drawn towards German culture).

The theme of travel suggests that the rejection of homeliness and parochial values is at the heart of both writers' reading of decadence, a departure from the naturalistic tendency to view characters as trapped in one place (as evident in *McTeague* and *Ethan Frome*). Both tales involve travel to and beyond the outer limits of Europe. Aschenbach travels to an Adriatic island before being drawn to Venice where he falls in love with Tadzio (a Polish boy whose name Aschenbach is forced to guess from a number of exotic sounding alternatives) and where he contracts Asiatic cholera. Michel and Marceline go on honeymoon to North Africa (where Michel discovers a passion for Arab boys); they travel outside Europe, return to France and then travel again via Italy (noticeably Michel 'gives up' Venice) to Algeria.[19] Both journeys produce profoundly destabilising effects on the protagonists: Venice physically paralyses Aschenbach even as it frees his desire, and Michel contracts tuberculosis on his first trip to Africa and then suffers from psychotic restlessness later in the narrative. Travel not only symbolises the fragility of early twentieth-century European identity when it is propelled to the edges of the Continent, but also symbolises the fascination with, and threat of, the cultural Other: for Michel Arabic, and for Aschenbach Eastern European and Asian culture. Just as Aschenbach imagines 'the glinting eyes of a crouching tiger' in his vision of exotic travel, so too is Michel's sensibility refined 'at the touch of new sensations' on his arrival in Tunis.[20] The twin themes of the 'foreign' and the 'estranged' suggest what Kristeva calls 'the hidden face' of identity which 'lives within' and threatens to 'wreck' the individual. Aschenbach's and Michel's heightened awareness of their new environments and their own physical changes are both an acknowledgement of Otherness (the foreign within themselves, as well as the cultural Other) and symptoms of the illnesses which threaten their existence. In *Strangers to Ourselves* (*Etrangers à nous-mêmes*, 1988), Kristeva introduces the notion of living on the border between familiarity and strangeness as a positive mode of existence that co-affirms similarity and difference: a new 'path' that emerges only if one has 'the strength not to give in'.[21] Whereas Aschenbach is eventually overwhelmed by his disease, Michel discovers therapeutic understanding and resilience from within his illness.

Second, both novellas reveal a decadent fascination with literal and psychic doublings: Aschenbach meets a demonic stranger who inspires him to travel; he watches with a 'spasm of distaste' the dandified young-old man when he arrives in Venice, whom he later literally becomes when he is 'made over' with cosmetics; and he encounters a surly gondolier and a grotesque street musician, both of whom are projections, distortions, debasements of, and therefore threats to, Aschenbach's identity.[22] As Stuart Burrows argues, Aschenbach very soon enters 'into a completely visual world, one where moral questions are subsumed by his delight in being "absorbed in looking"'.[23] In *The Immoralist* Michel and Marceline have a relationship of reversals: Michel contracts tuberculosis on honeymoon and is nursed by Marceline, and when she falls ill later in the narrative he is forced to nurse her (although he does this rather badly). In addition, Michel and his friend Ménalque (modelled on Wilde, whom Gide first met in Paris in 1891 and then on a trip to Algeria in 1895) have a dialectic relationship, offering a series of counterpoints without reconciliation: whereas Ménalque preaches heroism and courage ('I maintain the sensation of a state of precariousness, by which means I aggravate, or at any rate intensify, my life'), Michel toys with his philosophy but later embodies 'precariousness' as an unheroic mode of existence.[24] Nietzsche's 'transvaluation of values', in which the true moralist becomes the immoralist or, conversely, the immoralist becomes the true moralist in an age of suspect morality, is an important thread weaving through the tales. However, both stories can be read as critiques of Nietzschean individualism: Aschenbach embraces the Dionysian principle in an orgiastic dream towards the end of his illness, but at the risk of himself and his art, and Michel adopts Ménalque's heroic decadence at the expense of his wife, only later to realise the possible alternative of a more immanent, or banal, decadence.[25] Third, both tales deal with homosexuality as a shock and challenge to the psychic worlds of the two protagonists. Aschenbach's discipline as artist is carried out with fanatical effort: he writes in solitude with an almost religious fervour and with an altar-like pair of 'tall wax candles in silver candlesticks placed at the head of his manuscript'.[26] At first, his appreciation of Tadzio is described in purely aesthetic terms, but underlying this is an unrequited carnal desire for the boy, corresponding to the corporeality Aschenbach denies in himself. By way of contrast, Michel expresses his naïveté at the beginning of his narrative: he is twenty-four when he marries Marceline and claims to have 'barely cast a glance at anything but books and ruins'.[27] When Michel falls ill Marceline innocently brings the 'dark-complexioned' Arab boy Bachir with 'large silent eyes' to tend to him; however, Michel immediately feels 'embarrassed' when he notices the boy's nakedness under his thin garments.[28] Although Michel's homosexual impulses are less repressed than Aschenbach's (he is fascinated by many of the boys: Ashour, Lassif, Lachmi, and especially Moktir), the novellas offer a number of comparisons: the protagonists fall for adolescent boys despite themselves; they are narcissistic in their self-obsession; and the mother figure is significantly absent in both tales, being but a distant figure in *The Immoralist* (she dies when Michel is fifteen in comparison to the narrative presence of Michel's dying father), while Aschenbach's mother has been long absent (she is the daughter of 'a director of music from Bohemia' and is described as possessing 'darker, more fiery impulses' than his German clergyman father).[29] The oscillation between the similarity of same-sex love and the differences between the protagonists and their paramours (in terms of physicality, nationality and age) makes homosexuality an important symbolic site.

Lastly, both tales deal with the intersection of corporeality and illness, evident in the descriptions of decadent sensuality of North Africa and Venice and the preoccupation with the physical body. The type of illness contracted by the two protagonists is crucial for understanding their respective characters: Michel's tuberculosis is figured as a spiritual disease (one that Mann later mines for its symbolic riches in his high modernist novel *The Magic Mountain*, or *Der Zauberberg*, 1924), whereas cholera destroys Aschenbach from the base upwards. This opposition between a wasting illness that attacks the lungs and a disease which infects the bowels and intestine is characteristic of the relative ages of the two protagonists (Michel in his mid-twenties and Aschenbach his mid-fifties) and their respective sensibilities. Crucially, the stage in the narrative when the illnesses become manifest determines the fate of the individuals: Michel's tuberculosis emerges while on his honeymoon early in the novella and he is nursed back to health by Marceline, whereas Aschenbach seems compelled to stay in Venice even after he suspects a cholera outbreak and detects the 'mouldy smell of sea and swamp'.[30] Had Aschenbach left Venice and had Michel fended for himself, their outcomes may have been very different.

The symbolic resonances of tuberculosis and cholera are analogous to the oppositions between tuberculosis (TB) and cancer which Susan Sontag discusses in her essay *Illness as Metaphor* (1978): 'TB takes on qualities assigned to the lungs, which are part of the upper, spiritualized body, [while] cancer is notorious for attacking parts of the body (colon, bladder, rectum ...) which are embarrassing to acknowledge.'[31] Although tuberculosis is often figured as a Romantic disease that prioritises the spiritual over the corporeal (dissolving 'the gross body' and rendering 'the personality' ethereal), the illness does not prevent Michel from acknowledging the importance of his physical existence: 'I am going to speak at length of my body. I shall speak of it so much you will think I have forgotten my soul.'[32] In contrast, Aschenbach spends the first half of his Venetian trip sublimating carnal desire in an aesthetic appreciation of Tadzio: 'there, like a flower in bloom, his head was gracefully resting. It was the head of Eros, with the creamy lustre of Parian marble.'[33] Even though he detects Tadzio's 'jagged and pale' teeth with their 'brittle transparency', he does not acknowledge this morbid fascination until cholera has reduced him to nightmarish visions of carnal excess.[34] Aschenbach's cholera, which would be fascinating to Huysmans's Des Esseintes, does not usher in a sustainable decadent lifestyle, in contrast to Michel's more conventional Romantic illness. In this way, Aschenbach's denial of corporeality and Michel's respect for his body, at least partially, determines their ability to confront abjection.

Abject decadence

In *Powers of Horror* Kristeva begins from the position (developed from Mary Douglas's sociological work *Purity and Danger*, 1967) that the formation of binary oppositions in the Symbolic order structures a stable social, moral and linguistic system, but also implies a conflict between, and the impossible separation of, the socially acceptable (the morally edifying) and the abject (filth). Kristeva argues that any conviction, whether aesthetic, moral or spiritual, contains within it a trace of its own subversion. However, most individuals erect boundaries to ward against contradictions that would undermine choice or prevent them from acting in a way that roughly conforms to behaviour deemed to be socially acceptable. Following Kristeva's psychoanalytic argument, these desires belong to the unruly and chaotic world of pre-Oedipal corporeality which the socially-constructed self overcomes by behaving appropriately. Noticeably, Michel and Aschenbach develop two techniques for staving off such unruly elements. First, they attempt to control their personal environments by relying on ritualistic action: Aschenbach's discipline as a writer, his candlesticks and his daily walks, and Michel's meticulous care of his body. Kristeva considers such rituals as attempts to maintain the borders between cleanliness and filth, or between health and illness, but she argues they are 'flimsy protections against disintegration'.[35] Second, they try (yet fail) to transcend the banality of their situations, Aschenbach with monumental vision and Michel (until the end of the tale) with an affirmation of hedonistic sensuality.[36]

Kristeva argues that if social identity is formulated by the construction of a 'clean and proper' body (corresponding to the imperatives of the Symbolic order and the bourgeois ideology of self-determination) then 'the abject' – the filth of bodily processes like ingestion, egestion and putrefaction – becomes 'the jettisoned object, is radically excluded and draws [the individual] towards the place where meaning collapses'.[37] The acquisition of language in which one can place and describe oneself in the Symbolic order also represents a casting away of the bodily functions which are ontologically prior to, and which enable one to adopt, this place. Paradoxically, then, following this Lacanian position, in constructing the clean and proper body one denies the very dimension which makes identity possible. The feeling of abjection that emerges at times of anxiety and emotional crisis is an ambivalent awareness of the limits of sanity/health as a double experience of horror and fascination, in which the individual is drawn to the limit beyond which social identity collapses and at the same time repelled by the terrifying abyss of non-identity.[38] This sense of wavering is evident as both protagonists attempt to impose their heroic existence on the flux of psychic life. Michel wishes to throw off the restraints of his social identity that 'education had painted on the surface' and to discover the 'very flesh of the authentic creature that had lain hidden beneath it': he investigates his naked body for the first time and 'experiences a delicious burning' in his search for 'a wilder, more natural state'.[39] However, his attempt to transform himself from the 'bookworm' into the self-styled hedonist results not in 'pleasure' but the 'fear' that his 'mind had been stripped of all disguise, and it suddenly appeared redoubtable'.[40] Aschenbach styles himself as a virtuous and heroic writer but continues to suffers bouts of wretchedness: his book, *A Study in Abjection*, is a moral treatise condemning 'an age indecently undermined by psychology', but his life is 'haunted by an impulse that had no clear direction' and 'a fleeting sense of dread, a secret shudder of uneasiness'.[41]

In Lacanian thought, the polymorphous world of early childhood is a fragmentary unification of what the adult views as divided and distinct; the boundary of the body does not exist in the manner in which one articulates 'me–you', 'subject–object', or 'inside–outside', but the jettisoning of this pre-Oedipal unity is necessary if the child is to take its place in the Symbolic order. At such time, the disorderly, unclean and anti-social elements must be, to a greater or lesser extent, overcome or sublimated. The degree of such renunciation is dependent on specific cultural conditions and social expectations (for instance, the widespread attitude to homosexuality in Western Europe at the *fin de siècle*), but it most often leads to psychic conflict, as the individual attempts to purify him- or herself from the very baseness which forms identity. However, because a renunciation of the abject does not mean its annihilation, Kristeva explains that: 'there looms, within abjection, one of those violent, dark revolts of being, directed against a threat that seems to emanate from an exorbitant outside or inside, ejected beyond the scope of the possible, the tolerable, the thinkable. It lies there quite close, but it cannot be assimilated.'[42] Michel and Aschenbach fail to locate the source of their impulses, but anxiety continues to loom within their psychic world to disturb their self-constructed identities and their moral frame of reference. Kristeva argues that the abject has no object which can be identified with the self or a desired Other, but it has a tangible presence that manifests itself as a 'sudden emergence of uncanniness which ... now harries me as radically separate, loathsome. Not me. Not that. But not nothing, either. A "something" that I do not recognize as a thing.'[43] In other words, the abject is a point of disruption in the self that cannot be wholly elided with, or directed towards, a desire to travel to a particular place (Biskra for Michel and Venice for Aschenbach) or the desire for another (Moktir and Tadzio).

By applying Kristeva's insights to the two novellas it becomes clear why Aschenbach is overwhelmed by his vision of Tadzio, whereas Michel emerges from Marceline's death with an new orientation toward life. Kristeva argues that the sublime (associated with the European Romantic preoccupation with immensity and magnitude) is an attempt at controlling abjection: 'the abject is edged with the sublime. It is not the same moment on the journey, but the same subject and speech bring them into being.'[44] Aschenbach cannot contend with the looming feeling of abjection because he invests all his emotion in the resplendent vision of Tadzio:

> And to behold this living figure, lovely and austere in its early masculinity, with dripping locks and beautiful as a young god, approaching out of the depths of the sky and the sea, rising and escaping from the elements – this sight filled the mind with mythical images, it was like a poet's tale from a primitive age, a tale of the origins of form and of the birth of the gods.[45]

Aschenbach's vision of the Polish boy's classical body releases his mind 'from the elements' as he attempts to transcend the bodily world for the mythological Platonic realm of ideas. However, this vision only temporarily satisfies his 'longing for the unarticulated and immeasurable, for eternity, for nothingness'.[46] Aschenbach's fantasy is increasingly troubled by his unacknowledged physical desire for Tadzio; his spiritual vision is undermined by the corporeality (symbolised in the cholera epidemic) he denies in himself and which eventually consumes him. In this way, he is rendered impotent by his inability to either consummate his desire or release himself from his fixation on Tadzio. Abjection creeps up unawares and manifests itself too late in the narrative for him to contend with.

Although Michel's early commitment to heroic decadence hinders a full acknowledgement of abjection until the end of the tale, his obsessions are mercurial and many-faceted: he is narcissistic in his self-love; he swings between tenderness for Marceline and feelings of superiority over her; he is surprised by his desire for Arab boys but he does not become fixated on any particular paramour; and his relationship with Ménalque fuses sexual game-playing with intellectual skirmishing. This is not to assert that Michel does not suffer from abjection, but he manages to diffuse desire across a libidinal continuum rather than invest all his feelings in a sublime fascination for an unattainable love (see Chapter 5 for further discussion of this idea). In line with what

Mann describes as Gide's 'hobgoblinism', Michel lives an existence of dissimulation and contradiction without trying to reconcile conflicting elements in a consistent life-style. He does not attempt to assimilate the 'glimmerings of a thousand lost sensations' that arise from the depths into monumental vision, but acknowledges 'that even during those early studious years they had been living their own latent, cunning life'.[47] Unlike Aschenbach, Michel does not endeavour to stop 'the hemorrhage' of the abject (although he experiences haemorrhages during his tuberculosis). Rather, at the end of the tale he manages to keep 'open the wound' in a therapeutic mode of existence: in Kristeva's words, a 'heterogeneous, corporeal, and verbal ordeal of fundamental incompleteness'.[48]

Books and ruins

The Immoralist and *Death in Venice* explore the manner in which the protagonists' ruined lives – Michel's abject nihilism that emerges after Marceline's death, and Aschenbach's abject demise into the 'inert, deep-sunken' figure on the beach – are symbolised by ruined language.[49] It is important that both protagonists are literary men (Aschenbach is a respected writer and Michel lectures on ancient history and archaeology) because Kristeva claims that the sublimated forms of literature, art and music explore the manner in which the abject returns to haunt those processes which try to purify it. She is particularly interested in modernist literature (she lists Dostoevsky, Proust, Artaud, Kafka and Céline, with Gide a notable exception), and she claims that certain types of 'literature may also involve not an ultimate resistance to but an unveiling of the abject'.[50] Abjection, then, is the attitude of the subject who recognises the impossibility of purification, an attitude which Kristeva claims is most productively explored in modernist aesthetics. Both novellas are ultimately concerned with 'books and ruins'. This is particularly relevant for considering the role of abjection in the texts as inscribing the demoralisation of the protagonists and the ruination of language in which their individuality and desires are structured.[51] As Kristeva asserts, modernist writing in particular concerns itself with 'an elaboration, a discharge, and a hollowing out of abjection through the Crisis of the Word'.[52]

Early on in *The Immoralist* Michel claims that 'nothing attracted me [to Tunis] except Carthage and a few Roman ruins'.[53] After his first disappointing visit to the amphitheatre of El Djem he returns to the ruins and searches 'in vain for inscriptions on the stones'.[54] That night his illness worsens as he begins to spit blood, almost as if his body has taken on the character of the ruined amphitheatre. Later in the narrative, during a visit to Syracuse, Michel avoids the ruins because 'every thought of the festivals of antiquity made me grieve over the death of the ruin that was left standing in their place; and I had a horror of death'.[55] This abject recoiling from ancient culture informs Michel's lectures, in which he describes late Latin culture as:

> welling up in a whole people, like a secretion, which is at first a sign of plethora, of a superabundance of health, but which afterwards stiffens, hardens, forbids the perfect contact of the mind with nature, hides under the persistent appearance of life a diminution of life, turns into an outside sheath, in which the cramped mind languishes and pines, in which at last it dies. Finally, pushing my thought to its logical conclusion, I showed Culture, born of life, as the destroyer of life.[56]

Michel's realisation that most forms of culture serve only to secure the 'sheath' of life, instead of life itself, stimulates him to devote less interest to both ruins and books: on their later journey through Italy Michel and Marceline travel with eight trunks, but there was one Michel 'never opened in the whole journey, entirely filled with books'.[57] By the end of the narrative Michel has entirely renounced books and archaeological research in favour of a minimalist lifestyle of ruination which has its own simplistic beauty.[58] This enactment of an abject decadence not only prefigures the French Surrealist interest in the 'poeticisation of the banal' in the 1920s (as discussed in Chapter 3), but offers an aesthetic counterpoint to the kind of heroic stance espoused by Ménalque in *The Immoralist*.

By way of contrast, in the cultural ruins of one of the most glorious Renaissance cities, *Death in Venice* plays out a number of issues that Aschenbach fails to confront. In his book *A Study of Abjection*, Aschenbach proclaims his 'renunciation of all moral scepticism, of every kind of sympathy with the abyss'. However, his stylistic 'purity, simplicity and symmetry' that complements his 'moral resoluteness' stimulates the narrator to question the 'two-faced' nature of writing, which often hides the 'resurgence of energies that are evil, forbidden, or morally impossible' behind the veil of moral intention.[59] This understanding is very similar to Michel's realisation that the trappings of culture often shroud real life with the illusion of it, but crucially it is only the narrator who understands this point in *Death in Venice*. Aschenbach is drawn to Venice as 'a city irresistibly attractive to the man of culture, by its history no less than its present charms', but the narrator warns the reader that we should be suspicious of this 'glib empty talk'.[60] Indeed, the Venice in which he finds himself is overrun by commercialism and ridden with pestilence: a city fallen from aesthetic grace to its ruinous state as a commercial tourist trap. It is not that Aschenbach does not detect these signs (they come to him in his half-memories of Plato's *Phaedrus* as the 'tissue of strange dream-logic') but, rather, he fails to act on his decision to leave the city.[61] Instead he resurrects the sublime vision of Tadzio from the ruins of Venice and bolsters up his decaying body by 'cosmetically brightened lips' and by acquiring a straw hat and scarlet necktie. Ironically, in this cosmetic transformation into a parody of the late nineteenth-century dandy, Aschenbach gives himself over to the abyss which he had earlier renounced. His last experience of cholera-induced feelings are 'waves of dizziness, only half physical, and with them an increasing sense of dread, a feeling of hopelessness and pointlessness'.[62] However, although Aschenbach's symptoms resemble Michel's condition at the end of *The Immoralist*, Aschenbach is too sick to cultivate an existence that can contend with such emotions as he collapses under the weight of his ruination.

Both *Death in Venice* and *The Immoralist* are preoccupied with the possibilities as well as the impossibilities of enacting the border between morality and abjection that Kristeva discusses in *Powers of Horror*. This symbolic border takes on various forms in the narratives as the protagonists hover uncertainly between two states of being: caught between horror and fascination and the desire to be mobile; between the need to retain identity and the blurring of borders between self and Other (especially in terms of sexual proclivity); and between the unruly aspects of corporeality and spiritual vision. This state is most powerfully symbolised by Michel's fascination with (and fear of) shadows, and Aschenbach's vacillation between conscience and desire during his aborted attempt to leave Venice.

Since the abject is a point of disruption (according to Kristeva, not being subject, object, or non-object) it erodes distinctions between structural oppositions (intellect and passion, conviction and inclination, morality and immorality) rather than reconciling them. Although these dichotomies are discernible in both novellas, the ways in which Gide and Mann explore abject decadence diverge significantly. Aschenbach's inability to deal with the contradictory impulses of responsibility and inclination (or Apollonian control and Dionysian desire) leads inexorably to his death, whereas Michel (after Marceline's death) continues to lead a kind of 'shadow' life, or what Kristeva calls a 'forfeited existence':

> It is simply a frontier, a repulsive gift that the Other, having become alter ego, drops so that 'I' does not disappear in it but finds, in that sublime alienation, a forfeited existence. Hence a jouissance in which the subject is swallowed up but in which the Other, in return, keeps the subject from foundering by making it repugnant. One thus understands why so many victims of the abject are its fascinated victims – if not its submissive and willing ones.[63]

Even though Michel is often blind to his own motives, the first-person mode of narration reveals more about his psyche than the detached third-person narrative voice discloses about Aschenbach. The standard reading of the conclusion of *The Immoralist* is that Michel justifies his story and actions to his friends who are themselves readers of his story: 'We felt, alas, that by telling his story. Michel had made his action more legitimate.'[64] However, the ending can be read more productively as Michel's attempt to accept his shattered life in a ruined world by embracing the shadow-line that so fascinated him earlier in the tale.

Michel continues to live a 'forfeited existence', whereas Aschenbach is invaded and finally overcome by his desire and illness. In other words, Michel embraces the courage to transgress or live dangerously (but not heroically) at the limit, whereas Aschenbach (except for his dream of a Bacchanalian orgy) is rendered aimless after his self-discipline has been eroded by his confrontation with a decadent Venice. Jonathan Dollimore argues that this kind of courage is not continuous with the morally virtuous and disciplined Victorian hero, but embodies the decadent spirit of demoralisation: the courage to 'liberate' the self 'from moral constraint rather than dispirit'.[65] Dollimore argues that Gide learnt this sense of demoralisation from Wilde; but 'whereas for Wilde transgressive desire leads to a relinquishing of the essential self, for Gide it leads to its discovery, to the real self, a new self created from liberated desire'.[66] However, although the language of authenticity permeates the early sections of *The Immoralist*, Michel's new-found ability to lead a 'forfeited existence' suggests a different kind of selfhood from that conceived in essentialist terms. Crucially, after Marceline's death, it is not heroic transgression that Michel embodies but a banal negotiation of borders and lines between memories and action, intellect and passion and homo- and heterosexuality, or what Kristeva calls the life of the borderlander: 'there, I am at the border of my condition as a living being'.[67] Despite his trials and losses Michel improvises a demoralised code of ethics that engages with the abject, whereas Aschenbach is totally debilitated by excessive bodily drives. In his ruined state Michel confronts the impermanence of the modern world; his forfeited existence has its own existential authenticity but is still in the process of becoming.

> What frightens me, I admit, is that I am still very young. It seems to me sometimes that my real life has not begun. Take me away from here and give me some reason for living. I have none left. I have freed myself. That may be. But what does that signify?[68]

Michel claims earlier in the narrative that 'the miscellaneous mass of acquired knowledge of every kind gets peeled off in places like a mask of paint, exposing the bare skin',[69] but at the end he is reduced to a series of sexual encounters and the ritual of repeatedly cooling pebbles in the shade and then warming them in his hand. This is not a ritual that protects him from reality, but a way of comprehending the limits of his fragile and 'broken' life still under threat from the hedonistic forces that earlier consumed him. Even though he lives 'for next to nothing in this place', it is the 'next to nothing' which still gives his life some meaning.[70] He finally abandons his books for life in order to cultivate this ruined existence. The final image of Michel's minimalist life-style gestures towards what Walter Benjamin describes as Gide's mercurial talent for disguising his ethical agenda in his aesthetic aims, in order better to challenge the roots of 'moral indifference and lax complacency'.[71] As such, ultimately the elements in Gide's writing that most appeal to Mann do not actually conform to his pattern of 'precarious harmony' as they cannot be reconciled by aesthetic wizardry or the Joycean paring of fingernails. Rather, they are embodied in Michel's life as an enactment of banal decadence that confronts contradiction, fragmentation, liminality, unruliness and prodigality without recuperation: in short, a decadent mode of existence that faces the moral abjection of modernity even though it can never overcome it.

Part II
Symbolic Centres of Modernism

3
Extremist Modernism: The Avant-Garde and the Limits of Art

(Tzara, Huelsenbeck, Breton, Aragon)

By the 1910s the decadent impulses of the European *fin-de-siècle* had bifurcated into, on the one hand, the provocative posturing of the cosmopolitan avant-garde and, on the other, strains of Symbolism evident in the high modernism of (in Europe) Proust and Joyce and (in America) Fitzgerald and Faulkner. In *The Symbolist Movement in Literature* (1899), the English critic Arthur Symons dismissed decadence as 'the *maladie fin de siècle*', an 'interlude, half a mock-interlude' in the 'serious' development of Symbolism, which for him represented the 'attempt to spiritualize literature, to evade the old bondage of rhetoric, the old bondage of exteriority'.[1] Rather than adopting a blasé decadent attitude to culture, Symons argued that if art has taken the place of religion as the only rejuvenating force in a world of uncertainty, then the artist must accept both the 'heavier burden' of liberty and 'the duties and responsibilities of the sacred ritual'.[2] However, this fusion of religion and morality offered a solemn form of aesthetic responsibility which was undesirable to writers fashioning more experimental cultural forms free from the narrow 'duties' of art. If the passivity which Walter Pater and Symons describe – 'the delight of feeling ourselves carried onward by forces which it is our wisdom to obey'[3] – enables the artist to tap into an imaginative world beyond the conventionally moral or worthy in a search for the *'l'image peinte, l'épithète rare'*, then Symbolist poetics can be seen to foreshadow the aesthetic experiments of Dadaism and Surrealism in war-shocked Europe.[4] But, if Symons means the artist should be beholden to a religious imperative to create within fixed parameters, then many modernist writers in the 1910s and 1920s evidently dismissed the more doctrinal aspects of Symbolism. Although the decadent image of the artist as rebel or deviant continued to have currency in the mid-

1910s, the Romantic icon of the artist as high priest of the sublime was on the wane.

This chapter considers the transition between these two forms of aesthetic modelling: the late-Romantic transmutation of spiritual matter into Symbolist art, as epitomised in Stéphane Mallarmé's poetry of 'incantation', and the more prodigal and chaotic practice of the European avant-garde.[5] If Symbolism and decadence lag after their time as post-Romantic cultural manifestations, then the avant-garde is always ahead of its time, portending what is, or what might be, possible. This reorientation towards what Peter Osborne calls 'time-consciousness' reflects a reconfiguration of disparate modernist currents into new aesthetic forms more suited to their place in time than their predecessors.[6] Osborne defines the 'time-consciousness of modernity' as a state of 'perpetual transition' which interrupts the myth of linear historical progress by dissolving the notion of the present as the leading moment of the past into 'a process of pure presencing'.[7] Whereas decadent writers like Huysmans and Baudelaire tended to see time as a mortal curse, the early twentieth-century avant-gardists were excited about the possibilities of art as a revolutionary experience which interferes with and disrupts the temporal order at special (but unpredictable) moments of aesthetic and moral awareness. But, while the numerous avant-garde manifestos seem to promise a clean break from the past, traces of Symbolist aesthetics are evident in the ecstatic revelations of the Dadaists and Surrealists.

As exponents of 'extremist modernism', Tristan Tzara and André Breton devised new modes of expression to harden the soft edges of Symbolism, while continuing to explore the tensions between art and morality.[8] Georg Lukács argued famously that in their emphasis on form, many modernists offered negative and amoral responses to modernity. However, a more receptive view would suggest that avant-garde writers actually illuminated and creatively worked through the problematic distinctions between morality, immorality and amorality. If amoral is defined as having 'no moral quality', then Lukács's argument has some validity; however, it is this moral negation that extremist modernists explored in order to create value out of destructive impulses, a tendency which David Harvey calls 'creative destruction' set against the 'destructive creation' of modernisation and the moral nihilism of the Great War.[9] As the American artist Robert Motherwell argued in his influential collection, *The Dada Painters and Poets* (1951), avant-garde art plays destructive and constructive tendencies off one another: 'modern art ... had its destructive side only in order to recover for art human values that existed in art before and will again, but to which conventional or "official" art remain insensitive'.[10]

While Symbolist poets such as Mallarmé positioned enigmatic symbols at the centre of their poetry, the writers discussed in this chapter complicate the very notion of a 'centre' by which their art can be structured or explained. But, rather than dispensing with symbolic centres, the four avant-garde writers considered here – the German Dadaist Richard Huelsenbeck, the Romanian poet Tristan Tzara and the French Surrealists André Breton and Louis Aragon – deployed symbols as devices which fractured the formal limits of their work and gestured towards the possibility of a new aesthetic that would be, as Gertrude Stein proposed, 'irritating', 'annoying' and 'stimulating'.[11] Extremist modernists were particularly interested in the hidden life of objects, the materiality of words, and the ways in which defamiliarising techniques could facilitate new perceptions that undermine an anthropocentric view of life and help to reposition the subject in a denser and noisier world of images, textures and sounds. Only when the avant-garde became the 'official' face of modernism, when it became what Tzara called a 'precise, everyday word', did it sacrifice the potential to decentre and reorient aesthetic perception in this way. Before avant-garde practices became heavily politicised in the 1930s and its artefacts were canonised as museum pieces in the 1950s, the creative energies of Dadaism and Surrealism enabled their exponents to reassess the role of the artist by provoking 'from the intellectual and moral point of view'.[12] As *agents provocateurs* the European avant-garde artists cannot, as Breton argued, be simply categorised as either 'constructive or destructive'; rather, as Tzara claims, they mingle their 'caprices with the chaotic wind of creation'.[13] By focusing on these attempts to interrupt the twin dialectics of destruction and creation and of amorality and morality, the modernist avant-garde can be depicted as an interventionist moment within the time-consciousness of modernity.

The poetics of Dada: Tzara and Huelsenbeck

The emergence of an international avant-garde in the mid-1910s was heralded by the International Exhibition of Modern Art (the Armory Show) in early 1913 sponsored by the Association of American Painters and Sculptors and held at Sixty-ninth Regiment Armory in New York City. At the same time, the photographer Alfred Stieglitz provided exhibition opportunities to American and European artists at his Camera Work Gallery, making New York a rival centre to Paris as the showcase capital of modern art. A sweeping away of traditional art forms and hostility toward the past were evident in the mixed-media creations of the European émigrés Marcel Duchamp and Francis Picabia, who found in Manhattan an exciting multiculturalism not present in Europe until during the Great War. The spirit of artistic adventure in the new bohemia of Greenwich Village, exemplified in the most famous of the exhibits at the Armory Show, Duchamp's 'Nude Descending a Staircase' (painted in 1912) and fused with the revolutionary ideas of the philosophical anarchist Emma Goldman, inspired a spirit of non-conformism and widespread disdain for orthodox aesthetics. The response from the public was a mixture of curiosity, bewilderment and declamation, with the *New York Times* proclaiming that 'this movement is surely part of a general movement ... to disrupt, degrade, if not destroy, not only art but literature and society too'.[14] The twin aims of the practitioners to challenge perception and to revolutionise artistic form led to a knee-jerk reaction from journalists who deemed the exhibits intrinsically immoral. Despite these negative reviews, many artists acclaimed the Armory Show a creative success as the first organised exhibition of twentieth-century extremist modernism. But, it was not until Dadaism was given its name in Switzerland in 1916 that artists collectively begin to consider seriously the moral implications of their new practice.

Looking back on European creativity in the 1910s, Richard Huelsenbeck stated in a 1970 American lecture that 'Dada was a protest without a program ... We protested the system, without ever offering alternatives. Dada was a moral protest not only against the war but also against the malaise of the time.'[15] The experiments of Huelsenbeck, Hans Arp, Marcel Janco, Hugo Ball and Tristan Tzara are usually viewed as nihilistic examples of anti-art in contrast to what they deemed to be an unhealthy bourgeois reverence for art: what Peter Nicholls calls 'a posture of absolute indifference' to 'the complete bankruptcy of the West's intellectual tradition'.[16] Despite Huelsenbeck's claim that Dada was a moral protest, 'the malaise of the time' infected conventional morals that Tzara condemned for being divorced from 'real' life. Tzara's claim that 'morals have an atrophying effect, like every pestilential product of the intelligence' mirrors the moral inertia Norris and Wharton had earlier tackled from the perspective of naturalism.[17] But, in their fracturing of narrative and poetic form and disdain for art, knowledge, morality, social progress, law and science, Dadaist anti-art represented an outright assault on all the previously cherished values of Western culture. As Tzara proclaimed in 1918 in the most famous of his seven Dada manifestos, under the subheading 'Dadaist Disgust': 'Every product of disgust that is capable of becoming a negation of the family is *dada*; protest with the fists of one's whole being in destructive action.'[18] This 'organized insulting' of bourgeois culture is stylised in its aggression (although not as partisan as Filippo Marinetti's Futurist manifestos) and shot through with nihilism.[19]

The German artist Kurt Schwitters divided Dadaism into two kinds: 'kernel' Dada epitomised in the abstract work of Tzara, and the 'husk' Dadaists led by Huelsenbeck, whose radical experiments in Berlin became politicised in the late 1910s.[20] For Schwitters, kernel Dada laughs at its own demise whereas husk Dada (more directly German) learnt to be more progressive in its social struggle, even though Huelsenbeck (annoyed with this distinction) claimed that his socialist commitment had a 'human basis' and was not motivated by explicit political goals.[21] Despite these differences and Tzara's and Huelsenbeck's later hostility to each other (Huelsenbeck was particularly critical of Tzara's nihilistic spirit and his 'ownership' of Dadaism),[22] early Dadaist proclamations were consistent in promoting radical art as an 'ironic and contemptuous response to a culture which had shown itself worthy of flame-throwers and machine-guns'.[23] In the drive for simplicity they were particularly hostile to the novel as a bourgeois art form and more interested in the fictive potential of performance art, dance, poetry and song (especially *chants nègres*) to fashion primitive modes of expression. The cosmopolitan fertility of Zurich during and immediately after the war was the perfect place to devise art that could give reign to 'free expression' and attack the foundations of what they perceived to be a decadent bourgeois culture.[24] In the spring and summer of 1916 the Cabaret Voltaire (run by Hugo Ball) was the scene of Tzara's 'crafty grin' and Huelsenbeck's 'college-boy insolence', with Hans Richter claiming their strangely-costumed and noisy performances were 'unhindered by moral scruples'.[25] Along with their early artistic collaborators, Tzara and Huelsenbeck did not eschew all forms of morality; they merely refused to accept moral value as an inherited given.

The most famous anecdote concerning Dadaist irreverence for conventional morality recounts an incident when the Dadaists (in their late phase) found in a Parisian café a wallet left by a waiter. After discussing the alternatives, they decided not to return the wallet because this would have been acting in accordance with conventional morality, so the French poet Paul Eluard kept it while the group decided what to do. The wallet was returned to the waiter the following day, but Eluard later complicated the story by claiming it had been stolen from a priest and presented to the waiter as a gift. This anecdote suggests that in their refusal to adhere to bourgeois moral codes, the Dadaists sought another set of principles on which to base their morality. But, in their inability to devise an alternative to giving back the wallet (moral action) or effectively stealing the wallet (immoral), they are faced only with undecidability, or what Robert Motherwell calls 'the complete inability of Dada to enter on the practical plane'.[26] Whatever the truth of the anecdote, the attempt to cloak the incident in the uncertainty and comedy of Eluard's story of the priest suggests that the best response the group could muster was a theatrical gesture or hoax. While Helena Lewis views this *'acte gratuit'* in political terms as a thinly disguised empathy towards the poor, it is more productive to explore the moral implications of the Dada performance as an example of the serious 'practical joke'.[27] On this model, there would be little difference between this café incident, a public performance, or (in Huelsenbeck's words) 'the bartender in the Manhattan bar, who pours out Curaçao with one hand and gathers up gonorrhea with the other' as illustrating the transformation of 'ideas' into 'life'.[28] The major weakness in this claim is that the Dadaists found difficult to sustain what Huelsenbeck calls living 'only through action', because moral decision-making proved incommensurate with their desire to fashion a playful in-between world. In other words, as Peter Osborne comments, 'if the experience of the "truly new" can only be momentary' how can it inform materialist issues of 'identity and action'?[29]

While a certain spirit of nihilism, an 'I-don't give a damn attitude of life', pervades European Dadaism from its beginnings in 1916 in Zurich to the early 1920s in Paris (and, to a certain extent, in New York and Berlin), a number of affirmative aesthetic energies can be identified to balance its more destructive tendencies; energies which Nicholas Zurbrugg terms *'ante*-art' (as opposed to *'anti*-art') that promise 'new modes of positive creativity'.[30] For example, despite Tzara's militant aggression, he celebrates the 'interweaving of contraries and of all contradictions' in his 1918 Dadaist Manifesto, which he ends with the capitalised flourish 'LIFE'.[31] Another example of this affirmatory impulse can be found in Huelsenbeck's first contribution to Dadaism, 'The New Man' ('Der neue Mensch') published in *Neue Jugend* in May 1917, in which he promotes the *'homo novus'*, not as an embodiment of Nikolai Chernyshevsky's new rationalism attacked by Dostoevsky (see Introduction), but as an antidote to the posturing of 'bad revolutionaries':

> We have heard too much of the dialogues of the dead, our ear has received too much that is artificial, and we run now the risk of losing our inner self. *Words, words, too many words* – silence must rise, the ear must ready itself for the orphic of most sacred nights. Days change into nights, gods fall from their thrones, that, however remains which makes us human and grow. We are required to look deep into ourselves to understand man, what can be made out of him; there one sees the synthesis of capabilities and all things human.[32]

The widespread Dadaist disdain for meaningful language, from Huelsenbeck's criticisms of 'the dialogues of the dead' to the multilingual babble of Hugo Ball's phonetic poems and to Tzara's proclamation 'NO MORE WORDS!',[33] represents an assault on all naturalised values that have been elevated to the status of truth. Instead of striving for sense and the *mot juste*, in this passage Huelsenbeck claims that we should prepare ourselves for silence and wonder as the rejuvenating forces in a confusing world of signs. However, despite the Dadaist intention to divorce words from their naturalised meanings, as Beckett and Ionesco discovered thirty years later in their minimalist writings, Huelsenbeck is forced to rely on words to gesture towards his Symbolist description of the 'sacred night'. Similarly, Ball's account of one of his own performances of 'verses without words' begins as a clarion call for nonsense poetry in which the material texture and noise of the words (*le bruit*) overrides meaning, but actually results in a withdrawal into 'the innermost alchemy of the word' to conserve for poetry 'its most sacred domain'.[34]

Although Huelsenbeck's declamations echo Tzara's 'disgust' for moribund traditions, the German writes of a certain imperative, or 'requirement', which pushes him to nurture human 'capabilities' in order to see 'what can be made out of him'. Echoing Nietzsche's contempt in *Human, All Too Human* (1878) for conventional morality as the slavish veneration of custom ('to be moral, correct, ethical means to obey an age-old law or tradition'),[35] Huelsenbeck does not attempt to transcend the human condition by advocating a form of aestheticised will-to-power, but reassesses the parameters of 'the human' as a transvaluation of values. In a 1956 essay, 'Dada', Huelsenbeck provides one of his clearest expressions of the role of Dada for excavating the human condition:

> The Dada attitude is basically the paradox of forgetting the human in order to reveal it all the more penetratingly. The relativity of everything human is shown, and art has to adjust to it. Inhumanity is viewed as part of the human ... The division of human life into good and evil was rejected as a dangerous psychosis characteristic of the commercialized middle class in the nineteenth century. This 'new man' ... is a man of transcendence, by whom good and evil are no longer viewed from different standpoints. The moral and immoral are the relativized components of a total personality.[36]

Instead of pure nihilism then, Huelsenbeck's statement provides one example of the positive energies of Dadaism: a 'new integration' which counters the lazy conformity to convention of 'the burgher, the overfed philistine, the overfed pig, the pig of intellectuality, this shepherd of all miseries'.[37] Huelsenbeck's cultural stance mirrors the decadent aristocratic attitude to bourgeois complacency to a certain extent, but there is also a generative drive to renew values, rather than to indulge in the sensualities of the past. For him 'the Dadaist destruction of art is not just the clownish imitation of terrible events, but also an analytical anticipation of the processes one has to go through to reach the premise of all future artistic activity', which would be 'the total, human personality' not divided into specialised faculties or strict polarities.[38] Huelsenbeck's view of Dadaism (as an experimental movement which harnesses Nietzsche's transvaluation of values) embodies this longing for a new conception of humanity and 'the desire for a new morality' that could only emerge from a combined social and spiritual revolution.[39]

Although they offered different views of the transformative potential of Dada, both Tzara and Huelsenbeck move towards a conception of art divorced from the aesthetic verities of greatness, beauty or profundity. Walter Benjamin identifies the celebration of the banality of life as being central to early avant-garde practice, but the switch from artistic profundity to anti-aesthetic banality does not free Dada from what Tzara acknowledges to be 'the framework of European weaknesses'.[40] Tzara argues that even if Dada is 'still shit', this should not discourage the artist from shitting 'in different colours'.[41] Twisting Walter Pater's recommendation that the artist should burn with 'a gem-like flame', Tzara replaces the spiritualised aestheticism of art appreciation with the baseness of cultural defecation, while Hugo Ball played with 'shabby debris' and the first German Dadaist manifesto urged the artist to 'snatch the tatters of their bodies out of the frenzied cataract of life'.[42] Reflecting the underside of life explored in Mann's and Gide's decadent novellas and Kafka's modernist fable 'Metamorphosis' (*'Die Verwandlung'*, 1915), Huelsenbeck positions humans between 'apes and bedbugs' and Tzara muddies his art in the baseness of the human condition, instead of seeking an aestheticised realm which may transcend it.[43] As such, Tzara's art is neither one thing nor another – 'DADA is neither madness, nor wisdom, nor irony' – but constitutes a performance which on the surface appears facile, but cloaks the search for 'the central essence of things'.[44] It is difficult to ascertain where this search leads, partly because the spirit of Dada derives from the Nietzschean realm of lies, double negatives and creative tensions, and partly because Dada performance does not rely on the narrative progression of 'a talking and self-defining story'.[45] Rather than seeking solutions, the Dadaists devised a range of performances involving acted gestures, noisy declamation, multilingual babble, collage and other mixed-media ephemera, provoking questions about the status of, and relationship between, humans and objects: a series of performances in which Tzara argued 'both the insignificant gesture and the decisive movement are attacks' on convention.[46]

The anti-intellectual thrust of Dadaism was not merely an assault on intellectual pretensions, but represented a move towards the simplicity of primal noises and gestures. Instead of adhering to Kant's universal moral imperative which determines right behaviour, Tzara was sceptical of 'big' words such as 'Beauty, Truth, Art, Good, Liberty ... which claim to make everyone agree', but actually 'do not have the moral value and the objective force that people are used to giving them'.[47] In place of definitions and principles, Tzara commends plurality of meaning and diversity in life. What remains integral to the Dada 'state of mind' (and modernism more generally) is a moral sensibility that cannot be formalised into strict codes and rules without muting its potential.[48] Tzara's claim that 'Dada is more or less everywhere' is also applicable to his description of primal morality as a reservoir of ethical possibility. This gesture towards the mysterious source of morality as the hidden centre of Dadaist art echoes the Symbolism of Mallarmé and Baudelaire as an absent presence towards which poetic images can only hint. Just as Tzara claims that 'Dada is applicable to everything, and yet it is nothing, it *is* the point where *yes* and *no* meet', a kind of 'virgin microbe that insinuates itself with the insistence of air into all the spaces that reason hasn't been able to fill with words or conventions', so too is morality seen as an inexpressible reservoir of potentiality.

Even though Dadaist artists were virtuoso performers (in Hannah Arendt's sense of virtuosity: see the Introduction) in the creation of hybrid art forms, they welcomed elements of chance and accident as important ingredients in the creative process. Tzara's famous experiment of putting random words in a bag and rearranging them haphazardly provides an image of the artist as a 'prestidigitator ... who takes advantage of his own errors and of his faulty strokes to play tricks with them; he never has more grace than when he makes a virtue of his own clumsiness'.[49] Not only does this reconception of the artist distance the avant-gardist from the decadent aesthete, but it replaces the Romantic belief in the poet as divine creator with the artist as *bricoleur* who welcomes the flux of creative and moral energies from wherever they derive. In its most extreme form, the work of art would be a 'forgery', a 'hoax' or 'a fabrication not related to an author acting under the influence of a single impulse'.[50] The Dadaists were clearly cynical about acting on moral principles, but, as Gide demonstrated in his hoax novel, *The Vatican Cellars* (*Les caves du Vatican*, 1914), they did not simply swap moral principles for playful amorality or disdainful immorality, but tried to forge a creative mix of aesthetic and moral impulses. As Huelsenbeck claimed in 1920:

> The Dadaist ... is no longer a metaphysician in the sense of finding a rule for the conduct of life in any theoretical principles, for him there is no longer a 'thou shalt'; for him the cigarette-butt and the umbrella are as exalted and as timeless as the 'thing in itself.' Consequently, the good is for the Dadaist no 'better' than the bad – there is only simultaneity, in values as in everything else.[51]

While the illusion of simultaneity can be enacted in stage performances or created through the montage editing of Sergei Eisenstein's film aesthetic, decisions must be made in a world of moral consequences (as the Parisian wallet incident demonstrates). It is this inability to reconcile the spheres of art and action which partly contributed to the collapse of the Dadaist project. By 1920 the German Dadaists had become explicitly political in their support of communism as 'the destruction of everything that has gone bourgeois', while the Paris Surrealists, under the leadership of André Breton, became more interested in the creative potential of dreams for offering an alternative moral *kosmos* to the public world of decision-making and action.[52]

Forms of Surrealism: Breton and Aragon

Whereas the Dadaists were reticent about stating a positive artistic agenda for fear of adopting the language of bourgeois practicality, Breton insisted on the serious 'moral' goals of Surrealism for dealing with the 'principal problems of life'.[53] However, like the Dadaists, Breton wanted to redescribe the terms of moral involvement. In the First Surrealist Manifesto of 1924, he declared his interest in 'psychic automatism' as the true function of thought free from 'any control exercised by reason' and 'exempt from any aesthetic or moral concern'.[54] The links with Dadaism are obvious in this statement: the dislike for rationalism and conventional ethical codes in both movements forced a reorientation of the artist's moral role. However, Dadaists such as Tzara disliked the mysticism of Surrealism (Walter Benjamin called it a manifestation of the 'last trickle of French decadence'),[55] together with Breton's emphasis on 'the omnipotence of the dream', the word-association games he developed from psychoanalytic practice and the automatic writing experiments he shared with Philippe Soupault. Conversely, while Breton's statements echoed the combative proclamations of Tzara, he criticised Dadaist performances for simply trying 'to create as much confusion as possible in order to bring the misunderstanding between participants and public to its highest pitch'.[56] Breton was particularly critical of Tzara (although Tzara's name is included in support of the first two Surrealist manifestos of 1924 and 1930) for his unwillingness to step into line with 'the practical methods' and 'common goals' of the movement. This desire to 'recognize value ... wherever it exists' distanced Surrealism from the nihilistic currents of Dadaist aesthetics, in order to propel art in 'the direction of human liberation'.[57] Although Breton and Aragon moved away from their belief in the autonomy of art in the 1930s towards an active engagement with communism as a means to anchor the ethical and political directives of Surrealism, it is interesting to compare the moral implications of their practice up to the early 1930s with the more chaotic statements of the Dadaists.

Although the emergence of Surrealism in Europe (and less dramatically in America) cannot be credited solely to Breton, he represented the movement's most persistent and forceful voice. His 1924 Surrealist manifesto marked the crystallisation of a number of artistic experiments over the previous three years, setting out an agenda to prove that Surrealism was 'more than an intellectual pastime'.[58] In his 1929 preface to the First Manifesto, Breton argues that Surrealism was a timely intervention in the still new century, but he admits that 'we're in bad, we're in terrible shape when it comes to time'.[59] He is forced to reassess the dynamics of temporality because time does not unfold rationally in a stable universe, but flits through 'an imperceptible world of phantasms, of hypothetical realizations, of wages lost, and of lies', a world evocative of Paris as a surrealistic city in which, for Benjamin, 'ghostly signals flash from the traffic'.[60] Breton equates this alternative temporal order with the world of childhood characterised by simultaneity and 'the perspective of several lives lived at once': a world of play which may enable the adult artist to keep pace with the 'fleeting, the extreme facility of everything'.[61] However, foreshadowing Lacan's theorisation of the Symbolic order, Breton argues that most adults lose the ability to live comfortably in fractured time around the age of twenty, at which point they enter the world of prosaic reality. He looks to the imagination as a faculty that can dispense with the 'realistic attitude' to life and offers the artist some 'intimation of what *can be*' rather than what 'is' at the present time.[62] The opening up of the future reflects the Dadaist attitude to liberating the sphere of the possible, but Breton's aim is more optimistic in its search for the 'revelation' of the 'marvelous' in which reality and dream intertwine.[63] His desire to fold extremes into each other, at which point 'life and death, the real and the imagined, past and future, the communicable and the incommunicable, high and low, cease to be perceived as contradictions', contributes to his project to disrupt the logic of Hegel's dialectic by constantly reconfiguring image structures and accepted taxonomies of meaning.[64]

Breton's famous Surrealist anecdote included in the 1924 manifesto is almost a parody of Romantic revelation, concerning a vision he experienced in 1919 in which a 'disembodied phrase ... *was knocking at the window*'.[65] Breton recalls that the phrase – 'there is a man cut in two by the window' – was accompanied by a faint image in which the man and window appear together as an 'apparition' moving in space. This verbal-visual example of what Breton calls the 'extreme degree of immediate absurdity' suggests that the dream-like realm is usually encountered in solitude far removed from public consciousness. He writes about the preparation of the poet for such bizarre revelations, an introspective awareness of which, as he summarised in his 1930 manifesto, is 'nothing other than the dizzying descent into ourselves, the systematic illumination of hidden places and the progressive darkening of other places'.[66] Although Breton uses psychoanalytic language alien to Dadaism (because psychoanalysis claimed to be able to discover the unconscious 'truth'), this assertion undercuts the notion of a self-aware artist whose receptivity gives him a capacious understanding of life. Indeed, it is the materiality of language (rather than the power of the artist) that animates the phrase at the window and issues in a ghostly world of Otherness as revenants from the past and portents of the future.

In this spontaneous realm of colliding images, 'value' is created not by external criteria but by 'the beauty of the spark' which forces the artist into a 'complete state of distraction' where he must attend to the absurd relationship ('the difference of potential') between disparate images.[67] Rather than the 'spark' deriving from the poet's sensitivity, as it would for Pater, it stems from the supercharged images themselves that erupt to form new and strange linguistic combinations. This notion is reinforced by the Surrealist poet Paul Eluard in his claim that:

> Images are, images live, and everything becomes image. They were long mistaken for illusions because they were restricted, were made to undergo the test of reality, an insensitive and dead reality, when reality should have been made to undergo the test of its own interdependence which makes it alive, active, and perpetually moving.[68]

For Eluard, the chance encounters between images spark off new relations just as the collision of atoms create new molecular structures; only if the movement between elements is prohibited will images crystallise into 'dead reality'. On this phenomenological model inspired by Henri Bergson, the artist should ensure that perpetual motion is maintained, but cannot claim with any justification that the dynamism derives from within: the artist is only the observer of a greater reality (a *sur*-reality) and the receptacle of flux. Both Breton and Eluard claim avant-garde artists are copiers, not in a prosaic realist sense, but as figures who 'go on making objective, what it has not been and is not yet possible to make objective – everything'.[69] They do not possess the divine power attributed to Romantic poets, but with their 'eyes wide open' they can help transform perceptions of the possible and the impossible. For Michel Remy, this belief does not provide a 'technique as such' for the Surrealists, 'but only an unbounded series of *strategies*, aimed at destabilizing the gaze and conducted from as many angles as possible'.[70] Although Jürgen Habermas has argued that avant-garde strategies actually fail to impact on the public sphere of morality, Breton returned repeatedly to statements urging a radical reconsideration of the basis of morality as what Robert Desnos calls 'the meaning of life' and not 'the observation of human laws'.[71] Breton argued in the first manifesto that however difficult it is for him 'to accept the principle of any kind of responsibility', he admits that the avant-gardist will be held publicly accountable for his work, even if the artist were to deny authorship and argue that 'he is at least as foreign to the accused text' as those making accusations.[72] He claims that if Surrealism received widespread support a 'new morality' would emerge to replace 'the prevailing morality, the source of all our trials and tribulations'. Breton states this more clearly in his 1930 manifesto in his claim that avant-garde success can only be 'carried out under conditions of moral asepsis which very few people in this day and age are interested in hearing about'.[73] Elsewhere, he argues that the sister spirits of 'nonconformism' and 'demoralization' preside over Surrealist activity, suggesting that the products will always be unexpected and unhindered by conventional limitations; the Surrealist attacks the same blank wall that Dostoevsky's Underground Man faced, 'refuses to admit defeat, sets off from whatever point he chooses, along any other path save a reasonable one, and arrives wherever he can'.[74] Such activity may be anarchic in its intentions, but Breton offers his art as a gift to the reader: 'What I have done, what I have left undone, I give it to you.' Breton's voice is abrasive in his role of moral saboteur, but in these rare moments of humility he admits the modern world cannot be defeated by the cunning that Joyce's Stephen Dedalus seeks, but only traversed with the belief that fresh image constellations may spark new perceptions and through a wholesale revaluation of morality.

Michel Remy discerns that the basis of Surrealism is 'revelation by any method', implying it develops Symbolist impulses rather than offering a clean break with the past.[75] In Breton's prose trilogy *Nadja* (1928), *Communicating Vessels* (*Les Vases communicants*, 1932) and *Mad Love* (*L'Amour fou*, 1937) the 'enigma of revelation' is explored in terms of the artist's own libidinal drives, oscillating between the dreamscape and the world of unexpected erotic encounters and lucky finds.[76] At the beginning of *Nadja*, Breton suggests chance and coincidence are more important in allowing him access 'to an almost forbidden world of sudden parallels' than the versatility of the writer.[77] The flashes of insight he gains into his own identity are forced upon him after his chance meeting and irresistible attraction to Nadja. Rather than ending in abjection and death, *Nadja* differs from Gide's and Mann's homoerotic tales in depicting Breton's gradual drifting away from his obsession with Nadja's enigmatic beauty towards a meditation on the mysteries of existence. *Nadja* develops Breton's understanding of the therapeutic potential of art by, first, attacking the reader's expectations of what constitutes literary and moral value ('any action which requires a continuous application and which can be premeditated') and, second, by offering a tale which embodies what Susan Sontag calls the 're-education of the senses'.[78] Although Breton leaves himself open to attacks on his fickleness (he finds Nadja 'fascinating because mad', but she 'is then disappointing, because she is not interesting enough'[79]), their love affair forces him to question the power of desire to transform the prosaic world into one bristling with libidinous energies. Moreover, his affair with Nadja interrupts his time-consciousness in the same way that the avant-garde wished to disrupt the linearity of historical continuity, compelling him to rethink the patterns of his life. Breton is left humbled and demoralised in the face of beauty which 'consists of jolts and shocks, many of which do not have much importance, but which we know are destined to produce one *Shock*, which does. Which has all the importance I do not want to arrogate to myself.'[80]

In the second book of the trilogy, *Communicating Vessels*, Breton argues that dreams are the necessary link between the objective world of facts and the interior world of emotions as a mediating *kosmos* of latent energies. The realisation that the door to dreams is already 'half opened' enables the poet to act as mediator between the two worlds.[81] On this model, the avant-garde practitioner must lose him- or herself by submitting to subliminal forces beyond individual or social control before the role of artist as revolutionary agent can be forged. As Breton explores in *Mad Love*, these forces are beyond any rational comprehension but, when accessed, the dream world begins to leave traces in the real world as phantoms of what may be possible. The 'subtle, fleeting, and disquieting' elements of chance help to erode the habitual world of order and routine, charging it with psychic energy and the animism Breton experienced in his vision of the sliced man at the window, offering a bridge between sleeping and waking and illuminating 'the most faltering of human steps' with 'an intense light'.[82] His interest in the liminal dream-state in *Communicating Vessels* is imaged as a 'capillary tissue' which guarantees 'constant exchange in thought ... requires the continuous interpenetration of the activity of waking and that of sleeping' rather than keeping the two realms conceptually separate.[83]

What makes this idea interesting for considering morality in avant-garde thought is that Breton believes the passive world of dreaming and the active world of waking are false distinctions, 'a fiction' that can only be reconfigured by building a bridge that is both aesthetic (transforming dreams into poetic images) and moral (a 'will to change' the social world of relations).[84] By living on the boundary between dreaming and waking as a Foucauldian limit experience (like Gide's Michel), Breton is persuaded of the need to free himself from 'emotional and moral scruples'.[85] If the bridge were purely aesthetic then the artist would create without principle, and if it were purely moral then he would act without inspiration: only a 'foolproof knot' links 'this process of transformation with that of interpretation', allowing him to find a place in the real world and act with a regard for others in it.[86] Breton wishes to replace the codification of particular social roles with a vision of 'fleeting existence', to discover the place of the artist as a moral agent in 'the center of a new order'.[87] The reservoir of energies into which he is eager to tap provides channels for art, morality and love as intertwined 'communicating vessels' in a world of Others; as he says in *Mad Love*, 'still today I am only counting on what comes of my openness, my eagerness to wander in *search* of everything, which, I am confident, keeps me in mystical communication with other open beings'.[88] Even if his relationship with Nadja falls short of these revolutionary ideals, as he states clearly in *The Immaculate Conception* (1930), co-written with Paul Eluard, 'reciprocal love ... is what creates interplay between unfamiliarity and habit, imagination and the conventional, faith and doubt, perception of the internal object and the external object'.[89]

Before the rift between Louis Aragon and Breton in 1932 and before he began writing in a socialist-realist vein in 1933 (after joining the Communist Party in 1927), Aragon shared with Breton the belief that this kind of radical revolution of consciousness could only result from the liquidation of what Benjamin calls 'the sclerotic liberal-model-humanistic ideal of freedom'.[90] To this end Aragon attacked the basis of French society: the literary establishment (he called Gide a 'bothersome bore' and Dada an 'old legendary monster'[91]); the French military (he was convicted in 1932 of inciting soldiers to mutiny); French wit; and bourgeois values (claiming that 'in France everything ends in rhetorical flourishes').[92] In his two most provocative statements of artistic intent, the Preface to *The Libertine* (*Le Libertinage*, 1924) and *Treatise on Style* (*Traité du Style*, 1928), he attempted to be as scandalous and profane as possible in order to shake his readers out of their apathy (echoing Zola's Preface to *Thérèse Raquin*). Like Breton, Aragon claims he is on 'the side of the mysterious and the unjustifiable'; he embraces the forces of chance and opposes 'the traditional concept of beauty and good', but his writing is often more playful and prodigal than Breton's work: for example, 'at times I was like a child loose among machines: I pulled down handles just to see what would happen ... For a time I was at the mercy of these surprises.'[93] Aragon moves quickly from artistic anarchism to a realisation that 'the feeling of being out of one's depth in a fairy tale atmosphere' should impel the artist to stop 'living by proxy' and fight for an alternative set of values. For him, the process of writing is an authentic moral act that offsets the impulse to commodify ideas into simple homilies to be consumed by the public.

In his short prose sketch, 'A Man', published in *Little Review* (1923), Aragon links artistic introspection with the emergence of personal morality: 'the man opens his skull ... then with satisfaction shakes his head without his hands: noise. Thus morals begin.'[94] The sketch suggests that personal experience is the only true source of morality, as opposed to abstract philosophical ruminations that can never provide a 'satisfactory foundation' for ethics.[95] Because 'M' (the letter representing 'a man') has no distinguishing characteristics, he represents a prototypical being existing in a world of pre-social flux, in which he has neither 'duties' nor 'rights' and in which only improvised gestures offer the key to unlocking a moral life.[96] M finds in the holes 'cut in his morality' a freedom that enables him to invent himself as a performer, dancer or 'stage manager', rather than adopting the role of philosopher or intellectual.[97] Twenty-six axioms are offered as cornerstones for rules of action (from the serious 'man acts only through goodness' to the bizarre 'man does not understand french'), but few of them make sense in their own right and even fewer in combination with the others. Instead, they are likened to cards shuffled in a pack with the images on the cards blurring into one another. His only recommendation for a moral life is to accept that the 'edges of a word are blurred',[98] to shuffle the pack in an individualistic way and to discern the 'lacy association of ideas' by dealing fresh combinations and glimpsing in them traces of the future.[99] The sketch ends with the destructive image of an 'explosive which will destroy the world' with M at the detonator, with the will to activate the bomb 'in spite of laws, century old, dictated by fear of this unique event'.[100] This revolutionary anarchism may suggest that the only antidote for constrictive morality is a clean sweep (inspired by Mikhail Bakunin), but Aragon's other prose pieces from this period offer a more positive view of moral potentiality.

In *Paris Peasant* (*Le Paysan de Paris*, 1926), for example, Aragon shares with Breton (following Poe and Baudelaire) a belief that love produces the kind of triumphant surreality that can revolutionise the realm of the actual by intermingling dreams and real life. In most Surrealist writing, from the erotic poems of Eluard, to Breton's *Mad Love* and Aragon's *The Libertine* (in which he claims 'I think of nothing but love'[101]), love provides the transformative counterpoint to the apocalyptic imagery at the end of 'A Man', offering a glimpse of 'a door' in the real world behind which stretches a 'marvellous landscape'.[102] Aragon upholds love as the means of tapping into this hidden realm, with the mystical image of woman as the receptacle of the unknown. Like Breton's image of the man sliced by the window and the ghostly figure of Nadja, Aragon's image of the woman offers a 'secret stairway' towards 'poetic knowledge' that supersedes the 'vulgar forms of knowledge ... under their guise of science or logic' by moving towards a *kosmos* in which taxonomies and laws of reality no longer hold. In this metaphysical realm of abstraction only the image has a concrete reality and it is towards this 'perception of the concrete' that he argues the mind gravitates.[103] Aragon does not praise an abstract veneration of women, but a love of the 'adorable, peculiar quality' of the individual woman:

> What is marvellous is that I should have fled from womankind towards this woman. A vertiginous crossing: the incarnation of thought, and there I am, I cannot conceive of a greater mystery. Yesterday I clutched blindly at empty abstractions. Today a single person dominates me, and I love her, and her absence is an intolerable pain, and her presence ... Her presence passes my understanding, for every aspect of her, her very power over me, springs from a source beyond nature.[104]

Here, metaphysics is not a escape into a realm of ineffectual musings divorced from action, but enables Aragon to reorient the parameters and the values of 'the real' in an act of 'reciprocal love'.[105] Although Rudolf Kuenzli argues that 'the surrealists lived in their own masculine world, with their eyes closed the better to construct their male phantoms of the feminine' with the woman being little more than a 'child muse' or 'erotic object',[106] it is Aragon's celebration of the particular woman which redirects the destructive impulses evident in 'A Man' to a moral pattern in which he feels inspired to act with and for another. The concept of 'the feminine' remains a problem in Breton's and Aragon's formulations of their art (at a time when female artists were seeking their own 'self-definition and free artistic expression', as discussed in Chapter 5),[107] nevertheless the Surrealist emphasis on the poetic image and mystical love as rejuvenating forces feed into the avant-garde appropriation of Symbolist incantation as an untapped reservoir of moral regeneration. Indeed, despite the differences between Dadaist and Surrealist poetics, their unified aim to recompose the role of modernist art led them away from the destructive energies stimulated by the Great War towards a creative revaluation of morality as a hitherto latent revolutionary force.

4
Moral Regeneration and Moral Bankruptcy: Conrad, Faulkner and Idiocy

One of the distinctive traits of literary modernism is its exploration of both the possibilities and the limits of representation. When the narrator of George Eliot's *Middlemarch* (1872) interrupts her realistic account of provincial English life to consider the representational qualities of the novel, she compares fiction writing to a series of seemingly random scratches on a mirror or 'surface of polished steel', which transmute into a set of discernible images when illuminated by a central consciousness: 'place now against it a lighted candle as a centre of illumination, and lo! the scratches will seem to arrange themselves in a fine series of concentric circles around that little sun'.[1] In this passage Eliot provides a thumbnail sketch of literary realism, but she also foreshadows the modernist interest in tracing the scratches on the mirror, not to offer the illusion of an integrated image ('the flattering illusion of a concentric arrangement'), but to explore the random points of intersection as they appear.[2] For example, in *Mimesis* (1947) Erich Auerbach takes the brown stocking worked on by Mrs Ramsay in Virginia Woolf's *To the Lighthouse* (1927) as the central metaphor for a text that unravels itself in the act of narration: 'no one is certain of anything here: it is all mere supposition, glances cast by one person upon another whose enigma he cannot solve'.[3] Developing the poetics of French Symbolists such as Mallarmé, many modernists used the symbolic centre as an organising principle in their narrative – for example, Henry James's *The Golden Bowl* (1902) – and as a way of indicating the flaws in mimetic representation. This twin aesthetic does not cancel itself out: unlike a New Critical approach which would seek to discover the central structuring paradox to make rational sense of a poem or novel, as the previous chapter on the avant-garde demonstrated, an aesthetic mode which hovers around a present, but enigmatic, centre helps to further the modernist writer's exploration of the limits of representation. Although a linear genealogy of modernist aesthetics cannot do justice to the complex groupings of artists who moved sometimes in sympathy with, and at other times in antagonism to, mimetic forms, in *The English Novel from Dickens to Lawrence* (1970) Raymond Williams traces nineteenth-century literary production in England to what he distinguishes as a crisis point in the 1890s. One of the distinctive changes he detects is a definite shift from the 'Condition of England' novel with its emphasis on social problems and its reformist narrative trajectory (the domain of middle-class writers such as Dickens and Gaskell), towards the emergence of a 'new self-conscious experimental minority' represented by the *fin-de-siècle* aesthetes and the late novels of Henry James.[4] Although his writing is often experimental, Conrad also bridges the transition identified by Williams from predominantly moralistic Victorian concerns embodied in literary realism to the 'tension within language and form' preoccupying many writers publishing in Europe and America between 1915 and the mid-1930s.[5] Conrad's novel of political intrigue and anarchism, *The Secret Agent* (1907), is an exemplary fiction that can be positioned productively between these two modes: it is both reliant on nineteenth-century realism and melodrama but also foreshadows the more deliberate experimentalism of high modernism.

In order to discuss Conrad's fusion of social critique, aesthetic inquiry and the problematics of representation in *The Secret Agent* this chapter falls into three sections. The first part focuses on Conrad's use of irony and ambiguity as destabilising tropes, with particular reference to his appropriation of the ideas of the Italian phrenologist and criminologist Cesare Lombroso. The second section deals with the idiot figure, Stevie Verloc, more explicitly. Stevie acts as the symbolic centre of *The Secret Agent* but his presence does not explain the novel or help to lighten its dark aesthetic; rather, his complex role subverts the Lombrosian framework that Conrad deploys to highlight the moral implications of a narrative full of inept policemen and amoral anarchists. The third section compares Conrad's use of the idiot figure as a symbolic centre of moral regeneration with William Faulkner's portrayal of the congenital idiot Benjy in his high modernist novel *The Sound and the Fury* (1929). Benjy is less the sympathetic moral centre of the novel and more the most obvious symptom of moral bankruptcy in the post-bellum American South. Whereas Conrad drew on the Romantic figures of the noble savage and the holy fool (evident in the work of Rousseau, Wordsworth and Dostoevsky among others), Faulkner avoids this mode of representation in favour of symbolic naturalism to convey the stasis and paralysis of the Compson family. Nevertheless, although Conrad and Faulkner wrote twenty years apart and on opposite sides of the Atlantic, it is productive to compare the ways in which they explore the limits of representation by using the idiot figure as a technique for highlighting the mimetic and moral problematics of their fictional worlds. As Andrew Gibson comments in relation to Conrad's *Heart of Darkness* (1901), 'the ethical interinvolvement of representation and anti-representation [is] to locate an ethics in their complex interdependences, their engagements, collusions, struggles with one another'.[6] As such, the symbolic loci of *The Secret Agent* and *The Sound and the Fury* enable the authors to explore the possibilities of moral regeneration and the realities of moral bankruptcy within the material folds of their writing.

A language for idiocy: *The Secret Agent*

In his 1920 Preface to *The Secret Agent*, Conrad claimed famously that 'ironic treatment alone would enable me to say all I felt I would have to say in scorn as well as pity'.[7] This 'treatment' is most obviously present in the narrative voice which conveys the tone of declamation and deflation that pervades the novel. However, the persistently caustic tone spares a sympathetic space for the characters of Winnie and Stevie, the wife and brother-in-law of the anarchist-cum-shopkeeper Adolf Verloc. The structural complexity of the narrative and the discernible, but elusive, narrator draw attention to the novel as a 'told' tale. However, the beguiling subtitle 'A Simple Tale' and Conrad's dedication to H. G. Wells (with whom Henry James had a running debate about the limitations of what James considered low journalistic fiction), 'affectionately' offers 'this simple tale of the nineteenth century' to the reader as a straightforward story. While disarming irony may lurk in the subtitle, the dedication corroborates the idea that behind the apparent formal intricacies is a book with a simple moral message. However, this message remains ambiguous, as the text opens up moral possibilities that it fails, or, by virtue of its ironic tone, it refuses to confirm. In this manner, the book is suspended on an axis that moves between the strong social impetus of the nineteenth-century novel (offering a critique of the corruption at the heart of, and the complicity between, police and terrorist systems) and the intricate symbolic patterns of literary modernism.

In his study of the historical and political context of *The Secret Agent*, Brian Spittles argues that Conrad's interpretation of the bomb outrage, which provides the central action for the novel and shakes the *agent provocateur* and the arbiters of law out of their common indolence, juxtaposes two fundamental Edwardian concerns. He discerns that the codes of respectability and stability inherited from Victorian morality actually conceal corrupt social foundations: 'beneath the casual social and political confidence there existed a nervousness about the maintenance of order'.[8] As a fictional development of Disraeli's description of the 'two nations' of Victorian Britain, *The Secret Agent* depicts the social melting pot of Edwardian England in terms of collusive conspiracies and splintered interests, where solidarity and collective sympathy cannot thrive. The web of secrecy connecting opposing interest groups is finally disrupted by the physical and 'incomprehensible' impact of the bomb.[9] Spittles argues that many of the older generation living in Edwardian London would vividly remember the violent protests of the late 1880s and 1890s and, together with the political upheavals across the Irish Sea and on the Continent, would have feared more radical demonstrations closer to home. Rather than being a reactionary writer, Conrad's claim that his tale belongs to the 'nineteenth century' provides a way of reading the novel as a reconstruction of a late-century event with the insight of early-century fears.

In a 1906 letter, Conrad responded to John Galsworthy's reading of the manuscript of *The Secret Agent* by stressing the formal artifice of the book: 'the whole thing is superficial and it is but a tale. I had no idea to consider Anarchism politically, or to treat it seriously in its philosophical aspect; as a manifestation of human nature in its discontent and imbecility.'[10] This remark can be interpreted as a modest disclaimer, for Conrad goes on to presume that a polemic on anarchism 'would be the work for a more vigorous hand and for a mind more robust, and perhaps more honest than mine.'[11] His claim that honesty is linked to intellectual rigour may be disarming, but by strategically avoiding a univocal narrative voice he indicates his willingness to use irony to present at least two perspectives simultaneously, with the ostensible meaning being shadowed by its hidden signification. This does not mean that Conrad eschews ethical responsibility for formal game-playing; rather, he hints that the ironist can provide a more trustworthy and less imperious perspective than the Cyclopean dogmatist does, by offering a greater range of readerly responses.[12] For example, the Russian emissary Vladimir disdainfully claims that 'you can't count upon their [the middle classes'] emotions either of pity or fear very long'.[13] Here the echo of Conrad's own statement concerning 'pity and scorn' indicates that if no single response can be trusted, then perhaps only at the locus where two emotions meet can one approximate to a faithful reading. Although it is impossible to disambiguate Conrad's language, he seems sincere in his reluctance to treat the topic of anarchism with the rigour of a politician or philosopher. He seems more interested in producing a work of fiction that seeks aesthetically to transform and critically to synthesise a number of historical, philosophical and scientific sources.

Although Conrad's comment to Galsworthy is presented as a disclaimer ('the whole thing is superficial and it is but a tale'), it helps to identify the central thematic concern of the novel as a study of 'human nature in its discontent and imbecility'. Just as Dostoevsky (for whom Conrad expressed his dislike, but whose structural technique and characterisation he shares to a large degree) provided at least one other idiotic character besides Prince Myshkin in *The Idiot* (in the guise of Rogozhin, Myshkin's adversary and double), Conrad portrays a city containing a variety of moral and neurological idiots. By engaging with Darwinian ideas, which had found a popular manifestation in the writings of Lombroso, Conrad exposes what he conceives as the imbecility behind many political plans. In his persistent doubts concerning positive political action he shared with Dostoevsky a sceptical conservatism that finds its voice through the idiot-figure. Although Martin Seymour-Smith argues that Thomas Mann exaggerated his claim that Stevie Verloc would have been 'inconceivable' without Dostoevsky's Myshkin, he discerns a link between these characters, the Kirilov twins in *The Devils* (1872) and the disturbing figure of Conrad's Professor. These two perspectives – the formal and the literary historical – indicate that Conrad, like Dostoevsky, was concerned with exploring the semantic and the symbolic uses of idiocy. Conrad's use of irony, on the level of plurality, mirrors the slippery location of 'idiocy' in the clinical rhetoric of the time and, on the level of denunciation, also indicates the prevalence of idiocy and imbecility as terms of social abuse.

In his Preface to the novel Conrad recalls the historical 'attempt to blow up the Greenwich Observatory'.[14] The attempt failed (as it does in the book) with the body of the anarchist, Martial Bourdin, discovered blown to pieces by the bomb. Conrad cites his friend as remarking 'that fellow was half an idiot. His sister committed suicide afterwards.' In this instance, the anarchist's idiocy may derive either from retardation or what Conrad describes as the 'criminal futility' of the affair. Either way, the comment provided Conrad with his imaginative focus. In a letter to Marguerite Poradowska he contrasted the idiot with the 'convict' or criminal: 'it is only the elect who are convicts – a glorious band which comprehends and groans but which treads the earth amidst a multitude of phantoms with maniacal gestures, with idiotic grimaces. Which would you rather be: idiot or convict?'[15] This passage is open to two readings: either it is better to be a criminal than an idiotic and mindless phantom 'with maniacal gestures', or there is no real distinction between convict and idiot, except perhaps for the criminal's feeling of grandiose selfhood. Of course, the idea that one could choose to be an idiot is absurd, but the rhetorical ambiguity points towards the ironic narrator of *The Secret Agent*.

Conrad's juxtaposition of criminality and idiocy derives from the work of Lombroso, forming the scientific undercurrent of novel. In an entry in the encyclopaedic *Twentieth Century Practice of Modern Medical Science* (1897), Lombroso claims both idiocy and criminality are rooted in cranial degeneracy, an idea he developed in *Man of Genius* (1891).[16] The association of 'great men' with chaotic mental states leads Lombroso to suppose that because 'traits of genius are so often found in mentally unsound persons' it is not surprising that 'lunatics have not infrequently held the destinies of nations in their hands and furthered progress by revolutionary movements'.[17] The notion that 'idiocy, epilepsy and genius, crimes and sublime deeds were forged into one single chain' prefigures Conrad's ambiguous association of idiocy and criminality.[18] Following this model, anarchists and radical statesmen (here Lombroso cites Napoleon as an example) would be conceived as 'lunatics' for attempting to revolutionise social order. *The Secret Agent* suggests so many parallels and associations between police, anarchists and idiots that, to some extent, Conrad can be seen to adhere to this model. Moreover, both criminal and idiot share anatomical characteristics that Lombroso interprets as a throwback to atavistic beings. But here Lombroso and Conrad differ fundamentally: for the Italian criminologist the crania of those classified as primitive savages become the cornerstone for his ideas of degeneracy, whereas in *Heart of Darkness* Conrad had already shown narrative sympathy for the 'prehistoric' African natives over European colonists.[19] For Conrad, the 'heart of darkness' is a primitive, pre-conscious impulse that cannot be colonised either by white traders or by scientific classification and, as Andrew Gibson states, 'its ethical force is intricately linked to what it does not or cannot say, or breaks off from saying'.[20]

In his sensitive reading of *Heart of Darkness*, Gibson extends this discussion by arguing that Kurtz's sense of possessiveness ('my ivory, my station, my river, my –') and his command of language 'permits no encounter with the other' because he occupies and 'seeks to encompass the whole'.[21] In contrast, Patricia Waugh suggests that the Africa which the narrator, Marlowe, encounters is very different from the Kurtzian perspective as 'a place so radically alien that his normal linguistic categories seem to dissolve as they are projected onto it in an attempt to discover significance'.[22] She argues that Marlowe is uncertainly 'caught between two responses': first, 'an impulse towards identification, the possibility that in surrendering up his language and culture ... to it, he might discover some archaic form of mind or nature which would provide an alternative universal foundation' and, second, 'an impulse towards the absolute retention of his own cultural categories' as a 'means of protection'.[23] If Kurtz's totalising perspective is replicated in the phrenological certainties of Lombroso's system, then Marlowe's ambivalence can be detected in the exploration of *The Secret Agent* into the psychology of primitive instincts, without suggesting that these instincts would necessarily stimulate a superior mode of being.

Conrad's 'destructive hatred of civilization' evident in both novels is tempered only in *The Secret Agent* by the figures of Stevie and Winnie who, although they are extinguished during the action of the novel, briefly suggest a moral life otherwise absent in the murky streets of London.[24] The opposition between civilisation and primitivism seems to be based on Lombroso's essay 'Atavism and Evolution' (1895), in which the Italian describes a deadlock between the forward-moving forces of development and the regressive forces of biological degeneracy, with humans evolving only fitfully, if at all.[25] The Manichean polarity of light/good and darkness/bad is here given a Darwinian slant, with neither pole ever dominating for very long. Although Conrad can be seen to make use of this model, he not only reverses the Lombrosian polarity – now atavism is associated with light and regeneration – but, through his ironic and parodic narrative voice, he undermines the oppositions. Instead of the nostalgic tone in Eliot and Lawrence, who can be read to juxtapose a lost spiritual world with a stagnating present, Conrad positions atavism in the midst of the moral quagmire of London. If Stevie is an embodiment of lost innocence, he is more a symbolic antidote to the novel's pessimism than a lament for a better or more natural civilisation.

To borrow Linda Hutcheon's phrase, *The Secret Agent* can be read as a 'complicitous critique'[26] of Lombroso, relying on his typology of characters but challenging his categorical distinctions. So, while the characters in the novel tend to be two-dimensional, Conrad questions Lombroso's idea that character (whether thief, murderer or degenerate) is wholly genetically determined. Verloc's double or triple life (secret agent, police informer and husband) indicates that characters play roles rather than crudely representing types. Typology is crucially important in the representation of Stevie who, with his vacant stare and drooping lower lip, conforms to Lombroso's stereotyped description of idiocy.[27] But, as this chapter discusses, Conrad does not confine idiocy to clinical retardation, but situates the 'authentic' idiot in a different symbolic space from the other idiotic characters (although it is uncertain whether Stevie's idiocy is congenital or the result of parental beating). Like Dostoevsky's Myshkin, Stevie is uniquely located, both textually and mentally, and so offers a symbolic alternative to the seedy and dismal life of the London anarchists. But the possibilities of moral regeneration are shattered by the explosion which causes Stevie's death and leads to Winnie's suicide. With the literal death of these characters (and with them the symbolic death of hope), all that remains at the end of the novel is the bleak and disturbing scene of Comrade Ossipon 'inclining towards the gutter' and 'the incorruptible Professor' walking 'like a pest in the street full of men'.[28]

Vocal resistance to Lombroso's theories in the novel is limited to the decrepit anarchist Karl Yundt, who is himself described as a degenerate type and, in Winnie's view, a 'disgusting old man'.[29] When Ossipon suggests that Stevie's drawings are 'typical of this form of degeneracy ... very characteristic, perfectly typical', Yundt retorts 'Lombroso is an ass.'[30] In a moment of dramatic irony tinged with dark comedy, Ossipon responds to this 'blasphemy' with a 'vacant stare', one of the very characteristics that marks Stevie as an idiot. Yundt follows his retort with a diatribe against Lombrosian criminal anthropology. For Yundt, the criminal is not determined by the genetic deformity of ears, teeth and forehead, but is a victim of social law. He turns Ossipon's typology of idiocy against his revered master Lombroso and, in so doing, blurs the parameters of classification. However, if Ossipon and Lombroso can both be dismissed as shams then so can Yundt for, despite his violent rhetoric, 'he had never in his life raised personally as much as his little finger against the social edifice'.³¹ The possibility that Yundt speaks with an authorial voice is undermined by his physical decrepitude and indolent anarchism.

Vladimir is another character who, like Yundt, uses hyperbolic and highly charged language. In his meeting with Verloc in the second chapter his spleen is vented against all sections of British liberal society. Initially, like Tzara in virulent Dadaist mode, he attacks the property-loving 'imbecile bourgeoisie' who, in their moral lethargy, are complicit with 'the very people whose aim is to drive them out of their houses'.³² Vladimir and the Russian embassy wish to cause an event that would 'administer a tonic' to the Milan Conference (where the European governments are to form a treaty on terrorism), because the hard-liners view the English political system as too tolerant of anarchists. In order that the Russians can deal with their own anarchists, Vladimir demands an outrage that will shake the English out of their lethargy. He aims to scare the middle classes, blinded by their 'idiotic vanity' over material goods, by organising an act of terrorism that has all 'the shocking senselessness of gratuitous blasphemy'.³³ In order 'to raise a howl of execration' the attack must be unmotivated and purely terroristic.³⁴ Instead of attacking a church or art gallery, an assault which could be passed off as the work of fanaticism, Vladimir orders Verloc to 'have a go' at astronomy. A terroristic attack on pure science in the form of the 'first meridian' at Greenwich would represent 'the most alarming display of ferocious imbecility'.³⁵ Vladimir has no sympathy with the anarchists in England, but will use them to provoke the 'intellectual idiots' into make noises at the Conference. In fact, he rails disdainfully against the middle classes, anarchists and politicians alike, for he sees them all to be politically stupid.³⁶

The novel supports this view to some degree but, later, Vladimir is thrown by the efficiency of the police system, when Heat fortuitously stumbles upon evidence and promptly solves not only the bomb mystery but catches the 'dog-fish' (Vladimir) behind the 'sprat' (Verloc).³⁷ The Assistant Commissioner also detects the traces of a planned enterprise in the 'peculiar stupidity and feebleness' of the affair.³⁸ Through an 'inspired inference' his conclusion turns out to be fair, although his premise is, at this stage, erroneous. What is more interesting is that the 'stupidity' which Vladimir perceives in the English police system is here turned against its grand castigator. Indeed, not only are the adjectives 'stupid', 'imbecilic' and 'idiotic' so prevalent in the novel their impact is dissipated, but Conrad seems to be radically testing the nature of language. As Allan Hunter argues, this 'perception of language is post-Saussurean, words are suspended in a purely relativistic framework, and can be made to mean anything, as well as disguising almost anything'.[39] The dissipation of fixed meaning is illustrated in Winnie's obsessive thoughts that, like a ghastly mantra, in their repetition cease to signify. Also, in the newspaper in which Ossipon reads the news of the bomb, outrage about her suicide bastardises any sincere emotions that could be attached to the event. The newspaper Ossipon keeps in his pocket does not even carry current news; it is ten days old. Its phraseology – '*An impenetrable mystery seems destined to hang for ever over this act of madness or despair*'[40] – becomes a torturous refrain during Ossipon's final meeting with the Professor, recalling the narrative interjection a few pages earlier when the reader is told: 'as often happens in the lament of poor humanity rich in suffering but indigent in words, the truth – the very cry of truth – was found in a worn and artificial shape picked up somewhere among the phrases of sham sentiment'.[41] This sham sentiment bypasses the 'cry of truth' for sensationalist language and dilutes the moral tragedy of Winnie's suicide. Moreover, the journalese of the press extinguishes the notion that words correlate with that which they claim to describe. The 'impenetrable mystery' derives more from linguistic uncertainty and the loss of stable meaning than it does from the formal complexity of the narrative. Only the Professor, as he calls 'madness and despair to the regeneration of the world', can be sure of the language he uses.[42] For him language is all sham because it belongs to social institutions that only he, in his reliance on death, and Stevie, in his idiocy, can circumnavigate.

Idiocy and the limits of moral potency

Although Stevie's schooling places doubts over the clinical status of his idiocy, he is presented with all the conventional manifestations of an idiot figure. The novel encourages the reading that he is the victim of the society that produces him, as the son of an alcoholic father and the innocent victim of a pitiless plot. Lombroso would claim the signs of Stevie's degeneracy can be traced to his father's alcoholism. Similarly, Faulkner uses Benjy Compson, the idiot figure in *The Sound and the Fury*, to symbolise the mental decay and moral paralysis of a once-prosperous white family in Mississippi. However, as I will discuss in the remainder of this chapter, while Conrad preserves idiocy as a state of innocence, Faulkner does not allow Benjy, together with the other white characters in the novel, to escape with any virtue.

Whereas Benjy is a symptom of moral degeneration, Stevie can be read as the sympathetic centre of *The Secret Agent* as he pathetically illustrates the deprivation he laments. For Stevie, helplessness stimulates his faculty of perception and makes him an illustration of what he perceives. He spends his evenings 'drawing circles, circles; innumerable circles, concentric, eccentric; a coruscating whirl of circles that by their tangled multitude of repeated curves, uniformity of form, and confusion of intersecting lines suggested a rendering of cosmic chaos, the symbolism of mad art attempting the inconceivable',[43] as if, in his compulsive obsession, he is attempting to symbolise the psychic chaos he perceives in and around himself. Ossipon, as a disciple of Lombroso's *Man of Genius*, interprets this art as being typical of degenerates. It is noticeable that in the 'tangled multitude of repeated curves' and its 'confusion of intersecting lines', the drawings are diametrically opposite in form to Lombroso's strictly ordered classification of degenerates. As such, Stevie represents a physical embodiment of all that he perceives to be wrong in society, as his body contorts to the violence of Karl Yundt's rhetoric:

> Stevie knew very well that hot iron applied to one's skin hurt very much. His scared eyes blazed with indignation: it would hurt terribly. His mouth drooped open. ... Stevie swallowed the terrifying statement with an audible gulp, and at once, as though it had been swift poison, sank limply in a sitting position.[44]

Because he cannot distinguish between language and the physical pain it describes, Yundt's rhetoric has the virulence of real 'hot iron' on Stevie's body. As he swallows the statement the moral poison of the words becomes chemical poison that debilitates him. He understands the physical sensation associated with words (rather than their meaning) primarily because he exists outside the received semantic order: for him violence is not encoded in rhetoric but is an intensely felt physical pain.

Stevie expresses his pain only in 'half words' and emotive apostrophes: 'Too heavy. Too heavy', 'Walk. Must walk', 'Bad! Bad!', 'Poor. Poor'.[45] These words convey an acute sense of sensation and a strong, yet barely articulate, morality. Because he cannot voice his protest verbally, Stevie physically responds to the violence he hears: 'his vacant mouth and distressed eyes depicted the state of mind in regard to the transactions that were taking place'.[46] The droop of Stevie's lower lip represents a simple physical response to the complicated illness he perceives in Yundt's view of society. Conrad thus makes use of these stereotypical idiotic traits not to verify Stevie's degeneracy, but to inscribe an image of a drooping society on to Stevie's body, as if Stevie's condition is a direct reflection of an idiotic social system. He oscillates between feelings of indignation and rage and moments of helpless vacancy. Although the reader is informed that Stevie is not subject to fits (and cannot be considered epileptic like Dostoevsky's Myshkin), he does have luminous mental states in which he intuits social disorder and after which he relapses into limp vacancy. He has neither the language with which to express his insights nor the power to carry out any act of reform. Instead, his physiognomy reflects the disorder he feels.

Despite his sensitivity to other people's misery, Stevie's morality is incapable of being channelled into meaningful action. For example, when Winnie's and Stevie's mother leaves the Verloc household for an almshouse in order to lessen the financial burden on Verloc and to secure Stevie's future (an act which actually creates the family conditions that lead to the bomb plot), at the sight of the cabman whipping his horse Stevie jumps out of the carriage to lighten the load. In so doing he mirrors his mother's altruism in her move to the almshouse and Winnie's selfless love for her brother. But he can do nothing for the deprivation of either horse or cabman:

> He could say nothing; for the tenderness to all pain and all misery, the desire to make the horse happy and the cabman happy, had reached the point of a bizarre longing to take them to bed with him. And that, he knew, was impossible. For Stevie was not mad. It was, as it were, a symbolic longing.[47]

His only plan of action is to replicate the tenderness Winnie has shown him, but he knows of its practical impossibility. Stevie also realises that the cabman only maltreats the horse because he has been driven to violence through poverty and misery. Indeed, there seems to be no chance of practical reform in such a society, not even the anarchist's clean sweep. The last resort is a pathetic childhood wish to take both cabman and horse to bed with him. Although Stevie's innocence is preserved in the novel and gives him insights into social problems ('bad world for poor people'), his physical meekness prevents him from acting on them.[48]

Stevie's idiocy can, in part, be explained by considering his interaction with others. His degeneracy, if he is degenerate, is a result of his father's depravity and the beatings he received as a child; his tenderness is a consequence of Winnie's care and affection; and his violent reactions, letting fireworks off in a 'pitch of frenzy' and 'futile bodily agitation', are stimulated by the anarchistic rhetoric and activities he hears and sees around him.[49] He thus appears as a *tabula rasa* on to whose body the madness of society is imprinted. However, he is more than a textual imprint, as his bodily symptoms strongly suggest a mind struggling to make sense of disorder and a moral conscience that futilely wishes to right wrongs. After the explosion, when the reader is told the bits of Stevie's body are mixed with inorganic matter – 'limbs, gravel, clothing, bones, splinters – all mixed together' – the author appears to suggest that on a molecular level Stevie's body is recycled into the world he has confronted but failed to change.[50] But the hole created by the bomb is more than a textual hole: it represents both a gap in the temporal narrative (as the chronology shifts in the centre of the novel) and a chasm in the lives of the figures who have interacted with Stevie.

The only difference, the novel implies, between normality and 'madness and despair' is the depth and angle of perception. Until Winnie is forced to look into things and trouble 'her head about' the violence of the bomb blast, Stevie is alone in attempting to unravel the complex world of the novel.[51] After Winnie discovers the fate of her brother she enters a similar psychopathological world to the one he had recently inhabited. If Stevie's degeneracy is inherited from his father, Winnie can also be seen to share in this legacy, but her symptoms are hysterical rather than idiotic. As she steels herself to murder her husband, 'the resemblance of her face with that of her brother grew at every step, even to the droop of the lower lip, even to the slight divergence of the eyes'.[52] At this moment she is simultaneously an impassioned sister who believes her husband has brutally murdered her brother and also Stevie's alter ego, now given agency and the motive to seek revenge. Previously Yundt's comment that the capitalists 'are nourishing their greed on the quivering flesh and blood of the people' had caused Stevie immense pain, and now he literally becomes the hapless victim of this society as the joint of meat that Verloc carves.[53]

If Stevie lacks the capacity to act, then his 'agent' Winnie, with carving knife in hand, can restore a glimmer of moral justice. As soon as the murder is committed 'her extraordinary resemblance to her late brother had faded, had become very ordinary'.[54] Only at the climax of Winnie's grief is she transfigured into her brother. But Conrad weaves intimations of this moment in the slow dramatic movement of the murder scene: Winnie speaks like a 'corpse' and the 'red-hot iron' that had pained Stevie is transformed into 'white-hot iron drawn across' her eyes.[55] Moreover, by deploying Lombroso's rhetoric, the narrator informs the reader: 'Mrs Verloc had put all the inheritance of her immemorial and obscure descent, the simple ferocity of the age of caverns, and the unbalanced nervous fury of the age of bar-rooms.'[56] Stevie's atavism is mirrored by the actions of his vengeful sister as she releases immensely felt primitive emotions. As such, Lombroso's association of atavism with degeneracy is presented in this scene as the only potent force in an otherwise limp world. When the Professor claims in the last scene of the novel 'all passion is lost now. The world is mediocre, limp, without force', he unintentionally gestures towards the forceful passion of Stevie and Winnie, now extinguished. Their primitive instincts have provided the cannibals of Yundt's society with 'quivering flesh'.

In the scenes following the murder Winnie becomes as obsessive in her thoughts as Stevie in his drawings. Even Ossipon's classificatory system is overturned when he is surprised by the nature of the murder: 'he was excessively terrified at her – the sister of a degenerate – a degenerate herself of a murdering type'.[57] Ossipon classifies the sister as he had previously done the brother but, after his meeting with Winnie, he also enters the half-world of psychopathology: Winnie is transformed into a snake of death in his mind; he walks mindlessly though the streets of London; he lies immobilised in a foetal position; and later 'he was beginning to drink with pleasure, with anticipation, with hope. It was his ruin.'[58] His negroid features and the hints of alcoholism render Ossipon a victim of the very system to which he subscribes. Moreover, as he faces his fear – the fear that he is similar to the 'perfect' degenerate – he is described as being 'half frozen' and 'half dead', echoing the half-wit Stevie speaking 'half words'.[59] Ossipon's leap from the train to escape his doom directly parallels Stevie jumping from the Cab of Death in everything but motive. This contrast is illuminating. Stevie's altruistic leap is from a pre-industrial horse and cab, while Ossipon selfishly jumps from a railway carriage: the definitive symbol of technological modernity. If, as Conrad suggests, this is a tale of the nineteenth century, then Stevie's role as a primitive moralist is favourably contrasted with the disciple of modern systematic thinking.

As the symbolic centre of the novel Stevie is the true secret agent, his shadow moving in a strange arc through the later sections of the narrative. He appears to be a radically unstable character but, in his simplicity and innocence, he offers a counterpoint to the dubious morality of the anarchists, politicians and police. Although he is neither wholly an incarnation of a Christ-figure, nor a fully-blown Romantic noble savage, there are hints of potential regeneration that can be glimpsed before chemical nihilism blows him apart. Stevie's slight physique is set against the other characters, while his death can be seen as sacrificial. Although these traits may suggest a heroic figure stripped of his strength or a noble savage deprived of his nourishing contact with Nature, Conrad does not allow such analogies to permeate the novel. One reason for this can be gleaned from a letter he wrote in 1898 in which he claims 'faith is a myth and beliefs shift like mists on the shore'.[60] Accordingly, Stevie is an embodiment of Conrad's shifting ironic voice and, as such, his force is both destabilising and regenerative: he disturbs the strict classification of Lombroso's and Ossipon's systems and recoups some moral optimism, however short-lived, within the bleakly 'mediocre' modern world he inhabits.

Idiocy and moral bankruptcy: *The Sound and the Fury*

Faulkner's *The Sound and the Fury* marked the beginning of his truly experimental phase of fiction writing, in which he moved beyond the relatively straightforward representation of his version of Mississippi (Yoknapatawpha County) to the disturbing mindscapes of his major novels between 1929 and 1936. Whereas the semantic uncertainty of *The Secret Agent* reveals a growing modernist tendency to treat the novel as an aesthetic object which has a problematic relationship with the world it describes, *The Sound and the Fury* uses multiple perspective, formal dislocation and the dissociation of words from meaning as an expression (to quote Myra Jehlen) of 'the author's profoundly discordant view of Southern life' harbouring 'extreme, unresolvable contradictions'.[61] Jehlen argues that 'Faulkner's tensely uncertain attitude toward the South' was at its most extreme in the late 1920s and 1930s, stimulating him to explore 'the limits of perception and language' and 'to pierce false masks ... which he is coming more and more to realize have distorted Southern reality'.[62] The novels of this phase are organised around the question of what 'Southern reality' might be and whether it has an existence outside its myths. As with *The Secret Agent*, formal innovation is used in *The Sound and the Fury* to defamiliarise the conventional relationship between reader and text in order to highlight the uncertainties of history and identity.

Faulkner's novel depicts the genetic and moral decline of the Compsons, a family of Southern landed aristocracy 'driven to suicide by the vicissitudes of modernity and the collapse of the Southern tradition'.[63] The disintegration of the Compson family indicates a family 'who were decaying, going to pieces', but their decline implicates the whole history of the South just as *The Secret Agent* exposes subterfuge in the Edwardian social system.[64] Like Zola's Rougon-Macquart family, the Compson dynasty is genetically bankrupt, the collapse of cultural and genetic order symbolised by the incest motif running through the novel. The alcoholism and invalidity of the Compson parents (along with the parasitic dependency of Uncle Maury) are signs of such decay that manifests itself in the three brothers as idiocy (Benjy), insanity (Quentin) and brutal sadism (Jason). Each brother represents the end of the dynastic line: Benjy is castrated by Jason; Quentin in his incestuous wanderings and eventual suicide reveals an unwillingness to look outside himself; and Jason is only interested in sexual exchange with prostitutes. Even their sister, Candace (or Caddy), is thought to be promiscuous as Jason rails against her whorish activities. Caddy's daughter is the product of casual copulation and is described by Faulkner in his 1945 appendix as 'nameless at birth and already doomed to be unwed from the instant the dividing egg determined its sex'.[65] In this way *The Sound and the Fury* shares with Norris's *McTeague* a profoundly naturalistic perspective in which Benjy's idiocy is a symptom of the decline of his family and culture, rather than a moral antidote to it.

Unlike *The Secret Agent* Faulkner's novel offers no glimpse of regeneration from such decline, although the figure of 'endurance', the black servant Dilsey who narrates the fourth part of the novel (as well as the emergence of the Southern Renaissance in the 1930s), indicates that degeneration and death also imply a 'starting over, creation and growth'.[66] It may seem surprising that Faulkner chooses modernist techniques to convey the decline of an old family, but the form of the novel suggests traditional values must be re-interpreted through the experiences of modernity. Far from Faulkner's historical fiction being, like Walter Scott's Waverley novels, mythologised chronicles of cultural history, the emphasis is placed on the anxieties of related individuals forced to construct identities out of broken and ruined fragments. *The Sound and the Fury* is presented as a four-part novel, the first three parts being in the first person and the fourth narrated in the third person with Dilsey the main focus. Unlike the controlling voice of the realist novel, there is no centre of authority or moral voice that lucidly clarifies what is related. The reader has to search harder for a moral focus; the text becomes heavier, dripping with potential meaning and symbolic resonance; the textual voices become more anxious, questioning, uncertain, even noisy and belligerent. Like *McTeague*, the novel suggests that the primal screams of animals lie just beneath the social façade as wounded identities struggle to survive.

Each section of the novel illuminates, and is reflected by, the others, but for the purposes of this chapter I will focus on Benjy's narrative which represents the reader's first impressions of the Compson family and provides an introduction to the anti-mimetic qualities of the novel. The reader-response critic, Wolfgang Iser, claims that 'Benjy differs from most other idiots in literature mainly because he is seen from the inside and not from outside. The reader sees the world through his eyes and depends almost exclusively on him for orientation.'[67] Moving from Conrad's Stevie to Faulkner's Benjy is a journey inwards from the interpretation of behaviour to the interior language of consciousness. Instead of the narrator interpreting Stevie's drawings, Benjy is given a muffled voice of his own. In *The Secret Agent* the reader, to a large extent, shares the same interpretative space as the ironic narrator, whereas in *The Sound and the Fury* Benjy is the narrator: there is no mediating voice. It can be claimed that Faulkner's attempt to render the idiot's consciousness is unsuccessful. Although he is dumb and nearly deaf, Benjy uses correct grammar, 'speaks' without phonetic idiosyncrasies and identifies objects his three-year old mind could not possibly name. But Faulkner, instead of making the impossible leap into another alien consciousness, stresses the experiential nature of Benjy's world and his unconscious language of desire. For example:

> In the corner it was dark, but I could see the window. I squatted there, holding the slipper. I couldn't see it, my hands saw it, and I could hear it getting night, and my hands saw the slipper but I couldn't see myself, but my hands could see the slipper, and I squatted there, hearing it getting dark.[68]

The modulation of Benjy's phrases is similar to Gertrude Stein's technique of 'continuous present' (see Chapter 5), and roughly corresponds to Bergson's *la durée* as a stream of mental becoming. But, unlike the other modernist Bergsonians, Proust and Woolf, whose protagonists experience a fluid time flowing from past into future, Faulkner's idiot cannot differentiate between distinct temporal moments. Homologous to Stevie's capacity to distinguish rhetorical from physical violence, Benjy cannot distinguish remembered experiences from actual ones.

Benjy is more than the sum of his experiences and his identification with other voices. Indeed, the voices he 'hears' are (more or less) internal voices, manifestations of his unconscious, even though later evidence associates them with real people. In Benjy's narrative Faulkner seems to be questioning the binary categories of outside/inside, object/subject, and, by deploying the idiot's mind as a textual vehicle, he questions the relation between language and the world. The passage quoted above illustrates this point. Although the darkness of the room obscures all sight, the window implies an outside world while firmly locating Benjy on the inside. He focuses on Caddy's old slipper that he 'sees' through his hands, almost to the point where he feels it as an extension of his own body. Because the presence of the slipper really only corresponds to Benjy's impression of it, it becomes part of his identity just as a limb would. In the psychoanalytic language of Melanie Klein, he unconsciously introjects the slipper and it becomes part of his identity.[69] While he is locked in a continuous present, he does understand feelings associated with loss (the absence of Caddy, her slipper and the deviation from routine) and although he has no moral sense, his sentience can be felt in the pain of loss: the loss of his sister and his inability to assert his struggling identity.

In the first section of the novel Benjy is not presented as a limited or retarded mind struggling to make sense of an outside world, but as a primitive identity that cuts across the categorical distinctions of mind and matter. It is only when the reader is presented with the other stories, in particular the third-person narrative of the fourth section, that Benjy can be labelled an idiot. Indeed, it is only when we step into the larger social framework of the Compsons' world – from private to public – that the need to form a stable identity becomes important. Although from the outside Benjy has no identity, the narrative insight of the first section suggests his primal, or child-like, identity is structured around his desire for Caddy. The reader is invited to engage with Benjy's sense impressions, but the use of italicisation stresses the textuality of the experience and so checks the impulse towards identification; in Iser's words: 'the result for the reader is that he experiences Benjy's perspectives not only from inside – with Benjy – but also from the outside, as he tries to understand Benjy'.[70] The need to question the reality of Benjy's experiences encourages us to continue reading to understand more about the public world that Benjy's limited mind cannot understand. Faulkner's acknowledgement of this need to map private and public worlds coherently may be one of the reasons he resorted to a third-person narrative in the final section. As we respond to the neurological idiot's consciousness, the reader's other position – an outsider looking into the textual mind of the idiot – turns the text into an aesthetic object and Benjy into a symbolic device. As such, the text becomes the threshold to a repository of meanings on the fulcrum between mimetic representation and aesthetic autonomy.

As the opening section is told from Benjy's private perspective, a physical description of him is not provided until the last section of the novel. When the reader finally encounters Benjy it takes a moment to realise that this is the same person who has been presented with a complex psychic life:

> Luster entered, followed by a big man who appeared to have been shaped of some substance whose particles would not or did not cohere to one another or to the frame that supported it. His skin was dead looking and hairless; dropsical too, he moved with a shambling gait like a trained bear ... His eyes were clear, of the pale sweet blue of cornflowers, his thick mouth hung open, drooling a little.[71]

Because the reader has prior knowledge of Benjy, his physical aspect takes on another dimension: the particles that do not 'cohere to one another' are both physical and, figuratively, the mental flux of Benjy's experiences. Moreover, the passage implies that the physique of the idiot cannot be described without recourse to traditional descriptions of idiots. The authorial control of language reduces Benjy's psychic complexity to his ghastly appearance as a physical oddity. Instead of a tale told by an idiot, it is a tale told by the masters of language: the narrator and the other Compsons who have the final word over those subordinated by it (in *The Sound and the Fury*, the blacks and the idiot).

Although Benjy is innocent in that he is the victim of idiocy and his guardians, he is not a moral 'agent' like Conrad's Stevie, and neither are we permitted to see him as a martyr figure, despite the Christian associations of his age (thirty-three) and the Easter setting. The

Romantic scheme in which the idiot is conceived as a primitive being allows Conrad's Stevie to remain largely uncontaminated by the moral decay of his world. In direct contrast, Faulkner does not allow Benjy's idiocy to grant him any nobility or moral worth. His three-year-old mind may render him innocent but he is a Compson, and like his brothers he is narcissistic and self-seeking. His primal identity is rooted deeply in genetics and environment and, rather than embracing change, Benjy bellows when any alteration occurs to his routine. Towards the end, when Luster rides the surrey around the statue of the Confederate soldier from left to right, Benjy begins to roar, the departure from his usual experience evoking feelings of distress and disorientation. If social and mental order is restored at the end of *The Sound and the Fury* when Jason swings the carriage around the statue the right way, it is at the expense of the innocent morality of Stevie Verloc. Of course, Benjy does not have the power to impose direction on his own experiences; his boundaries are artificially imposed by the fence, the prohibitions of his guardians and, eventually, by the walls of the Jackson State Asylum. His one encounter with the Burgess girl, when he attempts to speak with a meaningful voice of his own (and he is 'trying to say'), accounts for the abortion of his sexual identity.[72] At the end, although his screams may be meaningless, the description of 'horror, shock; agony eyeless' conveys the disorientation of a sentient being who cannot bear to experience anything out of the ordinary and who, like the post-bellum white South he inhabits, cannot grow up.[73] Like Stevie with his compulsive drawings, Benjy's mind is locked inside a pattern of repetition to which he is a helpless victim. But, unlike Stevie, Benjy's childish world is not a primitive symbolic centre set against a morally bankrupt society, but crucially indicative of moral decay.

Part III
Sexual and Cultural Difference

5
American Expatriate Fictions and the Ethics of Sexual Difference

(Stein, Hemingway, Miller, Nin)

At the same time that Breton, Joyce and Faulkner were redefining the symbolic centres of modernism in the interwar period, another diverse group of writers and artists was exploring metropolitan cultural centres as a means for exploring the aesthetics and ethics of cultural and sexual difference. As the next chapter discusses, many European writers, including Franz Kafka and Federico García Lorca, were attracted to mythologising America (and especially New York) as a site of creative possibility. Conversely, another major transatlantic trend was for American writers to embark on the 'dangerous pilgrimage' (as Malcolm Bradbury calls it) of leaving their homeland, either permanently in the case of Gertrude Stein or temporarily for Ernest Hemingway and Henry Miller, as a rejection of what they deemed to be the worst excesses of American Progressivism.[1] Unlike many Europeans burdened by the geographical proximity of war, for these American writers and others, such as Ezra Pound, Anaïs Nin and Djuna Barnes and the African-American poets Langston Hughes and Countee Cullen, Europe, and more specifically Paris, became the primary imaginative site of cultural transformation in the early twentieth century. Paris allowed them a sexual and writerly freedom they felt had been compromised at home with the rise of hostile social trends, including the public disdain for the Armory Show, the rise of Prohibition after the Great War, and the mass arrests stemming from the Red Scare of 1920. Although New York, London and Paris were the three major 'world cities' at the turn of the century, Americans were drawn to the café life and romantic charm of Paris after those in service had glimpsed it briefly during the War. The excitement of Paris could be equalled in America only in Greenwich Village and the artistic salons of Alfred Stieglitz, Mabel Dodge and Walter Arensberg. One view of New York was a 'mongrel' city that positively minimised, rather than maximised, racial and gender distinctions (see Chapter 6),[2] but for white and black writers alike Montmartre and the Left Bank in Paris offered an escape from rigid moral codes and capitalist expectations.

American interest in European culture had grown steadily following the literary nationalism of the American Renaissance in the 1830s and 1840s, when Ralph Waldo Emerson called for a rejection of European models of writing in favour of promoting nativist literature. Although Melville, Hawthorne and Twain all developed relationships with Europe, not until Henry James in the late nineteenth century did American writers begin to consider the moral implications of a transatlantic culture. As his career developed James leaned increasingly towards Europe, but as an internationalist writer, in novels such as *The Ambassadors* (1903), he rejected fully neither American nor European culture, continuing to explore their interrelationship and dependency upon each other. Alice Gambrell describes one of the defining features of transatlantic modernism as a 'simultaneous distance from and intimacy with the subjects of their own inquiry'.[3] This notion of cultural traffic and the blurring of national boundaries is a useful starting point for considering American modernists in Europe: from Whistler and James in the late nineteenth century, to Stein and Hemingway in the 1910s and 1920s. The transatlantic journey was not a simple one-way affair for any of these artists, but provided a fluid symbolic site for investigating the complex interaction between European and American culture. Gambrell's theme of 'familiar strangeness' characterises the work of all these artists as a simultaneous intimacy with, and distance from, a single cultural perspective.[4]

Iain Chambers develops this analysis of cultural traffic in *Migrancy, Culture, Identity* (1994); he argues that the mobility of modernist ideas creates a geographical and figurative zone of 'transit', not only problematising the linear trajectory of the journey but making the final homecoming 'an impossibility'.[5] Deploying similar language to Gambrell, Chambers argues: 'to come from elsewhere, from "there" and not "here", and hence to be simultaneously "inside" and "outside" the situation at hand, is to live at the intersections of histories and memories, experiencing both their preliminary dispersal and their subsequent translation into new, more extensive, arrangements among emerging routes'.[6] Themes of cultural transit and dislocation are common in modernist aesthetics, inscribing what Chambers calls the 'drama of the stranger' as central to the form and content of American expatriate fiction.[7] The work of James, Hemingway, Miller and Nin are full of what Kelly Cannon calls 'in-between' characters who 'must learn both the limitations and the potential of their habitat' by developing formal *and* moral strategies for contending with cultural difference.[8] Fictions such as *The Sun Also Rises* (1924), *Tropic of Cancer* (1934), avant-garde poems such as Stein's 'Geography' (1923), and Nin's early diaries exploit what Paul Gilroy has defined as the symbolic fluidity of the Atlantic as a space of cultural multiplicity, both a site of expanding possibilities and a zone of threat and strangeness: a place of fictional 'wandering between geographical, sexual, and ideological worlds'.[9]

The view of 'homeland' as an anchor for personal identity and moral orientation is a perspective American expatriate writers treated with extreme suspicion: for Miller, New York was 'a whole city erected over a hollow pit of nothingness', whereas for Nin, America was no more her homeland than was Spain (in terms of her family background) or France (where she spent much of her adult life).[10] The internationalism of these writers developed the initial stimulus of the pan-European avant-garde (discussed in Chapter 3) and marks their place in an intricate network of crosscultural influences that cannot easily be reduced to a straightforward national tradition. For example, Stein was as much influenced by the post-Impressionism of Cézanne, Matisse and Picasso as by the modern psychology of her Harvard instructor, William James. Although Malcolm Cowley's eye-witness account of Americans in Paris, *Exile's Return* (1934), is important for locating what Donald Pizer calls the 'mythic expression of American self-exile', the tags 'Lost Generation' and 'American Exile' do not adequately convey these writers' complex relationship with both European and American culture.[11] While the term 'expatriate' is not without its political implications, as Arlen Hansen has argued, the term is useful as it 'implies a deliberate, freely made decision to leave Chicago or Chelsea and move, at least temporarily, to Paris'.[12]

As this chapter discusses, the expatriate rejection of a particular understanding of America as gendered aggressively male informs their exploration of what the French feminist Luce Irigaray has called 'an ethics of sexual difference'.[13] Although Hemingway and Miller are most often seen as masculinist writers, this chapter argues that particularly in their fiction from the 1920s and 1930s they, like Stein and Nin, consciously surrender to the 'magnetism' of Paris to explore the interface between alternative gender identities and moral impulses.[14]

Paris thus becomes a symbolic site for freedom, nourishment and mobility and, as a consequence, self-exile becomes both an expression of American alienation and a means to aesthetic fulfilment.[15] This does not mean that Paris is never treated critically: in *The Sun Also Rises* and *Tropic of Cancer* the city is part of the modern panorama of malaise and despair; in Fitzgerald's short story 'Babylon Revisited' (1931) it is the scene of guilt and loss; and for Nin it is often a place of sexual danger. However, compared with the puritan orthodoxies and the capitalist pressures they believed to be endemic to provincial and urban America, Paris offered a wealth of imaginative possibility.

American masculinity and angelic ethics

By the turn of the century the archetypal American hero had metamorphosed from the frontiersman as the coloniser and cultivator of land to the engineer as the designer and builder of cities. Despite their professional differences, pioneers and engineers worked skilfully and ingeniously with the physical world, embodying masculine values learnt in the Civil War and nurtured in the Progressive era. Ann Douglas in *The Feminization of American Culture* (1977) describes the 'redemptive' endeavours of feminists and clerics in the second half of the nineteenth century, but she detects that they did little to halt, or to redirect, the development of a patriarchal country being 'propelled so rapidly toward industrial capitalism'.[16] The introduction of the word 'masculinity' into the *Century Dictionary* by 1890 indicated more than just a separation of domestic and public spheres along gender lines. As Kim Townsend argues, the emphasis on patriotism, leadership and the sporting life promoted at Harvard University suggested a widening of the divide between gender values: 'if a man felt he was about as manly as he could be – or his efforts about as intense as his constitution could bear – he could relax them so long as he could be sure that women remained relatively womanly'.[17] By the early 1890s the future president Theodore Roosevelt (Harvard Class of 1880) was proclaiming that American men should continue to work and fight hard, following Frederick Jackson Turner's address at the Columbian Exposition of 1893 that marked the official closing of the frontier. Roosevelt's emphasis on sport and manual labour as benchmarks of 'the strenuous life' (the title of his Presidential Address from 1899) characterised his belief that skills learnt in frontier experience could be transferred directly to urban and industrial expansion. In the face of modern nervousness and the rise of neurasthenia among the urban middle classes, Roosevelt recommended that by embracing the 'primitive masculine' Americans could galvanise their passions and energies into industrial and imperial achievement. Roosevelt's almost adolescent insistence on manly endeavours and his own enactment of frontier fantasies during his trips West illustrate his concern about the foundations of universal morality and the direction of social progress in the face of Darwinism and the economic depression of the mid-1890s. Indeed, the fear that American urban culture may become feminised by suffragette movements is reflected in the insistence of Henry James's Southern stalwart Basil Ransom in *The Bostonians* (1886) that he must save his sex 'from the most damnable feminization' in the face of Olive Chancellor's strident feminism. Ransom exclaims:

> The whole generation is womanized; the masculine tone is passing out of the world; it's a feminine, a nervous, hysterical, chattering, canting age, an age of hollow phrases and false delicacy ... The masculine character, the ability to dare and endure, to know and yet not fear reality, to look the world in the face and take it for what it is ... that is what I want to preserve, or rather, as I may say, to recover.[18]

James's narrator comments that 'these narrow notions' are the residue of Ransom's Civil War ideology, characterising him as an 'intense conservative' who feared 'the encroachment of modern democracy'.[19] Similarly, in his reinvention of the modern Western hero, as Gail Bederman notes, Roosevelt's ideal of the ranchman countered the fears of a feminised culture by blending the savage's natural 'strength and vigor' with 'the superior manliness of the civilized white man'.[20] Developing the fashionable rhetoric of Social Darwinism, Roosevelt was concerned that untamed savagery would lead to regression into passivity (described as an overcivilised femininity) or would degenerate into barbarity (racialised primitivism). The modernist language of flux, fluidity and change, espoused by Henry Adams and the James brothers (William echoes Roosevelt's 'strenuous' rhetoric at times, but not his ideology), served as a counterpoint to these rigid gender and racial dichotomies, but did little to dilute their potency until the mid-1910s when the tangible consequences of urban capitalism were beginning to be felt.[21] Nevertheless, although Roosevelt's ideas had wide currency at the turn of the century, his emphasis on masculine values barely disguises his anxiety about the foundation of right behaviour, an anxiety later amplified by Americans protesting against the Great War on moral grounds (for example, Randolph Bourne) or witnessing its carnage directly (including Hemingway and John Dos Passos).

In his influential book *The End of American Innocence* (1959), Henry May argues that even though America did not enter the Great War until 1917, the realities of war marked a fault line between the Victorian world-view in the late nineteenth and very early twentieth century (epitomised by that champion of American moral realism, William Dean Howells) and the forging of a modern American sensibility. This distinction marks a shift from the idealism of the Harvard scholar Josiah Royce to the scepticism of Randolph Bourne, the premier American intellectual of the First World War. By the mid-1910s, Bourne had added his support to the collective voice of the *Dial* as 'freely experimental, sceptical of inherited values, ready to examine old dogmas and to subject afresh its sanctions to the test of experience'.[22] As May notes, the youthful rebellion and radicalism of the years preceding the war (including Stieglitz's experimental New York exhibitions) were reflected in the publications *New Republic* and *Seven Arts* (for which Leo Stein, Gertrude's brother, wrote important essays), but were already on the wane when the *Dial* produced its new manifesto in early 1917. As an active contributor to this 'Lyrical Left', Bourne himself (quite literally) challenged the Harvard emphasis on masculine prowess in the shape of his hunchbacked and dwarfed body (caused by a botched birth and spinal tuberculosis).[23] Even though Victorian cultural impulses can be traced into the 1920s, Bourne's essays written in late 1917 on the moral consequences of war ('The War and the Intellectuals' and 'A War Diary') form a radical reassessment of the moral, national and gender values of modern American life. For example, in his much-quoted essay on the status of American immigrants, 'Transnational America' (1916), Bourne argued for a moral rejection of 'weary old nationalism' and its emphasis on imperial values, in search of a 'new key' in which America would find fruition 'not as a nationality but a transnationality, a weaving back and forth, with the other lands, of many threads of all sizes and colors'.[24] The weaving of threads as a model for social and intellectual reform replaces the gender dichotomies of the Progressive era with a vision of ethnic and interpersonal plurality, providing a way of rethinking 'what Americanism may rightly mean' behind Roosevelt's veneer of masculine bravado.[25]

American expatriate writers such as Stein and Hemingway embodied

Bourne's call for a 'vivid consciousness' by extending his reappraisal of the relationship between nationality and moral life into the aesthetic sphere. As experimental writers they developed Iain Chambers's idea of the 'drama of the stranger' by subverting dominant ideologies and testing the stability of boundaries between personal and national identities. A huge body of critical work surrounds both figures, but the moral implications of their literary experiments have received scant attention as a way of grounding their artistic practice. Indeed, a composite sexual identity characterises their work (as well as Miller's and Nin's fiction), combining 'active' masculine language with poetic exuberance, later described by French feminists as a central feature of *écriture féminine*. Abstract work such as 'Tender Buttons' exemplifies Stein's development of a 'queer' aesthetic by undermining gender dichotomies, and *The Sun Also Rises* contains two figures – the wounded and impotent Jake Barnes and the boy-like flapper Brett Ashley – who blur the strict gender roles often attributed to Hemingway's characters. While their styles are very different, both writers sensed that formal innovation would enable them to explore the intersection of psychological, sexual and moral impulses more readily than realistic narrative forms.[26] But, before addressing Stein's and Hemingway's fictional exploration of sexual difference, it is useful to consider Luce Irigaray's work for understanding the relationship between desire and morality in modernist writing.

Desire and morality were usually considered as polar opposites in late nineteenth-century America (as in Victorian Britain), the former being associated with indulgence, selfishness and sin and the latter with restraint, control and moderation. In her collection *An Ethics of Sexual Difference* (1984), Irigaray argues that these conventional groupings serve to gender moral theory (together with political theory and philosophy) as male, while 'women are left the so-called minor arts: cooking, knitting, embroidery, and sewing; and, in exceptional cases, poetry, painting, and music'.[27] As one of the most influential voices in nineteenth-century America, Margaret Fuller bemoaned this sanctioning of gender roles in *Woman in the Nineteenth Century* (1845) in which man becomes 'the master of time' and woman the overseer of domestic space, but not until the 1890s, with writers such as Charlotte Perkins Gilman and Henry Adams, was the model systematically challenged. Irigaray also rejects the idea of sexual specificity by suggesting that gender binaries and the 'space-time' of the 'living subject' should both be reconceived in terms of 'containers, or envelopes of identity' rather than fixed entities.[28] Echoing Bourne's 'Transnational

America', she believes that such a reconception will transform the way in which individuals and social units relate: as she claims, 'this change in perspective is, precisely, a matter of ethics'.[29] As Stein explored in transcultural pieces such as 'Geography', this kind of relatedness can be conceived in terms of a 'borderlander' identity both inside and outside a national culture, or in terms of desire and sexual attraction which 'makes possible speech, promises, alliances' between separate beings: a 'half-open' existence that develops the Romantic understanding of the self as both receptive to, and co-extensive with, its environment.[30]

Irigaray argues that ethics can emerge out of the rethinking of sexual difference as mutually complementary, rather than combative, and by reconceiving the parameters and the relevance of 'the masculine' and 'the feminine' as essentialising terms. The either–or logic (corresponding to the gender dichotomies of Progressive America) that places divisions and limits on concepts and social spaces alike suggests an atomised world of distance and opposition, rather than of sexual intimacy. Irigaray suggests that 'the maternal-feminine' can intervene in a traditionally male world of right behaviour (in which impulse is resisted in favour of good sense), to reveal a realm of libidinal attraction that belongs neither to male nor female, but exists in the plenum of overlapping identity-envelopes. Such a realm has its obvious dangers when one individual subjects another to his or her power, with 'the one who offers or allows desire' usually 'engulfing the other'. But, Irigaray suggests, rather than accepting a binary model of empowerment and submission, the existence of a third term in 'relation to the divine, to death, to the social, [or] to the cosmic' can limit narcissism and self-aggrandisement at the expense of the Other and open a space for mutual interaction that echoes Breton's conception of 'mad love': the 'rubbings between two infinitely near neighbors that creates a dynamics'.[31] Irigaray hopes to replace the dialectic model of master–slave with a model based on what she calls the 'first passion': a sense of wonder or joy 'which beholds what it sees always as if for the first time, never taking hold of the other as its object. It does not try to seize, possess, or reduce this object, but leaves it subjective, still free.'[32] Rather than founding ethical practice on the repudiation of desire, this theory (influenced by the Romantic belief that moral reform must stem from within) implies that morality emerges from the intertwining of selves as an excess, a threshold, 'an alchemical site' that cannot be contained either by the self or by a union of selves.[33]

On this model, morality is co-extensive with the discovery of the self in the Other as an angelic 'messenger of ethics', revealing a primitive level of human awareness. This is better associated with the primal sense of touch as a coming and going between selves, than with the higher sense of sight that divides the visual field into subject and object.[34] In the essay 'An Ethics of Sexual Difference', Irigaray contrasts her angelic ethics of intimacy with the neutral ethics of classical philosophy and the nineteenth-century natural sciences, in which the human subject is understood to be universal and ungendered. While Irigaray illustrates her ideas with distinctly feminised images – the meeting of vaginal lips and the touch of the placental membrane – she admits that the only way such an ethics could be mobilised is through interaction and a giving over the self to the Other: 'it can be accomplished only through the combined efforts of the two halves of the world: the masculine and feminine'.[35] Her theory raises questions about monogamy and fidelity, but she is less concerned with normative ethics than with reconceiving a meta-ethical sphere based on sexual difference that is anterior to moral behaviour. What makes literary fiction useful for developing Irigaray's conception of angelic ethics is its exploration of the transformations the self undergoes. Fiction offers an exploratory zone in which the individual can test relationships with others. Even in those fictions in which the individual appears dominant and active (as Roosevelt's manly fantasies suggest), the boundaries between self and Other are always under threat. Like Bourne, Irigaray hopes to establish an ethics of difference through union (rather than the erasure of difference in unity): 'a "we are" or "we become", "we live here" together'.[36]

Stein's and Nin's feminist agendas are evident in their fracturing of the boundaries of the domestic sphere and their exploration of alternative models of femininity which free the angel from the house, but it is also productive to consider Hemingway and Miller in the light of French feminist ideas. In *The Gender of Modernity* (1995) Rita Felski discusses the feminisation of some strains of modernism, claiming that 'just as nineteenth-century ideals of progress, heroism, and national identity became identified with a somatic norm of healthy masculinity, so the motif of the feminized male offered a provocative refusal of such ideas'.[37] However, Felski remains cautious that 'male appropriations of feminine textuality', whether in terms of decadent, avant-garde or high modernist writers, 'may coexist with undisguised expressions of anxiety and hostility towards women'.[38] Such anxiety does inform the fictions of Hemingway and Miller, but in their Paris writings in particular they transgress gender boundaries and move towards a libidinally fluid notion of sexual identity. While the American expatriate fictions discussed here rarely reach Irigaray's dialogic ideal, the four writers reject the orderly masculine world (reflected in the Progressive values of post-bellum America) in favour of a mode of existence based on self-transformation and sexual metamorphosis (imaged in the creative alchemy of Paris) achieved by exploring the interface between desire and morality.

Primitive identities in Stein and Hemingway

Stein's *Three Lives* prefigures Irigaray's fusion of critique and fiction (in, for example, Irigaray's poetic homage/critique *Marine Lover of Friedrich Nietzsche*; *Amante Marine*, 1980) by exploring the ways in which ambiguity emerges from the moral certainties of late nineteenth-century America with its emphasis on work and self-discipline. 'The Good Anna', the first of the three tales based on the aesthetic model of Flaubert's *Three Tales* (*Trois contes*, 1877), examines the way in which Anna's goodness is eventually perverted from within. The apparent simplicity of the narrative, set in Baltimore and recounting Anna's domestic life as an industrious German serving-woman who 'had always a firm old world sense of what was the right way for a girl to do', disguises a complicated and ironic relationship between narrator, character and reader.[39] Anna's insistence on her own goodness (as opposed to her lazy mistresses) becomes a means of justifying her industrious actions as morally right. Her hatred of waste is reminiscent of Norris's descriptions of Trina McTeague as she descends into psychopathology, while her pinched face and emaciated body imply that bourgeois morality can be a poisonous force, rigidifying gender boundaries instead of opening up to the Other in line with Irigaray's model of angelic ethics. If Anna is an angel in the house, she is an angel imprisoned by her own strict moral codes and lack of compassion (even though her subservient role implies that her economic relationships to others are imprisoning). Stein's use of an unsettling narrator in *Three Lives* – in turns sympathetic towards and disdainful of her characters, sometimes knowing and at other times seemingly ignorant or naïve – echoes the Dadaist insistence that modernist morality must be located somewhere ontologically quite different from where nineteenth-century bourgeois ideology would insist. Indeed, Stein's development and gradual movement away from the naturalistic mode of Norris and Dreiser reflects the Dadaist disdain for naturalism as 'a psychological penetration of the motives of the bourgeois' which 'despite all efforts of resistance, brings an identification with the various precepts of bourgeois morality'.[40]

Although Anna's lack of introspection echoes the failings of McTeague and Ethan Frome, *Three Lives* has a peculiar narrative rhythm deriving from the use of phrases and paragraphs as basic structural units: the repetition and modulation of phrases lend the prose a fluidity that recreates a retrospective dynamic even as the narrative progresses. Rather than the narrator seeking to 'penetrate' Anna's motives in naturalistic fashion, her own actions succeed in undermining her cherished beliefs. The initially casual use of the epithet 'good' to describe Anna's character as morally upright is destabilised by repetition and its use in different contexts: the good Anna does chores for other people's 'own good' (defined by her moral standards), she cannot tolerate any opposition to her authority, and she contrasts her ideal of goodness with what she considers to be bad (Mrs Lehntman's 'affair') or 'evil' (the corrupting influence of the doctor).[41] Moreover, Anna's rigid polarities – she divides the world into strict categories of good and bad, thin and fat – actually transform her into a rigid type: 'already the temper and the humor showed sharply in her clean blue eyes, and the thinning was begun about the lower jaw, that was so often strained with the upward pressure of resolve'.[42] Flaubert's use of negative implication – for example, his use of 'simple' in 'A Simple Heart' (*'Un coeur simple'*) – becomes a dominant motif in *Three Lives*, which challenges bourgeois notions of morality and habitual ways of seeing the world. The impression of flux created by narrative fluidity and shifting point of view acts as a countercheck to the stasis that blights the lives of Stein's three major characters: 'The Good Anna', 'Melanctha' and 'The Gentle Lena'.

Stein succeeded in countering Anna's ideological limitations in her work, first, by developing an open fluid style from William James's phenomenological psychology, particularly evident in 'Melanctha' and her epic *The Making of Americans* (begun in 1903 and published in 1925) and, second, by transmuting the method of Cézanne's and Picasso's post-Impressionistic aesthetics into the cubist work 'Tender Buttons'. This fusion of American psychology and French modernist art marks Stein's work as being distinctively transatlantic. Moreover, her interest in what James calls 'fine-grained' consciousness (contrasting with rigid either-or logic) and the procreativity of Picasso's work (what Stein describes as a 'bringing out of himself') reveals her desire to feminise the theories of her male mentors.[43] Her emphasis on fecundity and creativity in her Paris writings – what she calls in her lecture 'Composition as Explanation' (1926) an 'elaboration of the complexities of using everything and of a continuous present and of beginning again and again and again' – reveals a strong moral impulse in her work. Rather than using ethical language (that which Irigaray describes as the stronghold of male theory) or depicting fully-formed individuals distinct from, or in conflict with, each other, Stein devises a number of overlapping identity-envelopes.[44] As Linda Mizejewski argues, writers such as Kate Chopin, Gilman and Woolf shared this reaction to the 'cultural expectation of enduring consciousness'; they tended to reject 'identity writing' (which seeks to establish 'meaning') in favour of 'entity writing' ('a process of concentration, or intensification') in which woman becomes both self and Other.[45] Even though Stein returned to an identifiable mode of characterisation in *The Autobiography of Alice B. Toklas* (1933), in poems such as 'Lifting Belly' and 'Pink Melon Joy' real figures are transformed into a poetic palate of emotions, geometric figures, and kinetic nodes, presented as fragments of a libidinal performance that problematises, rather than erases, gender difference.

Stein experimented with a variety of literary styles in the 1910s and 1920s while resident in Paris, but the composition of 'Tender Buttons', most daringly challenged both the conventions of narrative and the possibility of representing the world accurately through language. Like *Three Lives*, it is divided into three parts, 'Objects', 'Food' and 'Rooms', but the sequence is really a collection of fragments structured by the juxtaposition of images and the modulated repetition of nouns and phrases; this 'insistent' or 'incantatory' style suggests a regression from the poise and erudition of Victorian writing to a primitive mode of emblematic repetition.[46] Marianne DeKoven describes 'Tender Buttons', as an 'attempt to re-create her still-life subjects in pure language, using not words that "mean it" but words that are "equivalent to it"'.[47] The use of pre-Symbolic language reveals a primitive aesthetic in which objects are kinetically suspended in spatial relationship to each other. For Robert Motherwell this would represent a shift from 'sequence' ('a-b-c-d') to 'simultaneity' ('a=b=c=d') in which narrative is temporarily frozen in order to privilege the unstable perceptual moment.[48] As DeKoven argues, despite its unconventional aesthetic, 'Tender Buttons', is not a piece of Dada nonsense. Instead, the paratactic structure of the fragments offer a liminal or 'semi-grammatical' aesthetic hovering between referential meaning and the auto-telic function of language: 'the fact that it is *semi-* rather than *un*grammatical is what makes it readable, viable, valid as an option for literature'.[49]

'Tender Buttons' offers a revisionist account of the female domain of the household in which everyday objects take the place of human agents as identity-envelopes. Rather than housekeeping being an oppressive activity, it is full of unusual connections and surprising revelations that unearth a hidden world beneath the familiar contents of the house. For example, her description of 'A Petticoat' – 'A light white, a disgrace, an ink spot, a rosy charm' – provokes the reader to make connections between descriptive terms that suggest a certain kind of sexual identity, balancing the morally-charged 'disgrace' with the amorous 'rosy charm'.[50] Instead of encouraging the reader to enter a world of static things, the objects release electrical charges and subliminal currents in their relation to each other (paralleling the 'charge' of Breton's surreal visions). Stein's insistent style overcomes the divisions between past and future and between familiarity and strangeness, prefiguring Irigaray's feminised description of open libidinal flow. As Norman Weinstein argues, the descriptions vary in speed and density to defamiliarise the reader's perception of a stable domain of known objects, food and space.[51] This technique embodies Lacan's view of the child's primitive world in which naturalised distinctions have yet to spoil enjoyment of polymorphous sensation and word play. But, rather than encouraging pure indulgence, here, as in later pieces such as 'Identity A Poem' (1936), Stein encourages the reader to search for possible links between objects to discover the implications they have for sexual agency. Often she poses questions – 'An increase why is an increase idle' and 'What is the wind, what is it' – as injunctions demanding that the reader takes the pleasure of the text seriously.[52] This strange mid-world between nonsense and sense, between desire and responsibility, offers the reader an opportunity to blend the sensual pleasure of reading with the moral critic's sensitivity to what Stein calls the 'justice and likeness' of things.[53]

While Hemingway was not as flamboyant as Stein in terms of formal innovation, he shared her disdain for literary and moral convention and her interest in exploring the familiar strangeness of contemporary life. *The Sun Also Rises* (also published as *Fiesta*) dramatises the philosophical tensions between despair and rejuvenation among the expatriate community in Paris. The image of the sun is repeated in the second of two epigraphs, linking the experience of postwar Paris to the world of the Old Testament philosopher in Ecclesiastes who mourns the futility of life for offering no significance to his pitiful existence. The philosopher moans that life is useless and knowledge is like chasing the wind; just like Hemingway's characters, he seeks happiness and pleasure through the conventional routes of drinking and debauchery, but these do not satisfy him and real pleasure proves elusive. Despite his scepticism and despair he eventually comes to faith in God by testing the truth of the proverbs and folklore told to him. This analogy suggests that *The Sun Also Rises* can be read as a proto-existential novel, testing the fundamental values of life in the face of American modernity and the cataclysm of war.

Hemingway's use of the epigraph from Ecclesiastes – 'One generation passeth away, and another generation cometh; but the earth abideth forever' – offers human solace in the realisation that the world remains constant despite devastating changes to it. This reading sets the passage in optimistic contrast to the first apocalyptic epigraph from Stein that evokes the sense of futility in the aftermath of the War: 'You are all a lost generation'. Mirroring the paralysis experienced by Wharton's Ethan Frome and Newland Archer, towards the start of Hemingway's novel the American Jew Robert Cohn exclaims to the narrator Jake Barnes: 'Don't you ever get the feeling that all your life is going by and you're not taking advantage of it?'[54] The counterbalance of optimism and despair in the epigraphs marks *The Sun Also Rises* as an ambivalent novel: on one view it can be seen as a retreat to the Spanish countryside and the bullrings of Pamplona to escape from the emptiness of the modern metropolis and 'fake European standards', but on another it can be seen as a profound meditation on a world which remains 'bright and clear' even though it is 'inclined to blur at the edges'.[55] The conflict between New World optimism and European experience characterises *The Sun Also Rises* as an 'insider-outsider' novel (to use Alice Gambrell's phrase[56]) which charts the formation of transatlantic identity through the character of Jake Barnes. It is uncertain whether Jake has had his 'prick shot off' (as Hemingway suggested in one of his letters), but he seems incapable of receiving sexual satisfaction, reflecting the feelings of impotence and hopelessness expressed by the philosopher in Ecclesiastes. Jake's injury symbolises the difficulty of forging meaningful relationships with other 'suffering' and 'morally wounded' characters.[57] Paris may have offered Hemingway more cultural and sexual freedom than the American Mid-West, but the marks of barbarity in Europe were too fresh to ignore.[58] Nevertheless, although for much of the narrative Jake is presented as a spectator looking at a European culture to which he feels he does not properly belong (despite partly identifying with it), and he feels at odds with the other American expatriates in Paris, later on he manages to affirm his humanity by participating in the simple activities of fishing and swimming.

The dominant reading of Hemingway's European writing is as a symbolic development of the American frontier story, where the activity of a single self-reliant man is contrasted with the oppression of government, the brutality of revolution and the corrupting influence of politics.[59] Hemingway's world is certainly characterised by ungrounded morality (Jake ponders confusedly, 'that was morality; things that made you disgusted afterwards. No, that must be immorality') and devalued language (like the Dadaists, Hemingway was suspicious of 'abstract words such as glory, honor, courage, or hallow'), but in *The Sun Also Rises* neither are gender identities stable.[60] Jake's impotence and the British aristocrat Brett Ashley's androgynous persona (at once sexually assertive, promiscuous and confused) are just two examples of a psychological landscape in which gender roles are marked by uncertainty and characters interact at cross-purposes. Jake and Brett are described early on as 'strangers' to each other and to themselves; indeed, Jake wonders if Brett 'really saw out of her own eyes at all'.[61] The characters may appear to each other as hard-boiled during the day, but at night or alone their uncertainty and fear is impossible to conceal. As Malcolm Cowley argues, in a frightening world in which characters are pursued by their own demons perhaps the only 'chance for safety lies in the faithful observance of customs they invent for themselves': the 'magical ceremonies' of boxing, swimming, fishing and bull-fighting.[62] Rather than shoring up masculine boundaries, these primitive rituals form part of a mythical interaction with nature, with simple devices (hands, rods, gloves) and with others. The simplicity of these actions is embodied in the stark style that Hemingway develops; his 'true declarative' sentences, repeated phrases and modulated rhythms offer a concrete expression of primal emotions.[63] The primitive values of Spanish country life and imaginative interaction with nature mirrors Hemingway's own desire to be truthful as an antidote to the shiftless existence of his American expatriate characters in Paris. Moreover, this drive to tell the 'truth' is reflected in Jake's desire to be an *aficionado* of European culture, combining passion, commitment and spiritual affinity with the land.[64]

If Hemingway's search for the elusive grail of 'grace under pressure' and his fiction writing in the 1920s and 1930s offered a means of proving masculine integrity (exaggerated, as Joe Moran notes, in the way Hemingway's masculinist persona was later constructed by 'celebrity' publicity in *Life* and *Time* magazines[65]), a much more androgynous aesthetic has been detected in his later work by the critics Mark Spilka and Rose Burwell.[66] For example, in his novel *The Garden of Eden* (written in 1948–59, published in 1986) the destructive power of 'the feminine' towards the male artist is dramatised in the actions of the androgynous character, Catherine, who desires to exchange sex-roles and to 'cross-fertilize' David's (her lover's) imagination. But, rather than *The Sun Also Rises* being grouped squarely in Hemingway's masculinist phase, Spilka detects unanswered questions in the novel about alternative gender roles to those endorsed by Progressive American sexual norms. The 'unmanning' of Jake due to his wound is in conflict with the manly behaviour of Brett who dons a male felt hat and actively pursues the Spanish picador, Romero. F. Scott Fitzgerald's comment that Jake wears a 'moral chastity belt' contrasts to Brett's 'style-setting creativity' and, rather than a simple heterosexual relationship, Spilka suggests that Jake 'wants Brett in a womanly way', even to the extent that she becomes 'the woman Jake would in some sense like to be'.[67] If Jake's primitive rituals can be defined as masculinist, then his interaction with Brett certainly problematises traditional gender identities. Their relationship can be described in terms of Irigaray's identity-envelopes in which the two personalities meld and fold over into each other. This is especially relevant as the narrative is told retrospectively by Jake, suggesting that Brett is a projection of his psychic and sexual longing; his angelic love transcends the baseness and rivalry of his relationships with male characters, revealing his commitment to a set of intimate values outside his rational control and even to the detriment of his self-integrity. Rather than the story being Jake's solipsistic fantasy, the liveliness of Brett's character and the diastolic movement of the novel, in which the characters repeatedly part and meet company, suggests an interactive relationship far beyond physical attraction. In this way, as James Nagel comments, Jake's 'confessional' narrative can be read as his attempt to learn 'how to live in the special circumstances of his world'.[68]

Just as the novel's two epigraphs are neither wholly optimistic nor pessimistic (mirroring the counterpoints in Stein's experimental work), so Jake expresses both his undisguised hatred of and jealousy towards Robert Cohn and Brett's fiancé, Mike Campbell, and his almost transcendent, but self-lacerating, love for Brett. Although Jake betrays 'his personal values' by actively complying in Brett's affair with Romero, in his own desire to be an *aficionado* he perhaps confuses his selfless love for Brett with his fantasy of Spanish authenticity.[69] Here, Spilka's reading of the novel as a troubled meditation on gender identity ties in with the confusion between Jake's expatriate passion for 'true' European culture and his sexually open (yet non-consummated) relationship with Brett. After Brett's relationship with Romero has ended and she has decided to go back to Mike, Jake responds immediately to her telegram. Although he never clearly expresses his motives, his desire to be near her is too intense to be explained as simply a willingness to offer her emotional comfort. Jake and Brett are both wounded, partly by their own actions and partly because their behaviour does not meet the expectations of the other characters. Despite their affinity they realise a regular heterosexual relationship would not work for them; nevertheless, their symbolic and physical intimacy at the end of the novel – 'Brett moved close to me. We sat close against each other' – suggests an overlapping of identity and a self-sacrificing, almost angelic, commitment to each other.[70] The moral implications of such commitment are left hanging as the text (like Stein's fiction) provokes the reader to work through the consequences of the characters' actions. Indeed, this provocation to the reader parallels Hemingway's final comment in his other Paris novel, *The Torrents of Spring* (1925), which he describes as his 'secret history' of American identity. He warns the reader that 'when you're travelling abroad alone ... you simply cannot be too careful ... I will just say a simple farewell ... and leave you now to your own devices.'[71]

Sexual creativity in Miller and Nin

In the 1930s Henry Miller and Anaïs Nin began to develop Stein's and Hemingway's interest in exploring the interstices between traditional gender identities in forms of writing that blurred fiction with autobiography. This section discusses the different ways in which Miller and Nin problematised national and gender identities, but first there are a number of striking parallels in their work which should be noted: they entered into a fraught relationship in Paris (documented in Nin's extensive journal); they were both intensely interested in sexuality; and both adopted the Austrian analyst Otto Rank as their mentor for exploring the possibilities and dangers of living a full artistic and sexual life. Furthermore, their work bridges the linear form of the *Bildungsroman* and the modernist novel of psychic disintegration without fitting neatly into either category: Miller's work is loose and picaresque in its wandering, whereas Nin developed a diaristic and fragmented form of telling stories. Miller's work from the 1930s is much more despairing than Nin's diaries and short stories, but for both writers creativity emerges from fusing life and art, rendered through first-person personae who are, as Michael Woolf argues, impressionistic in their outlook and promiscuous in their relationships.[72] In this way, they explore the Romantic themes of growth, freedom and self-creation, but plumb sexual experience more deeply than their literary predecessors. The mythic space of Paris is important in defining the symbolic topos of their work: the river Seine at the end of Miller's *Tropic of Cancer* suggests a psychic flow which the artist may harness, whereas for Nin the city is an erotic playground for testing a variety of sexual roles. As Donald Pizer notes, Paris is not 'an incarnation of some specific insight into experience' but stimulates 'an intensity of response to various kinds of experience'.[73] Although they both emphasise individual expression and can be criticised for being narcissistic, their writings really come alive in their interaction with others; while Nin is more emotionally sensitive than Miller, they both explore the sexual and moral consequences of encountering the Other.

Miller was particularly interested in Nietzsche's theory that socially-given borders must be transgressed if the individual is to follow his or her own desires. In *Tropic of Cancer*, Miller describes the nothingness which he has become, divorced from his homeland and without moral bearings – 'I made up my mind that I would hold on to nothing, that I would expect nothing' – but out of this nothingness emerges a new being: 'The dawn is breaking on a new world in which the lean spirits roam with sharp claws'.[74] Such descriptions suggest that he views character both in a biological sense (as creature) and in an imaginative sense (as creator), a combination which helps individuals to adapt to new environments. On this theme, in a letter to his friend James Laughlin in June 1938, he distinguishes modernist experimentation from conventional novel writing: 'the difference between literature for consumption and literature as art lies in this constant effort to express what has been derived from experience (of all sorts) and is real. It isn't a question of honesty, even, or sincerity; it's beyond that. It is in the very nexus of creation.'[75] This idea of going beyond truth and 'sincerity' means he refuses to accept conventional wisdom on issues of gender and national identity and marks his commitment to explore the unassimilable elements of the self. As Michael Woolf claims, Miller's fiction replaces the American Progressive archetype of the self-made man with that of the 'un-made' man, who must relinquish a safe identity before he can rediscover himself.[76] It seems that only by adopting the double identity of creature and creator can he prevent himself being stifled by despair and the threat of death. While in much of his work he parallels Hemingway's attraction to danger and death by adopting an aggressive masculine stance in which he poses as a predatory beast, elsewhere he responds sensitively to the fluid 'chaos' of creative life with a much more androgynous voice. For example, at the beginning of *Tropic of Capricorn* (1939) he writes: 'From the beginning it was never anything but chaos: it was a fluid which enveloped me, which I breathed through the gills.'[77] Rather than regressing to masculine barbarity, Miller's emphasis on primitive experience – the bestiality of the predator or the androgynous fish – reveals a double or multiple life as potentially liberating. Moreover, whereas Roosevelt's cult of masculinity is intertwined with Progressive values, when Miller's characters assert their aggression it is usually associated critically with destructive and asocial impulses in the self that cannot be successfully eradicated.

It is not easy to rescue Miller's writing from the charges of misogyny (and, at times, anti-Semitism) levelled at him by the likes of Kate Millett (who criticises his 'unlimited scope for masculine aggression'), because many of his fictional encounters can be interpreted as debasing the feminine Other.[78] One consequence of the abjection embraced by Gide's Michel at the end of *The Immoralist* can be gauged in the dashed expectations of Miller's characters (when all the heroes are dead) and the hatred and despair they have for the postwar world. However, at other times, this Dadaist nihilism is counterpoised by great tenderness and humility in his artistic expression. For example, at the start of *Tropic of Cancer* he states:

> It is to you, Tania, that I am singing. I wish that I could sing better, more melodiously, but then perhaps you would never have consented to listen to me. You have heard the others sing and they have left you cold. They sang too beautifully, or not beautifully enough.[79]

The composition of a virtually formless novel ('a prolonged insult, a gob of spit in the face of Art'[80]) allows him to distance himself from the constraints of pleasing melody, conventional character construction and the expectation that the reader will be edified by the story.

In a world that is 'rotting away' this kind of beautiful fiction would be an act of deception, luring the reader into a fantasy that fails to deal with conflict, unhappiness and disillusion as fundamental aspects of postwar identity. For Miller, only by 'digging around in the dark, with nothing but instinct to guide' him can he create a fiction 'full of odds and ends, bric-a-brac' that speaks to modern identity as having no stable parameters.[81] This act of blind creation has ramifications in terms of national identity – his persona in *Tropic of Cancer* is homeless and dissolute – and in terms of gender identity: at different times he becomes amoeboid, animalistic, feminised and corpse-like. Total dissolution seems only to be prevented by the physical life-force of Paris that sustains his private metamorphoses and enables him to fuse the creaturely and creative aspects in himself. If at times he asserts heroically his moral freedom ('I am only spiritually dead. Physically I am alive. Morally I am free'; 'If anybody ... is pursuing his own destiny like an arrow, it is me'[82]), at other moments Paris inspires in him a much more tempered commitment to the destitute and the lowly: 'when spring comes to Paris the humblest mortal alive must feel that he dwells in Paradise'.[83] Miller's development of a transformative and expansive self is stimulated by the creative energy of Paris and provides him with a fictional strategy for exploring those darker elements of identity and personal interaction usually eschewed by social moralists.

If Miller's fiction can be interpreted as an extravagant masculinist enterprise in which the self becomes expansively creative and in which angelic intimacy is only an unrealised dream, then Nin explores the way in which the unified self can splinter into different aspects 'without the disintegration which usually accompanies it' as 'each fragment had a life of its own'.[84] Both Miller and Nin construct fictional selves that proliferate future possibilities and enlarge the boundaries of reality. But, whereas Miller fictionalises his Paris experience in his writing, Nin distinguishes diary-writing from fiction in that the former represents a discursive 'laboratory' in which one can check 'realities' against 'illusions'.[85] Her diary allowed her some freedom from reality, enabling her to keep touch with the self behind the roles which society induced her to play: 'I had to find one place of truth, one dialogue without falsity.'[86] This does not imply that she believed there is an essential self behind these roles; indeed, switching between different written forms prevented her personae from rigidifying into particular types (as represented by Stein's 'The Good Anna'). Nin links creative development with sexual liberation as a way of overcoming inhibiting fears and preventative barriers in the self. Moreover, like Miller and Irigaray, in her journals she displays her interest in the doubleness of experience: 'henceforth I travel two ways, as sun and as moon. Henceforth I take on two sexes, two hemispheres, two skies, two sets of everything. Henceforth I shall be double-jointed and double sexed.'[87] At times Nin is a ghostly angel moving through other characters' lives, whereas at others her body becomes a site for sexual demand. Indeed, just as Nin's writing is full of bisexual expressions that enable her to transgress the conventional sphere of femininity, she becomes the living embodiment of Irigaray's claim that 'a sexual or carnal ethics would require that both angel and body be found together'.[88]

In *Henry and June*, a collection of her diaristic entries from 1932 to 1936 concerning her relationships with Miller and his wife June Mansfield, Nin problematises Miller's 'frank sensualism' by portraying him, at times, as sensitive to female experience and, at others, 'caricatural' in his complete ignorance of her needs.[89] In describing her very different relationships with the Millers and her European husband Hugo, Nin draws from a rich palette of emotional energies that follow from such tangled dependencies. While her feelings for Miller are very strong, they are represented in more conventional terms than her love for June which 'overstep[s] normal boundaries' and can only be described as 'a secret language' full of 'undertones, overtones, nuances, abstractions, symbols'.[90] Like Stein, Nin moves towards a kind of 'entity writing' in which her identity is often submerged in the libidinal currents she describes. The labyrinth of Parisian back streets, in turn exciting and dangerous, serves as a metaphor for this emotional maze. When she began therapy with Otto Rank in the early 1930s Nin described her life as a labyrinth with no discernible shape and characterised herself as a 'failed work of art' with no way of connecting her split selves.[91] Rather than striving for psychic harmony, Rank encouraged her to dramatise her conflicts by improvising new personae in her writing. Hence, in *Henry and June* she responds to life 'extravagantly' by plunging into invented roles and by proliferating different kinds of sexual experience.[92] Only through such extravagance can she express the many identities she detects in herself and come to the blissful joy that Irigaray describes as the exuberant meeting of Otherness. In contrast, Nin admits that June's 'unethical, irresponsible' and, at times, demonic behaviour cannot sustain this search for Otherness; she detects in June 'the power to destroy' and in herself 'the power to create'.[93] Here, Nin displays her sympathy with the more affirmative currents of the European avant-garde (perhaps stimulated by her relationship with Antonin Artaud) in her fusion of art and everyday life. Indeed, June's almost nihilistic sexual freedom contrasts with Nin's description of herself as 'a fettered, ethical being, in spite of my amoral intellect'.[94] Nin harnesses the psychic flow of Miller's writing to a commitment to remain open to the Otherness in herself and in other beings; only through mutuality with both sexes does she believe that she can experience the blissful joy of sexuality.

This pursuit of joy that cannot be contained in conventional frames of reference is the central uniting factor in American expatriate writing of this time, exemplified by Nin's search for alternative selves: 'I enlarge and expand my self; I do not like to be just one Anaïs, whole, familiar, contained.'[95] Formal innovation and the portrayal of characters more as identity-envelopes than fully-fleshed monads are devices that these writers use to blur strict gender, cultural and national identities and to draw the reader into a more complex understanding of the way in which language can open up different sexual, psychic and ontological spaces. If one modernist response to normative gender expectations is illustrated in the perversity of decadent writers, the American expatriates can be seen to 'queer' relationships even further in their exploration of primitive identities, suggesting that heterosexual and bisexual expressions can be equally creative. Nevertheless, despite their similarities the four writers *can* be paired along gender lines in their responses to Paris: for Hemingway and Miller, Paris is a physical and flexible space reflecting their hunger for new experiences and their desire to experience authentic European culture, whereas for Stein and Nin the city is more of a shadowy substratum for their exploration of fragmented identities within the self. This aside, as Donald Pizer argues, Paris stimulated in these writers a collective 'belief in change and multiplicity as the dynamic core of life' that their expatriate experience charged with an ethical current to forge relationships against the grain of conventional morals. Indeed, even if the blissful joy they desire can only be a supreme fiction or, at best, a fleeting epiphany in the postwar world, Irigaray's 'ethics of sexual difference' provides the moral backbone to their art as an 'overture to a future that is still and always open'.[96]

6
The Blind Impress of Modernity: Lorca, Kafka and New York

In his essay on moral perception, 'On a Certain Blindness in Human Beings' (1899), William James recalls an incident when, on entering a forest clearing in the Appalachian mountains, he encountered a farmer who had cultivated his land in a manner that struck James as repulsive. He describes the wanton destruction of the forest in forceful language: 'a ugly picture on the retina' divorced from any grace or beauty, a scene of 'denudation' and 'a sort of ulcer'.[1] However, after the initial shock of violent repulsion, he has a chance meeting with a mountaineer who helps him to see that his initial impulse was blind to the farmer's story of 'duty, struggle and success'. James begins to realise that his prejudice is both a perceptual blindness (a 'picture on the retina') and a form of cultural myopia that challenges his Romantic view of agrarian life. He admits his provincial values had prevented him from appreciating the signs of collective labour: 'I had been blind to the peculiar ideality of their conditions as they certainly would also have been to the ideality of mine, had they had a peep at my strange indoor academic ways of life at Cambridge.'[2] These two versions of blindness overlap in an intricate way: perceptual blindness derives from James's inability to 'see' cultural difference and his ideological prejudices prohibit him from affirming the farmer's condition of living. This incident is useful for considering the relationship between modernity and morality in providing a visual metaphor for theorising Otherness, and articulating what the anthropologist James Clifford calls the 'poetics' of cultural difference.[3] James detects the need to devise a code of behaviour that could maximise his capacity to respond to (and empathise with) a mode of existence removed from his familiar world. To this end, he realises that life is 'soaked and shot-through ... with values and meanings which we fail to realise because of our external and insensible point of view'.[4]

The American philosopher, Richard Rorty, interprets James's encounter and subsequent realisation as exemplifying the 'contingent' condition of modernity. Rorty argues that the modern condition necessitates a set of individual experiences deriving from matters of 'chance' and 'mere contingency', as opposed to the 'necessary, essential, telic, constitutive' trajectory of classical Greek culture and epitomising the social coherence of mid-nineteenth-century Europe.[5] If classical philosophy is characterised by ideas of necessity, fullness and awareness, qualities which embody the 'whole' man, then the 'fallen' condition of modernity can be described as a 'blind impress': a condition in which the 'fragmented' self is cursed with imperfect and limited vision. This distinction may seem crude, but Rorty deploys the phrase 'blind impress' in two more precise ways that help to differentiate Romantic from modernist ideas. First, 'blind impress' represents a post-Darwinian awareness that there is no universal design, in contrast to the Romantic belief in intrinsic natural order. Second, the term suggests the modern individual is unable to see outside his or her narrow perspective or to occupy another subject position, whereas Romantic thinkers emphasised the primacy of emotional openness and pathos. For Rorty, the 'blind impress' describes the subjective response to modernity, marking a shift from the scientific precision of the microscope to what Gillian Beer calls the 'imperfect vision' and 'extreme tenuity' of modern perception.[6] The visual theorist Victor Burgin translates this contingent experience into an explicitly optical language. He argues that whereas classical theories of representation offered 'the image' as 'a mirror' of 'an ordered reality' and an 'anticipation of a perfected reality', the fragments of the modern mirror are 'perpetually in motion' and 'reflect nothing reassuring'.[7] The horror James feels on entering the forest clearing is an expression of his incomprehension (in Rorty's sense) and lack of visual reassurance (in Burgin's description). If, as Rorty claims, Nietzsche was the first thinker to renounce the desire to attain an inclusive panoramic view of truth, exemplified by Emerson's Romantic image of the 'transparent eye-ball' and Kant's universal or foundational moral consciousness,[8] then it is important to consider the relation between contingency and morality for modernist writers.

Although James's theory of consciousness resembles Nietzsche's to a degree, they part company on crucial issues. Both thinkers focus on the way in which the individual psyche is sealed off from the perspective of others in a self-contained world of phenomena. This perspectivist position can be detected in the work of modernists who explored the way in which the individual's phenomenological world is detached from others who may share the same spatial vacinity. However, whereas Nietzsche seems to deliberately exclude the perspective of others in order to surpass the limitations of the self, the moral thrust of James's thought implies an Other (another person or another point of view) that prevents the closure of any phenomenological system. In other words, whereas Nietzsche's self-affirming doctrine of will-to-power represents one technique for contending with the 'blind impress' of modernity, by reflecting on the moral implications of his encounter James goes some way to acknowledging the Appalachian farmer's perspective, even though he continues to filter his understanding through a puritan lens of virtuous toil. If Rorty's 'blind impress' characterises the condition of the modern self, then James can be seen to acknowledge this condition and take a step further to devise techniques that can maximise the possibilities of responding to Otherness:

> And now what is the result of all these considerations ...? It is negative in one sense, but positive in another. It absolutely forbids us to be forward in pronouncing on the meaninglessness of forms of existence other than our own; and it commands us to tolerate, respect, and indulge those whom we see harmlessly interested and happy in their own ways, however unintelligible these may seem to us.[9]

Even if understanding is threatened with 'a certain blindness', once the hope of attaining a panoramic or God's eye view of the world is renounced, rather than dwelling on the impenetrable secrets of existence, the individual can begin to fashion ways of responding to, and acting with, others. This idea reflects James's interest in 'blind-sight' discussed in *The Principles of Psychology* (1890), a condition that bypasses direct perception and encroaches on the realm of intuitive or reflexive beholding. With this in mind, James concludes his essay thus: 'Hands off: neither the whole truth, nor the whole good, is revealed to any single observer, although each observer gains a partial superiority of insight from the peculiar position in which he stands.'[10]

In order to test the moral implications of James's 'certain blindness' and Rorty's 'blind impress', this chapter develops the theme of cultural transit by considering two examples of modernist writing which explore the lack or depletion of sight, in both perceptual and cultural senses. Much modernist literature describes the individual's failure to empathise with another's condition as a loss of moral fibre: Dostoevsky's Underground Man and the narrator of Knut Hamsun's *Hunger* (*Sult*, 1890) are both anxious about their inability to communicate or empathise with those people who share their physical worlds. However, in line with James's realisation in 'A Certain Blindness in Human Beings' and in contrast to Nietzsche's nihilism, signs of hope are evident in some strains of modernist writing, suggesting that a creative or moral response remains an often unfulfilled possibility. This kind of response can be discerned in the Hindu evocations at the end of *The Waste Land* or Lily Briscoe's 'moment of being' at the close of *To the Lighthouse*,[11] but this chapter considers work by Federico García Lorca and Franz Kafka for their dual emphasis on morality and cultural Otherness.

Although there are more differences between Lorca and Kafka than similarities, their distinctive responses to America provide a bridging focus for discussing their modernist aesthetics. Lorca's American experiences documented in *Poet in New York* (*Poeta in Neuva York*, 1940) are first-hand, whereas Kafka imagines his fictional version of *America* (*Amerika*, written in 1927) from a European vantage point. As Peter Brooker discusses in *New York Fictions* (1996), America, especially New York, provided a powerful symbol of the fledgeling twentieth century for many European writers who were drawn to it as a 'gateway city' between European and American culture.[12] Among European visitors to New York were Freud, Jung, Lorca and Maxim Gorky, while others, such as Kafka, Joyce and Musil chose to explore the lures of American culture and ideas from a distance. Although actual visitors are obviously more accurate in terms of cultural specifics, there is a certain parity between first-hand and imaginative accounts. For example, the bifocal visions of Lorca and Kafka fuse the inability to perceive clearly with the possibilities of imaginative 'seeing', a combination which is exacerbated by what Lorca calls the 'furious rhythm' of America and his struggle to learn a foreign language during his studies at Columbia University.[13] By comparing these two writers' work, it is possible to explore the moral implications of their simultaneous feelings of repulsion by, and fascination with, the modern city. Whereas James's encounter occurs in the relative solitude of the Appalachian mountains, the visual spectacle of Manhattan means the artist must negotiate between the physical topos of the crowded city (compounded by the rapid growth of skyscrapers between 1890 and 1930) and the possibilities of new cultural experiences.

Lorca's uncertain sexual identity and his hatred of imperial and partisan Spain directly parallel Kafka's own libidinal worries and his sense of being doubly removed from Czech culture as a German-speaking Jew. If this sense of alienation represents a feeling of not belonging to, or not being at home in, a dominant culture, then their American experiences provide a double take on the notion of exile: for Lorca, a self-imposed exile in New York to reorientate himself in relation to Spanish culture and, for Kafka, an imaginative exile in a fascinating, but hostile, alien environment. Whereas the American writers in Paris formed a displaced community, Lorca's and Kafka's exiles are fundamentally solitary. However, from its very inception America has been used as a potent metaphor for cultural exile; as Leslie Fiedler argues in *Waiting for the End* (1964): 'It is the dream of exile as freedom which has made America; but it is the experience of exile as terror that has forged the self-consciousness of Americans.'[14] This ambivalent notion of exile as both an unfortunate and a beneficial borderline experience also marks out the modern intellectual as being both inside and outside a culture, whether American expatriate writers in Paris or Europeans encountering American culture. Edward Said writes about such a condition of exile as being 'a challenge or a risk ... a positive mission, whose success would be a cultural act of great importance', by situating the writer in a specular relation to the other culture without becoming consumed or tainted by it.[15] This strong sense of exile – of '*willed* homelessness' – offers an 'enabling theory' of exile which aligns geographical and imaginative travel in a 'specular', but, for the individual aware of the contingent condition of modernity, not necessarily a clear-sighted, relationship to two cultures.[16] As this chapter discusses, Lorca in *Poet in New York* and Karl Rossman, Kafka's protagonist in *America*, give themselves over to American culture, almost to the point of self-sacrifice, in order to devise moral connections between cultures and to resist aligning themselves with nationalistic sympathies or 'the coercive tendencies of fixed, indigenous identities'.[17] Their conditions of exile are not fully rationalised in either text; rather, this borderline position is primarily experiential, in which assured self-consciousness is held in abeyance (or is banished as being an unreal spectre of Enlightenment thought) in order to imaginatively behold the Other.

Lorca's geometric anguish and blind vision

Lorca's posthumously published poem collection *Poet in New York* charts his visit to New York from the spring of 1929 to May 1930. He was encouraged to leave Spain after suffering an emotional breakdown earlier the same year and the signs of his troubled mind are evident in the chaotic and threatening images that convey his impressions of the city. Throughout the poem sequence Lorca's urban experience is rendered explicitly in visual terms, reflecting the distorted Expressionism of Picasso, Miró and Dalí more than the subtle Impressionism of Renoir and Monet. Instead of privileging the clear vision of the artist, in his earlier lecture 'Thoughts on Modern Art' (1928) Lorca distances himself from late nineteenth-century Impressionism for which, he argued, 'sight was a slave to what it saw, and the soul of a painter was a sad creature chained to his eyes, having no space or criteria of its own, unlike the souls of poets and musicians'.[18] Although both optical and cultural blindness are conditions to avoid, visual distortion offers the artist a freedom to surpass orthodox modes of representation on a level that reflects the modernist rejection of conventional moral codes. In *Poet in New York* and the pictures he drew while in the city – for example, 'Self-Portrait of the Poet in New York' in which the boundaries between the poet and the city blur at the edges – Lorca attempts to distance himself from old ways of seeing and the tyranny of the eye by merging himself with the city.[19] Rather than uncritically celebrating urban life, this stance allows him to dismantle the conventional subject–object dichotomy between the 'seer' and the 'seen' in order that, in his jumble of imagery, he might discover the secret 'pictorial centre' of objects (analogous to James's blind-sight) that he claims 'the copy artist cannot perceive'.[20]

The first poem in *Poet in New York*, 'After a Walk' ('*Vuelta de paseo*'), provides a good example of this technique of optical immersal. He claimed later that the poem was composed after he had 'wandered alone' through Manhattan, 'exhausted by the rhythm of the huge electric billboards of Times Square'.[21] The title of the poem implies that the poet needs time to absorb the experience before he can muster an expression of the city as an 'after image', but he is wary about translating sense-data into rational understanding. The opening line 'Cut down by the sky' (repeated as an apostrophe in the closing line of the last of five short stanzas) suggests a violent vertical force that strikes down the poet from above. Instead of providing light and generativity, with a violent 'cut' the sky delays the emergence of the speaking subject until the fourth line of the first stanza:

> Cut down by the sky.
> Between shapes moving toward the serpent
> and crystal-craving shapes,
> I'll let my hair grow.[22]

The reader is given no sense of exact location here (in contrast to Lorca's prose description of his wanderings in his lecture); the people of the city are reduced to 'shapes' who crave enlightenment, but move inexorably towards a malevolent 'serpent' that consumes the city by obliterating the source of light. The poet's response to the anonymity of city life in the fourth line hovers between defiance and blasé flippancy (an attitude identified by Georg Simmel in his classic sociological essay 'The Metropolis and Mental Life', 1901), as if he too cannot locate himself spatially within the city except as a passive object ('I'll let . . .') into which the shapes bump and metamorphose in the last stanza: 'Bumping into my own face, different each day.' The middle three two-line stanzas begin 'with . . .', which may be read as a muffled articulation of a wounded community, but actually emphasises the isolation and fragmentation of city life. The string of violent images – 'the amputated tree that doesn't sing'; 'the child with the blank face of an egg'; 'the little animals whose skulls are cracked'; and 'a butterfly drowned in the inkwell' – hover between a description of identifiable, but damaged, organisms and creatures who have been so fatigued that they have been reduced to the status of things. The ugly juxtaposition of images conveys the poet's sense of despair; facing this city-island 'dressed in rags, but with dry feet' he struggles to connect with his older European identity.

As a collection, *Poet in New York* hovers between an exploration of the objects and images of the city and a meditation on the adjustments the poet has to make to his self-identity. Just before leaving Spain, in a letter to his friend Carlos Morla Lynch, Lorca wrote that 'New York seems horrible, but for that very reason I'm going there. I think I'll have a very good time.'[23] Here Lorca expresses his feelings in the face of the 'horrible' city, but also the benefits he hopes to accrue from his visit: 'this trip will be very useful to me'.[24] In another letter written on voyage to America, Lorca expressed his reservations about his trip in the form of self-doubt – 'I look in the mirror of the confining cabin and I don't recognize myself. I seem to be another

Federico' – as if he must ritually shed his European skin in order to adopt a new hybrid form.[25] This idea is reinforced on his arrival in New York, which he sees as 'Babylonic, cruel and violent' but filled with 'a great modern beauty'.[26] Lorca's reassessment of his identity during the Atlantic crossing enables him to focus on a city which 'from far away seemed gigantic and disordered' but which, on closer inspection, has a 'symphonic' quality.[27] This notion of a horrific, but beneficial, experience provides a way of reading the poem sequence as an attempt to develop a visual and moral language for describing New York, linking the innocence of child-like wonder with the hard-headedness of the cultural critic abroad in a hostile environment. He claims that an honest 'lyrical reaction' may enable him to 'escape through the murky edge of the looking glass of day more quickly than most children'.[28]

Lorca believed his journeys through the city would lead him to uncover hidden truths among the urban debris. For example, 'After a Walk' opens with an image of the violent sky which blinds the innocent child ('with the blank face of an egg'), but which cannot 'amputate' the poet's ability to make sense of this chaos. Throughout the sequence the poet struggles to maintain his identity, but this is characterised as much by his inability to see as a visual description of urban spectacle: for example, the third poem in the sequence, 'Dawn' ('*La aurora*'), describes 'four columns of mire/and a hurricane of black pigeons/splashing in the putrid waters'.[29] Whereas Eliot describes *The Waste Land* as a place of spiritual drought, Lorca's New York City is a sea-island that obliterates light and renders its inhabitants blind, both to the sky which it devours and the surrounding countryside which it hides beneath its urban cloak. In 'Dawn', 'morning and hope are impossible' in a city which buries light 'under chains and noises'; the crowds can only avoid obliteration by keeping their distance from the urban serpent and staggering 'sleeplessly through the boroughs/as if they had just escaped a shipwreck of blood'.[30] If Eliot's spiritual drought is symbolised by a lack of fresh water and the fetid canal of the Fisher King, Lorca views the 'unanswered sea'[31] which surrounds the island as the real potent force, but guarded by what he describes in the titles of two more poems as the 'pissing multitude' of Manhattan and the 'vomiting multitude' of Coney Island.[32]

Another example of diminished sight is evident in 'Blind Panorama of New York' ('*Panorama ciego de Neuva York*'), in which the poet once more describes his imaginative and perceptual blindness when faced with an alien panorama. To some degree this is true of all crosscultural experiences, but Lorca suggests that the experience of New York City epitomises a certain European blindness to America in the early twentieth century, a blindness which cannot be overcome either by simply embracing or rejecting an American identity. If 'panorama' suggests an inclusive vision, characterised by Walt Whitman's soaring views of Manhattan and Brooklyn Bridge, then Lorca's poem is testimony to the disorienting experience of the New York street plan and the overwhelming verticality of the skyscrapers, compounding his linguistic and cultural differences.[33] This is figured in 'Blind Panorama of New York' by incomplete images which metamorphose into broken spaces: 'the birds will soon become oxen/They could become white rocks'; 'the sky often shrugs them into ragged togetherness'; 'a tiny space alive in the crazy union of light'.[34] Here, as with James's encounter in the Appalachians, these images suggest that cultural blindness does not derive from a total lack of sight, nor a refusal to see, but rather an inability to grasp fully and represent adequately the alterity of the Other. In a city which shuts out light and atomises individuals, any encounters with strangers remain fleeting and darkly disturbing, lending Lorca's 'blind impress' an inherently modern feel.

On one level, Lorca's view of New York is conventionally Romantic and compares well with James's agrarian encounter. In 'Dawn', New York has 'four columns of mire',[35] in 'New York (Office and Denunciation)' ('*Neuva York (Oficina y denuncia)*') the city is a slaughterhouse of 'clouded blood ... that sweeps machines over waterfalls' and in 'Blind Panorama of New York' he displaces images drawn from the natural world, 'birds' and 'caterpillars', into an industrial cityscape of 'ash' and 'billowing smoke'.[36] However, although *Poet in New York* represents a sustained attack on the urban space in which the natural world is contaminated or perverted, New York actually galvanises his poetry into surrealistic life. An example of this is found in 'Dance of Death' ('*Danza de la muerte*') in which the poetic vision takes on the geometrical form of the city: 'A pure and manicured sky, identical with itself,/with the down and the keen-edged iris of its invisible mountains'.[37] Here, vision is sharp and acute, but he goes on to suggest a kind of blind-sight buried within these cool visions: 'the primitive impetus dances with the mechanical impetus, unaware, in their frenzy, of the original light'. The Romantic symmetry of vision and view – the 'seer' and 'seen' – is problematised by the poet's inability to define, or divine, the source of light. Indeed, as he qualified in his lecture 'A Poet in New York' (1932), the skyscrapers of New York, 'hostile to mystery and blind to any sort of play, shear off the rain's tresses and shine their three thousand swords through the soft swan of fog'.[38] The 'geometry' of the city and 'anguish' of the poet combine in a blind vision, revealing a primitive exuberance of natural dance and play. Lorca's anguished parade of fractured images cannot be separated easily from the geometric inspiration that stimulates his vision because, as Helen Oppenheimer comments, 'in New York ... there is no cause which is entirely positive and consequently none which is entirely negative. We therefore find a considerable number of half-forces'.[39]

Lorca describes the buildings of New York more explicitly in his lecture than he does in his poem sequence, in which they appear only as shadowy columns. Nevertheless, he continues to render them in poetic vein:

> The angles and edges of Gothic architecture surge from the hearts of the dead and buried, but these climb coldly skyward with a beauty that has no roots and reveals no longing, stupidly complacent and utterly unable to transcend and conquer, as does spiritual architecture, the perpetually inferior intentions of the architect. There is nothing more poetic and terrible than the skyscrapers' battle with the heavens that cover them.[40]

He contrasts the blind faces of the 'stupidly complacent' New York skyscrapers to the more 'spiritual architecture' of Granada, but describes the former as being more 'poetic' in their battle for dominance with the sky. Here, Lorca seems to show a greater sympathy with an America-inspired modern poetry than the late-Romantic Hispanic *modernismo* from which he had begun to distance himself. On the one hand, he describes the skyscrapers as having no spiritual roots and, on the other, he sees something inspirational in their brute juxtaposition with nature. The real lack of spirituality and morality which the poems bemoan derives from the fact that the skyscrapers are not adequate memorials for those workers who are now 'dead and buried' beneath the mass of steel and glass. Although *Poet in New York* was written after the 1929 Wall Street Crash (described as a 'rabble of dead money that went sliding off into the sea'),[41] the poems echo the earlier, more jubilant, verse of the Chicagoan poet Carl Sandburg in their celebration of the 'soul' of the city, absorbed from the forgotten and anonymous workers who built the skyscrapers.[42] Similarly, in contrast to the 'terrible' and 'cruel' sight of Wall Street, it is the inhabitants of New York who redeem the city in Lorca's eyes, especially the forgotten workers and immigrants: 'the Chinese, Armenians, Russians, and Germans' and the 'human warmth' of Harlem.[43]

Of the nine sections of *Poet in New York*, two are dedicated entirely to ethnic groups. The second section, entitled 'The Blacks' ('*Los Negros*'), comprises three poems focusing on Harlem life and the ninth, 'The Poet Arrives in Havana' ('*El Poeta llega a la Habana*'), introduces a single poem 'Blacks Dancing to Cuban Rhythms' ('*Son de negros en Cuba*'), which represents a joyful climax to the poem sequence by marking Lorca's escape from America during his visit to Cuba in the spring and summer of 1930. Together with 'Dance of Death' in the third section of the sequence, these poems offer a less self-preoccupied appraisal of American life than the other city poems, as Lorca sympathetically gives himself over to the black experience which he describes as 'the most delicate, most spiritual element' he encountered on his trip.[44] These four poems are much more rhythmical than the city poems, as he attempts to connect his passion for deep song (*cante jondo*) in his earlier Andalusian poems to the tempo and the pitch of African jazz and blues, in a similar way to the Harlem poet Langston Hughes who developed a poetic form mid-way between verse and song. But, rather than an uncritical celebration of ethnic rhythms, the poems highlight the difficulties and the moral pitfalls of the poet trying to give himself over to a foreign culture.

If the Harlem poems represent what David Johnston calls Lorca's 'search for community',[45] then the first poem of 'The Blacks' section, 'Standards and Paradise of the Blacks' ('*Norma y paraiso de los negros*') suggests a radical Otherness that cannot be bridged easily with empathy: throughout the blacks are continually referred to as 'They'. The first two stanzas begin 'They hate', followed by a series of images associated with Caucasian American culture: 'the bird's shadow on the white cheek', 'the conflict of light and wind', 'the great hall of snow' and 'the punctual handkerchief of farewell'. These images are contrasted to a darker set of cultural markers: 'the deserted blue', 'the swaying bovine faces', 'the deceitful moon of both poles' and 'the science of tree trunk'. Here, the language of primitivism both stigmatises the blacks as Other (the 'bovine faces' and naked 'torsos') and suggests a mysterious current ('the crackling blue') which can only be beheld intuitively or through fellow-feeling. However, rather than the African-Americans being little more than savages, that is a term Lorca reserves to describe white America, when in 'Dance of Death' he proclaims: 'Oh savage, shameless North America!/Stretched out on the frontier of snow.' Lorca's primary worry for the black New Yorkers is that they will sacrifice their 'primitive impetus' for 'the mechanical impetus' of the city and thereby forget the 'original light' of their culture.[46]

In the long second poem of this section, 'The King of Harlem' (*El rey de Harlem*), the poet shifts away from an outsider beholding another culture by adopting a bardic voice which moves between a description of urban conditions to visions of future triumph: an almost Blakean 'cry of encouragement to those who tremble and search',[47] but also a prophetic warning that the New York blacks should not become like the whites. The king of Harlem is both a carnival figure representing a lord of misrule (the white world turned upside down) and a servile 'prisoner in the uniform of a doorman' for whom the poet displays sympathy. Although Lorca returns to this figure throughout the poem, he continues to address the Harlemites as a collective ('the murmuring blacks'), which he must 'cross the bridges' to stand a chance of meeting. The language is surrealistic both in terms of the incongruity of images and the energy of the poem, and he again uses optical images to express his empathy with an oppressed culture that has been denied a leader: 'Oblivion was expressed by three drops of ink on the monocle./Love, by a single, invisible, stone-deep face.' Over two decades before the most prominent phase of the Civil Rights movement, Lorca writes in terms of love for overcoming the limitations of traditions that privilege white Euro-American culture ('a mob of headless suits'). While the optical device of 'the monocle' suggests a narrow vision obscured by the ink of civilisation, the 'invisible' love of intimate relationships may provide the potency to overcome the institutional barriers that still existed in 1930s America:

> To the left and right, south and north,
> the wall rises, impassable
> for the mole and the needle made of water.
> Blacks, don't look in its cracks
> to find the infinite mask.
> Look for the great central sun.
> Turn into a swarm of buzzing pineapple.

The transformation that can be brought about by a sense of collectivity may figuratively return the sun to a city lacking in light. Paradoxically, it is the deeper darkness of African-American culture that can banish the industrial darkness of Manhattan. Although the

Harlemites are urban dwellers, if they hold on to the 'murmur' of the jungle (echoing Marcus Garvey's 'Back to Africa' slogans) that the poet hears 'through tree trunks and elevator shafts', they can rescue themselves from cultural exile and regenerate the natural world which has been perverted by the processes of modernity.

The moral dilemma for Lorca is how to speak for the blacks without overstepping his own cultural relationship to them as a Spaniard abroad. In his accompanying lecture, he moves from the general to the particular, speaking of 'a black girl riding a bicycle' who exchanges looks with Lorca and a 'naked dancer' into whose eyes he stares, not in lust, but with human admiration for her 'inner certainty that she has nothing to do with that admiring audience of Americans and foreigners'.[48] Similarly, in his attempt to overcome the cultural chasm in the third poem of 'The Blacks', 'Abandoned Church (Ballad of the Great War)' ('*Iglesia abandonada (Balada de la Gran Guerra)*'), the poet adopts the voice of a father who has lost his son in the war and whose tragedy is heightened by the death of a race: 'the black heads of dying soldiers'.[49] There is no solace for the speaker, only the sense that if his son 'had been a bear' he might have overcome the 'crocodiles lying in ambush for him'. The poem ends not with the poetic intervention of a white European poet, but the empathy of a black nation 'who sleep and sing on street corners' for the father and who lament his loss as part of theirs:

> Once he had a son.
> A son! A son! A son
> who was his alone, because he was his son!
> His son! His son! His son

This biblical lament may bring no solace, but displays the empathy of an oppressed and struggling community for its individual members. As Lorca reveals in his New York lecture, there are certain barriers over which he will not be pushed: he too is 'here to fight ... hand to hand against a complacent mass ... and it does not matter if I am defeated'.[50] Mirroring James's 'a certain blindness', but shifting the register to an auditory realm, Lorca claims that 'where the blond Americans live, you sense a certain deafness: people who love walls that can shut out a stray glance', whereas in the 'black neighbourhood there is something of the constant exchange of smiles'.[51] This celebration of human exchange is the most moral dimension of Lorca's poem sequence, echoing James's delayed recognition of the

Andalusian farmer and prefiguring the philosopher Emmanuel Levinas's work on face-to-face contact with the Other.[52] In 'New York (Office and Denunciation)' the poet denounces 'everyone/who ignores the other half' and offers himself up 'as food for the cows'. This sense of cultural synergy is evident in his unreservedly joyful 'Blacks Dancing to Cuban Rhythms', in which the Latin rhythms of the Cubans are cultural reflections of 'the great Andalusian people',[53] as Lorca joins with their Cajun dance in celebration of a living culture, not jeopardised by the cold rationality of the city's 'huge machine'. Rather than waiting for the 'sterile sunshine' to return to New York, this last poem gestures towards Lorca's aesthetic and moral ideal: 'the wide-awake and true poem where beauty and horror and the ineffable and the repugnant may live and collide in the midst of the most incandescent joy'.[54]

Kafka: the man who vanished

If Lorca's poems are both stimulated and tarnished by the shadow of New York, then Kafka's fictional exploration of America is marked with the same ambivalence. Kafka was attracted to the idea of America as an imaginative panorama in his work-in-progress novel 'The Man Who Vanished' (*'Der Verschollene'*, written in 1912–13), published posthumously in 1927 by his friend Max Brod with the title *Amerika*. Although Kafka did not visit America, he had three cousins and two uncles living there and his cultural knowledge derived from reading James Fenimore Cooper, Karl May, Franklin's *Autobiography*, Dickens's *Martin Chuzzlewit* and an article by Arthur Holitscher, 'America Today and Tomorrow', attacking American social values and advertising culture in particular (published in the German periodical *Neue Rundschau*, March 1912). The imaginative possibilities of America were obviously very strong for Kafka: where could Kafka's protagonist, Karl Rossman, go to disappear from Europe other than into the cultural void of America? For Kafka, America epitomised the worst excesses of mass industrialisation, where the rational factory systems of Frederick Taylor banished cultural exuberance and quashed individual freedom. Moreover, as Michael Löwy claims, Kafka's 'moral and religious hostility to industrial, capitalist 'progress' is accompanied ... by a nostalgia for traditional community, for organic *Gemeinschaft*', a communal ideal not possible in what he imagined to be the 'invasive' streets of New York.[55] Mark Anderson indicates a number of interesting inaccuracies in *America* that cannot be explained away by Kafka's lack of first-hand knowledge of the country. For example, Liberty holds a sword rather than a flame; on his arrival in the city Rossman pays for a meal with pounds rather than dollars; and the narrator 'stubbornly refuses to name any famous street, building, or tourist sight that would allow its readers to recognize and find themselves in the space Karl Rossman traverses'.[56] For these reasons, despite his own limited knowledge of America, Kafka can be seen to explore the symbolic and cultural potential of a naïve European abroad for very deliberate aesthetic ends.

Written from within the heart of Europe, Kafka's work-in-progress novel seems far removed from Lorca's immediate experiences of New York, but nevertheless displays striking similarities in style and content. Lorca's *Poet in New York* and Kafka's *America* are comparable on four main issues. First, Kafka's original plan for the novel was to narrate the story of two brothers, one of whom travels to America while the other remains trapped in a European prison, indicating Kafka's interest in exploring cultural exile. The novel offers a bifocal vision of early twentieth-century immigrant life which mirrored fiction documenting actual passages of European Jews to America, such as Mary Antin's *The Promised Land* (1912) and Henry Roth's *Call It Sleep* (1934: see Chapter 7 below), by combining a mixture of European roots and American dreams that parallel Lorca's geometric anguish. Second, whereas the 'pale-faced' American self-exiles Pound and Eliot felt more at home indulging in high European culture and Stein and Hemingway relished a loosening of moral restrictions in Paris, Lorca's poem sequence and Kafka's incomplete novel both attest to the disorientation felt by many Europeans in the face of accelerating Americanisation. This dimension is particularly apparent in the form of their respective work. Although *Poet in New York* offers a weave of thematic threads, the poems do not constitute a narrative sequence as such, thus suggesting an experience of dislocation. Similarly, *America* is an incomplete novel, with which Kafka struggled from its early stages and later abandoned. These fractured narratives formally complement the blurred and imperfect vision of the writers when faced with the enormity of New York City. Third, both Lorca's poetic persona and Kafka's protagonist adopt roles of innocents abroad. Although neither writer is as satirical as Mark Twain's or Henry James's narrators in *The Innocents Abroad* (1869) and *The American* (1877), who highlight their American protagonists' shortcomings and European myopia by emphasising cultural naïveté and innocent foolishness, Lorca and Kafka deploy their characters as receptacles of cultural difference. Prior to his New York trip, Lorca's experiences of modernity had been limited to his university life in Madrid with Luis Buñuel and his reading of Breton's Surrealist manifestos, whereas Kafka's work was beginning to reflect the full force of Europe straining under industrial, bureaucratic and urban growth, inflected by more personal feelings of ethnic and family persecution. Despite the biographical differences of the two, both writers represent the bewildering effects of America by deploying Surrealist techniques. However, reflecting the jubilant tone of some of Lorca's poetry, Max Brod notes that Kafka was willing to acknowledge that *America* 'was more optimistic and "lighter" in mood' than his other writings.[57] Lastly, their respective work displays a troubled sexuality manifested through a series of erotic encounters in *America* (what the critic Frederick Karl calls 'undirected sexuality') and the displaced libidinal experiences of Lorca's New York poems.[58]

America opens as the protagonist Karl Rossman enters New York harbour on a German liner, forced to leave Europe after being seduced by a servant girl who had given birth to his child. A complex mixture of naïveté – the innocent seduced by his parent's employee – and sexual experience combine to make Rossman an unstable and shadowy figure who spends much of the first chapter, 'The Stoker', on board the liner searching for his lost belongings, his umbrella (symbolising male potency) and luggage (a symbol of personal identity). On seeing New York harbour, 'a sudden burst of sunshine seemed to illuminate the Statue of Liberty, so that he saw it in a new light, although he had sighted it long before'.[59] A mixture of familiarity and virginal experience suggests a tension within Karl's psyche which is projected on to the mythical site of Liberty Island: 'the arm with the sword rose up as if newly stretched aloft, and round the figure blew the free winds of heaven'.[60] All Karl's personal and sexual insecurities are figured in the image of the threatening, but nevertheless, sublime Statue, as she holds a sword rather than a flame: a threatening symbol of authority rather than a promise of freedom. His only verbal response to the scene is the utterance 'So high!', which, despite its inadequacy, serves to suggest a soaring angle of vision. The sublimity of the scene is thrown into sharp relief by the 'swelling throng of porters' who push Karl towards the rail of the liner where he seems likely to fall.[61]

Despite Karl's claim that he is 'quite ready' to go ashore and take his first step on American soil, he is distracted from disembarking by the realisation that he has left his umbrella 'down below'. Here, the reader is confronted with the verticality of vision opposed to the descent into the ship ('below decks') to retrieve his umbrella. Rather than any panoramic description of Manhattan (bearing in mind Kafka's limited knowledge of the city), the narrator describes a characteristic Kafkaesque geographical and psychological landscape – 'endless recurring stairs, through corridors with countless turnings' where he loses himself 'completely' – which result in delaying Karl's actual arrival in American for the remainder of the first chapter, during which time he meets the ship's stoker and encounters his Uncle Jacob.[62] This opening description illustrates the 'blind impress' Karl experiences as a result of his ethnic and personal insecurities at the moment he is greeted by the icon of American independence and freedom. Karl's initial impression of New York is not unlike the interiorised cityscapes in which the characters of Kafka's other fiction find themselves: most notably, Gregor Samsa in 'Metamorphosis' (1915) and Josef K. in *The Trial* (*Der Proceß*, 1925). The failure of Karl's imagination is spatially mapped out in the dark labyrinthine ways of the ocean liner, acting as a horizontal symbolic counterpoint to the verticality of the city before him.[63]

The reader is encouraged to interpret Rossman's movements below decks as symptomatic of his feelings of disorientation when faced with a new culture, but they can also be read as a strategy, subconsciously devised, by which he prepares himself for the confusion of his altered circumstances, acting out a number of spatial and interpersonal moves in the bowels of the liner. This view of the first chapter develops Michael Löwy's reading of *America* as a novel of 'negative messianism' and 'negative anarchism' in a more positive direction.[64] For Löwy, the novel simply offers a 'critique of a world entirely devoid of liberty' with 'the positive "beyond" of this world ... radically absent'.[65] Although the novel provides no metaphysical comforts, *America* can be read as an attempt to explore possible ethical devices with which to contend with the general lack of morality in Karl Rossman's America. In other words, if the novel is read less as a political critique of American capitalism and more as an exploration of moral anarchism as an antidote to the dehumanising forces of modernisation, then *America* can be read alongside Lorca's New York poems as a work galvanised by the systems it critiques.

The second chapter of the novel is the only one to take place inside New York, the subsequent chapters moving away from the metropolis in widening circles. Unlike the arrival of other poor European immigrants to New York who must learn by 'hard experience', Karl falls under the protection of his uncle and quickly 'became used to his new circumstances'.⁶⁶ Although his first visual experiences of the city are from the safety of his apartment, there seems to be a permeable membrane between inside and outside which positions Karl as a borderline experiencer. Moreover, rather than offering him a 'vantage point', his balcony 'allowed him here little more than a view of one street' and a 'constant stream of traffic'. Human life on the street is reduced to the movement of particles in a system and the 'inextricable confusion' of the traffic hits Karl's 'dazzled eye as if a glass roof stretched over the street were being violently smashed into fragments at every moment'.⁶⁷ The shock and violence of the city echoes Lorca's poetic descriptions and here the 'flood of light' offers Karl little more clarity than the darkness and mire that Lorca encountered. His uncle warns him that these initial impressions are bound to be 'unreliable' and he frowns upon Karl when he finds him gazing at the city, as if he already knows, as an assimilated European immigrant, that the confusion cannot be optically sorted out and will only lead to his nephew's 'ruination'.

Mark Anderson is particularly interested in the way traffic ('*Verkehr*') is represented in America as an economy of confusion as much as exchange: from Karl's early experience of street traffic which changed 'its direction every minute', to the confusing exchange of European and American ideas, to the movement of lifts in his later role as lift boy in the Hotel Occident and, as Anderson argues, to 'the "traffic" or "commerce" of the sexes'.⁶⁸ As for Lorca, Kafka's view of perception cannot be located at a fixed point but as a series of sensations in constant movement.⁶⁹ With this in mind, if the modern city provides the artist with 'a stage for theatrical performance', then 'the big city as a theatrical, depersonalized space marked by its "traffic" and hence by the problem of "accident" – of *Unfall*, but also "contingency" (*Zufall*), chance, and death – ... is the double optic through which Kafka's early texts view the modern world'.⁷⁰ As such, *America* offers the same double view of the New York as Lorca's *Poet in New York*: while the city's impersonal systems and 'the problem of "accident"' epitomise the contingency of modern urban life, its theatricality offers aesthetic attractions to those who can immerse themselves in the environment with enough protection to prevent themselves being completely lost in it.⁷¹

Replicating Karl's initial view of the traffic from his balcony, his American journey is not unidirectional. Although he moves away from the city, from Mr Pollunder's labyrinthine house in the country outside New York to his final train ride towards Oklahoma, like his experiences in the bowels of the ocean liner, his journey is picaresque in its wandering and uncertain in its goal.[72] One of the main reasons why Karl's exile in America is so strange is because he believes he 'no longer has a home' (compounded later when he loses the only photograph of his parents) and therefore no fixed point from which to gauge distance or direction.[73] After his uncle has spurned him for disobeying orders, on leaving Mr Pollunder's country house Karl 'could not tell with certainty in which direction New York lay [because] he had paid too little attention to details which might have been useful to him now'.[74] One of the lessons he had learnt on the liner was that space and direction cannot be adequately mapped and so, faced with this dilemma, he chooses 'a chance direction and set[s] out on his way'.

If there is a purpose to Karl's journey, other than the task of finding work, food and shelter, it is his doomed efforts to help others. Despite his early realisation that 'in this country sympathy was something you could not hope for', he oscillates between responding sensitively to others and bolstering self-regard when he receives little in return. For example, Karl visits Mr Pollunder's country house to please his host but only incurs the wrath of his uncle and, on meeting two immigrant travellers (the lazy Irishman Robinson and fiery Frenchman Delamarche) on his journey away from New York, Karl offers unconditional friendship, but is robbed and later treated contemptuously by them. Although this can be partly explained as a symptom of cultural naïveté and the persecution complex that dogs most of Kafka's protagonists, for Karl fellow-feeling is a moral response as he proves later when, working as a lift boy, he sacrifices his tips to help Robinson who reappears drunken and needing a bed. Because he leaves his lift service momentarily to help the Irishman he is dismissed from the job by the authoritarian Head Porter and is accused of acting 'without thinking' to make matters worse.[75] As such, Karl's dilemma replicates the modern crisis in morality, with the gap between moral intention and the results of acting forever widening. Whereas Lorca's New York poems recount his solitary wanderings in which he has the freedom to imaginatively encounter African-American culture, Kafka's protagonists live in a universe in which they constantly collide with authority figures or systems that undermine individual agency. Only when Karl is offered a 'decent life' by joining Nature Theatre of Oklahoma, with its place for everyone and in which profession is of little importance (although there are still gradations of work), does he enter a symbolic space that allows him to identify with another culture without threat of persecution.[76] Although Karl's train journey towards Oklahoma seems at last to have some purpose (interestingly, he has the window seat on the train offering a 'view'), because the novel is incomplete one is left to wonder whether he would at last find some moral direction and, in the words of Max Brod, discover 'his freedom, even his old home again and his parents, as if by some celestial witchery'.[77]

Just as Lorca moves towards an act of poetic self-sacrifice in his Harlem poems, Karl also comes to position himself sympathetically with the subaltern. The nickname he uses on joining the travelling theatre is 'negro' (a name he had been given when working as a lift boy in the Hotel Occident) which, although he later regrets not using his own name, positions him alongside other 'destitute' characters which the theatrical group is willing to employ. This is not to claim that Karl emerges from the novel as a fully-fledged moral protagonist, but that his struggle to act performatively on behalf of, and to sympathetically align himself with, the Other, implies a moral conscience struggling to assert itself in a hostile environment. Karl's perceptions of America are periodically marred by either too much light or too little: under both conditions his blindness becomes a metaphor for not being able to assimilate with a culture which continuously denies him an identity other than that of worthless immigrant. It seems that only by occupying an equivalent lowly status within the American cultural system – the 'negro' – can Karl begin to overcome these polar optics and reforge his identity. On this level, when Kafka claimed fiction writing was like 'closing' his eyes, it is less a refusal to 'see' and more a willingness to project the psychic conditions of being the Other (even though his protagonists bear a close resemblance to him).[78] Similarly, Lorca continually stresses how little he knows about the world ('I know hardly anything at all'), but he is adamant that he will 'always support those who have nothing' and he retains the hope that a redeeming 'light should come down from above'.[79] In this same interview Lorca goes on to describe himself as an educated middle-class European, but only with the erasure of combative boundaries between insiders and outsiders does he believe that 'justice for all' can be brought about: not by the subaltern capitulating to the dominant culture or by the observer 'possessing' the space of the Other, but by a mutual willingness to see the position of one another. Neither *Poet in New York* nor *America* shows the fruition of such justice, or the kind of cultural education this would entail, but by deploying metaphors of sight and blindness, they indicate that in the mythical land of opportunity (New York acting as a synecdoche for America) a certain blindness can offer either the curse of limited vision or the opportunity to close one's eyes and imagine the Other.

Part IV
Modernist Trickery

7
The Modernist Picaresque: Moralists without Qualities
(Musil, Hesse, Hurston, Roth)

Most critics agree that European and American writing produced in the 1930s has an uncertain relationship with modernism of the 1910s and 1920s on two main counts.[1] First, there was a general cultural and generational shift from the highly wrought formalism of Joyce, Stein and Woolf in the 1920s to the looser literary styles of Samuel Beckett, Albert Camus and Henry Miller in the late 1930s. Second, the 1930s was a period of economic and political transition in which socially-engaged writers such as Bertolt Brecht and John Steinbeck deliberately reacted against the formal complexity and the perceived pretensions of high modernism, or, in the cases of W. H. Auden and John Dos Passos, harnessed experimentalism to ideological goals. Rather than dividing these two modes into the camps of late modernism and anti-modernism, it is perhaps better to view 1930s writing as part of a mobile transatlantic culture in which defining categories of nationhood, community and personal identity were reconfigured. Although there is a hard-headedness to much 1930s writing and a renewed interest in social realism, a range of European and American writers continued to question the conventions of narrative representation by exploring artistic trickery and theatrical performance in their fiction. The next chapter deals with the tensions between aesthetic, moral and political concerns in Klaus Mann's theatrical novel, *Mephisto* (1936), in which he rebelled against what he saw as the political evasion in the fiction of his father, Thomas Mann. Before that, this chapter discusses modernists who were interested in rejuvenating the literary picaresque as a narrative of trickery, particularly Robert Musil and Herman Hesse in Central Europe (selected from other European writers, such as Jaroslav Hašek and Camilo José Cela) and Zora Neale Hurston and Henry Roth in America (amongst Faulkner, Steinbeck,

Nathanael West and James T. Farrell). Although these writers developed the picaresque form for different artistic ends, the traditional mode in which the protagonist devises an alternative set of values to mainstream social morals remained central for them.

The picaresque has very precise cultural and historical roots in sixteenth-century Spain, but since then it has mutated into a number of literary strains that explore the ongoing tensions between stifling social values and disaffected individuals. In its original mode as a Spanish narrative of roguery, the picaresque tale follows the adventures of the *pícaro*, whose inclinations towards wayward living and moral proclivity position him (and it is almost always a 'he') in opposition to (often questionable) qualities of virtue and decency. Most picaresque narratives form a series of loosely connected episodes in the life of the *pícaro*, who usually narrates his adventures retrospectively, or whose encounters are recalled by a secondary figure who discovers records of the character's life. Picaresques tend to be digressive and rambling as the *pícaro* wanders nomadically through various communities, revelling in his ingenuity as he deals with exacting encounters. There is some critical disagreement as to the essential qualities of the *pícaro*. Generally he is thought to be a delinquent figure who, although he transgresses social and moral values, is essentially non-violent, or he is seen as a character whose roguish tendencies are redeemed by a good heart and compassion.[2] There are enough historical versions of the picaresque (from *Lazarillo de Tormes*, 1554, to Defoe's *Moll Flanders*, 1722 – a rare example of the female *pícaro* – and Twain's *The Adventures of Huckleberry Finn*, 1884) to defend either view of the *pícaro* as rebel or ultimate conformist. But many critics agree the figure is a prototype of the anti-hero, furnishing writers with a vehicle for ridiculing dominant social beliefs while sustaining the reader's interest in the *pícaro*'s adventures. The picaresque is a loose narrative form (neither purely comic or tragic) involving a hotchpotch of caricature, burlesque and satire to attack dogma, hypocrisy and high seriousness. Due to this hybridity it has been open to creative distortion, with a range of writers adopting it to serve different cultural and ethnic agendas.

In the early twentieth century, a version of the picaresque re-emerged following a latent period in the nineteenth century when the *Bildungsroman* and the moral seriousness of the realist novel conspired to banish it as an acceptable narrative mode. The reaction by modernist writers against literary propriety and, specifically, the upward and prospective trajectory of the bourgeois narrative usually resulted in impressionistic, fragmented and chaotic forms. This reaction is evident in two anti-novels discussed in previous chapters: Kafka's *America* and Miller's *Tropic of Cancer* both display picaresque traits of the winding narrative and the anti-hero as protagonist. Particularly in Germanic writing, the *pícaro* emerged in a number of guises as a bastard offspring of the self-cultivated hero, from the innocent abroad (Karl Rossman in *America*) and the morally suspect anti-hero (Musil's Ulrich in *The Man Without Qualities*), to the schizophrenic artist (Harry Haller in Hesse's *Steppenwolf*, 1927) and the master of deception (in Thomas Mann's *Confessions of Felix Krull, Confidence Man*, 1954). The modernist picaresque usually deals with issues of cultural displacement, with Kafka working on the borders of the German tradition and Mann spending twenty years in exile, while ethnic American exponents such as Zora Neale Hurston and Henry Roth felt uncomfortable working with mainstream modes of American fiction. The picaresque offered these writers a flexible narrative form, enabling them to test the strategies their protagonists improvised to deal with social disdain or public rejection. As such, the modernist picaresque combines the quick-wittedness of the traditional *pícaro* with an exploration of the psychic chaos caused by the perceived erosion of customs or the corruption of justice. Philip Melling describes the topos of the modernist picaresque as:

> a blind, formless, emotionally stunted world, which moves in so many aborted directions at once that it is unable to intelligently assume control of its energies. In this whirling chaos characters work on their destinies but are prohibited from working them out ... The spliced and dislocated narrative traces, retraces, tracks and doubles back on the experiences of the people in order to expose a life of flux and the banal repetition of events.[3]

Few modernist *pícaros* are thoroughly despicable and some are very sympathetic, such as Roth's David Schearl in *Call It Sleep* (1934) and Hurston's Janie Crawford in *Their Eyes Were Watching God* (1937), but their behaviour is thrown into relief by their marginal status and their questioning of core social values.[4] As Camus and Ionesco explored in *The Outsider* (*L'Etranger*, 1942) and *Rhinoceros*, an awareness of the banality and absurdity of life, combined with oppressive social forces, often stimulates the protagonists to doubt their faith in humanity. Modernist picaresques do not resolve psychic dilemmas through heroic exertion, but exaggerate existential indeterminacy by forcing the protagonists to question social value and to test moral certainties.

The tension between individuality and social convention is explored in modernist picaresques through three related themes: wilfulness, evil, and the law. Previous chapters have discussed the modernist interest in freedom and transgression, but modernist picaresques fuse these themes with an exploration of the danger and excitement of bending or breaking the law. The evil Dorian Gray encounters when he rejects natural order and sinks into an amoral world of decadence – in which he is both free (in improvising his own value system) and unfree (he is still shackled to his portrait) – is different only in its sensuously heightened state from that experienced by many *pícaros*. For example, as a picaresque offspring of the decadent hero, Thomas Mann's Felix Krull chooses not to view the world from a 'diminished point of view', as he fears this will lead to the paralysis of hereditary determinism or the nihilistic belief that nothing is 'worth while'.[5] Instead, Krull is attracted instinctively to seeing the world from a magnified perspective as 'a great and infinitely exciting phenomenon, offering priceless satisfactions'. In such a world the *pícaro* can exert himself as an active agent using trickery to reap his rewards, but at the risk that wilfulness and the pursuit of advancement may lead to self-serving egotism and the loss of moral bearings. While modernists such as Mann celebrate transgression and dissidence as a rejection of stifling convention, when the transgressor denies basic human rights or acts solely out of self-interest evil often emerges as a destructive or diabolic force (as the next chapter discusses). In this way, the renewed interest in the picaresque develops the modernist revaluation of traditional notions of heroism and the possibilities of, as well as the impediments to, right action in a dislocated world.

In German philosophy, both Kant and Schopenhauer argued that evil stemmed directly from human wilfulness and self-interest. Schopenhauer claimed that 'the will' is the primary source of misery in the world and if individuals are to liberate themselves from bondage they must cultivate a denial of the will. On this view, rather than seeing evil as the absence of good, it actively manifests itself in the political and moral spheres as the disobedience to and transgression of law. Whether this is expressed in terms of Promethean courage or criminal villainy, as Joan Copjec argues, individuals cannot explain (or excuse) their behaviour by claiming it results from necessity, irrationality or psychic paralysis, for 'if we act badly, out of self-interest, this is because we have *chosen* to be influenced by external concerns'.[6] However, while Kafka's protagonists are ridden by the guilt of wrongdoing, the modern *pícaro* tends to assert his relative freedom by justifying his deeds as mischievous. This does not mean that blind disregard for consequence always follows for, as Kant conceded, the will to act does not necessarily bring about worse results than capitulating to natural or social law. Indeed, as William James argued, Schopenhauer's pessimistic understanding of wilfulness can be seen as 'an abandonment of the better possibility for sheer inaction'.[7] One reason why deception and trickery are often picaresque traits is because the *pícaro* discerns that sanctioned morality often masks a set of prohibitions and imperatives that may deceive the individual into serving others' interests (as Kafka's Josef K realises as he passively faces the law). Perhaps it is better to confront social rules with one's own repertoire of trickery and risk acting perversely or waywardly, if the moral consequences transpire to be qualitatively little different from when obeying moral law as absolute good. This issue of the instability of evil and morality can be detected in the modernist picaresque, from Mann's versatile Felix Krull to Steinbeck's retarded Lennie in *Of Mice and Men* (1937). There is no exemplary version of the modernist picaresque, mainly because it emerged on either side of the Atlantic in distinct ways: European tales tend to be psychological investigations of marginalised individuals, whereas American writers reworked postfrontier stories of mobility and physical adventure. Nevertheless, despite cultural variations, these disparate strains reveal striking parallels on moral issues of wilfulness, evil and the transgression of law.

The modernist picaresque in Europe: Musil and Hesse

In *A Bend in the River* (1979), V. S. Naipaul's postcolonial reworking of Conrad's *Heart of Darkness*, the narrator suggests that the *modus operandi* of modern protagonists who are 'doers' (rather than 'thinkers') is not 'to be good' by adhering to social rules, but 'to make good' either in terms of individual gain or the testing of personal values against experience.[8] On this model, as Dostoevsky discovered in attempting the impossible feat of creating a 'perfectly good' character in *The Idiot*, 'to be good' is only ever an ontological ideal. In contrast, 'to make good' is always in transition, with the state of 'goodness' either a deferred goal or part of the myth of divine completion. While this ethos often leads to imperialist aspirations (critiqued by both Conrad and Naipaul) or what Musil calls the bourgeois 'social duty' of 'pushing' ahead,[9] rather than locating goodness in the heroism of the nineteenth-century protagonist (the 'great men' championed by Thomas Carlyle in England and by Ralph Waldo Emerson in America), modernist writers tended to be more interested in the trickery of characters entrenched in the mire of mortality who cannot (or do not want to) extricate themselves from the ambivalence and perversity of human action.

Evil and corruption are always threats (both from within and without) in a world in which morality lacks firm foundations and cannot be defined adequately either in terms of moral law or an ethos of the greatest social good. However, the picaresque themes of self-belief and experiential value develop both the Romantic interest in imaginative encounter and the American pragmatic emphasis on the strategies and techniques individuals devise to achieve particular short-term goals. Although it is possible to argue that Romanticism and pragmatism are cultural opposites, particularly in America the emphasis on experience provides a central link between the two traditions of inquiry (most notably in the thought of New England intellectuals such as Emerson and William James). The modernist picaresque displays affinity with both traditions, but its critique of heroism is comparable to the more banal model of existence that many modernist writers offered as an alternative to the grandiose heroism of 'the great man'. Indeed, in the two European picaresque tales discussed here – Musil's *The Man Without Qualities* and Hesse's *Steppenwolf* – the protagonist is neither a worthy literary hero nor a charismatic individual who appeals to the reader by force of personality or by performing great deeds. Despite the obscurity and foibles of the modernist *pícaro*, these texts force the reader to confront moral incertitude by exposing them to the evils and suspect morality of the protagonist's social world.

In *The Man Without Qualities* (1930–42) Robert Musil suggests that the pressures of 'everyday heroism' cause modern protagonists great concern, often contributing to their wayward lives on the fringes of society, or leading to the flouting of 'right-doing', like Dostoevsky's Underground Man.[10] Living in the State of Kakania, described as a super-modern (almost Americanised) version of Austria, Musil's 'man without qualities', Ulrich, decides to take time out from social affairs on the eve of the Great War precisely because he cannot determine what such 'everyday heroism' should be. Although the city where Ulrich lives is not explicitly Vienna, it similarly promotes material success and bourgeois security at the expense of intellectual pursuits (despite Vienna having become a great artistic centre by 1900). Musil uses these topographical elisions to amplify the identity crisis that he detected in the Austrian-Hungarian empire in 1914, which Karl Kraus had called the 'experimental station for the end of the world'.[11] As a fellow Austrian, Musil shared with Kraus a deep suspicion for the 'cultivated artifice' of Viennese society that masked ulterior commercial and imperialist motives.[12] As soon as Ulrich recognises this social masquerade he stops 'wanting to become a young man of promise'. Instead, he adopts an 'inverted life-style' and embarks on a moral holiday to reflect more clearly on the social pressures to which he is subjected.[13] Echoing other modernist protagonists, he senses that morally sanctioned codes really only exist for the interest of the few who benefit from conformism. For example, after being beaten badly in a brawl, Ulrich realises

> that there was desperately little use in ... diminishing stupidity and knavery by any greater or lesser piece of progress; for the measure of all that is disagreeable and bad is instantly made up again by new forms of the same thing, as though the world was always sliding back with the one foot while it takes a step forward with the other. If only one could discover the secret cause of this, the secret mechanism of it! That of course would be vastly more important than being a good man according to obsolescent principles.[14]

He worries about the fate of social progress as war approaches and realises that reform would not necessarily diminish senseless violence and may, in fact, just replicate it. These thoughts lead to his disaffection with the 'worthy' professions of engineering, mathematics and the army – the perplexities of which Musil deals more directly in his earlier *Young Törless* (*Die Verwirrungen des Zöglings Törless*, 1906) – and the social codes he inherits from his father (who is described as a man *with* qualities). If *The Man Without Qualities* is a quasi-picaresque work which, as Musil commented in a 1926 interview, may 'provide help in understanding and coming to terms with the world', it does so not by planting Ulrich into a respectable role in Viennese society, or showing his attempts to attain this through roguery, but by dramatising two colliding ideologies, neither necessarily better or worthier than the other.[15]

Musil wrote a number of essays in the 1910s dealing with the ethical implications of art, and throughout *The Man Without Qualities* he blends essayistic and novelistic modes of writing. Despite the book's length it is very much an anti-epic in the mode of Joyce's *Ulysses*, in which banal and everyday behaviour supplants heroic action defined in traditional terms.[16] The real dilemma in Musil's work is how to relate the individual's psychic life to the world of everyday action; as Ulrich comments: 'in this country one acted ... differently from the way one thought, or one thought differently from the way one acted'.[17] Traditionally the *pícaro* has no problem in acting, responding intuitively without worrying about consequences, with survival instinct or inherent roguery preventing his demise. However, even though the modernist *pícaro*, such as Felix Krull, often moves through an expansive world of adventure, in European writing he is usually troubled by the same dilemma that paralyses naturalistic characters: namely, the possibility of acting meaningfully with limited resources. Ulrich's Kakania is described as a place where events 'just sort of happened' and 'world-shaking adventures' degenerate into 'drunken young [men] roistering about a wide empty square'.[18] Perhaps one escape route from the paralysis of Chekhov's students and Eliot's Prufrock is, to use Musil's phrase, by 'living hypothetically' and by adopting the mantle of the trickster. The trickster does not simply replicate the traditional 'image of manliness' (which Ulrich rejects as an 'ideological spectre'), but embodies paradox and embraces possibility at the same time.[19] It is this role of trickster that Ulrich learns to adopt in *The Man Without Qualities*, guiding him away from the lures of wealth and social status 'towards everything that inwardly enriches him – even though it may be morally or intellectually taboo' (mirroring the Austrian analyst Otto Rank's advice to Anaïs Nin).[20] However, the trickster is not a safe persona. Living 'against the grain' may help to alleviate oppressive circumstances, but it can also lead to an existence which drifts 'along without any constraint'.[21] The danger in such a move is that the protagonist may become a self-serving egoist who is as morally reprehensible as those who act blindly under the smoke screen of social morality.

As the narrative progresses, Ulrich is drawn towards the mentally unstable character Moosbrugger, a psychopath and murderer, whose will to act throws Ulrich's inverted life into stark relief. Under Cesare Lombroso's phrenological scheme Moosbrugger should appear as a degenerate type, but his face is described as expressing 'good-hearted strength and the wish to do right'.[22] Just as Conrad ironically subverts the rigid system of Lombrosian phrenology in *The Secret Agent* (see Chapter 4), Moosbrugger's smile is frustratingly ambiguous: 'it might have been an embarrassed smile, or a cunning one, an ironical, treacherous, grieved, mad, bloodthirsty or uncanny one'.[23] The psychiatrists that examine him cannot match his seemingly 'kind face' with his murderous impulses; they categorise him periodically 'as a case of dementia praecox, as a paranoic, an epileptic, a manic depressive' and then as sane.[24] Neither is criminality a suitable description for a figure who believes his acts are not maliciously wilful, but come 'towards him the way birds come flying along'.[25] Rather than being inarticulate like Norris's McTeague, the contradictions in Moosbrugger's personality – a strange admixture of brutality, intelligence, perversity and inconsistency – confound the psychiatrists and jury alike. He is condemned for murder (although Ulrich thinks he should only be convicted for manslaughter), but his trial is later reopened following a plea on grounds of insanity against the court's decision. The official line of jurisprudence is that 'the individual is either capable of acting contrary to law or he is not, for between contraries there is no third of middle term'.[26] While Moosbrugger is certainly guilty of denying another's right to live, because he exists in a 'transitional state' between sanity and madness he cannot be justly convicted on a legal model based on 'precision'.[27] As such, Moosbrugger is the ultimate trickster figure in *The Man Without Qualities*; his actions are reinterpreted from every perspective and his elusive character cannot be pinned down.

The trial of Moosbrugger helps Ulrich understand the failings of the legal system in dealing with elusive 'human questions' such as 'beauty, justice, love and faith' because it attempts to rationalise action into strict categories.[28] Just as 'character' is formed from the repetition of particular and identifiable traits, jurisprudence is based on concepts which force an individual's often contradictory motives into a rigid mould. In contrast, for Ulrich 'nothing, no ego, no form, no principle, is safe ... there is more of the future in the unsolid than in the solid, and the present is nothing but a hypothesis that one has not yet finished with'.[29] Ulrich finds the best expression of this understanding in the essay form itself that allows one to view human problems from many sides, without reducing transitory flux to fixed concepts or arriving at definite conclusions. On this model, 'all moral events took place in a field of energy the constellation of which charged them with meaning, and they contained good and evil just as an atom contains the potentialities of chemical combination. ... Ulrich felt himself capable of every virtue and every kind of badness.'[30] Such a world is certainly more authentic than one based on the either–or logic that structure legal judgements and ethical categories, but it becomes a dangerous place when the valency of good and evil is blurring with each other. Just as Musil's love of the essay form can be seen as an 'attempt' (*essai*) to dramatise existential confusions, so Ulrich's adventures test the values of patriotism, solidarity and love. Moreover, Ulrich attempts to exist in a 'floating' state without falling back on the 'senile form' of social morality which he believes can prevail only with 'a loss of ethical force'.[31] This does not mean he ever fully masters such a state (if mastery implies control and order) and, indeed, the planned end of the novel, in which he and his beloved sister Agathe mystically unite in a garden, may imply that such an attempt is frustrated in its realisation. Nevertheless, Musil's picaresque draws the reader into exploring the possibilities (if not the full realisation) of living hypothetically in the 'large experimental station' of early twentieth-century Europe.[32]

Where Musil explores the tensions between civic order and the inner life of the mind, Herman Hesse's *Steppenwolf* examines the artist's relation to language and the problems of interpretation that stem from psychic fragmentation and existential bewilderment.[33] The novel is interesting not just in its appropriation of psychoanalytic and mystical ideas (via Carl Jung), but by testing the reader with the same experiential dilemmas that the ageing protagonist, Harry Haller, encounters. The first section of the book frames the strange story of Haller's schizophrenic world with an objective account of events related by the nephew of his landlady. The nephew adopts a bourgeois view of Haller as an intriguing outsider. When he later learns he is a shape-shifting 'wolf of the Steppes' he cannot make the leap from his world of factuality to the mysterious realm of the Steppenwolf. Even when he discovers some private notes that offer him access to Haller's mind he refuses to enter the 'other world' that Haller inhabits.[34] While he detects in the notes more than the 'pathological fancies of a single and isolated case of a diseased temperament', when he listens to Haller's description of modern chaos when 'two ages, two cultures and religions overlap' he does so clinically, without internalising the situation to include himself.[35]

Hesse invites the reader to steer away from the nephew's interpretation of Haller and his presumption that all morals are 'safe and innocent'. This reading, in fact, is a misinterpretation of Haller's expressed belief that the barbarity of contemporary European society in tolerating 'certain evils' results from a loss of vitality and a 'feeling for itself'. Haller is not an inspirational philosopher (offering a diluted mixture of Schopenhauer, Nietzsche and Jung), but his ideas mark out a similar symbolic space between two worlds and two identities to that experienced by Ulrich. Indeed, Haller's condition as part-man and part-beast inscribes a strange mid-world that the reader experiences as a tension between safe (critical) and ravenous (sensual) roles. But, as the reader slowly realises, neither role will necessarily lead to success in the games Haller is forced to play in the Magic Theatre. Like the strict gender divisions problematised by American expatriate writers, *Steppenwolf* reveals that the neat dichotomy between man and beast is based on false logic.

Hesse uses the introductory section to warn against a 'safe and innocent' reading of the novel when he states, 'the story of the Steppenwolf pictures a disease and crisis – but not one leading to death and destruction, on the contrary: to healing'.[36] The choice for Haller (and the reader) is to remain in the factual world of the nephew, or to enter a world of psychic possibility in which he must arm himself with the interpretative strategies to channel primordial desire. As Haller walks through 'one of the quietest and oldest quarters of the town' he recognises a familiar wall with 'a small and pretty doorway with a Gothic arch in the middle' that he cannot remember to have been there before.[37] A sign states the Theatre is 'NOT FOR EVERYBODY' and warns that entry is 'FOR MADMEN ONLY'.[38] While Haller may meet these criteria, at this stage he has little chance of playing without first nurturing strategies of survival. Rather than learning these lessons from bourgeois institutions, he is taught by mysterious figures of a fringe subculture. Three characters in particular – the prostitute Maria, the dancing instructor Hermine and the jazz-playing Pablo – teach him to tap into hidden psychic resources and instruct him that every personality is 'a manifold world ... a chaos of forms, of states and stages, of inheritances and potentialities'.[39] Haller is scared by this constantly shifting personality; he would rather be either wolf or man, but the 'Treatise on the Steppenwolf' reveals he is essentially neither.

Although he is much older than Ulrich, Haller is not an exemplary hero who moves from understanding to achievement on the model of the *Bildungsroman*. Early on in the novel he confronts his multiple identity not with courage, but with despair, despite his teacher's help. Pablo and Hermine show him the way of the ravenous sensualist, widening his experiments with narcotics, dancing, jazz and sexual adventure which, as Michel discovers in *The Immoralist*, may counteract bourgeois certainties and lead towards a decadent, if abject, life. Behind the door in the Magic Theatre labelled 'BUILDING-UP OF THE

PERSONALITY', Pablo teaches Haller that the 'separation of the unity of personality into these numerous [chess] pieces passes for madness' in conventional terms, but also allows him to experience the deeper recesses of his psychic world. The chess pieces symbolise the schizophrenic type, who has been marginalised or locked away (with the growth of asylums in nineteenth-century Europe) to prevent the bourgeoisie from 'hearing the cry of truth'.[40] The Theatre suggests that to be free of the psychotic clash between opposing forces, Haller must embrace the schizophrenic chaos of art and game-playing and unlock his latent ability to reconfigure identity. As he begins to experience these alternatives his imaginative life is enriched and he discovers 'in the tender beauty of the night many pictures of my life rose before me who for so long had lived in a poor pictureless vacancy'.[41] As soon as he realises that any arrangement of the chess pieces is only *one* permutation (or one 'picture') and can be changed, he begins to view his *psychomachia* with the liberating humour that can overcome it. On a Freudian interpretation of laughter as hydraulic release, this would entail 'withdrawing the energy from the release of unpleasure' or aggression 'and transforming it, by discharge, into pleasure' as a means of averting tragic inevitability.[42]

If, on one level, the novel indicates a range of techniques that Haller can adopt to alter his destiny as one torn between alternatives (with man and wolf taking it in turns to exercise power over one another), so the reader is invited to learn the same devices of psychic displacement and existential acceptance. To do this the reader must dismantle the dichotomy of fact and fiction and the segregation of realist and fantasy worlds in order to step inside the game-world. Henri Bergson would describe this act as being homologous to the psychic expenditure of laughter as 'a kind of secret freemasonry' or the 'complicity with other laughters, real or imaginary'.[43] If fact and fiction become intertwined in the process of experiencing *with* Haller, the only way out of the paradox of equivalences is by laughing with the text. Just as Haller learns to reject the shallow categories of the nephew and to explore the possibilities of the Magic Theatre, so the reader puts him- or herself at risk by experiencing the indeterminacies of the text and becoming, to use Wolfgang Iser's phrase, 'co-partners' with it. In Iser's view, although readers must make inferences to understand a text, any single interpretation is only a partial fulfilment of it, as 'the semantic possibilities ... always remain far richer than any configurative meaning formed while reading'.[44] Iser claims that in the classic realist novel the process of interaction is an unconscious or tacit one.

Only in modernist writing does 'the very precision of the written details ... increase the proportion of indeterminacy; one detail appears to contradict another, and so simultaneously stimulates our desire to "picture"'. In moulding the text into a particular reading (or 'picture') there is always an excess of detail, but *Steppenwolf* suggests that 'freemasonry' can provide a technique for acknowledging this excess without inhibiting interpretation or paralysing action.

However, it is in Iser's notion of co-partnering that Haller ultimately fails. When he sees Pablo making love to Hermine he cannot redirect his emotion by realising the fictionality of the scene, but in a jealous rage stabs Hermine, who (in Romantic vein) turns out to be nothing but a symbolic extension of his self. In killing Hermine he severs his shadow self in a dramatic struggle to remain on stable ground. Rather than devising a new code of morality, Haller's intense struggle with himself re-emerges at various times as despair, amorality and jealousy as he breaks the rules of the game to stab Hermine. With this act, the Immortals who oversee the Theatre condemn him to eternal life, to re-live the interpretation process until he can play the game proficiently. This judgement does not represent the reimposition of immutable law, but embodies the sense that Haller has betrayed himself by giving way to destructive emotions. The task for the reader is not to make the same error as Haller in mistaking the absurdity of the modern world for predetermined tragedy, or confusing liberating laughter for struggle with the self. Only by reassessing the text-world as a marginal arena where reality and fiction bleed into each other can the reader learn to live with the indeterminacies and shifting value systems that corrode Haller's resolve. Just as Moosbrugger represents the darker possibilities of Ulrich's hypothetical world, Haller possesses a peculiar sensitivity to the Otherness in himself as both wolf and man. With encouragement Haller is willing to play the game of possibilities, but at the last he misjudges the gravity of his condition. While the winning move would be laughter and acceptance, he is overcome with jealousy and violence.

The modernist picaresque in America: Hurston and Roth

While there are strong thematic and formal links between high modernism and the re-emergence of the picaresque in European writing, the tradition of the picaresque in American literature is intertwined with the nineteenth-century frontier narrative. Just as the frontier stories of Cooper and Twain emphasised the peculiar qualities of landscape and the trials of the protagonist in forging an existence in the face of exacting circumstances, so 1930s novels such as Faulkner's *As I Lay Dying* (1930) and Steinbeck's *The Grapes of Wrath* (1939) use the picaresque form to emphasise the complex relationship of character and environment in the aftermath of the 1929 Stock Market Crash. On this view, Steinbeck's Tom Joad can be seen to embody what Philip Melling describes as the complex mixture of 'attractive criminality, destitution and rebellious poeticism' that characterises much American writing in the Depression years.[45] The wandering narratives charting mass migration in the 1930s and the loss of regional identification were the perfect vehicles for postfrontier themes that reflected the experience of the rootless *pícaro*. The hobo and the marginal man are common characters in Depression literature, undergoing trials usually caused by force of circumstance rather than inherent mischief. As variants of the 'pioneer misfit' these figures enabled American writers to combine frontier themes – 'the thrill of the open road, the scent of coming danger, the romance of a character who yearns to escape the limitations of the moment'[46] – with a reconsideration of human ontology in a period in which the optimism of the early twentieth century had given way to profound psychological and economic pessimism. If character is no longer rooted in place, then the 'damaged survivor' offers an appropriately unstable notion of identity for writers dealing with domestic cultural issues, analogous to the displaced identities explored by American expatriate writers.[47] As Melling succinctly writes: the American *pícaro* 'is an outgrowth of society and a victim in flight from it; a creature who justifies his peripatetic status ... in terms of a native idiom of space as change'.[48]

The issue of hybrid identity for African-American writers such as Richard Wright and Zora Neale Hurston, and Jewish-Americans such as Henry Roth and Nathanael West, were played out in the 1930s and early 1940s through protagonists caught between social law and an alternative set of values born out of their experience of cultural difference. Whereas William Dean Howells firmly located social ethics in terms of truth and beauty in the post-bellum period, for modernist writers morality is always provisional, existing in the interstices between social regulations and spiritual lore. For ethnic writers grassroots folklore provides a different type of cultural cohesion to official law, serving less as a set of regulations and more as a repository of ancestral wisdom, encouraging individuals to sustain relationships in families and communities. However, as the last chapter discussed and the examples of Steinbeck's *In Dubious Battle* (1936) and sections of

Dos Passos's *U.S.A.* (1938) illustrate, while solidarity with others (in trade union activity, for example) subordinates the will of the self to a greater cause, the tyranny of the group is often deemed to be a more profound threat to moral integrity than the waywardness of the individual caught between better and worse alternatives. As such, despite their awareness of different cultural, regional and ethnic pressures, Hurston's *Their Eyes Were Watching God* and Roth's *Call It Sleep* offer a peculiarly American mode of fiction that simultaneously celebrates and critiques individualism. Their protagonists travel from obscurity to self-acceptance, devising a repertoire of psychological and pragmatic tricks to test their own experience as social outsiders.

Zora Neale Hurston derived much of her literary impetus from the creativity of Harlem Renaissance writers such as Alain Locke and Langston Hughes, combining their interest in a 'black aesthetic' with her own professional interest in anthropology and folklore. Although she was educated in Washington, DC, and New York, Hurston was drawn back to the all-black town of her birth – Eatonville, Florida – which continued to provide a personal touchstone for her work. This mixture of urban creativity and dedication to African-American vernacular and local myths enabled Hurston to blend her interest in individual and collective identity with the art of storytelling. Her collections of folk myths *Mules and Men* (1935), West Indian legends in *Tell My Horse* (1938) and other local and cultural tales, collected as *Go Gator and Muddy the Water* (1999), display Hurston's ability to tell engaging stories that explore a number of related themes: creation myths, adventure stories, initiation rites, and tales of racial strength. One recurring figure in these stories is the trickster figure who emerged most popularly in the South in the tales of Br'er Rabbit. It is not surprising that Hurston was drawn to the figure as 'survivor and transformer' by embodying the trickster in her female protagonist, Janie Crawford.[49] If folklore is conceived as an expression of racial savagery, then the attraction of African-American writers to trickster tales could be explained out of identification 'with the witty creature to whom nature had assigned an inferior position'.[50] However, this contentious view of folklore overlooks the fact that tricksters survive through a mixture of 'cleverness, guile and wit', transforming their status as potential victims into mischievous protagonists who can out-manoeuvre hostile predators.[51] From this perspective trickster tales represent little more than stories of criminal defiance of law, but from the disenfranchised slave's perspective 'the actions of the trickster reflect a situational moral code for survival', emphasising 'the importance of creativity and inventiveness in dealing with situations peculiar to the slave–master relationship'.[52]

Hurston's work is full of characters who survive on their wits by devising an internal sense of right behaviour that defies imprisoning social codes. Although Janie Crawford displays resolve and there is an identifiable ethical undercurrent to Hurston's non-fiction writing, she rarely writes in terms of 'morality' and 'ethics', mainly because she uses African-American vernacular and less formalised folk expressions. Rather than highlighting the work's moral content (as in Hesse's and Musil's fictions), these idioms encourage the reader to respond more closely to ambivalent behaviour and the consequences of action. However, Hurston was deeply interested in circumstances that test characters, moving beyond simple protest writing to sketch out techniques for personal and racial survival. For example, in her autobiographical sketch, 'How It Feels to Be Colored Me' (1928) she refuses to see herself as 'tragically colored' or to 'weep at the world' for not offering her the same opportunities as white Americans.[53] She claims she is 'too busy sharpening my oyster knife ... living in the jungle way' to be self-pitying for too long, and learning strategies to overcome the subordination she would otherwise feel as a black woman.[54]

These strategies of survival find a less personal expression in her piece on 'Characteristics of Negro Expression' (1934), in which she describes a mixture of black aesthetic forms (angularity, asymmetry) and primitive creativity (dancing, adornment) as exemplifying both the wiliness of the trickster hero and 'the adaptability of the black man' who reinterprets everything and for whom 'nothing is too old or too new, domestic of foreign, high or low'.[55] She also evokes the folk figure, Jack, a close cousin to the animal trickster whose adventures she describes at length in *Mules and Men*. Because Jack dwells 'on borders ... between worlds' he has the capacity to outwit even the Devil and God through a mixture of mimicry, inventiveness and quick-wittedness.[56] This notion of folk hero as 'possibilitarian' reflects Ulrich in *The Man Without Qualities*. But, whereas Kakania and the world of *Steppenwolf* paralyse Ulrich and Haller, African-American trickster tales have an internal momentum propelling characters towards interpersonal conflict.

The African-American critic June Jordan describes *Their Eyes Were Watching God* as 'the prototypical Black novel of affirmation' in its exploration of the possibilities for a black woman of being simultaneously independent and deeply in love with a man.[57] The tale is told retrospectively by Janie to her friend Phoebe. It begins with her grandmother's advice to her as a girl to marry well and moves through Janie's two unsuccessful sexual relationships with neglectful men (the first with Logan Killicks, a lazy farmer, and the second with Joe Starks, a self-made man who rises to town mayor) who 'squeeze' her into domestic roles 'tuh make room' for their personalities, to her third relationship with the trickster figure Tea Cake Woods.[58] Tea Cake helps to liberate Janie after the death of Joe Starks by propelling her away from the linear trajectory of marriage and the dead-end of domesticity towards a dynamic picaresque template of exuberance, energy and risk. Tea Cake possesses the trickster traits of wiliness and gambling and remains elusive throughout the narrative, while his roughness is tempered by Janie's spiritual vitality. Even though she is prone to jealousy and he is not always sympathetic to her needs, their symbiotic relationship casts both characters as American *pícaros* (with aspects of Tea Cake's trickery rubbing off on Janie), while their mutual love transforms their isolation into a supportive emotional life.

On one level, Tea Cake displays traditionally masculine traits and his values remain suspect – he steals from Janie and encourages the attention of another woman – but, on another level, he mirrors Janie's androgynous personality. At the beginning of the novel she appears in overalls (thought to be inappropriate for her age, gender and class) and he is initially described as having 'lean, over-padded shoulders and narrow waist'.[59] This gender confusion is underlined by the references to animals in the narrative: the yellow mule that is ceremoniously buried by the townsfolk represents freedom to an imprisoned Janie (as a black woman she is 'de mule of the world') and, serving the same function as Moosbrugger in *The Man Without Qualities*, the rabid dog that bites Tea Cake (while he is protecting Janie) symbolises his trickster lifestyle taken to an exaggerated degree. The moral dilemma that Janie faces is whether to kill the man she loves when Tea Cake is afflicted by demons, develops a bestial 'queer loping gait' and becomes dangerously psychotic.[60] While Haller in *Steppenwolf* makes the wrong move by committing murder, Janie is given no choice but to shoot Tea Cake as he attacks her with a pistol. In the ensuing trial, Janie

> tried to make [the jurors] see how terrible it was that things were fixed so that Tea Cake couldn't come back to himself until he had got rid of that mad dog that was in him and he couldn't get rid of

the dog and live. He had to die to get rid of the dog. But she hadn't wanted to kill him.⁶¹

Although she is judged not to have committed 'cold blooded murder', like Moosbrugger she fears only 'misunderstanding'. Indeed, she later hears a group of men discussing the fact that she was only let off because it was a black man she killed: '"Well, long as she don't shoot no white man she kin kill jus' as many niggers as she please."'⁶² After resisting the drudgery of her first two relationships and fighting the evil demons that have taken possession of Tea Cake, Janie confronts a legal system that acquits her only because she is deemed to have committed a 'minor' crime against one of her own race. However, despite her lover's tragic death, the novel concludes with a moment of jubilation as Janie expresses her cosmic identity in a mystical vision when she dances with the spirit of Tea Cake. This sense of expanding identity reflects Hurston's comments in 'How It Feels to Be Colored Me' when she refers to herself as 'the cosmic Zora ... the eternal feminine with its string of beads'.⁶³ While Janie's flight of metaphysical fantasy may be interpreted as evasion of social reality on the same level as Ulrich's garden retreat, it serves to indicate that out of the hotchpotch of different cultural experiences (what Hurston calls 'a brown bag of miscellany propped against a wall') Janie manages to transform her life from 'a jumble of small priceless and worthless' things into a treasure-trove of moral and spiritual value.⁶⁴

Henry Roth's novel of Jewish immigrants in New York, *Call It Sleep* (1934), also explores the possibilities of basing a moral and spiritual existence on experiential values, rather than relying on scriptures, teachers or parents for guidance. Roth joined the Communist Party in 1933, but he realised that a literary exploration of psychological doubt and existential fear should not be subordinated to ideological ends, as exemplified by other Jewish-American left-wing writers such as Michael Gold in *Jews Without Money* (1930). His political commitment did not sit easily with his aesthetic interest in the high modernism of *Ulysses* and *The Waste Land*. While he was attracted to Joyce's and Eliot's mode of aesthetic detachment, *Call It Sleep* is very much an 'imminent' novel in which the tumult of the 1930s is strongly felt (even though it looks back to the wave of East European immigration in the first decade of the twentieth century). Roth felt strongly that paralysis and 'immobilization' could occur either through the author having too much detachment from the characters or by being committed too firmly to a cause.⁶⁵ Only in the middle ground between art and politics did he feel able to express the 'give-and-take, the vitality, the dynamics of living among your own people' and the possibilities of forging a moral existence.[66]

The three novels previously discussed in this chapter focus on characters in various stages of adulthood, whereas *Call It Sleep* uses modernist experimentation to focus on the troubled childhood of David Schearl, who is portrayed from the ages of six to eight growing up in an ethnic ghetto in New York's Lower East Side. David feels alienated not only from his abusive father, but also from the two cultural templates available to him as a East European Jew in New York: Judaism and Americanism. On the one hand, the social obligations and the high seriousness of orthodox Judaism threaten David's spiritual essence, while, on the other, linguistic and class barriers prevent him attaining a roving urban identity. Although Steinbeck's novels offer a more direct representation of the 'marginal man' in the Depression years hampered by poverty, class and rootlessness, the themes of the two writers are similar. In the course of the novel David experiences a strange rites of passage caught between Old and New World values, where he must learn strategies of survival to contend with the difficult circumstances into which he is thrown. Like *Their Eyes Were Watching God*, Roth's episodic novel becomes picaresque by degrees as the narrative grows in complexity (using a mixture of formalist, Symbolist and Surrealist techniques) as it traces the clash between cultures, ethnicities and value systems. David's immigrant experience clearly mirrors Kafka's Karl Rossman (although David's world is characterised by noise and Rossman's by sight), but also provides a bridge between Jewish- and African-American writers, whom Adam Zachary Newton describes as often being 'partners in catastrophe' and whose 'narratives of loss and ruin ground and legitimate a substitutive story of spirituality gained through time'.[67] Caught between catastrophe and redemption, both Hurston's and Roth's novels combine strains of American optimism with a jeremiadic concern that the values which promise a better future have been lost or are overlooked in daily life. While neither writer portrays characters lacking in quality in quite the way Musil and Hesse do, neither Janie nor David possess any mark of social distinction (true even when Janie becomes the wife of the town mayor), apart from the repertoire of strategies they learn from experience that enable them to survive in hostile environments.

The conflict in David's world derives directly from his relationships with his father and mother, both of whom hide significant events from him: his father's violent motivations and his mother's adulterous relationship with a gentile in Europe (the latter casting doubt over David's legitimacy). This world of secrecy and mistrust forces David to piece together fragments of conversation to contend with his linguistic confusion. As he listens to his aunt and mother speak in guarded tones 'he wondered if they understood each other. Maybe it was like Yiddish and English, or Yiddish and Polish ... Secrets. What? Was wondering. What?'[68] Without parental or moral guidance David must sift through hints, signs and gestures that conceal secrets but do not seem to lead anywhere:

> And what was it about, he wondered. What did those Polish words mean that made his mother straighten out so? Intuition prompted him. He divined vaguely that what he had just heard must be linked to the sparse hints of meaning he had heard before, that stirred him at first so strangely and afterwards scared him. Now perhaps he might learn what it was about, but if he did, something might change again, be the something else that had been lurking all the time beneath the thing that was.[69]

At first David is 'tempted to avoid' such detective work and quickly learns to 'trust nothing'. But, in this slippery language he feels 'a danger that was also a fascination' as he begins to piece together scraps of Yiddish, Hebrew, Polish and English.[70] Like Conrad's Stevie, the fragments of this polyglot babble are reflected in the half-words he uses to describe his identity: 'Can see and ain't. Can see and ain't. And when I ain't, where? In between them if I stopped, where? Ain't nobody. No place. Stand here then. BE nobody.'[71] This expression of extreme ontological uncertainty pushes David to the verge of death later in the novel but, whereas Harry Haller is overcome by uncontrollable jealousy, David's resourcefulness and innocence help him to become a good interpreter whose gains his moral bearings from raw experience.[72]

As the law of Judaism does not speak to his condition (despite his almost biblical experience of exile), David must improvise his own values from scraps of scripture, other religions (he is attracted to his friend Leo's Catholicism), street culture, New World intuition and tales of Old World lore. The influence of *Ulysses* can be detected throughout *Call It Sleep* (even though Roth thought Joyce took linguistic playfulness too far), especially in the way the Irish writer transformed 'the sordid and squalid' into art.[73] Just as Janie must rely on 'a jumble of small priceless and worthless' things to base her life on, David searches among the debris of the city to make connections between his own identity and the objects he encounters:

> Only his own face met him, a pale oval, and dark, fear-struck, staring eyes, that slid low along the windows of stores, snapped from glass to glass, mingled with the enemas, ointment jars, green globes of the drug-store – snapped off – mingled with the baby clothes, button-heaps, underwear of the drygoods store – snapped off – with the cans of paint, steel tools, frying pans, clothes lines of the hardware store – snapped off. A variegated pallor, but pallor always, a motley fear, but fear. Or he was not.[74]

This dramatisation of David's 'fear-struck face' links to Adam Newton's suggestion that the twin themes of *Call It Sleep* are identification and misrecognition. Because urban objects threaten to mingle with his subjectivity, just like Ulrich, Haller and Janie, David can only mature by avoiding the snares of false identities and the 'illth' of the city (to recall Ruskin's phrase). Although, on this model, *Call It Sleep* can be read as a novel of American cultural assimilation, David's status as an in-between character is essential for his development as a moral, if still fledgeling, agent.[75]

The theme of doubleness explored by American expatriate writers becomes in *Call It Sleep* a fraught clash between ethnic and national identities that explodes into a babel of (to David) virtually meaningless language. In the midst of such chaos David must realise his own autonomy, but also his partial rootedness in all these fragments. His near-death experience on the railroad nearly consumes him entirely ('battering his skull with a beak of fire, braying his body within pinions of intolerable light'), but he fights back, 'the last screaming nerve clawing for survival'.[76] This experience teaches him to centre himself within his marginality, rather than allowing his insignificance to push him to the edge of oblivion: in other words, to realise he is both self and Other. Sleep periodically threatens to overwhelm him as a kind of restful dormancy that clouds understanding, makes him blind and deaf to reality and stifles action. Although sleep is never an evil force (unlike his father's abusive rages), it does lull him into forgetfulness and, at times, passivity. David's moral quest in the novel is to distinguish reality (and the obligations and opportunities that it brings) from sleep; to learn not always to succumb to dreams, but not to heroically dismiss them as unnecessary either. His recognition that these zones of existential and moral life overlap stimulates his final ambivalent feeling of 'strangest triumph, strangest acquiescence'. Rather than embodying the *pícaro* as perpetual shape-shifter, then, David's final state of in-betweenness suggests that the most important technique for survival the modernist protagonist can learn is to steer a middle course between autonomy and acceptance, between trickery and responsibility, and between agitation and Otherness.[77]

8
Myths of the Magician: Klaus Mann, Thomas Mann and Nazi Germany

Modernist writers were obsessed by the artistry of the mask. Masks enabled them to explore psychological complexities without resorting to an elusive 'unconscious' language, while also acting as symbolic devices for exposing what they believed to be moral falsities. The naturalist plays of Ibsen, Strindberg and Eugene O'Neill, for example, sought to critique the deceptive masks characters wore either through their own weakness or by adhering to dubious standards, while Hesse, Woolf and Nin used masks more creatively to explore hidden impulses that fragment the stable boundaries of personal identity, and ethnic writers such as Hurston and Langston Hughes detected in masks a way of tapping into folkloric identities that exist prior to, and often in conflict with, legitimised social roles.[1] By the early 1930s, with the rise of fascism in Central Europe, this interest in masks encouraged writers to link the public and private dimensions of their art more explicitly, as political vicissitudes became increasingly entangled with the idiosyncrasies of individual human behaviour. The grand theatrical stages and elaborate public performances Mussolini and Hitler used to create their aura of leadership were open to critique perhaps only through the 'safe' aesthetic game-playing that Orson Welles perfected in his high modernist film *Citizen Kane* (1941). Just as the 'literary magician' Filippo Marinetti (as Huelsenbeck called him) used performative masks in his Futurist writings to aestheticise his extreme political beliefs,[2] so the fascist leaders magically transformed their imperial aspirations into appealing myths of nationhood and collective strength to gain popular support.

Liberal and left-wing German writers, such as Klaus Mann and Bertolt Brecht, were also interested in literary masks as a means of exposing the tyranny of fascism. Although both were forced into exile for their dissident beliefs, masks enabled them to explore the seductions of Nazism without abandoning their own moral and political commitments.[3] The mythic figure of the magician was of particular interest to Klaus Mann. He followed his father's intriguing fable 'Mario and the Magician' ('*Mario und der Zauberer*', 1929) by assessing the attractions and the dangers of theatrical and political masquerade in his late modernist novel *Mephisto: The Novel of a Career* (*Mephisto: Roman einer Karriere*, 1936). Masking and magic are used in 'Mario and the Magician' and *Mephisto* to critique fascist ideology and artistic fakery, despite the conflicting political and personal values of the two writers. Indeed, as this chapter discusses, the family romance of the Manns is interesting in itself for exploring the ideological and aesthetic impulses that both father and son saw as endangering the very moral integrity that might rescue Europe from another total war. Whereas versatility helps the modernist *pícaro* (discussed in Chapter 7) to emerge as a resilient, if wounded, agent, in the Faustian tales of Thomas and Klaus Mann trickery leads their characters into moral and spiritual danger.

Mephisto was published in Amsterdam in 1936 with Klaus Mann in exile from Nazi Germany, but was not published in Germany until the early 1960s (when it provoked a lawsuit). This *roman à clef* (or *Schlüsselroman*) is, in part, a diatribe against the rise of the Third Reich in the early 1930s and also an attempt to document the turbulent cultural scene in Germany over the previous twenty years. It charts the meteoric rise of the actor Hendrik Höfgen whose early revolutionary aspirations and theatrical ideals are squandered in his desire for fame. Höfgen's careerist drive stems from his feelings of anonymity as a provincial actor at The Hamburg Arts Theatre (at a time when Munich and Berlin were the chief theatrical centres), whose desire for recognition leads him to abandon his mistress and friends. The fact that his early dreams of forming a Revolutionary Workers' Theatre are never put into practice suggests that what was possible in 1918, with the November Revolution, had little chance of succeeding in the second half of the 1920s in the face of profound economic depression. Although many of his theatrical colleagues leave Germany for France and America in the early 1930s, Höfgen clings desperately to German tradition and language, without which he believes himself to lack talent or identity. The acclaim Höfgen seeks in his career leads him to pander to the 'gods of the Underworld': the thinly disguised figures of the club-footed Minister of Propaganda, Josef Goebbels, portrayed as 'the overlord of the spiritual life of millions', and the corpulent Air

Force General and Prime Minister, Hermann Göring, who has a face of 'raw, formless meat'.[4]

The character of Höfgen was based on Klaus's former brother-in-law, the actor Gustaf Gründgens, whose success on stage and in the Weimar films *M* (Fritz Lang, 1931) and *Liebelei* (Max Ophüls, 1932) propelled him to stardom in Germany.[5] Not only was Klaus's sister Erika divorced from Gründgens in 1929, but the two men had a brief affair in the mid-1920s when they performed together in Klaus's play *Anya and Esther* (1925). The bitterness that stemmed from these broken relationships was exacerbated when Klaus and Erika left Germany sticking firmly to their liberal-socialist principles, while Gründgens developed his career under the auspices of the Third Reich with his appointment as manager of The Prussian State Theatre in Berlin in 1934.[6] The novel is faithful to Gründgens's career, but it demonises the actor as a self-serving egoist, whose most triumphant theatrical role, Mephistopheles (in a centenary version of Goethe's *Faust*, directed by the Nazi Lothar Müthel in 1932–3), provides a metaphor for his Faustian pact with the Third Reich. Although the novel is melodramatic and overwrought in places, its modernist aesthetic derives from Klaus's and Gründgens's interest in theatrical masks and what the critic Marcel Reich-Ranicki calls the 'dark, pathological, marginal spheres of existence.'[7]

Friedrich Luft describes Gründgens as an actor who 'appeared in ever changing masks' and associates him with 'sinister plots, terror, the pathological and the endangered' (as true of Lang's *M* as it is of Goethe's *Faust*).[8] Similarly, in his autobiographical book *The Turning Point* (1942), Klaus describes Gründgens as

> a neurotic Hermes ... haunted by his vanity and persecution mania, and a frantic desire to please. There was something very grand and very pathetic about him. He was mangled by inferiority complexes. His face, without the mask of make-up, was strangely wan, as if covered with ashes. He glittered and suffered and seduced. He wanted to be loved, but no one loved him.[9]

The narrative voice of *Mephisto* credits Gründgens's fictional self, Höfgen, for his theatrical versatility, but portrays him, to use Musil's phrase, as a man without qualities or, at least, without substance. As Musil claimed, such a man was not wholly evil, 'only that the good was adulterated with a little too much of the bad, the truth with error, and the meaning with a little too much of the spirit of accommodation'.[10]

It is not so much that Höfgen lacks character (even though the cultural prophet in *Mephisto*, Theophilus Marder, comments that 'what the modern world lacked was men of character'), but that his earlier political commitment is subsumed by what Musil calls the 'dazzling seductions of art' and the mercurial profession of acting.[11] In his greatest role as the shape-shifting Mephistopheles, Höfgen merges completely with his stage persona: he is billed as 'the strange son of Chaos' and plays Mephistopheles as 'a tragic clown, a diabolical Pierrot' and an 'elegant jester'.[12] The tricks of his trade are clearly theatrical accomplishments, but the narrative invites the reader to question the moral ramifications of such intense acting and explore how much of the man remains outside his dramatic roles. Both Brecht and Walter Benjamin argued that the 'law of the lie' is a defining feature of theatrical illusionism and the kind of intense acting that Höfgen perfects, bedazzling the audience and denying them the critical distance to consider the social and political pressures that mould events.[13] While Klaus Mann does not quite mirror Brecht's 'A-effect' in distancing the reader from the events of the story, the narrator's criticisms of Höfgen have the same result. Whereas Brecht used the 'technique of taking the human social incidents to be portrayed and labelling them as something striking ... not just natural' to empower the spectator to 'criticise constructively from a social point of view', Klaus engages the reader's emotions in the tale but at crucial times breaks the frame of the story to reveal parallels between Höfgen's shortcomings and the state of German culture.[14] Indeed, the theme of endangered identity (both private and public) is at the heart of an interpretation of *Mephisto* as an exploration of the myths, lies and seductions of Nazi Germany. Parallels between characters and particular historical people are strikingly evident in places, but Klaus intended the novel not as a *Schlüsselroman*, but as a study of the intellectual as arch-betrayer. Moreover, in his desire 'to expose and analyze the abject type of the treacherous intellectual who prostitutes his talent for the sake of some tawdry fame', *Mephisto* can be seen to develop the theme of abjection explored in *Death in Venice* and by his uncle Heinrich Mann in *Small Town Tyrant* (*Professor Unrat das Ende eines Tyrannen*, 1905), filmed in the Weimar period as *The Blue Angel* (*Der blaue Engel*, 1930).[15] Although Klaus was not as materialist in his outlook as Brecht or Benjamin, rather than just exploring the intersection between ethics and aesthetics (as his father did), Klaus identifies Höfgen's abjection as a direct consequence of his collusion with the dominant political forces in Nazi Germany.

Mephisto is marked by an ambivalent narrative voice (slightly more involved than the narrator of *Death in Venice*), at times displaying sympathy towards the protagonist and, at others, mocking his vanity and shallowness. The narrator appears to share with Höfgen's first wife, Barbara, a simultaneous attraction and repulsion for 'this ambiguous, versatile, highly gifted, sometimes touching, sometimes almost repellent creature', with descriptions such as, 'his eyes were icy and soft like the eyes of a rare and royal fish who had jewels in place of eyes', epitomising this ambivalence.[16] The novel reads as a satirical *Bildungsroman*, recounting Höfgen's rise to fame from the 1920s to 1936 and charting his descent into the satanic court of his benefactors. As such, Klaus shared with Brecht and Benjamin a commitment to knowing 'the man of today; a reduced man, a man kept on ice in a cold world' by subjecting him to 'tests and observations' in the novel.[17] The Prologue (set in 1936) emphasises the close relationship between theatrical performance and political acting: from the outset, Höfgen is presented as the diabolic companion of Goebbels, Göring and Göring's wife, Lotte Lindenstahl, as 'four powers of this land, four wielders of force, four actors'.[18] The blurring of art and military politics is illustrated by a swastika 'made of diamonds' and tanks and machine guns 'faithfully recreated in marzipan' to celebrate Göring's birthday.[19] The narrator stresses that the ostentatious display of wealth only thinly disguises what Benjamin describes as the aestheticisation of politics, subjugating the attendants with magical power and figuratively forcing them 'to their knees'.[20] The State Opera House had been sprayed with 'clouds of artificial fragrance' for the occasion, which, as the narrator comments, prevents the people 'from inhaling another odor: the stale, sweet stench of blood, permeating the entire country'.[21] The power politics of Nazism are increasingly apparent as the novel traces Höfgen's career; although he masters the stage-art of the trickster, beneath the shimmering aura of this state occasion lurks the dark force of the Führer-magician.[22]

As a late modernist novel, *Mephisto* blends mythic elements of earlier modernist fiction with the political commitment of much 1930s European writing, in a story of excessive individualism and careerist overreaching. It is useful to consider it as a 'magico-political tale', a phrase taken from the subtitle of a late eighteenth-century Gothic story by Cajetan Tschink, translated as *The Victim of Magical Delusion* in 1795. As two moralistic tales warning of the danger of confusing reality for what is ideal and mistaking art for illusion, both Tschink's story and *Mephisto* focus on individuals whose imaginative urges override good sense and consideration for others.[23] In so doing, although Klaus desired to expose fascism, he realised that neither the actor's nor the politician's mask can simply be removed to reveal the raw truth lurking beneath in the manner Brecht intended of his epic theatre. Indeed, the Mephisto-mask that Höfgen wears cannot be torn away, for 'under the greasepaint his eyes now had the steady gaze of despair'.[24] Nevertheless, the Faust myth does enable Klaus to explore the cultural and social conditions emerging towards the end of the Weimar period and serves to question the whole rhetoric of Faustian heroism. Instead of Faust being portrayed as a Promethean hero, Klaus suggests that Faustianism is symptomatic of a society in decline: 'The European genius has often been prone to treachery and corruption. Given to adventures and experiments, the *homo europaeus* is always in danger of going astray, of losing his moral equilibrium.'[25]

This chapter examines two types of metamorphosis relating to a reading of *Mephisto* as a modern European tale of moral un/masking. The first transformation concerns a reworking of the Mann family romance, in which Thomas plays a significant role as bourgeois patriarch, national writer and author of 'Mario and the Magician'; and the second concerns the appropriation (and partial distortion) of the Faust myth in Klaus's magico-political tale. *Mephisto* is clearly didactic in places, but its appeal derives as much from its exploration of the complex relationship between art, ideology and morality as it does from Benjamin's materialist description of the theatricality of politics. For example, the 'hell of shame' that Höfgen describes to his wife Barbara just before their marriage turns sour stems from his isolated world of narcissism, in which he cannot commit to anything outside himself.[26] His expression of shame seems to be a tacit acknowledgement of other people, but his unwillingness (or inability) to act on this recognition suggests that his entrapment in Nazi Germany does not derive from commitment, but from a selfish attempt to preserve himself (given the only other real alternative is to leave Germany). Höfgen realises too late that in his careerist motivations he has colluded with Nazi propaganda and facilitated the death of his friends. As a consequence, he is reduced to the amoral and dependent world of childhood as he cries in his mother's lap at the end of the novel.[27] These shifting values are closely related to the theme of transformation that suffuses the aesthetic, moral and political dimensions of the tale but, rather than *Mephisto* embodying the mid-1920s ideal of *Neue Sachlichkeit* as a cool assessment of modern German society (a movement Benjamin criticised in his essay 'The Author as Producer'), the cultural contradictions of the 1930s are firmly embedded in its aesthetic design.

Family myths: the magician

Written in English while in exile, Klaus's autobiographical book *The Turning Point* offers a semi-fictional recreation of the past in the modernist style of Proust and Gide. However, this is no celebration of childhood innocence. Despite the 'provincial coziness' of his early years, the book explores the bewildering experience of growing up in Germany during the 1910s and 1920s.[28] Developing Proust's semi-autobiographical meditations on memory, Klaus claims that recollections can distort or misrepresent the past, but they are nevertheless 'compelling, powerful and fleet and often are the only experiences which stand between the individual and "chaos"'.[29] The prologue reveals his interest in 'sources' and 'secret influences', his voice wavering between an 'individual life' and the cultural identity of 'we', suggesting a movement beyond the modernist preoccupation with individuality: 'Where does the story begin? Where are the sources of our individual life? What secret influences have shaped our profiles, gestures, and emotions? What whim or wisdom has provided us with the abundance of contradictory features inherent in our character? Where do we come from? Who are we?'[30] He claims that 'our individual destinies are interwoven in a vast mosaic' of collective cultural myths which partly determine the roles available to individuals, but he admits it is usually 'something weirder and greater' than a single mind can grasp. Rather than outlining a naturalistic view of character determined by inherited patterns and environmental forces, Klaus mythologises his life as a crucial moment between past and future (corresponding to Benjamin's concept of *Jetztzeit* as 'the presence of the now' and Arendt's dynamic theory of history as containing past traces and future portents).[31] Haunted by 'crimes whose name and gravity we do not know', he claims that his generation must accept their 'time-consciousness of modernity' (as Peter Osborne terms it: see Chapter 3) and the burdensome responsibility of influencing 'future generations', by responding sensitively to the social explosions his own generation were encountering. By framing an account of his childhood with this declaration of collective responsibility, Klaus suggests a transformative layering of lives, where individual and cultural identities merge into, and are constantly thrown into conflict with, each other: as he states, 'nobody, nothing is disconnected'.[32]

The first chapter, 'The Myths of Childhood, 1906–1914', describes his early feelings towards his father as ones of awe and uncertainty, tinged with fear. Klaus depicts Thomas as a milder version of Kafka's tyrannical father: he was intolerant of dirty fingernails and bad table manners, and the Mann children were not allowed to make any noise when he worked or took his nap. Aside from Thomas as a strict bourgeois parent, Klaus's and Erika's nickname for him was *Zauberer*, or 'the Magician' (also a popular name for Max Reinhardt, appointed Director of Deutsches Theatre in 1905), because the children believed he possessed secret powers.[33] This nickname derived from an incident when Klaus was plagued by 'the evil whisper of nightmares' and his room 'was invaded by apparitions'.[34] His father advised him to ignore the ghost or tell it to leave; if this failed then he should warn the spectre that his 'father is very irritable and just doesn't like to have ugly spooks in his house'.[35] On heeding this advice the 'spook presently dissolved', an incident which convinced Klaus that his father possessed 'superhuman insight and influence'. Despite the clarity of his recollection, the adult Klaus questions the 'tokens, secret cues and signs that come to us from nobody-knows-where', revealing that this episode has been transformed into a mythic fable of threat, power and parental care.[36]

Although Klaus associated his father with the positive memories of storytelling, 'the aroma of cigars and eau de Cologne', piano music and 'long rows of books', he records that his father's stern manners intensified during the war, when he seemed to Klaus to conceal an 'ominous secret'.[37] Now, the magical secrets of childhood are transformed into darker threats that Klaus admits he only dimly recognised at the time. Nevertheless, the pensive and introspective figure of his father stimulates him to wonder in what 'dangerous piece of witchcraft' was he involved: 'had he sacrificed the serene realm of his tales for the sake of black magic?' These questions are inflected by Klaus's later political differences from his father and his anger that Thomas did not publicly denounce Hitler and Nazism as a national disease earlier than 1932. The composition of *Reflections of an Unpolitical Man* (*Betrachtungen eines Unpolitischen*, 1918) during the First World War, in which Thomas skirts around the issue of political commitment in favour of the heroic aloofness of the artist, struck Klaus as being one of his father's most diabolic acts.[38] From one modernist perspective, Thomas's unpolitical stance was an attempt to preserve an inner aesthetic life away from the demands of the public sphere: a cultural existence that secures personal and intellectual freedom at a remove from state interference. However, for Klaus (the adult writer), his father's position derived from the fickleness of his political position and a refusal to see the realities of a time that Auden (who married Erika in 1935) described as 'this hour of crisis and dismay'.[39] But, as the shifting narrative voice of *Mephisto* confirms, Klaus did not simply abandon his father's use of disruptive irony in favour of materialist critique. Ambiguity for Klaus is not an evasion of ethical-political commitment, but provides a means for dealing with the complex cultural transformations occurring in Germany from the late nineteenth century.

In a 1925 letter to Erika, Thomas admits that Klaus had a 'sizable Z. complex, among other things'.[40] This 'Z. complex', or magician syndrome, suggests that not only did he and Klaus have a problematic relationship (Thomas's repressed homosexuality compared to Klaus's more overtly gay lifestyle), but father and son shared an obsession with the figure of the magician. For both, the magician is an agent of control, whose versatility is matched only by the ominous secrets he was thought to conceal behind his theatrical mask. For Thomas, the figure of the magician manifested itself in his fable 'Mario and the Magician'. Set in Italy's Torre di Venere, the story focuses on the theatrical performance of the conjuror and hypnotist Cipolla who asserts his will over an enraptured audience through 'intimidation, bluff, brow beating and a mixed bag of "artistic" tricks and technical illusionism'.[41] The reputation of Cipolla precedes him, with his aura bewitching the audience long before he appears on stage. Even though the tale is told retrospectively with a degree of detachment, and the narrator justifies his desire to experience the magician's art on grounds of bravery, the lure of the magician's aura can be detected in the following rhetorical questions:

> Shall we strike sail, avoid a certain experience so soon as it seems not expressly calculated to increase our enjoyment or our self-esteem? Shall we go away whenever life looks like turning in the slightest uncanny, or not quite normal, or even rather painful and mortifying? No surely not. Rather stay and look matters in the face, brave them out; perhaps precisely in so doing lies a lesson for us to learn.[42]

Whether these thoughts represent an active decision to watch Cipolla's performance or a justification of passivity is open to question. Nevertheless, the themes of theatrical illusionism and self-deception are tightly woven in Mann's story, through the theme of will power (and the evils of mind control), to such an extent that the 'complete seriousness' of Cipolla's stage persona also inflects the narrative tone. As such, there seems to be little to distinguish the modernist art of storyteller and Cipolla's sleight of hand apart from the end to which they are directed: Cipolla's for monetary gain and Mann's for moral exposure.

The narrator is sceptical as to whether or not Cipolla has planted accomplices in the audience whom he calls forward to practise his trickery, but he does share the audience's feelings of awe mixed with unease as the magician makes 'fleering and derogatory' comments and projects his air of 'calm superiority'.[43] Cipolla's conjuring in the first part of the show gives way to hypnotic experiments and what the narrator describes as 'one long series of attacks upon the will-power, the loss or compulsion of volition'.[44] Despite the complex relationship between the narrator and Cipolla, he is at pains to emphasise that behind the veneer of entertainment the magician's dark art and power of the will are at root fascistic, only to be halted in the final scene by the gunshots of the liberal humanist Mario whose sincerity spares him from the hypnotist's power.[45] If 'Mario and the Magician' powerfully exposes the barbarism and manipulation which lies hidden beneath the veil of mystification, mirroring Benjamin's exposé of Hitler's persona as 'so much luster surrounding so much shabbiness',[46] the other side of magic in Thomas Mann's work is evident in his earlier modernist epic, *The Magic Mountain* (1924). The refined spirituality of Hans Castorp's Alpine retreat may conceal dark and disconcerting forces, but (as the mystical celebration in the chapter 'Snow' demonstrates) it also has the potential for spiritual renewal. The difference between these two examples is that in *The Magic Mountain* the magical forces are not in the possession of a human being as they are for Cipolla, whose potential to be corrupted by power leads to dire consequences.

Klaus's *Mephisto* develops many of his father's ideas but goes beyond them in an act of political and moral commitment. Thomas claimed he did not want his tales to be considered 'political satires'; in the case of 'Mario and the Magician', he asserted: 'I would ... rather see the significance of the little story in the ethical than in the political.'[47] Thomas's decision to set his story in Italy may suggest he was nervous about critiquing the emergence of German fascism, or that he was seeking to expose a general human condition (given that the tale preceded by three years the Nazis becoming the largest political party in Germany). Either way, his refusal to align aesthetics with politics was seen as a major weakness for Klaus. To redress this issue, *Mephisto* is full of references to magic, often directly related to the wielding of political power, or the exertion of coercion over others: Goebbels adopts a smile to 'soften the dreadful spell he cast about him'; Göring keeps a 'fairy queen' for company and a 'mystic veil' conceals his real intentions behind his flabby mask-like face; and the Führer (who disappears almost completely) is described as a wielder of 'black magic'.[48] Höfgen's early magical powers are confined solely to the stage; only when he becomes 'a colourful, magical figure' behind the footlights does he cast aside the undistinguished mantle of provincial actor.[49] He desires to become a 'star' because it offers the actor a magical aura, but, as the narrator suggests, he does so by risking his integrity. Later in the novel, as Director of the State Theatre, Höfgen begins to exert his magic in real life, but in true Mephistophelean fashion such power is only apparent: Göring's enchantment with Höfgen's Mephistopheles on stage is short-lived, followed by an intolerant and curt dismissal of the actor's requests to spare his friend's life. Even though it may be argued that Höfgen displays bravery by remaining in Germany where he could theoretically subvert the system from within (implied by Gründgens's biographer Curt Reiss), as Elizabeth Houston argues, it is 'debatable as to whether the artistic resistance' (for example, in his restless portrayal of Prince Hamlet) 'translates fully as effective political resistance' given the cultural control of the State both in terms of theatrical production and propagandist machinery.[50]

The moralistic dimension of *Mephisto* suggests the actor's magical qualities are crucial for his success, but when associated with too much power they lead to a corrupt and dangerous art. Klaus's relationship with his father parallels this dimension of the story: the magic which helps banish Klaus's childhood ghost leaves him in awe, but when Thomas starts to hide 'ominous secrets' of a political nature, his son's respect soon recedes. On this level, the novel suggests that it is dangerous to separate culture, politics and ethics into distinct spheres of activity: for Klaus, only an act of socialist commitment can help reunite the spheres and guard against the dark art and control of the magician. But, this interpretation of the novel is only a partial one. As Reich-Ranicki makes clear Höfgen is not simply a 'comic-strip villain': his 'protean nature contained as much coquetry as shrewdness, as much grace as corruption' and, as Director of the State Theatre, he does not simply surrender to National Socialist propaganda.[51]

Klaus's world is not a Manichean universe, but one in which good and evil, commitment and evasion, slide over and merge into one another: a series of secret doors and false bottoms which, as Hesse comments in his author's note on *Steppenwolf*, lead the individual to 'disease and crisis'.[52] Unlike Hesse and his father, Klaus's world is without redemption: the shape-shifting does not resolve itself in epiphany or spiritual unity, but ends in dissolution and abjection. For these reasons, rather than being an 'adolescent intellectual' (as Reich-Rinicki calls him) and despite his geographical distance from Germany, in *Mephisto* Klaus attempts to untangle the complicated web of mythic connections and to face the distressing reality of German social and political transition.[53]

Cultural myths: Faustian transformation

The Weimar period gave rise to a renewed interest in the Faust myth, especially in the new medium of cinema. The hugely popular German film, *The Student of Prague* (*Der Student von Prag*, 1913), directed by Stellan Rye and starring Paul Wegener (remade twice in the 1920s), and F. W. Murnau's *Faust* (1926), starring Emil Jannings, offered fresh cultural perspectives on the Faust myth. *The Student of Prague* explores the life of the double self popular in post-Romantic literature, fusing the stories of Poe and Hoffman with a reworking of the Faust myth. As a classic illustration of German Expressionism, the film portrays the gothic psychodrama of a young student, Balduin, who sells his mirror image to a demonic sorcerer, Scapinelli, for endless wealth. After the Faustian pact, Balduin's reflection takes on an independent double life with the malevolent intent to destroy him. When Balduin finally shoots his alter ego after being plagued by him for so long, he actually murders himself and his double survives as the diabolic companion of Scapinelli. Murnau's *Faust* is more faithful to the Faust legend in its medieval setting, but it shares with *The Student of Prague* a symbolic emphasis on the metamorphosis of Faust into a young man after the pact and the reversal, when he is transformed back into an old man at the end of the film. This interest in metamorphosis can be traced through the many European versions of the Faust myth (including Wilde's *Dorian Gray*), but it becomes a dominant theme during the Weimar period, which the film critic Siegfried Kracauer reads as a manifestation of 'the deep and fearful concern with the foundations of the self'.[54] The questioning of Faustian heroism during this period intensified the modernist subversion of the *Bildungsroman* and the critique of nineteenth-century heroism, suggesting that psychic exploration could no longer be equated with progressive social values but, as these two films suggest, with disintegration and dissolution of identity.

In *All That Is Solid Melts Into Air* (1982), Marshall Berman offers a modernist perspective on Goethe's *Faust* (which lurks in the background of these two film versions) by reading it as a 'tragedy of development' *par excellence*.[55] Berman discerns three major metamorphoses in the narrative of *Faust* which also structure the development of Höfgen's career in *Mephisto*. On Berman's reading, Faust becomes in turn a dreamer, a lover (in Part I, 1790) and a developer (in Part II, 1832), suggesting a heroic movement away from self-obsession towards the larger world of social mobility. In this interpretation of *Faust* as an archetypal story of modernity, in its 'affinity between the cultural ideal of *self*-development and the real social movement toward *economic* development', Berman argues that Faust-the-magician positively transforms 'the whole physical and social and moral world he lives in', but at 'great human cost'.[56] Faust's heroism is linked to his search for knowledge beyond the limits of the 'stagnant and closed' medieval society, but he only achieves this at the expense of real self-knowledge: 'he cannot bear to confront anything that might cast shadows on his brilliant life and works'.[57] Höfgen also lacks self-knowledge as he follows the three phases of Goethe's *Faust*, shifting from his early dreams of a revolutionary socialist aesthetic, to his love for his black mistress Juliette, his safe marriage to Barbara (the daughter of a privy councillor), and to his role as cultural developer as theatrical director in Berlin. However, whereas Goethe's Faust was, as Ian Watt argues, a 'great traveller' and 'free of national or local loyalties', Höfgen feels uncomfortable outside Germany and would rather be imprisoned in Berlin than seek the relative freedom of exile in Paris or Hollywood.[58] As such, *Mephisto* drains the heroism from Goethe's *Faust* by aligning Höfgen's rise in social status with his descent into a morally blind and, to a large extent, self-imposed personal hell.

If *Mephisto* questions, or discards, the heroism of Goethe's *Faust*, it offers two other distortions of the Faust myth which clarify Klaus's interest in magic: first, the reversal of moral polarities in the shape of the good and bad angels (deriving from Marlowe's *Tragical History of the Life and Death of Dr. Faustus*, 1593) and, second, the deployment of the *Doppelgänger*-motif, in which Höfgen plays the roles of both Faust and Mephistopheles. Both developments suggest that it was no longer possible to relay European myths straightforwardly in the

1930s, or simply to tear away masks to expose the ideology of false consciousness. Just as Joyce, Eliot and Broch structured their expressions of modernity with reference to the fragments of well-worn myths, so Klaus uses reversal and distortion as defamiliarising techniques to expose the illusionism of cultural stories that have been given the status of truth.

Marlowe's *Dr. Faustus* is a late morality play which, as the title page of the earlier German text *History of Dr John Faust (Historia von D. Iohan Fausten*, 1587) states, offers a 'terrifying instance', a 'horrible example' and a 'friendly warning to all arrogant, insolent-minded, and godless men'.[59] In Marlowe's play, the Good and Bad Angels are outward manifestations of Faustus's conscience and his appetite for intellectual and physical indulgence: the Good Angel urges restraint and warns against 'that execrable art' of magic in the early scenes, whereas the Bad Angel goads him into action and encourages him to dabble in 'that famous art/Wherein all nature's treasury is contain'd'.[60] In *Mephisto*, the angels are not so much choric figures or catalysts for Höfgen's stage magic, but barometers of his passions and aspirations: Barbara, Höfgen's 'good angel', whom he marries for her Aryan credentials, and Juliette, his 'black Venus', lover and tormentor who appeals to his more perverse, but also more authentic, appetite.[61]

Höfgen does not abandon Juliette for racist reasons, but because Barbara's distinguished family background and temperate nature offer him more stability and social status. However, it is Höfgen 'who demanded with such soulful eloquence that she play the part of his good angel', rather than Barbara accepting the role because of her intrinsic goodness.[62] Their marriage soon degenerates into a passionless affair, compounded later when he realises that she is not of pure German stock anyway. Although Barbara has a mask-like and 'impenetrably serene face' ('she never wore makeup and had no pretensions to being a *femme fatale*'), it is she who feels 'duped' by Höfgen's initial show of genuine passion, concluding that 'probably he is incapable of love.'[63] The narrator does not blame either of them exclusively, but halfway through the novel Höfgen's 'good angel' has already become 'his bad conscience'.[64] By way of contrast, Höfgen's relationship with Juliette is full of passion and mutual dependency: the sado-masochistic games they play do not disguise their deep need for each other. Juliette's face is described as an 'awesome mask of a strange god' and her primitive feelings are 'enthroned in a secret place'. However, unlike Barbara's indifference, her 'savage caress' did Höfgen 'good', suggesting a destabilisation of moral values.[65] Juliette may be his true lover (like Gretchen in Goethe's *Faust*), but for the sake of cultural security Höfgen abandons her for Barbara, and to preserve his own career he agrees to her deportation by Nazi officials. The 'propaganda of disgust', promoted by Nazism to purge German culture of what its sympathisers perceived to be 'foreign bodies' such as Juliette (by enforced exile, torture or death), returns to haunt Höfgen.[66] He has more integrity than to judge his former lover by her skin colour, but he still colludes in her deportation, an act that denies his moral instinct and eventually pushes him towards a state of dissolute abjection.

The second symbolic transformation in *Mephisto* is the manner in which Höfgen plays the role of both Faust, the careerist overreacher whose nemesis is cultural imprisonment, and Mephistopheles, the pander and tempter in the court of the Third Reich. Although the two roles are linked to distinct realms – Mephisto on stage, Faust in real life – the novel (like *The Turning Point*) emphasises the confusion of art and life to such a degree that it leads to a blurring of the two personalities. For example, when the prime minister sees Höfgen in *Faust* for the first time he invites him up to his box. Höfgen trembles when he thinks of seeing 'the demigod face-to-face', but the masks they wear (Höfgen's grease paint and Göring's 'mystic veil') make such an intimate encounter impossible.[67] Interestingly, the view of the box is presented from the audience's perspective. After speaking for a while, the prime minister laughs and:

> with an expansive gesture Höfgen threw wide his arms under his cloak, making it seem that he had grown black wings. The man of power slapped him on the back. A respectful murmur went around the orchestra ... The prime minister had risen. There he stood in all his magnitude, his shining bulk, and stretched out his hand to the actor. Was he congratulating him on his magnificent performance? It looked more like the sealing of a pact between the potentate and the actor. In the orchestra people strained their eyes and ears. They devoured the scene in the box above as though it was the most exceptional entertainment, an entrancing pantomime entitled 'The Actor Bewitches the Prince.'[68]

Here, Höfgen carries the role of Mephistopheles off-stage with him and seems to bewitch the prime minister into signing a diabolic pact. At this moment the power differential appears to be erased or even reversed, but the reader (unlike the watching audience) is informed that, in his dual role of Faust and Mephisto, Höfgen's 'happiness' is tinged with 'nausea'. As Mephistopheles, Höfgen fulfils Göring's desire to create a 'German national hero' (he even shaves his balding head to mirror the General), but later it becomes apparent that Höfgen's Faustian power is only superficial when the prime minister dismisses his requests.[69] This radical confusion of the roles of Faust and Mephistopheles is powerfully dramatised in the Hungarian director István Szabó's film adaptation of *Mephisto* (1981). The camera movement back and forth between the mask-like faces of Göring and Höfgen in this scene suggests a blurring of the figures: because they wear virtually the same mask, it leads the spectator to ask who is making a pact with whom? However, the scene also emphasises Höfgen's diminished power: the opening of his black wings is seen from the distance of the theatre stalls as a pathetic act compared, for example, the beginning of Murnau's *Faust* in which Mephistopheles' cloak shrouds the whole of Wittenburg.

This scene crystallises Klaus Mann's interest in metamorphosis, magic and the intertwining of the aesthetic, moral and political spheres, all deriving from a moment in German culture in which there was no clear moral agenda, and no politically safe public roles to adopt. Dispensing with the heroism of Goethe's Faust and the damnation of the early Faust stories, the novel offers no escape from the world of Nazi Germany, but neither does it provide absolute retribution for Höfgen. What *Mephisto* does expose is the banal reality that lies beneath the veil of German culture in the 1930s. The reader is told that 'the magic of his [Höfgen's] personality made people overlook the fact that he was putting on weight', but we are not allowed to ignore this: he is simply 'the monkey of power, a clown to entertain murderers'.[70] Similarly, when finally the Führer appears towards the end of the novel he is satirised mercilessly: 'Power incarnate had an insignificant receding forehead, over which fell the legendary greasy strand of hair, and dead staring eyes. The face of Power was putty-white, bloated, porous. Power had a very ordinary nose – a vulgar nose, thought Hendrik, in whom awe was now mixed with repulsion, even scorn'.[71]

Mephisto does not completely dispense with the allure of theatricality or illusionism (matching Klaus's and Thomas's preoccupation with the art of magic), but the novel goes some way to dislodging the mask from the actor (to echo Brecht's and Benjamin's aesthetic and political aims). The feelings of 'awe', 'repulsion' and 'scorn' experienced by Höfgen when he meets the Führer are emotions the reader is invited to expend during the course of the narrative, but not without indulging fully in this mythical story of self-empowerment. As a powerful interpretation of the tale, Szabó's film version of *Mephisto* reads back through history by translating the final scene of the novel (in which Höfgen is abjectly reduced to an infant as he cries with his mother) into a moment of excruciating torture when the spotlights are turned on the actor in the newly completed Nuremberg stadium. The film ends with the same words as the novel, with Höfgen exclaiming: 'What do men want from me? Why do they pursue me? Why are they so hard? All I am is a perfectly ordinary actor ...'[72] Whereas the novel closes with a moment of existential retreat and moral evasion (Höfgen speaks 'in a fine grieving gesture'), in the film the spotlights of Nuremberg blind the frightened actor so much he can barely see. This scene provides a metaphor for reading *Mephisto* as, to use Benjamin's phrase, a 'dramatic laboratory' of cultural and moral inquisition. On one level, modernist fiction enables Klaus Mann to explore the blinding magic of cultural and political theatricality, and, on another level, it provokes the reader to look history straight in the eye.[73]

Conclusion: Liberating the Fear of Modernity

Whereas Thomas Hardy's Tess could barely articulate her 'ache of modernism', in *Jude the Obscure* (1895) another of Hardy's tragic characters, Jude Fawley, manages to give voice to his fears and desires, despite his equally humble background and propensity to 'ache a good deal'.[1] Early on in the novel the young Jude realises that as he grows up he must contend with the noises and jolts of modernity: 'all around you there seemed to be something glaring, garish, rattling, and the noises and glares hit upon the little cell called your life, and shook it, and warped it'.[2] Despite his worries, Jude's major obstacle to realising his vision of scholarly life is caused less by the onset of modernity and more because he was born too early, when men from working-class backgrounds still had little chance of being accepted into the University at Christminster (Hardy's name for Oxford). Jude is baffled by a world that will not accept him on his own terms, but he continues to pursue his dream. Even before this frustration emerges, while waiting for a package of Latin texts that would help him begin his studies, Jude ponders over the possibility of devising 'a rule, prescription, or clue of the nature of a secret cipher' that would change 'one language into another set of signs'.[3] The narrator criticises him for attempting to transmute 'an aggrandizement of rough rules to ideal completeness' and Jude, after perusing his textbooks, also realises 'that there was no law of transmutation' that can alleviate 'years of plodding'.[4] Here, the 'secret cipher' corresponds to Jude's pursuit of scholarly learning. But it is precisely the tension between the search for a prescriptive rule to anchor moral life and the realisation that only heuristic techniques can help reorientate the self in particular circumstances that surfaces dimly in Jude's mind. Despite this insight, Jude cannot shake off his transcendent vision of

Christminster's cloisters. Had he realised that this vision would also be his death knell he might have embraced the possibilities of modernity more eagerly, surrendered his notion of 'ideal completeness' and so increase his chances of improvising 'rough rules' to hold at bay the fateful patterns directing his life.

While Hardy sacrifices Jude and Tess at the altar of naturalism, their demise is at least partially offset by the more affirmative outlooks of other modernists who learn, as Kafka expresses in his diary, that existing moral standards are often 'too high'.[5] Rather than this insight leading to complete demoralisation, some modernist protagonists succeed in devising a moral life by adapting, without fully capitulating, to their environment. As the previous chapters discuss, such reorientation comes about by rejecting the upward trajectory of the *Bildungsroman*, by lowering 'ontological pretensions', and by adopting a more banal and horizontal existence in which high ideals are rejected as hangovers from an unrealistic age.[6]

Banal existence for modernists rarely entails the renunciation of imagination and a passive acceptance of reality,[7] but the coming to terms with a world that may appear new and exciting on the surface but often masks a 'fear of void' (as Zygmunt Bauman describes it).[8] Few writers would choose to surrender the creative potential of art, as this would lead back to the imprisoning isolation of Dostoevsky's *Notes from Underground* or the inarticulate world of Frank Norris's *McTeague*. Moreover, acquiescence would mean surrendering the possibility of improvising moral devices that could reorientate individuals within meaningful social relationships. While some critics argue that modernism focuses too centrally on individual experience (for example, Georg Lukács and Alasdair McIntyre discern a moral solipsism running through it),[9] the tangled web of aesthetic, moral and political modernist impulses provides a vision of individuals 'knotted' together. The intractability of these interpersonal knots has led Stanley Cavell to argue that moral commitment derives from resisting solipsism and recognising and adjusting to others.[10] Clearly, this is no easy task; but, as Richard Bernstein has argued, when faced with 'the alterity of "the Other" ... without such acknowledgement and recognition no ethics is possible'.[11]

While it may be possible to live a meaningful and banal low-level existence, as Musil's Ulrich realises in *The Man Without Qualities*, the absence of a 'secret cipher' leaves characters to contend with a disconcerting world of uncertainty:

He possessed fragments of a new way of thinking, and of feeling, too, but the glimpse of something utterly new, which had at first been so intense, had blurred with the increasing number of details; and after believing that he was drinking from the fountain of life, he discovered that he had drained almost all his expectations to the dregs.[12]

Although Ulrich's feelings are not unique among modernists and they may lead to what Kafka calls a 'rat's nest of miserable dissimulations',[13] the absence of sustainable moral laws also opens up the possibility for individuals to rework personal codes without being bound to socially sanctioned morality. It seems only a morality that is flexible enough to contend with the 'glaring, garish, rattling' world that Hardy's narrator describes in *Jude the Obscure* will enable the individual to negotiate a route between deterministic forces and self-aggrandising freedom. In *Life in Fragments*, Bauman describes this attitude as an 'ethically unfounded morality', by which he means a pliable code of existence that lacks 'official stamps certifying its propriety' and for which morality cannot be 'logically deduced'.[14] On this model, the end of 'the era of ethics' does not 'herald the end of morality' for the very reason that modernist writing provides an internal critique of modernisation, in its exploration of alternative moral passages between individual belief and shared values.[15] Bauman uses the phrase 'morality without ethics' specifically to designate late twentieth-century life (at least in Western Europe and North America), which he describes as 'a jungle deprived even of the jungle law'.[16] Some commentators have argued that a century after the modernist moment we are now free of the anguish of modernism. However, Bauman's argument that postmodernism 'cannot but include and incorporate modernity' into its diversity links the dilemmas of modernist writing to one of the central features of postmodernity, in which individual and collective responsibility remain bound up with an obligation to the Other.[17] While the (at least apparent) widening of cultural choice in the late twentieth century may increase the sensitivity to Otherness, it also leads back to some key modernist questions: what is authentic value? Are some choices more meaningful than others? What does it mean to act when one only has a provisional notion of the grounds for action?

It is one type of commitment to reject social morality for being prescriptive and to reconsider moral ideals for being too optimistic, but another to invent workable codes with which to reorient a 'life in fragments', while sustaining meaningful relationships across boundaries of strict identification. The danger is that, instead of breaching gender, racial and cultural divides, these codes may either serve to shore up boundaries and reinstate individuals as monads, or lead to a 'valueless' free-floating lifestyle. These individualistic attitudes may seem inherently postmodern, but Jürgen Habermas does not see them as recent phenomena, arguing that they are actually rooted in modernity. As he states: 'the new value placed on the transitory, the elusive and the ephemeral, the very celebration of dynamism, discloses a longing for an undefiled, immaculate and stable present'.[18] Whether Habermas is correct in identifying the roots of such 'longing' is open to debate, but he does argue convincingly that the 'anything goes' view of postmodernism is far from revolutionary and may actually feed into the hands of neo-conservative ideologues. Developing the distinction of the political theorist William Corlett, rather than the abandonment of ethical fixity leading to moral agency (in Corlett's terms, a 'giving in to' morality), this neo-conservative attitude may actually represent a 'giving up' to market forces.[19] Moreover, rather than the interface between art and morality providing a passage between personal expression and socio-political involvement, according to Habermas neo-conservatives celebrate 'the pure immanence of art ... in order to limit the aesthetic experience to privacy'.[20] Thus, morality is severed from creativity and an awareness of Otherness and becomes a depleted resource, or it is confused with the kind of instrumental reason that Adorno argued led directly to the Holocaust. Only if ethical devices are flexible enough to open up possibilities and robust enough to disturb the 'time-consciousness' of the present (to recall Peter Osborne's phrase) can they contribute to the reorientation of agency.[21]

In search of the 'third alternative': Wolf and Auster

There is not space in this Conclusion even to gesture towards the wide variety of European and American writers since the Second World War who have continued to test moral boundaries in their fiction. Although questions of political agency raised by socially-engaged writers seem to relate more directly to debates concerning oppression and liberation, postwar fiction has continued to address moral issues on both sides of the Atlantic. This suggests that the view of postmodernism as a mode of aesthetic game-playing is as one-dimensional as modernist writing being seen as an 'escape into aesthetics'.[22] The moral concerns of some postmodernist fictions do tend to be more diluted, mainly because (on the whole) the social morality they comment on is not as easy to codify as that which modernists attacked in the early twentieth century. But, this does not mean that postwar social morality has never been as strict as Victorian moralism: the witch-hunts under the edict of Republican senator Joseph McCarthy and the hostility to 'outsiders' in Cold War America have been visibly attacked in, for example, Arthur Miller's *The Crucible* (1953) and E. L. Doctorow's *The Book of Daniel* (1971), while the socialist values Eastern European writers were expected to promote in their work in the 1960s have been critiqued by Milan Kundera and Christa Wolf. However, conspiracy theories in the USA and the shift of social and ideological power to international corporations with media investments make it much more difficult to apportion blame for false consciousness, while it seems increasingly tricky to find time to ensure that practical techniques devised to contend with the acceleration of culture actually have ethical value. Given these conditions, many contemporary writers have been faced with the same dilemma that Saul Bellow expressed in 1963: 'It is hard to know what is meant by a moral novelist, or what people think they are talking about when they ask for commitment, affirmation, or messages.'[23]

With Bellow's statement in mind it is worth considering briefly two recent influential figures, the former German Democratic Republic (GDR) writer Christa Wolf and the Jewish New York novelist Paul Auster, who deal with the difficulties and possibilities of forging a moral passage from personal to public concerns in fiction that could be labelled either modernist or postmodernist, both in style and orientation.

As the most prominent literary voice to be heard from the GDR after the Second World War, Christa Wolf deliberately flouted the conformist principles of socialist realism and was sceptical about whether a liberal literary agenda was sustainable given the troubled political climate of the Cold War years. Especially after 1965, with the reinstatement of bureaucratic centralism in East Germany, Wolf began to question the tightening of cultural liberty in her own country and, more widely, the liberal ideals of freedom, equality, humanity and justice which (echoing the sentiments of the Dadaists and the American expatriates) seemed to have become hollow journalistic phrases. Her most famous novel, *The Quest for Christa T.* (*Nachdenken über Christa T.*, 1968), reconsiders issues of identity, morality and communication by probing the private lives of narrator and character, at a time when socialist writers were expected to subordinate personal concerns to the collective good. In *Christa T.* Wolf experimented with literary form by mixing biography, autobiography and fiction to explore how social control, destructive ideology and historical necessity conspire to prevent nurturing relationships. Based on the life of Wolf's friend Christa Tabbert (who died of leukaemia aged 35), Christa T. grows up in East Germany, but her child-like exuberance wanes as her socialist consciousness develops. This relationship between history and identity is often figured in Wolf through symbols of wounds or scars. As Myra Love discerns, in Wolf's early novel *Divided Heaven* (*Der geteilte Himmel*, 1963), the central character Rita avoids her wounds in order to grow up, whereas Christa learns that scars 'only still ache when one is forced to grow'.[24] Rather than ignoring these wounds or making them into a spectacle (allowing them 'to ache in order to draw attention to them'), Wolf suggests that working with pain is necessary to nurture receptivity and the possibility of healing. Similarly, the narrator's search for Christa T. is also a painful quest for a language to articulate the links between imagination and moral responsibility and between past and future, facilitated by intimate friendship and creative reciprocity.

The Quest for Christa T. could be considered modernist in its problematic appraisal of Christa's past and her eventual death (following the Germanic tradition of Mann and Kafka), or postmodernist in the sense that there is no stable 'truth' about Christa to be discovered, only versions or interpretations of the past. This pulling between past and future is explored further in the historical, and yet prophetic, novel *Cassandra* (*Kassandra*, 1983), in which Wolf draws historical parallels between contemporary forms of social control and the 'clear-cut distinctions' of Greek culture. She conveys these parallels through the troubled insights of Cassandra, the soothsaying daughter of the King of Troy:

> We have no name for what spoke out of me. I was its mouth, and not of my own free will. It had to subdue me before I would breathe a word it suggested. It was the enemy who spread the tale that I spoke 'the truth' and that you all would not listen to me ... It is the other alternative that they crush ... the third alternative, which in their view does not exist, the smiling vital force that is able to generate itself from itself over and over: the undivided spirit in life, life in spirit.[25]

This 'other' or 'third alternative' that Cassandra seeks mirrors Wolf's search for a route that avoids the perceived weaknesses of liberalism and the dangers of extremist politics, while linking personal morality with public life without subordinating one to the other. She does not suggest that morality is sustainable as a purely private affair; of necessity it involves a reorientation to, and the forming of tangible relationships with, others. In *Christa T.* the shifting relationship between the narrator and Christa is crucial for establishing links between personal and public relationships, implying that identities are not complete in themselves, but (paralleling Luce Irigaray) are open and interdependent envelopes that constantly slide over and through each other.

While her work seems to affirm the modernist emphasis on subjectivity and intimacy, in an essay from 1973, 'The Reader and the Writer', Wolf discerns strong 'relations between literature and social morality'. But she also claims that 'an author's social morality should not be limited to hiding from his society all he can of what he knows about it'.[26] Her interest in excavating secrets and mining the past in *Christa T.* and *Cassandra* does not represent an escape from the present, but the realisation that:

> Persistent, unflinching work is needed on those complexes, rooted in the past, which it hurts to touch: not so as to tie society's resources to the past unnecessarily, but to make them productive in the present. This task ... could lead to literary discoveries of a kind we do not expect.

The promise of these unexpected 'discoveries' makes literary creation worthwhile for Wolf, who as a 'writer of liberation' has been often misunderstood. The clarity of her moral vision is obscured by her alignment to the secret police in East Germany at the beginning of her career and she has been criticised for failing until after the fall of the Berlin Wall to publish her novella, *What Remains* (*Was bleibt*, 1990), which she wrote in the 1970s under surveillance. Whatever the outcome of these debates, as Myra Love argues, the ideas expressed in Wolf's fiction and essays perhaps do more to help reconnect the separate spheres (of morality, aesthetics and politics) than Habermas's idea of 'rational social communication'. It is precisely Wolf's emphasis on 'difference' and 'the sensuous and affective dimensions of human personality' that hold the key for bringing about the reorientation of personal and social morality.[27]

Where Wolf can be described as an outward-looking writer, forging links between personal experience, relationships and public life, Paul Auster's fiction is much more introspective. Although Auster does not amplify Jewish themes in his work, his fictions are often postapocalyptic; social worlds are pared down to a shadowy substratum and characters find themselves in impoverished environments full of 'shattered things'.[28] Auster has been identified as one of the most distinctive of American postmodernists,[29] particularly for the way in which, in *New York Trilogy* (1987) and *Leviathan* (1992), he strips away the social edifice to uncover 'some barer condition in which we have to face up to who we are. Or who we aren't.'[30] Auster mixes different generic codes – the city novel, the detective story, fictional autobiography, science fiction, the picaresque – but the crisis of identity (both personal and public) is the central theme running throughout his work. Auster's interest in developing a certain type of detective story (inspired by Poe's fusion of criminal investigation and the macabre) derives from his belief that detection tends to 'unveil more mysteries', rather than solving problems. For him, writers and detectives both begin with the impulse to pull 'objects and events' together and 'make sense of them'; but, whereas conventional detectives seek to avoid red herrings and solve puzzles, writers are often more interested in exploring obscure paths and blind alleys.[31] As such, the interlinked triad of stories in *New York Trilogy* reveal Auster's versatility in creating a frustrating and slippery urban world, in which personal identity becomes part of the 'mountain of rubbish' of contemporary life and in which characters have lost their 'sense of purpose' and 'the language whereby [they] can speak it'.[32] Under these conditions identity and value are constantly in doubt but never entirely eradicated, forcing characters and readers alike to confront metaphysical questions that modernity purported to overcome (or to banish) long ago.

Auster has claimed that his fictions 'are mostly concerned with spiritual questions' and 'the search for spiritual grace' (for example, the search for the father in *The Invention of Solitude* (1987) and *Mr Vertigo* (1994) suggests Jewish identity is a recurring, if understated, theme), but issues of moral agency also haunt his work.[33] For instance, the first character introduced in *New York Trilogy*, the writer Quinn, finds himself in a 'inexhaustible' city, even more incomprehensible than that faced by Kafka's Karl Rossman in *America*.[34] Quinn becomes caught up in a detection plot when, under the assumed name of the detective 'Paul Auster', he is hired to find a lost man, Boston Stillman. On discovering two versions of Stillman, one prosperous and the other 'gone to seed', Quinn realises his pursuit will be inevitably riddled with error:

> There was nothing he could do now that would not be a mistake. Whatever choice he made – and he had to make a choice – would be arbitrary, submission to chance. Uncertainty would haunt him to the end. At that moment, the two Stillmans started on their way again. The first turned right, the second turned left. Quinn craved an amoeba's body, wanting to cut himself in half and run in two directions at once.[35]

The inability to arrive at a practical solution that would enable Quinn to pursue the two Stillmans at the same time is not a spiritual or a purely practical issue, but framed in terms of a moral choice: would the pursuit of the destitute Stillman prove to be 'better' (in moral terms) than following the prosperous one? A similar dilemma is experienced by Peter Aaron, the narrator and detective in Auster's *Leviathan*, when he is faced with two conflicting stories: 'as soon as I accepted one story, I would have to reject the other. There wasn't any alternative. They had presented me with two versions of the truth, two separate and distinct realities, and no amount of pushing and shoving could ever bring them together.'[36] These incidents reflect the condition of modernist protagonists trapped between the imaginary world of possibility and the real either-or world of choice. Indeed, like Mann's Aschenbach or Hesse's Haller, rather than these incidents being dismissed as inconsequential, the hesitation between irreconcilable choices not only endangers Quinn's and Aaron's integrity, but also their very existence. In Auster's fiction these moments do not just threaten personal boundaries, but often represent what he calls the 'moral equivalent of death'.[37]

Far from working in a zone of safety then (to recall Michael Ignatieff's phrase), Wolf's and Auster's careers as writers and cultural commentators can be located in a realm of moral and personal danger, as they search for the elusive 'third alternative' to cement the passage between personal experience and social agency. While there are certainly postmodern elements in their fiction, the 'radical doubt' which Auster detects in the modernist avant-garde actually becomes a kind of saving uncertainty in his and Wolf's work, making provisional meaning possible without offering interpretative certainties.[38] Identity and relationships are fragile in their work, but sometimes uncertainty can work in favour of the characters. Indeed, it may actually be consolatory to realise, along with the narrator of *New York Trilogy*, that most 'lives seem to veer abruptly from one thing to another, to jostle and bump, to squirm ... inevitably we come to a place quite different from the one we set out for'.[39]

Moral agency and the 'outside'

While modernist writers (both early and late) often portray impotent characters debilitated by social and environmental pressures, the possibility of agency seems bound up in the ability to manufacture devices that can contend with powerful forces and facilitate alliances with others. The notion of moral agency is well-theorised in Michel Foucault's *Technologies of the Self* (1982) and his late essays on ethics, in which he discusses power not purely as a restrictive force wielded by institutions over individuals, but an 'agonic' structure that cements social relationships and creates the conditions for meaningful acts of resistance and solidarity. In the 1980s Foucault moved away from the panopticist model of power outlined in *Discipline and Punish* (1975), in which individuals are subject to intense social surveillance, to arguing that 'agonic' power is an enabling structure that 'no longer takes law as a model and a code' for defining social cohesion; power is 'a machinery that no one owns', but which can be deployed by individuals or social blocs in productive or counterhegemonic ways.[40] This does not mean individuals can be entirely self-governing, or that the codes one may improvise are entirely free from strains of social morality. Rather, the interplay between personal beliefs and shared values can stimulate techniques which can help to transform an individual's or a particular social group's material conditions. These 'practices of the self', as Foucault calls them, involve a mixture of creative energy and self-discipline: energy alone leads to psychic expenditure or unfettered licence, while discipline without creativity tends towards instrumental reason and an inability to compromise with others. On this view, morality is never a 'systematic ensemble' of rules or prescriptions, but a diffuse and 'complex interplay of elements that counterbalance and correct one another'.[41] In this jungle of counterforces it is easy to lose one's bearings, but in his later work Foucault returns to the intimate values of care, friendship and love for privileging relationships over individual desires. Rather than finding solutions to contemporary problems in models from the past (for example, Greek ethics or early Christian practices), like many of the modernist texts discussed in previous chapters and, more recently, in

Wolf's and Auster's fiction, Foucault's theories do not lead to 'apathy but to a hyper- and pessimistic activism' that is both affirmative and moral.[42]

However, there are problems with Foucault's account and, more broadly, with the idea of 'postmodern agency'. His notion of agonic power seems to lead back to the solitary and self-exiled figure of Joyce's Stephen Dedalus struggling with the nets of modernity, while the strategy of improvisation could be seen simply as a by-product of late capitalism. As such, conservative critics such as Francis Fukuyama take a more relaxed view of capitalism than Foucault and Habermas, seeing it both as an economic inevitability and the bulwark of postindustrial society. Rather than the forces of capitalism inevitably leading to the breakdown of community, by encouraging individuals to place 'self-interest ahead of moral obligation and being endlessly innovative through the replacement of one technology by another', Fukuyama (following the lead of the eighteenth-century thinker Samuel Ricard) suggests that 'members of commercial societies [have] developed long-term interests in industriousness, honesty, self-discipline, and a host of other small virtues'.[43]

Although it is easy to vilify Fukuyama for justifying the current social and economic order in the West, he actually sees capitalism as simultaneously improving and damaging moral relationships. For example, although people may 'acquire social connectedness in the workplace and learn honesty and prudence by being forced to work with other people on a long-term basis', private firms promoting these values may do so as a smoke screen to hide their strategies for keeping pace with market forces.[44] Strategies that seem on the surface to foster personal values of friendship and kindness may hide a deeper logic that merely affirms competitive impulses. Individuals acculturated in this environment are likely to confuse moral agency and an Other-orientated lifestyle with the policies of private agencies working towards favourable profit margins. With this in mind, Bauman argues that '*privatization* of all concerns has been the main factor that has rendered postmodern society so spectacularly immune to systemic critique and radical social dissent with revolutionary potential'.[45] The Foucauldian model of counterbalancing forces only has validity when alternatives exist 'outside' the all-devouring logic of late capitalism, otherwise the moral and aesthetic resources into which individuals can tap will run dry and economic forces alone will become the backbone for social relationships.

One recent model proposed by the Canadian critic Naomi Klein describes this notion of the 'outside' as stemming paradoxically from the heart of global capitalism. Klein's book *No Logo* (2000) represents an attack on 'the global logo web' and the veneer of brand advertising behind which, she argues, vast corporations hide.[46] By exposing the false economy of images that have come to dominate public life since the mid-1980s she attempts to express the 'anticorporate attitude ... emerging among young activists' (as seen, for example, in the mass demonstrations against trade laws at the Seattle World Trade Organization Millennial Summit in November 1999), which she hopes will lead to 'the next big political movement, a vast wave of opposition squarely targeting transnational corporations, particularly those with very high name-brand recognition'.[47] Klein studies the way in the 'corporate obsession with brand identity is waging a war on public and individual space', on the individual's freedom to choose without being manipulated, and on the very material conditions of work that create civic identity.[48] On her account, creativity is absorbed into advertising campaigns and aesthetics degenerate into public logos, becoming images of false consciousness rather than stimulating moral possibility. However, rather than resigning herself to the fact that the vast socio-economic machine will eventually crush liberty and the possibility of resistance, Klein sees the emergence of an alliance in the mid-1990s between 'ethical shareholders, culture jammers, street reclaimers, McUnion organizers, human rights hacktivists, school-logo fighters and Internet corporate watchdogs' who are beginning to demand 'a citizen-centred alternative to the international rule of the brands'.[49] The force of this resistance derives from the shared goals of cultural producers and moral campaigners, fighting together against a divisive socio-economic machine running out of control. Klein's vision is both realistic and farsighted. She does not resurrect the countercultural promises of the 1960s in which alienated middle-class youth rebelled against the perceived conformism of their parents, only for many to realign themselves with materialist values in the 1980s. Rather, she proposes a counterhegemonic alliance which is 'both high-tech and grassroots, both focused and fragmented' as a way of exercising the agonic power that Foucault describes.

This notion of an outside to a social and economic system that, as Bauman and Klein both argue, seems to have completely enveloped moral life appears to be a long way from the discussion in the Introduction of modernist protagonists attempting to bolster an inner life-world against invading forces. However, if following postmodern theory we see individuals as partly constitutive of the social codes through which they are acculturated, in a strictly regulated environment it would be impossible to preserve inner sanctity unless an outside experience filters in to counter dominant values. Indeed, this notion of 'outside' taps into the recent interest in 'outsider art' and provides a bridge between Wolf and Auster and early twentieth-century modernists, who felt themselves simultaneously inside and outside a cultural system, simultaneously constrained by it and free from it. If this kind of experience is no longer to be located in the socio-economic sphere as Fukuyama proposes (with communism drawing its last gasp), then perhaps, despite Klein's argument, only in relation to the creative/aesthetic sphere can morality retain its potency.

It is important to remember that aesthetic expressions of reciprocity and the representation of the Other are never 'non-cultural' and will always be inflected by the social conditions that shape a writer's ideological perspective. It seems that only writers who fall between the cracks of nationhood and fixed cultural identities will be able to preserve such ability. This is most obvious in the fiction of postcolonial writers such as Salman Rushdie and Bharati Mukherjee, indigenous writers such as Louise Erdrich in America struggling against the marginalisation of tribal values, or gay writers largely disenfranchised by a system which many feel reinforces 'compulsory heterosexuality' (to use the lesbian poet Adrienne Rich's phrase).[50] Although the centripetal pull of late capitalism may suck in even these writers, muting the force of their work by diluting radical difference within the mainstream, as long as they retain the status of 'the outsider' (without it simply becoming a media label) their work will remain in the fissures of a system which, by its very nature, cannot be perfectly self-regulating. While the 'moral agreement' that Alasdair MacIntyre discusses in *After Virtue* (1981) may be an elusive goal and arguments over ethical grounds are inevitable, a dissensus of voices might actually be more desirable for raising issues of identity and Otherness that keep moral debates alive.[51]

These aesthetic and literary concerns may seem to have little to do with recent moral debates and policy-making on both international and domestic issues: for example, the implementation of an International Criminal Court (ratified in 1998); intervention in Northern Ireland and the Baltic States; the 'Sarah's Law' campaign in the UK to name paedophiles in the wake of Sarah Payne's murder (August 2000); or the discussions in the media, church and courts about whether to surgically separate the conjoined twins Jodie and

Mary (with the inevitable death of Mary in November 2000) despite their Catholic parents' wish not to operate. While it is absurd to suggest these issues can be 'solved' by aesthetic means, Stuart Hall argues that literature and art do not just have 'a reflexive, after-the-event role' in working through moral conundrums (for example, the commodification of babies), but actually have 'a formative, not merely an expressive, place in the constitution of social and political life' (in this case, acting as a testing ground for medical ethics).[52] Rather than losing its force as a media spectacle or becoming corporately owned,[53] if experimental art retains its disruptive function it will encourage us to look outside emotive cases to address wider social implications. This notion of art being 'formative' of ideology and value leads directly back to the modernist emphasis upon what the art historian Colin Rhodes describes as 'the commonplace of experience that is too often overlooked'.[54] The reason why modernist writing (in its early and more recent manifestations) can relieve us from the aches and bruises of modernity is not by active forgetting or passive acceptance of reality but, as Christa Wolf writes, by continuing to dramatise 'the writer's struggle with himself ... to reach the limit of what he can say and perhaps cross beyond it at an unforeseeable point'.[55] This struggle between the 'commonplace of experience' and the 'unforeseeable point' suggests fiction will continue to offer a source of moral value by reminding us of ethical issues that just will not go away.

Notes

Introduction: modernity and the crisis of morals

1. Thomas Hardy, *Tess of the D'Urbervilles* (Harmondsworth: Penguin, 1978), p. 180.
2. Ibid., p. 180.
3. Ibid., p. 180.
4. 'General Preface to the Wessex Edition of 1912', reprinted in *A Pair of Blue Eyes* (London: Macmillan, 1975), p. 426.
5. Michael Wood, 'You Can't Go Home Again', in Paul Barker (ed.), *Arts in Society* (London: Fontana, 1977), pp. 26–7.
6. See Kathryn Pyne Addelson, *Moral Passages: Towards a Collectivist Moral Theory* (New York: Routledge, 1994).
7. Robert Musil, *The Man Without Qualities*, Volume 1, trans. Eithne Wilkins and Ernst Kaiser (London: Minerva, 1995), p. 8.
8. Alain de Botton, *The Consolations of Philosophy* (London: Hamish Hamilton, 2000).
9. Mike Jay and Michael Neve (eds), *1900: A Fin-de-siècle Reader* (Harmondsworth: Penguin, 2000), p. xi.
10. Wood, 'You Can't Go Home Again', p. 26.
11. *The Trial of Freedom*, written by Michael Ignatieff, directed by Nicola Colton, Channel 4 (31 October 1999).
12. See Ignatieff's *Virtual War* (London: Chatto & Windus, 2000).
13. James Joyce, *A Portrait of the Artist as a Young Man* (Harmondsworth: Penguin, 1992), p. 269.
14. Colin McGinn, *Ethics, Evil and Fiction* (Oxford: Clarendon, 1997), p. 176.
15. Ibid., p. 175.
16. Peter Nicholls, *Modernisms: A Literary Guide* (London: Macmillan, 1995), pp. 29–31.
17. This idea encapsulates the position developed by Zygmunt Bauman in his published lecture, *Postmodernity: Chance or Menace?*, organised by the Centre for the Study of Cultural Values, Lancaster University (1991).
18. See Stephen Kern, *The Culture of Time and Space, 1880–1918* (Cambridge, MA: Harvard University Press, 1983).
19. Charles Baudelaire, *Selected Writings on Art and Literature* (Harmondsworth: Penguin, 1992), pp. 403–4.
20. Theodor Adorno and Max Horkheimer, *Dialectic of Enlightenment* (London: Verso, 1979), pp. 24–5.
21. Fyodor Dostoevsky, *Notes From Underground/The Double* (Harmondsworth: Penguin, 1972), p. 16
22. Ibid., p. 21.
23. Ibid., p. 20; p. 41.
24. Ibid., p. 16.

25. Jack Clayton, *Saul Bellow: In Defense of Man*, 2nd edn (Bloomington, IN Indiana University Press, 1979), p. 61.
26. Dostoevsky, *Notes From Underground*, pp. 29–30.
27. Ibid., p. 43.
28. Joseph Frank and David Goldstein (eds), *Selected Letters of Fyodor Dostoyevsky*, trans. Andrew MacAndrew (New Brunswick, NJ: Rutgers University Press, 1989), p. 269.
29. Ibid., p. 269.
30. Dostoevsky, *Notes from Underground*, p. 123.
31. Ibid., p. 123.
32. See Colin McCabe, *James Joyce and the Revolution of the Word* (London: Macmillan, 1979); Randall Stevenson, *Modernist Fiction: An Introduction* (London: Harvester, 1992); Peter Nicholls, *Modernisms* (London: Macmillan, 1995).
33. Musil, *The Man Without Qualities*, Volume 1, p. 12.
34. Ibid., p. 12.
35. Peter Brooker (ed.), *Modernism/Postmodernism* (London: Longman, 1992), p. 132.
36. Ibid., p. 132.
37. Musil, *The Man Without Qualities*, Volume 1, p. 41.
38. McGinn, *Ethics, Evil and Fiction*, pp. 171–2.
39. Ibid., p. 172.
40. Georg Lukács, *The Meaning of Contemporary Realism* (London: Merlin, 1963), p. 20.
41. Ibid., p. 33.
42. See Fredric Jameson, *Marxism and Form* (London: Verso, 1972), pp. 160–205.
43. Eugene Ionesco, *Rhinoceros/The Chairs/The Lesson* (Harmondsworth: Penguin, 1962), pp. 12–13.
44. Ionesco, *Notes and Counternotes* (London: John Calder, 1964), p. 217.
45. Ionesco, *Rhinoceros*, p. 10.
46. Ibid., p. 79.
47. Ibid., p. 79.
48. Ibid., p. 83.
49. Ibid., p. 92.
50. Ibid., pp. 123–4.
51. Ionesco, *Notes and Counternotes*, p. 218.
52. Ibid., p. 218.
53. Ibid., p. 218–19.
54. Ibid., p. 219.
55. Hannah Arendt, *Between Past and Future* (Harmondsworth: Penguin, 1993), p. 153.
56. See J. Hillis Miller, *The Ethics of Reading* (New York: Columbia University Press, 1987); Stanley Cavell, *This New Yet Unapproachable America* (Albuquerque, NM: Living Batch, 1989); Simon Critchley, *The Ethics of Deconstruction* (Oxford: Basil Blackwell, 1992); Ewa Ziarek, *The Rhetoric of Failure* (New York: State University of New York Press, 1996); Robert Eaglestone, *Ethical Criticism: Reading After Levinas* (Edinburgh: Edinburgh University Press, 1997).

57. F. R. Leavis, *The Great Tradition* (Harmondsworth: Penguin, 1993), p. 9.
58. Ibid., p. 10.
59. Ibid., p. 196.
60. Bauman, *Life in Fragments* (Oxford: Basil Blackwell, 1995), p. 2.
61. René Wellek, 'Literary Criticism and Philosophy', *Scrutiny*, 5:4 (1937), 376.
62. Bauman, *Life in Fragments*, p. 8.
63. Ibid., p. 9.
64. J. Hillis Miller, *The Ethics of Reading*, p. 1.
65. Ibid., p. 3.
66. Cavell, *The Senses of Walden: An Expanded Edition* (Chicago, IL: University of Chicago Press, 1992), p. 25.
67. Cavell, *This New Yet Unapproachable America*, p. 20.
68. Cavell, *The Senses of Walden*, p. 65.
69. Ibid., p. 65.
70. Cavell, *Conditions Handsome and Unhandsome: The Constitution of Emersonian Perfectionism* (Chicago, IL: Chicago University Press, 1990), p. 46.
71. McGinn, *Ethics, Evil and Fiction*, p. 174.
72. Ibid., p. 177.
73. Cavell, *Conditions Handsome and Unhandsome*, p. 46.
74. Cavell, *This New Yet Unapproachable America*, p. 36.

1 Decadence, naturalism and the morality of writing

1. In *Masculine Desire: The Sexual Politics of Victorian Aestheticism*, Richard Dellamora argues that the dandy is often a sham aristocrat or a figure of 'middle-class uppityism' (Chapel Hill, NC: University of North Carolina Press, 1990), p. 200. For Huysmans and Wilde, however, the dandy (in its ennobled form) symbolised what Baudelaire calls 'a quintessence of character and a subtle understanding of all the moral mechanisms of this world', although this kind of untrammelled ideal is rarely portrayed as such in decadent texts: Charles Baudelaire, *Selected Writings on Art and Literature*, trans. P. E. Charvet (Harmondsworth: Penguin, 1972), p. 399.
2. Richard Lehan, 'The European Background', in Donald Pizer (ed.), *The Cambridge Companion to American Realism and Naturalism* (Cambridge: Cambridge University Press, 1995), p. 63.
3. Max Nordau, *Degeneration* (Lincoln, NB: University of Nebraska Press, 1993), p. 537.
4. Lehan, 'The European Background', p. 70.
5. Edgar Allan Poe, *Selected Tales*, ed. Julian Symons (Oxford: Oxford University Press, 1980), p. 184; p. 165.
6. Ibid., p. 265.
7. Henry James, 'Honoré de Balzac' (1875), in *The Critical Muse: Selected Literary Criticism*, ed. Roger Gard (Harmondsworth: Penguin, 1987), p. 92.
8. For two studies of the 'French Poe' see Patrick F. Quinn, *The French Face of Edgar Poe* (Carbondale, IL: Southern Illinois University Press, 1957) and John Weightman, 'Poe in France: A Myth Revisited', in A. Robert Lee (ed.),

Edgar Allan Poe: The Design of Order (London: Vision Press, 1987), pp. 202–19.
9. Baudelaire, *Selected Writings on Art and Literature*, p. 177; p. 184.
10. Ibid., p. 192; p. 184.
11. Ibid., p. 194; p. 191.
12. Ibid., p. 197.
13. Ibid., p. 203.
14. Ibid., p. 186.
15. Ibid., p. 19.
16. Rupert Hart-Davis (ed.), *Selected Letters of Oscar Wilde* (Oxford: Oxford University Press, 1989), p. 179.
17. John Ruskin, *Unto This Last and Other Writings*, ed. Clive Wilmer (Harmondsworth: Penguin, 1985), p. 209.
18. Ibid., p. 256.
19. Marcel Proust, *Against Saint-Beuve and Other Essays*, trans. John Sturrock (Harmondsworth: Penguin, 1994), p. 165.
20. Marcel Proust, *On Reading*, trans. John Sturrock (Harmondsworth: Penguin, 1994), pp. 10–11.
21. Ibid., p. 32.
22. Ibid., p. 49.
23. Jonathan Dollimore, *Sexual Dissidence: Augustine to Wilde, Freud to Foucault* (Oxford: Clarendon Press, 1991), p. 241.
24. Ibid., p. 240.
25. Joris-Karl Huysmans, *Against Nature*, trans. Robert Baldick (Harmondsworth: Penguin, 1959), p. 176. Des Esseintes echoes Baudelaire's description of 'counting-house morality' in his account of the rise of the imbecilic and frivolous bourgeoisie: see p. 217.
26. Ibid., p. 17.
27. Ibid., p. 19.
28. Ibid., p. 24.
29. Ibid., p. 25.
30. Ibid., p. 36.
31. Ibid., p. 46.
32. Ibid., p. 191; p. 28; p. 29.
33. Ibid., p. 74.
34. Ibid., p. 191.
35. Dollimore, *Sexual Dissidence*, p. 4.
36. Huysmans, *Against Nature*, p. 220.
37. Oscar Wilde, *De Profundis and Other Writings* (Harmondsworth: Penguin, 1986), p. 57.
38. Dollimore, *Sexual Dissidence*, p. 33.
39. Charles Whibley, *The Scots Observer*, 5 August 1890, in *Selected Letters of Oscar Wilde*, p. 81.
40. Wilde, *The Picture of Dorian Gray*, ed. Peter Ackroyd (Harmondsworth: Penguin, 1985), p. 3.
41. Hart-Davis (ed.), *Selected Letters of Oscar Wilde*, p. 85.
42. Wilde, *The Picture of Dorian Gray*, p. 17; Hart-Davis (ed.), *Selected Letters of Oscar Wilde*, p. 95.
43. Ibid., p. 23.

44. Colin McGinn, *Ethics, Evil, and Fiction* (Oxford: Clarendon Press, 1997), p. 124.
45. Ibid., p. 135.
46. Ibid., p. 139.
47. See Richard Chase, *The American Novel and its Tradition* (New York: Doubleday, 1957).
48. William Dean Howells, 'James's Hawthorne' (1880), in *W. D. Howells As Critic*, ed. E. H. Cady (London: Routledge & Kegan Paul, 1973), p. 53.
49. Frank Norris, *The Literary Criticism of Frank Norris*, ed. Donald Pizer (Austin, TX: University of Texas Press, 1964), p. 41; p. 40.
50. Ibid., p. 71.
51. Ibid., p. 43; p. 41.
52. Ibid., p. 51.
53. Ibid., p. xiv; p. xv; p. 8.
54. Ibid., p. 75.
55. Ibid., p. 98.
56. Ibid., p. xxi.
57. Émile Zola, *Thérèse Raquin*, trans. Andrew Rothwell (Oxford: Oxford University Press, 1992), p. 2.
58. Ibid., p. 2; p. 1.
59. Ibid., p. 3.
60. Huysmans, *Against Nature*, p. 184; Zola, *Thérèse Raquin*, p. 3.
61. Pizer, *The Cambridge Companion to American Realism and Naturalism*, p. 3.
62. Norris, *The Literary Criticism of Frank Norris*, p. 71.
63. Norris, *McTeague*, 2nd edn, ed. Donald Pizer (New York: Norton, 1997), p. 5; p. 6.
64. Ibid., p. 243.
65. Ernest Marchand, *Frank Norris: A Study* (Stanford, CA: Stanford University Press, 1942), p. 201.
66. Norris, *McTeague*, p. 21.
67. Ibid., pp. 21–2.
68. Stephen Crane, 'The Open Boat' (1897), in *The Works of Stephen Crane*, Volume 5, *Tales of Adventure* (Charlottesville, VA: University Press of Virginia, 1970), p. 69.
69. Norris, *McTeague*, p. 108.
70. Ibid., p. 171.
71. Ibid., pp. 205–6.
72. Ibid., p. 206.
73. Edith Wharton, 'Visibility in Fiction', *Life and Letters*, 2:11 (April 1929), 263.
74. Ibid., 268.
75. Edith Wharton, 'Fiction and Criticism', in *The Uncollected Critical Writings*, ed. Frederick Wegener (Princeton, NJ: Princeton University Press, 1996), p. 294; p. 297.
76. Edith Wharton, *Ethan Frome*, eds Kristin O. Lauer and Cynthia Griffin Wolff (New York: Norton, 1995), p. xi.
77. Ibid, p. xii.
78. Ibid., p. 3.

79. Ibid., p. 8.
80. Ibid., p. 6; p. 4.
81. Ibid., p. 12; p. 5.
82. J. Hillis Miller, *The Ethics of Reading* (New York: Columbia University Press, 1987), p. 4.
83. Wharton, *Ethan Frome*, p. 22; p. 23.
84. Ibid., p. 48.
85. Ibid., p. 35.
86. Ibid., p. 55.
87. Ibid., p. 68.
88. Wharton, 'The Writing of *Ethan Frome*' (1932), in *Ethan Frome*, p. 78.
89. Lionel Trilling, 'The Morality of Inertia' (1956), in *Ethan Frome*, p. 126.
90. Ibid., p. 127; p. 126.
91. Ibid., p. 127.
92. Ibid., p. 129.
93. Ibid., p. 128.
94. Proust, *On Reading*, p. 33; p. 34.

2 Books and ruins

1. Thomas Mann, *New York Times Book Review*, 19 August 1951, reprinted in Albert J. Guerard, *André Gide*, 2nd edn (Cambridge, MA: Harvard University Press, 1969), p. xxvii.
2. Ibid., p. xxvi. Even Gide wrote to Guerard to express his surprise that the critic rated *The Immoralist* so highly: David Walker (ed.), *André Gide* (London: Longman, 1996), p. 125.
3. Guerard, *André Gide*, p. xxvi; p. xxiv.
4. Mann was six years younger than Gide and displays the typical anxiety symptoms of a troubled younger brother, especially in his early period as a writer: Anthony Heilbut, *Thomas Mann* (London: Macmillan, 1996), p. 472.
5. Ibid., p. xxv.
6. From a letter sent to the critic Carl Maria Weber on 4 July 1920, in *The Letters of Thomas Mann, 1889–1955*, eds and trans. Richard and Clara Winston (Harmondsworth: Penguin, 1975), p. 94. Mann's original stimulus for *Death in Venice* came from the story of the ageing Goethe's desire for a girl he met at Marienbad baths and to whom he proposed: see Walter Stewart, '*Der Tod in Venedig*: The Path to Insight', *Germanic Review*, 53 (1978), 50–4.
7. Guerard, *André Gide*, p. 234.
8. Ibid., p. xxv.
9. Richard and Clara Winston (eds), *The Letters of Thomas Mann*, p. 94.
10. Thomas Mann, *Death in Venice and Other Stories*, trans. David Luke (London: Minerva, 1996), p. 194.
11. Julia Kristeva, *Powers of Horror: An Essay on Abjection*, ed. Leon S. Roudiez (New York: Columbia University Press, 1982), p. 13.
12. André Gide, *The Immoralist*, trans. Dorothy Bussy (Harmondsworth: Penguin, 1996), p. 15.
13. Ibid., pp. 7–8.

14. G. Norman Laidlaw, *Elysian Encounter: Diderot and Gide* (New York: Syracuse University Press, 1963), p. 16.
15. Charles Baudelaire, 'The Painter of Modern Life', *Baudelaire: Selected Writings on Art and Literature* (Harmondsworth: Penguin, 1972), p. 421.
16. Mann, *Death in Venice and Other Stories*, p. 267; Kristeva, *Powers of Horror*, p. 55.
17. Michel Foucault, *The Use of Pleasure*, trans. Robert Hurley (Harmondsworth: Penguin, 1992), pp. 8–9.
18. Mann, *Death in Venice*, p. 265.
19. Gide, *The Immoralist*, p. 65.
20. Mann, *Death in Venice*, p. 200; Gide, *The Immoralist*, p. 19.
21. Julia Kristeva, *Strangers to Ourselves*, trans. Leon S. Roudiez (New York: Columbia University Press, 1991), p. 5. Kristeva's notion of 'strength' does not correspond to the kind of religious or military discipline that Aschenbach shows in his writing – discussed by Harvey Goldman in *Max Weber and Thomas Mann: Calling and the Shaping of the Self* (Berkeley, CA: University of California Press, 1988) – but is an acknowledgement of the unruly and unassimilable elements within the self: Kristeva, *Strangers to Ourselves*, p. 1.
22. Mann, *Death in Venice*, p. 211.
23. Stuart Burrows, '"Desire Projected Itself Visually": Watching *Death in Venice*', in Deborah Cartmell et al. (eds), *Classics in Film and Fiction*, (London: Pluto, 2000), p. 141.
24. Gide, *The Immoralist*, p. 95.
25. Although Guerard also reads *The Immoralist* as a critique of Nietzschean individualism, my position regarding the ending of tale differs from his reading of Michel's final 'futile anarchy': Guerard, *André Gide*, p. 102; p. 99.
26. Mann, *Death in Venice*, p. 204.
27. Gide, *The Immoralist*, p. 15.
28. Ibid., p. 26.
29. Mann, *Death in Venice*, pp. 202–3.
30. Ibid., p. 231.
31. Susan Sontag, *Illness as Metaphor/AIDS and its Metaphors* (Harmondsworth: Penguin, 1991), p. 18.
32. Ibid., p. 20; Gide, *The Immoralist*, p. 33.
33. Mann, *Death in Venice*, p. 223.
34. Ibid., p. 228.
35. Kelly Oliver, *Reading Kristeva: Unravelling the Double-Bind* (Bloomington, IN: Indiana University Press, 1993), p. 58.
36. Gide, *The Immoralist*, p. 54.
37. Kristeva, *Powers of Horror*, p. 8; p. 2.
38. Such ambivalent feelings are analogous to Freud's classic definition of the uncanny (*unheimlich*) in which the foreign and the strange are found in, and implicated by, the everyday and the familiar. On this model, the uncanny represents a region within the homely which disturbs as 'that class of the frightening which leads back to what is known of old and long familiar': James Strachey and Anna Freud (eds), *The Standard Edition of the Complete Psychological Works of Sigmund Freud*, Volume 17 (London: Hogarth, 1964), p. 220.

39. Gide, *The Immoralist*, p. 51; p. 65.
40. Ibid., p. 57; p. 58.
41. Mann, *Death in Venice*, p. 206; p. 207; p. 209; p. 214.
42. Kristeva, *Powers of Horror*, p. 1.
43. Ibid., p. 2.
44. Ibid., p. 11.
45. Mann, *Death in Venice*, pp. 226–7.
46. Ibid., p. 224.
47. Gide, *The Immoralist*, p. 39.
48. Kristeva, *Powers of Horror*, p. 55; p. 27.
49. Gide, *The Immoralist*, pp. 155–9; Mann, *Death in Venice*, p. 267.
50. Kristeva, *Powers of Horror*, p. 208.
51. The way in which modernist literature reflects what Sontag calls 'the nihilistic energies of the modern era' and makes 'everything a ruin or fragment' means a study of these writers is pertinent for dealing with theories of abjection: cited in Liam Kennedy, *Susan Sontag: Mind as Passion* (Manchester: Manchester University Press, 1995), p. 11. As a point of comparison, Maud Ellman applies Kristeva's theory of abjection to Eliot's modernist lament *The Waste Land* in *The Poetics of Impersonality: T. S. Eliot and Ezra Pound* (Brighton: Harvester, 1987), pp. 91–113.
52. Kristeva, *Powers of Horror*, p. 208.
53. Gide, *The Immoralist*, p. 19.
54. Ibid., p. 20.
55. Ibid., p. 50.
56. Ibid., p. 90.
57. Ibid., p. 137; p. 140.
58. Michel looks forward to 'a land free from works of art; I despise those who cannot recognize beauty until it has been transcribed and interpreted' (ibid., p. 148). This position develops Walter Pater's dictum that 'to burn with this hard, gem-like flame' is to live an intense artistic life, whereas Michel attempts to discover such authenticity outside the cultural realm: Pater, *The Renaissance* (Oxford: Oxford University Press, 1986), p. 152.
59. Mann, *Death in Venice*, p. 207.
60. Ibid., p. 210.
61. Ibid., p. 265.
62. Ibid., p. 265.
63. Kristeva, *Powers of Horror*, p. 9.
64. Gide, *The Immoralist*, p. 157.
65. Jonathan Dollimore, *Sexual Dissidence: Augustine to Wilde, Freud to Foucault* (Oxford: Clarendon Press, 1991), p. 4.
66. Ibid., p. 13.
67. Kristeva, *Powers of Horror*, p. 3. This exploration of psychic borders is prevalent throughout French modernism, especially in Artaud, Bataille, Genet and Foucault, and may go some way to account for the different cultural inflection Gide and Mann place on decadence.
68. Gide, *The Immoralist*, p. 158.
69. Ibid., p. 51.
70. Ibid., p. 158.
71. Walter Benjamin, 'Conversation with André Gide' (1928), in Walter

Benjamin, *Selected Writings, Volume 2, 1927–1934*, ed. Michael W. Jennings, trans. Rodney Livingstone (Cambridge, MA: Belknap Press, 1999), p. 96.

3 Extremist modernism

1. Arthur Symons, *Selected Writings*, ed. Roger Holdsworth (Manchester: Carcanet, 1989), p. 77; p. 83.
2. Ibid., p. 84.
3. Ibid., p. 85.
4. Ibid., p. 77.
5. Stéphane Mallarmé, 'Crisis in Poetry' (1892–95), in *Mallarmé: Selected Prose Poems, Essays and Letters*, trans. Bradford Cook (Baltimore, MD: Johns Hopkins University Press, 1956), p. 43.
6. Peter Osborne, *The Politics of Time: Modernity and Avant-Garde* (London: Verso, 1995), p. 1.
7. Ibid., p. 157; p. 199.
8. This phrase is appropriated from Alan Young's book *Dada and After: Extremist Modernism and English Literature* (Manchester: Manchester University Press, 1981).
9. David Harvey, *The Conditions of Postmodernity* (Oxford: Basil Blackwell, 1991), p. 16.
10. Robert Motherwell (ed.), *The Dada Painters and Poets: An Anthology* (New York: George Wittenborn, 1951), p. xii.
11. Gertrude Stein, 'Composition as Explanation' (1926), in *A Stein Reader*, ed. Ulla E. Dydo (Evanston, IL: Northwestern University Press, 1993), p. 496.
12. André Breton, *Manifestoes of Surrealism*, trans. Richard Seaver and Helen R. Lane (Ann Arbor, MI: University of Michigan Press, 1972), p. 123.
13. Ibid., p. 124. Tristan Tzara, *Seven Dada Manifestos*, trans. Barbara Wright (London: John Calder, 1977), p. 110.
14. Cited in Milton Brown, *The Story of the Armory Show* (New York: Abbeville, 1988), p. 167.
15. Richard Huelsenbeck, *Memoirs of a Dada Drummer*, ed. Hans J. Kleinschmidt, trans. Joachim Neugroschel (Berkeley, CA: University of California Press, 1991), p. xviii.
16. Peter Nicholls, *Modernisms* (London: Macmillan, 1995), p. 224.
17. Tzara, *Seven Dada Manifestos*, p. 12.
18. Ibid., p. 13.
19. Motherwell (ed.), *The Dada Painters and Poets*, p. xviii.
20. Kurt Schwitters, *Merz* (1921), reprinted in Vassiliki Kolocotroni *et al.* (eds), *Modernism: An Anthology of Sources and Documents* (Edinburgh: Edinburgh University Press, 1998), p. 282.
21. Huelsenbeck, 'Zurich in 1916, As it Really Was' (1928), ibid., p. 209.
22. See John Elderfield's 'Afterword' to Hugo Ball, *Flight Out of Time: A Dada Diary*, ed. John Elderfield, trans. Ann Raimes (Berkeley, CA: University of California Press, 1996), pp. 238–55 for a discussion of the origins of Dadaism and the disputes between its practitioners.
23. Ibid., p. 209.

24. Ibid., p. 210.
25. Hans Richter, *Dada: Art and Anti-Art* (London: Thames & Hudson, 1997), p. 19; p. 20; p. 36.
26. Ibid., p. 115.
27. Helena Lewis, *Dada Turns Red: The Politics of Surrealism* (Edinburgh: Edinburgh University Press, 1990), pp. 13–14.
28. Huelsenbeck 'En Avant Dada: A History of Dadaism' (1920), in Motherwell (ed.), *The Dada Painters and Poets*, p. 28.
29. Ibid., p. 28.
30. Ibid., p. 9. Nicholas Zurbrugg, *The Parameters of Postmodernism* (London: Routledge, 1993), p. 2.
31. Tzara, *Seven Dada Manifestos*, p. 13.
32. Huelsenbeck, *Memoirs of a Dada Drummer*, pp. xxxiv–xxxv.
33. Tzara, *Seven Dada Manifestos*, p. 24.
34. Motherwell, *Dada Painters and Poets*, p. xx.
35. Friedrich Nietzsche, *Human All Too Human*, trans. Marion Faber and Stephen Lehmann (Harmondsworth: Penguin, 1994), p. 66.
36. Huelsenbeck, *Memoirs of a Dada Drummer*, pp. 139–40.
37. Ibid., p. 140; p. xxxvi.
38. Ibid., p. 140.
39. Ibid., p. 141.
40. Tzara, *Seven Dada Manifestos*, p. 1.
41. Ibid., p. 1.
42. Walter Pater, *The Renaissance* (Oxford: Oxford University Press, 1986), p. 152; Motherwell, *The Dada Painters and Poets*, p. 51; p. 40.
43. Motherwell (ed.), *The Dada Painters and Poets*, p. 29.
44. Tzara, *Seven Dada Manifestos*, p. 2; p. 1.
45. Ibid., p. 4.
46. Ibid., p. 27.
47. Ibid., p. 109.
48. Ibid., p. 111.
49. Henri Focillon, 'In Praise of Hands' (1948), cited by Motherwell, *The Dada Painters and Poets*, p. xxxvii.
50. Marcel Raymond, *From Baudelaire to Surrealism* (Paris: José Corti, 1985), p. xxviii.
51. Motherwell (ed.), *The Dada Painters and Poets*, p. 42.
52. Ibid., p. 42.
53. Ibid., p. xxvi; Breton, *Manifestoes of Surrealism*, p. 26.
54. Ibid., p. 26.
55. Walter Benjamin, 'Surrealism: The Last Snapshot of the European Intelligentsia', in *One Way Street and Other Writings*, ed. Susan Sontag, trans. Edmund Jephcott and Kingsley Shorter (London: Verso, 1992), p. 225.
56. Breton, *Manifestoes of Surrealism*, p. 171.
57. Ibid., p. 171; p. 172.
58. Ibid., p. 133.
59. Ibid., p. x.
60. Ibid., p. xi; Benjamin, *One Way Street*, p. 231.
61. Breton, *Manifestoes of Surrealism*, p. 3.

62. Ibid., p. 6; p. 5.
63. Ibid., p. 16.
64. Ibid., p. 123.
65. Ibid., p. 21.
66. Ibid., p. 137.
67. Ibid., p. 47; p. 37.
68. Paul Eluard, 'Poetry's Evidence', *This Quarter*, 5:1 (1932), 146.
69. Ibid., 148.
70. Michel Remy, *Surrealism in Britain* (London: Ashgate, 1999), p. 20.
71. Quoted in Breton, *Manifestoes of Surrealism*, p. 191.
72. Ibid., p. 44.
73. Ibid., p. 187.
74. Ibid., p. 47; p. 14; p. 46.
75. Remy, *Surrealism in Britain*, p. 19.
76. Breton, *Nadja*, trans. Richard Howard (New York: Grove Press, 1960), p. 15.
77. Ibid., p. 19.
78. Ibid., p. 59; Susan Sontag, *Against Interpretation* (New York: Farrar Straus & Giroux, 1982), p. 271.
79. Mary Ann Caws, 'Seeing the Surrealist Woman: We Are a Problem in Misogyny', in Mary Ann Caws *et al.* (eds), *Surrealism and Women*, (Cambridge, MA: MIT Press, 1991), p. 13.
80. Breton, *Nadja*, p. 160.
81. Breton, *Communicating Vessels*, trans. Mary Ann Caws and Geoffrey T. Harris (Lincoln, NB: University of Nebraska Press, 1990), p. 5.
82. Breton, *Mad Love*, trans. Mary Ann Caws (Lincoln: University of Nebraska Press, 1987), p. 24.
83. Breton, *Communicating Vessels*, p. 139.
84. Ibid., p. 115.
85. Ibid., p. 40.
86. Ibid., p. 128.
87. Ibid., p. 139.
88. Breton, *Mad Love*, p. 25.
89. Breton and Paul Eluard, *The Immaculate Conception*, trans. Jon Graham (London: Atlas Press, 1990), p. 101.
90. Benjamin, *One Way Street*, p. 236.
91. Louis Aragon, *Treatise on Style*, trans. Alyson Waters (Lincoln, NB: University of Nebraska Press, 1991), pp. 8–9; Aragon, *The Libertine*, trans. Jo Levy (London: John Calder, 1993), p. 19.
92. Ibid., p. 9.
93. Ibid., p. 16; p. 21.
94. Aragon, 'A Man', *Little Review*, 9:4 (Autumn/Winter 1923–24), 18.
95. Ibid., 19.
96. Ibid., 20.
97. Ibid., 22.
98. Aragon, *The Libertine*, p. 23.
99. Aragon, 'A Man', 22.
100. Ibid., 22.
101. Aragon, *The Libertine*, p. 10.

102. Aragon, *Paris Peasant*, trans. Simon Watson Taylor (London: Jonathan Cape, 1971), p. 211.
103. Ibid., p. 208.
104. Ibid., p. 209.
105. Breton and Eluard, *The Immaculate Conception*, p. 101.
106. Rudolf E. Kuenzli, 'Surrealism and Misogyny', in Mary Ann Caws *et al.* (eds), *Surrealism and Women*, pp. 18–19.
107. Gwen Raaberg, 'The Problematic of Women and Surrealism', ibid., p. 3.

4 Moral regeneration and moral bankruptcy

1. George Eliot, *Middlemarch* (Harmondsworth: Penguin, 1985), p. 297.
2. Ibid., p. 297.
3. Erich Auerbach, *Mimesis: The Representation of Reality in Western Fiction* (Princeton, NJ: Princeton University Press, 1953), p. 532.
4. Raymond Williams, *The English Novel from Dickens to Lawrence* (London: Chatto & Windus, 1970), p. 100.
5. Ibid., p. 101. Of course, this does not preclude reading nineteenth-century realist novels as illustrative of the problems of rendering 'reality', as Roland Barthes demonstrates in his reading of Balzac's story 'Sarrasine' in *S/Z*, trans. Richard Miller (New York: Hill & Wang, 1974).
6. Andrew Gibson, *Postmodernity, Ethics and the Novel* (London: Routledge, 1999), p. 55.
7. Joseph Conrad, *The Secret Agent* (Harmondsworth: Penguin, 1986), p. 41.
8. Brian Spittles, *Joseph Conrad* (London: Macmillan, 1992), p. 119.
9. Conrad, *The Secret Agent*, p. 67.
10. Allan Ingram (ed.), *Joseph Conrad: Selected Literary Criticism and 'The Shadow-Line'* (London: Methuen, 1986), pp. 78–9.
11. Ibid., p. 79.
12. Dwight Purdy suggests Conrad's narrative tone is both ironic and compassionate, combining to create a 'third quality' of depression which pervades the mood of the novel. See Dwight H. Purdy, '*The Secret Agent*: Under Edwardian Eyes', *Conradian*, 16:2 (1992), 1–17.
13. Conrad, *The Secret Agent*, p. 66.
14. Ibid., p. 39.
15. J. A. Gee and J. P. Sturm (eds), *Letters of Joseph Conrad to Marguerite Poradowska, 1890–1920* (London: Oxford University Press, 1940), p. 72.
16. It is interesting to note that Paul Sollier argues, in an article on 'Idiocy' in the same volume of the encyclopaedia as Lombroso's essay, that the category of 'idiot' is inadequate for describing a particular neurological condition, serving instead as an umbrella term for 'a large number of cerebral affections'; T. L. Stedman (ed.), *Twentieth Century Practice: An International Encyclopædia of Modern Medical Science*, Volume 12 (London: Sampson Low, Marston, 1897), p. 257.
17. Gina Lombroso Ferrero, *Criminal Man* (New York: Putnam's, 1911), p. 87.
18. Stedman, *Twentieth Century Practice*, p. 188.
19. Conrad, *Heart of Darkness* (Harmondsworth: Penguin, 1986), p. 68. A very different interpretation of Conrad's interest in primitivism is provided by

Chinua Achebe in 'An Image of Africa: Racism in Conrad's *Heart of Darkness*', *Hopes and Impediments: Selected Essays* (London: Heinemann, 1988).
20. Gibson, *Postmodernity, Ethics and the Novel*, p. 56.
21. Ibid., p. 60.
22. Patricia Waugh, *Practising Postmodernism/Reading Modernism* (London: Edward Arnold, 1992), p. 94.
23. Ibid., p. 94.
24. K. K. Ruthven, 'The Savage God: Conrad and Lawrence', *Critical Quarterly*, 10 (1968), 39.
25. Eugene S. Talbot, in *Degeneracy: Its Causes, Signs and Results* (London: Walter Scott, 1898), claims that the idea of a deadlock between progression and degeneration was one which Lombroso had borrowed from mainstream evolutionary writing. See also J. Edward Chamberlain and Sander Gilman (eds), *Degeneration: The Dark Side of Progress* (New York: Columbia University Press, 1986).
26. This is a central phrase in Hutcheon's *The Politics of Postmodernism* (London: Routledge, 1989), p. 12.
27. For two interesting appraisals of nineteenth-century stereotypes of idiocy and madness see Sander Gilman, *Pathology and Difference: Stereotypes of Sexuality, Race, and Madness* (Ithaca, NY: Cornell University Press, 1985) and *Disease and Representation: Images of Illness from Madness to AIDS* (Ithaca, NY: Cornell University Press, 1988).
28. Conrad, *The Secret Agent*, p. 269.
29. Ibid., p. 86.
30. Ibid., pp. 76–7.
31. Ibid., p. 78.
32. Ibid., p. 64.
33. Ibid., p. 67.
34. Ibid., p. 68.
35. Ibid., p. 68.
36. Ibid., p. 67.
37. Ibid., p. 200.
38. Ibid., p. 146.
39. Allan Hunter, *Joseph Conrad and the Ethics of Darwinism* (London: Croom Helm, 1983), p. 161.
40. Conrad, *The Secret Agent*, p. 266.
41. Ibid., p. 260.
42. Ibid., p. 269.
43. Ibid., p. 76.
44. Ibid., pp. 79–80.
45. Ibid., p. 168.
46. Ibid., p. 157.
47. Ibid., p. 165.
48. Ibid., p. 168.
49. Ibid., p. 5; p. 167.
50. Ibid., p. 196.
51. For example, the detective work of Inspector Heat and the Assistant Commissioner relies more on luck than guile, as they are complicit in maintaining the web of political secrecy.

52. Ibid., p. 234.
53. Ibid., p. 230.
54. Ibid., pp. 234–5.
55. Ibid., p. 223; p. 219.
56. Ibid., p. 234.
57. Ibid., p. 254.
58. Ibid., p. 269.
59. Ibid., p. 254; p. 168.
60. Conrad's letter to R. B. Cunninghame Graham, in *Letters to R. B. Cuninghame Graham*, ed. C. T. Watts (Cambridge: Cambridge University Press, 1969), p. 65.
61. Myra Jehlen, *Class and Character in Faulkner's South* (New York: Columbia University Press, 1976), p. 19.
62. Ibid., pp. 43–4.
63. Richard H. King, *A Southern Renaissance: The Cultural Awakening of the American South, 1930–1955* (New York: Oxford University Press, 1980), p. 111.
64. James B. Meriwether and Michael Millgate (eds), *Lion in the Garden: Interviews with William Faulkner* (New York: Random House, 1968), p. 127.
65. Faulkner, *The Sound and the Fury*, ed. David Minter (New York: Norton, 1987), p. 235.
66. Richard H. King, 'Framework of a Renaissance', in Doreen Fowler and Ann J. Abadie (eds), *Faulkner and the Southern Renaissance*, (Jackson, MS: University of Mississippi Press, 1982), p. 4.
67. Wolfgang Iser, *The Implied Reader* (Baltimore, MD: Johns Hopkins University Press, 1974), p. 136.
68. Faulkner, *The Sound and the Fury* (London: Picador, 1989), pp. 61–2.
69. See Melanie Klein, *Envy and Gratitude and Other Works, 1946–1963* (London: Hogarth, 1975).
70. Iser, *The Implied Reader*, p. 140.
71. Faulkner, *The Sound and the Fury*, p. 237.
72. Ibid., p. 45.
73. Ibid., p. 277.

5 American expatriate fictions

1. Malcolm Bradbury, *Dangerous Pilgrimages: Trans-Atlantic Mythologies and the Novel* (Harmondsworth: Penguin, 1996).
2. See, for example, Ann Douglas, *Terrible Honesty: Mongrel Manhattan in the 1920s* (London: Macmillan, 1997), p. 5.
3. Alice Gambrell, *Women Intellectuals, Modernism and Difference* (Cambridge: Cambridge University Press, 1997), pp. 4–5.
4. Ibid., p. 9.
5. Iain Chambers, *Migrancy, Culture, Identity* (London: Routledge, 1994), p. 4.
6. Ibid., p. 6.
7. Ibid., p. 6.
8. Kelly Cannon, *Henry James and Masculinity: The Men at the Margins* (London: Macmillan, 1994), p. 8.

9. Ibid., p. 5.
10. Henry Miller, *Tropic of Cancer* (London: Flamingo, 1993), p. 74.
11. Malcolm Cowley, *Exile's Return: A Literary Odyssey of the 1920s* (New York: Penguin, 1994). Donald Pizer, *American Expatriate Writing and the Paris Moment: Modernism and Place* (Baton Rouge, LA: Louisiana State University Press, 1996), p. xiii. A more sceptical, but limited, view of American writers in Paris can be found in Joseph H. McMahon's essay 'City for Expatriates', *Yale French Studies*, 32 (1964), 144–58.
12. Arlen J. Hansen, *Expatriate Paris: A Cultural and Literary Guide to Paris of the 1920s* (New York: Little, Brown, 1990), p. xx.
13. Luce Irigaray, *An Ethics of Sexual Difference*, trans. Carolyn Burke and Gillian C. Gill (London: Athlone, 1993).
14. Hansen, *Expatriate Paris*, p. xxi.
15. Paris was not always the fictional focus of expatriate writing; Hemingway commented that to view Paris one had to be elsewhere: 'Maybe away from Paris I could write about Paris as in Paris I could write about Michigan'; *A Moveable Feast* (New York: Scribner's, 1994), p. 6.
16. Ann Douglas, *The Feminization of American Culture* (New York: Macmillan, 1996), p. 12.
17. Kim Townsend, *Manhood at Harvard: William James and Others* (Cambridge, MA: Harvard University Press, 1996), p. 17; p. 25.
18. Henry James, *The Bostonians* (Oxford: Oxford University Press, 1998), p. 322.
19. Ibid., p. 323; p. 315; p. 181.
20. Gail Bederman, *Manliness and Civilization: A Cultural History of Gender and Race in the United States, 1880–1917* (Chicago, IL: University of Chicago Press, 1995), p. 176.
21. As Malcolm Bradbury notes, the internationalism of Woodrow Wilson's administration in the mid-1910s was succeeded in 1920 by the next president Warren Harding's emphasis on 'normalcy' and the restoration of domestic order: Bradbury, *Dangerous Pilgrimages*, p. 306.
22. *Dial*, 25 January 1917, 45, quoted in Henry May, *The End of American Innocence: A Study of the First Years of Our Own Time, 1912–1917* (New York: Knopf, 1959), p. 297.
23. For a comparison of Bourne and Stieglitz see Edward Abrahams, *The Lyrical Left and the Origins of Radicalism in America* (Charlottesville, VA: University Press of Virginia, 1986).
24. Randolph Bourne, 'Transnational America', *The Radical Will*, ed. Olaf Hansen (New York: Urizen, 1977), p. 262.
25. Ibid., p. 248.
26. Hemingway and Stein were not like-minded in their sexual views. Hemingway records Stein's criticism of male homosexual promiscuity while she preserved the sanctity of lesbian relationships, and he was horrified on overhearing her intimate exchange with her 'friend' Alice B. Toklas: Hemingway, *A Moveable Feast* (New York: Scribner's, 1994), p. 18.
27. Irigaray, *An Ethics of Sexual Difference*, p. 7.
28. Ibid., p. 5; p. 7.
29. Ibid., p. 117.
30. Ibid., p. 9; p. 18.

31. Ibid., p. 12; Irigaray, 'The Power of Discourse and the Subordination of the Feminine', *This Sex Which is Not One*, trans. Catherine Porter and Carolyn Burke (Ithaca, NY: Cornell University Press, 1985), p. 79.
32. Ibid., p. 13.
33. Ibid., p. 14.
34. Ibid., p. 16.
35. Ibid., p. 127.
36. Ibid., p. 129.
37. Rita Felski, *The Gender of Modernity* (Cambridge, MA: Harvard University Press, 1995), p. 95.
38. Ibid., p. 114.
39. Gertrude Stein, *Three Lives* (New York: Penguin, 1990), p. 13.
40. Quoted in Robert Motherwell (ed.), *The Dada Painters and Poets: An Anthology* (New York: George Wittenborn, 1951), p. 24.
41. Stein, *Three Lives*, p. 37.
42. Ibid., p. 16.
43. William James, *The Principles of Psychology*, Volume 1 (New York: Dover, 1950), p. 199; Gertrude Stein, 'Picasso', *Camera Work* (August 1912); reprinted in *A Stein Reader*, ed. Ulla Dydo (Evanston, IL: Northwestern University Press, 1993), p. 142.
44. Ibid., p. 499.
45. Linda Mizejewski, 'Gertrude Stein: The Pattern Moves', in Sandra Gilbert and Susan Gubar (eds) *The Female Imagination and the Modernist Aesthetic* (London: Gordon & Breach, 1986), pp. 43–4.
46. Marianne DeKoven, *A Different Language: Gertrude Stein's Experimental Writing* (Madison, WI: University of Wisconsin Press, 1983), p. 46.
47. Ibid., p. 67.
48. Motherwell, *The Dada Painters and Poets*, pp. 35–6.
49. DeKoven, *A Different Language*, p. 11. Hemingway offers a more cynical view of Stein's writing: 'she disliked the drudgery of revision and the obligation to make her writing intelligible'; Hemingway, *A Moveable Feast*, p. 16.
50. Stein, 'Tender Buttons', *Writings and Lectures (1911–1945)*, ed. Peter Meyerowitz (London: Peter Owen, 1967), p. 167.
51. See Norman Weinstein, *Gertrude Stein and the Literature of the Modern Consciousness* (New York: Ungar, 1970).
52. Stein, 'Tender Buttons', pp. 162–3.
53. Ibid., p. 198.
54. Ernest Hemingway, *The Sun Also Rises* (New York: Scribner's, 1986), p. 11.
55. Ibid., p. 115; p. 224.
56. Gambrell, *Women Intellectuals, Modernism and Difference*, p. 5.
57. Malcolm Cowley, 'Hemingway at Midnight', Introduction to *The Portable Hemingway* (New York: Viking, 1944), p. 317.
58. Hemingway's friend Harold Stearns (who returned to New York in 1925, while Hemingway returned to Michigan in 1926) was not always univocal in his support of expatriate antics. However, in *America and the Young Intellectual* (1921), even he comments that true 'moral restraint' can only derive 'not from the checking of desire but from the abundance of it; not from any denial of life, but from deeper sense of life's richness and

fulness': Harold Stearns, *America and the Young Intellectual* (Westport, CT: Greenwood Press, 1921), p. 76.
59. See Scott Donaldson, *By Force of Will: The Life and Art of Hemingway* (New York: Viking, 1977), pp. 109–10.
60. Hemingway, *The Sun Also Rises*, p. 149; Hemingway, *A Farewell to Arms* (New York: Scribner's, 1929), p. 196.
61. Hemingway, *The Sun Also Rises*, p. 27; p. 26.
62. Cowley, 'Hemingway at Midnight', p. 322.
63. Hemingway, *A Moveable Feast*, p. 12.
64. Hemingway, *The Sun Also Rises*, pp. 131–2. This concern with authenticity is reflected in Stearns's comment on the expatriate community: 'They are heartily tired of the fake. They want the real thing, and their sure instincts tell them that in Europe (not in England of course), even in the Europe that is dying from the follies and crimes of its old men, life can still be lived': Stearns, *America and the Young Intellectual*, p. 167.
65. Joe Moran, *Star Authors: Literary Celebrity in America* (London: Pluto, 2000), p. 27.
66. Mark Spilka, *Hemingway's Quarrel with Androgyny* (Lincoln, NB: University of Nebraska Press, 1990), p. 2. See also Rose Burwell, *Hemingway: The Postwar Years and the Posthumous Novels* (Cambridge: Cambridge University Press, 1996).
67. Spilka, *Hemingway's Quarrel with Androgyny*, pp. 202–4.
68. James Nagel, 'Brett and the Other Women in *The Sun Also Rises*', in Scott Donaldson (ed.), *The Cambridge Companion to Hemingway* (Cambridge: Cambridge University Press, 1996), p. 90.
69. Ibid., p. 98.
70. Ibid., p. 247.
71. Hemingway, *The Torrents of Spring* (London: Grafton, 1984), pp. 107–8.
72. Michael Woolf, 'Europe in the American Mind', in Philip John Davies (ed.), *Imagining and Representing America* (Keele: Keele University Press, 1996), p. 40.
73. Pizer, *American Expatriate Writing and the Paris Moment*, p. 136.
74. Miller, *Tropic of Cancer*, p. 104.
75. George Wickes (ed.), *Henry Miller and James Laughlin: Selected Letters* (London: Constable, 1996), p. 12.
76. Woolf, 'Europe in the American Mind', p. 40.
77. Miller, *Tropic of Capricorn* (London: Flamingo, 1993), p. 9.
78. Kate Millett, *Sexual Politics* (London: Virago, 1977), p. 313.
79. Miller, *Tropic of Cancer*, p. 10.
80. Ibid., p. 10.
81. Ibid., p. 33; p. 45.
82. Ibid., p. 104; Wickes (ed.), *Henry Miller and James Laughlin*, p. 13.
83. Miller, *Tropic of Cancer*, p. 74.
84. Nin, *Anaïs Nin Reader*, ed. Philip K. Jason (Chicago: Swallow, 1973), p. 301.
85. Ibid., p. 296; p. 299. There are certainly differences between Nin's diary and her short stories, but in her late long essay, *The Novel of the Future* (1968) she reflects on the 'mutual influence' of diary and fiction as two aspects of the same creative continuum.
86. Nin, *The Journals of Anaïs Nin, Volume 1, 1931–1934*, ed. Gunther

Stuhlmann (London: Peter Owen, 1970), p. 286.
87. Ibid., p. 191.
88. Irigaray, *An Ethics of Sexual Difference*, p. 17.
89. Anaïs Nin, *Henry and June*, (ed.) Rupert Pole (Harmondsworth: Penguin, 1990), p. 39; p. 13.
90. Ibid., p. 26; p. 68.
91. Nin, *The Journals, Volume 1*, p. 269.
92. Nin, *Henry and June*, p. 89.
93. Nin, *The Journals, Volume 1*, p. 29.
94. Nin, *Henry and June*, p. 31.
95. Nin, *The Journals, Volume 1*, p. 29.
96. Irigaray, *An Ethics of Sexual Difference*, p. 19.

6 The blind impress of modernity

1. William James, 'On a Certain Blindness in Human Beings', *Talks to Teachers* (Cambridge, MA: Harvard University Press, 1983), p. 134.
2. Ibid., p. 134.
3. See James Clifford and George E. Marcus (eds), *Writing Culture: The Poetics and Politics of Ethnography* (Berkeley, CA: University of California Press, 1986).
4. James, 'On a Certain Blindness', p. 150.
5. Richard Rorty, *Contingency, Irony and Solidarity* (Cambridge: Cambridge University Press, 1989), p. 26.
6. Gillian Beer, '"Authentic Tidings of Invisible Things": Vision and the Invisible in the Later Nineteenth Century', in Teresa Brennan and Martin Jay, (eds), *Vision in Context: Historical and Contemporary Perspectives on Sight* (New York: Routledge, 1996), pp. 90–1.
7. Victor Burgin, 'Paranoic Space', *In/Different Spaces: Place and Memory in Visual Culture* (Berkeley, CA: University of California Press, 1996), p. 120.
8. Ralph Waldo Emerson, 'Nature' (1836), in *Essays and Lectures* (New York: Library of America, 1983), p. 10. Also see Kant's *Groundwork of the Metaphysics of Morals*, trans. H. J. Paton (London: Routledge, 1995).
9. James, 'On a Certain Blindness', p. 149.
10. Ibid., p. 149.
11. For an exploration of this term see Woolf's 'A Sketch of the Past', *Moments of Being*, ed. Jeanne Schulkind (London: Grafton, 1989), pp. 72–173.
12. Quoted by Said in Maya Jaggi, 'Out of the Shadows', *The Guardian*, Saturday Review, 11 September 1999, 7.
13. Federico García Lorca, *Poet in New York* (Harmondsworth: Penguin, 1990), p. 185.
14. Leslie Fiedler, *Waiting for the End* (New York: Stein & Day, 1964), p. 84.
15. Edward Said, 'Secular Criticism', *The World, the Text and the Critic* (Cambridge, MA: Harvard University Press, 1983), pp. 6–7.
16. Abdul J. JanMohamed, 'Worldliness-without-World, Homelessness-as-Home: Toward a Definition of the Specular Border Intellectual', in Michael Sprinker (ed.), *Edward Said: A Critical Reader* (Oxford: Basil Blackwell, 1992), p. 99.

17. Ibid., p. 118.
18. Lorca, 'Thoughts on Modern Art', reprinted in Helen Oppenheimer, *Lorca: The Drawings* (London: Herbert Press, 1986), p. 128.
19. For a discussion of Lorca's New York paintings see Oppenheimer, *Lorca: The Drawings*, pp. 85–102.
20. Ibid., p. 130.
21. Lorca, *Poet in New York*, p. 186.
22. Ibid., p. 7.
23. Lorca, *Selected Letters*, ed. and trans. David Gershator (London: Marion Boyars, 1984), p. 146.
24. Ibid., p. 146.
25. Ibid., p. 148.
26. Ibid., p. 149.
27. Ibid., p. 151; p.155.
28. Lorca, *Poet in New York*, p. 185; p. 183.
29. Ibid., p. 11.
30. Ibid., p. 11.
31. Ibid., p. 186.
32. Ibid., p. 57; p. 53.
33. In his letters Lorca underplays both of these aspects: he claims he is able to 'adjust' himself to the city and he is 'making quick progress in English', which brush over the problems he had in adjusting culturally and linguistically to American life: Lorca, *Selected Letters*, p.151.
34. Lorca, *Poet in New York*, pp. 73–5.
35. Ibid., p. 11.
36. Ibid., p. 73.
37. Ibid., p. 47.
38. Ibid., p. 185.
39. Oppenheimer, *Lorca: The Drawings*, p. 86.
40. Lorca, *Poet in New York*, p. 185.
41. Ibid., p. 189.
42. See, for example, Sandburg's 'Skyscraper', published in *Chicago Poems* (1916), reprinted in Carl Sandburg, *Selected Poems* (New York: Gramercy Books, 1992), pp. 75–7.
43. Lorca, *Poet in New York*, p. 186; p. 189.
44. Ibid., p. 186.
45. David Johnston, *Federico García Lorca* (Bath: Absolute Press, 1998), p. 102.
46. Although Lorca can be accused of being a 'romantic racist' in his exoticising of the Harlemites, his empathy with their exiled condition follows his 'sympathetic understanding' of the plight of the Moors, Jews and gypsies in Spain which, he argued, 'all *granadinos* carry inside them': see Ian Gibson, *The Assassination of Federico García Lorca* (Harmondsworth: Penguin, 1983), pp. 22–3.
47. Lorca, *Poet in New York*, p. 189.
48. Ibid., p. 188.
49. Helen Oppenheimer notes that the mask, which recurs through Lorca's poems and drawings, links himself as the poet to the New York blacks: for example, in 'Dance of Death' he cries, 'The mask, look at the mask! How it comes from Africa to New York!'; Oppenheimer, *Lorca: The Drawings*, p. 91.

For my discussion of modernist masks see Chapter 8.
50. Lorca, *Poet in New York*, pp. 183–4.
51. Ibid., p. 187.
52. See the selections in the first section 'From Existence to Ethics' in *The Levinas Reader*, ed. Seán Hand (Oxford: Basil Blackwell, 1989).
53. Ibid., p. 198.
54. Lorca, *El Defens or de Granada* (7 May 1929), pp. 129–30; quoted in Richard Predmore, *Lorca's New York Poetry: Social Injustice, Dark Love, Lost Faith* (Durham, NC: Duke University Press, 1980), p. 6.
55. Michael Löwy, 'Libertarian Anarchism in *Amerika*', in Mark Anderson (ed.), *Reading Kafka: Prague, Politics and the Fin de Siècle* (New York: Schocken Books, 1989), p. 120; p. 121.
56. Mark Anderson, *Kafka's Clothes: Ornament and Aestheticism in the Habsburg Fin de Siècle* (Oxford: Clarendon Press, 1992), p. 107.
57. Franz Kafka, *America*, trans. Edwin Muir (London: Minerva, 1992), p. 255.
58. Frederick Karl, *Franz Kafka: Representative Man* (New York: Ticknor & Fields, 1991), p. 462.
59. Kafka, *America*, p. 12.
60. Ibid., p. 12.
61. Ibid., p. 12.
62. Ibid., pp. 12–13.
63. In his diary from 1917, Kafka resorts to an optical register when he describes 'The Stoker' as being Dickensian in its 'barbarism', but 'enhanced by the sharper lights I should have taken from the times [the early twentieth century] and the duller ones I should have got from myself': Kafka, *The Diaries of Franz Kafka, 1910–23*, ed. Max Brod (Harmondsworth: Penguin, 1972), p. 388.
64. Löwy, 'Libertarian Anarchism in *Amerika*', p. 122.
65. Ibid., p. 127.
66. Kafka, *America*, p. 42.
67. Ibid., p. 43.
68. Ibid., p. 54; Anderson, *Kafka's Clothes*, p. 109.
69. To substantiate this point, Mark Anderson cites Kafka's essay 'On Perception' ('*Über Apperzeption*') which was not published until 1966: ibid., p. 100.
70. Ibid., p. 101.
71. Anderson argues that 'theatricality' is more akin to the Parisian experience, whereas New York is 'cinematic' in its 'relentless movement of framed images': ibid., p. 120. It is perhaps better to consider the intermingling of 'the theatrical' and 'the cinematic' in early silent film for characterising the optical urban spectacle which Lorca and Karl Rossmann experience.
72. This uncertainty mirrors Kafka's declaration in a letter to Felice Bauer that the novel was 'falling apart' in front of him: 'I can no longer contain it ... it has recently become altogether too disconnected; wrong things appear and cannot be made to disappear': Franz Kafka, *Letters to Felice*, ed. James Stern and Jurgen Born (London: Minerva, 1992), p. 200.
73. Kafka, *America*, p. 42.
74. Ibid., p. 89.

75. Ibid., p. 167.
76. Ibid., p. 235; p. 234.
77. Ibid., p. 255.
78. Gustav Janouch, *Conversations with Kafka*, 2nd edn, trans. Goronwy Rees (New York: New Directions, 1971), p. 31.
79. Lorca, interview in *El Sol*, 15 December 1934; cited in Oppenheimer, *Lorca: The Drawings*, p. 115.

7 The modernist picaresque

1. For a reading of British literature in the 1930s see Maggie Clune *et al.*, 'Decline and Fall? The Course of the Novel', in *Literature and Culture in Modern Britain, Volume Two: 1930–1955* (London: Longman, 1997) and for a study of 1930s American writing see the third section of David Minter, *A Cultural History of the American Novel: Henry James to William Faulkner* (Cambridge: Cambridge University Press, 1996). See Ruth Brandon, *Surreal Lives: The Surrealists, 1917–1945* (London: Macmillan, 1999) for a discussion of French culture and the next chapter for a consideration of the transitions in German culture after the Weimar Period.
2. For readings of picaresque conventions see Robert Alter, *Rogue's Progress: Studies in the Picaresque Novel* (Cambridge, MA: Harvard University Press, 1964); Alexander Parker, *Literature and the Delinquent: The Picaresque Novel in Spain and Europe* (Edinburgh: Edinburgh University Press, 1967); and Richard Bjornson, *The Picaresque Hero in European Fiction* (Madison, WI: University of Wisconsin Press, 1977).
3. Philip Melling, 'Samples of Horizon: Picaresque Patterns in the Thirties', in Stephen W. Baskerville and Ralph Miller (eds), *Nothing Else to Fear: New Perspectives on America in the Thirties* (Manchester: Manchester University Press, 1985), p. 120.
4. Perhaps the closest modernist writers came to a truly despicable anti-hero is in the Spanish novelist Camilo José Cela's ironic novel *The Family of Pascual Duarte* (*La familia de Pascual Duarte*, 1942), dealing with the cataclysm of the Spanish Civil War as the eponymous anti-hero relates his violent tale while awaiting execution for murder.
5. Thomas Mann, *Confessions of Felix Krull, Confidence Man*, trans. Denver Lindley (Harmondsworth: Penguin, 1958), p. 13. *Felix Krull* was conceived at the same time as *Death in Venice* but only published posthumously in incomplete form.
6. Joan Copjec (ed.), *Radical Evil* (London: Verso, 1996), p. xi.
7. Ralph Barton Perry, *The Thought and Character of William James*, Volume 1 (Boston, MA: Little, Brown, 1935), p. 722. For a fuller discussion of Schopenhauer and James on wilfulness see Martin Halliwell, *Romantic Science and the Experience of Self* (London: Ashgate, 1999), pp. 42–50.
8. V. S. Naipaul, *A Bend In The River* (London: André Deutsch, 1979), p. 26.
9. Musil, *The Man Without Qualities*, Volume 1 (London: Minerva, 1995), p. 46.
10. Ibid., p. 26.
11. Karl Kraus, *Die Fackel* (1914), cited in Edward Timms, *Karl Kraus,*

Apocalyptic Satirist: Culture and Catastrophe in Habsburg Vienna (New Haven, CT: Yale University Press, 1986), p. 10.
12. Ibid., p. 26. In his earlier sketch 'A Man Without Character', Musil expresses the close relationship between 'character' and 'war': Musil, *Posthumous Papers of a Living Author*, trans. Peter Wortsman (Harmondsworth: Penguin, 1995), p. 113.
13. Musil, *The Man Without Qualities*, Volume 1, p. 46; Kraus, *Die Fackel* (1908), cited in Timms, *Karl Kraus*, p. 184.
14. Musil, *The Man Without Qualities*, Volume 1, pp. 25–6.
15. Quoted in Hannah Hickman, *Robert Musil and the Culture of Vienna* (London: Croom Helm, 1984), p. 3.
16. The three published volumes of *The Man Without Qualities* (1930, 1932 and 1943) can be described roughly in terms of: (1) Ulrich's reassessment of contemporary values; (2) the development of his creative life; and (3) the adventures resulting from such a life. The book is far too lengthy and eclectic to discuss in any detail here, so my commentary derives mainly from the first volume.
17. Musil, *The Man Without Qualities*, Volume 1, p. 34.
18. Ibid., p. 34; p. 36.
19. Ibid., p. 47; p. 296.
20. Ibid., p. 297.
21. Ibid., p. 176.
22. Ibid., p. 74.
23. Ibid., p. 75.
24. Ibid., p. 288.
25. Ibid., p. 75; p. 84.
26. Ibid., p. 287.
27. Ibid., p. 294.
28. Ibid., p. 294.
29. Ibid., pp. 296–7.
30. Ibid., pp. 297–8.
31. Ibid., 301; p. 298.
32. Ibid., p. 177.
33. Although *Steppenwolf* was published in 1927, it compares well with the other 1930s modernist picaresques discussed here, as well as prefiguring some of the major themes that Hesse explored in his fiction from the 1930s and early 1940s, especially *Narziss and Goldmund* (1930) and *The Glass-Bead Game* (*Das Glasperlenspiel*, 1943).
34. Herman Hesse, *Steppenwolf*, trans. Basil Creighton, revised Walter Sorell (Harmondsworth: Penguin, 1965), p. 20.
35. Ibid., p. 28; p. 27.
36. Ibid., p. 6. Like Musil's work, *Steppenwolf* can be understood, to use Mark Boulby's phrase, as an 'interpretative novel' (together with Hesse's early novel *Demian*, 1919), in which 'nothing is presented wholly free of the author's interpretative hindsight'; Mark Boulby, *Herman Hesse: His Mind and Art* (Ithaca, NY: Cornell University Press, 1967), p. 96. While there is certainly a deliberate aesthetic at work in *Steppenwolf*, it coaxes the reader to experience with Haller, rather than being didactic in the neo-classical mode of instructive literature.

37. Hesse, *Steppenwolf*, pp. 39–40.
38. Ibid., p. 41.
39. Ibid., p. 71.
40. Ibid., p. 71.
41. Ibid., p. 165.
42. Sigmund Freud, *Jokes and their Relation to the Unconscious*, trans. James Strachey (Harmondsworth: Penguin, 1976), p. 299.
43. Henri Bergson, *Laughter*, trans. Fred Rothwell (London: Macmillan, 1911), p. 6.
44. Wolfgang Iser, 'The Reading Process: A Phenomenological Approach', in David Lodge (ed.), *Modern Criticism and Theory* (London: Longman, 1988), p. 220.
45. Melling, 'Samples of Horizon: Picaresque Patterns in the Thirties', p. 112.
46. Ibid., p. 111.
47. Ibid., p. 113. While the American *pícaro* is normally male, as David Wyatt comments (and Zora Neale Hurston attests in relation to women): 'humanity is now stationed in the middle ... of history, and wandering is no longer a male but a human prerogative': David Wyatt (ed.), *New Essays on The Grapes of Wrath* (Cambridge: Cambridge University Press, 1990), p. 19.
48. Melling, 'Samples of Horizon', p. 115.
49. Jeanne Rosier Smith, *Writing Tricksters: Mythic Gambols in American Ethnic Literature* (Berkeley, CA: University of California Press, 1997), p. xiii.
50. John W. Roberts, 'The African American Animal Trickster as Hero', in A. LaVonne Brown Ruoff and Jerry W. Ward (eds), *Redefining American Literary History* (New York: The Modern Language Association of America, 1990), p. 100. Also see Roberts, *From Trickster to Badman: The Black Folk Hero in Slavery and Freedom* (Philadelphia, PA: University of Pennsylvania Press, 1989).
51. Ibid., p. 110.
52. Ibid., p. 110; p. 111.
53. Zora Neale Hurston, 'How It Feels to Be Colored Me' (1928), in Henry Louis Gates Jnr and Nellie Y. McKay (eds), *The Norton Anthology of African-American Literature* (New York: Norton, 1997), p. 1009.
54. Ibid., p. 1009.
55. Hurston, 'Characteristics of Negro Expression' (1934), ibid., p. 1025; p. 1024.
56. Smith, *Writing Tricksters*, p. 1.
57. June Jordan, 'On Richard Wright and Zora Neale Hurston: Notes Toward a Balancing of Love and Hatred', *Black World*, August 1974, 6.
58. Hurston, *Their Eyes Were Watching God* (London: Virago, 1986), p. 133.
59. Ibid., p. 146.
60. Ibid., p. 271.
61. Ibid., p. 278.
62. Ibid., p. 280.
63. Hurston, 'How It Feels to Be Colored Me', p. 1010.
64. Ibid., p. 1010. Whereas Mann's theatrical impersonator Felix Krull embodies one sense of the *pícaro* as fabricator, Janie weaves the fabric of daily life into a fulfilling spiritual vision.

65. Roth tried to write a proletarian novel as a follow up to *Call It Sleep* but felt inhibited by ideological obligation to the extent that it was never finished. An extract, 'If We Have Bacon', was published in *Signatures: Works in Progress*, 1:2 (1936), 139–58.
66. Roth, *Shifting Landscape* (London: Weidenfeld & Nicolson, 1995), p. 110.
67. Adam Zachary Newton, *Facing Black and Jew: Literature as Public Space in Twentieth-Century America* (Cambridge: Cambridge University Press, 1999), p. 5; p. 3.
68. Henry Roth, *Call It Sleep* (Harmondsworth: Penguin, 1977), p. 171.
69. Ibid., pp. 190–1.
70. Ibid., p. 191.
71. Ibid., p. 376.
72. The pessimistic outcome of *Steppenwolf* and the optimistic ending of *Call It Sleep* can partly be explained by the age difference between Haller (middle-aged) and David (youthful), reflecting, to a degree, the protagonists' ages and the moral focus of Mann's and Gide's novellas (discussed in Chapter 2).
73. Roth, *Shifting Landscape*, p. xxvi.
74. Roth, *Call It Sleep*, p. 376.
75. Newton, *Facing Black and Jew*, p. 48.
76. Roth, *Call It Sleep*, p. 417.
77. Ibid., p. 379. Here, David's state of being approximates to Emmanuel Levinas's description of the 'eternal vigilance which we cannot avoid by falling asleep'. See Levinas's 'There Is: Existence Without Existents', *The Levinas Reader*, ed. Seán Hand (Oxford: Basil Blackwell, 1989), pp. 29–36.

8 Myths of the magician

1. For example, in his essay 'Memoranda on Masks' (1932) Eugene O'Neill asked: 'what, at bottom, is the new psychological insight into human cause and effect but a study in masks, an exercise in unmasking?'; quoted by Egil Törnqvist in Michael Mannheim (ed.), *The Cambridge Companion to Eugene O'Neill* (Cambridge: Cambridge University Press, 1998), pp. 22–3.
2. Motherwell, *The Dada Painters and Poets: An Anthology* (New York: George Wittenborn, 1951), p. 27.
3. As the film historian Anton Kaes argues, despite becoming German exiles and having profound ideological differences with Nazism, émigrés such as Brecht and the Manns 'still passionately indulged in fantasies of Germany': Anton Kaes, *From Hitler to Heimat: The Return of History as Film* (Cambridge, MA: Harvard University Press, 1989), p. 72.
4. Klaus Mann, *Mephisto*, trans. Robin Smith (Harmondsworth: Penguin, 1995), p. 230; p. 11; p. 15.
5. Significantly, *Liebelei* (an adaptation from Arthur Schnitzler) was Ophüls' last German film before he went into exile in Europe and then America.
6. As Alexandra Richie comments: the 'story is also a metaphor for Berlin, and for all the people who sold their souls for the fame and fortune, security and success afforded by the new regime': Alexandra Richie, *Faust's Metropolis: A History of Berlin* (London: HarperCollins, 1998), p. li.

In addition to Gründgens, *Mephisto* mocks the poet Gottfried Benn (Benjamin Pelz), the actress Emmy Sonnemann (Lotte Lindensthal) and André Germain (Pierre Larue), who all stayed in Berlin to enhance their prospects under the new regime. The relationship between Klaus and Erika is dramatised in Andrea Weiss's and Weiland Speck's documentary film *Escape to Life: The Erika and Klaus Mann Story* (Germany/UK, 2000).
7. Marcel Reich-Ranicki, *Thomas Mann and His Family*, trans. Ralph Manheim (London: Collins, 1989), p. 153.
8. Quoted in Eberhard Spangenberg, *Karriere eines Romans: Mephisto, Klaus Mann und Gustaf Gründgens* (Munich: Ellermann, 1982), p. 26. Spangenberg discusses the controversy surrounding *Mephisto* after the end of the Nazi period: it was banned twice in Germany after Klaus's death in 1949 and a paperback version did not appear until the early 1980s.
9. Mann, *The Turning Point: Thirty-Five Years in this Century: The Autobiography of Klaus Mann* (London: Oswald Wolff, 1984), p. 116.
10. Quoted in the foreword to Volume 1 of Robert Musil's *The Man Without Qualities* (London: Minerva, 1995), p. xxviii.
11. Mann, *Mephisto*, p. 69.
12. Ibid., p. 152.
13. Walter Benjamin, 'The Country Where it is Forbidden to Mention the Proletariat', *Understanding Brecht*, trans. Anna Bostock (London: NLB, 1977), p. 40.
14. Bertolt Brecht, *Brecht on Theatre*, ed. John Willett (London: Eyre Methuen, 1964), p. 125.
15. Mann, *The Turning Point*, p. 282.
16. Mann, *Mephisto*, p. 77; p. 116.
17. Benjamin, 'The Author as Producer', *Understanding Brecht*, p. 100. Although there are parallels between their responses to Nazi Germany, Benjamin believed that both Heinrich and Klaus Mann placed too much emphasis on 'the will' and 'the intellect' (on this count they could only ever be counter-revolutionaries), rather than dealing directly with the proletariat and the material means of production. Despite this, Benjamin sent a number of manuscripts to Klaus while he was editor of *Die Sammlung* in Amsterdam, indicating that the rift was not unbreachable. See Momme Brodersen, *Walter Benjamin: A Biography*, trans. Malcolm R. Green and Ingrida Ligers, (London: Verso, 1996), pp. 213–15.
18. Mann, *Mephisto*, p. 17. It is important to note that although Gründgens remained in Germany in the 1930s and 1940s, his dealings with the Third Reich were not as close as the novel suggests. He was cleared of the label of 'Nazi sympathiser' and went on performing after 1945.
19. Ibid., p. 10.
20. Walter Benjamin, 'The Work of Art in the Age of Mechanical Reproduction', *Illuminations*, ed. Hannah Arendt, trans. Harry Zohn (London: Fontana, 1973), p. 243.
21. Mann, *Mephisto*, p. 9.
22. Benjamin defines 'aura' as 'the unique phenomenon of a distance, however close it may be', suggesting an aesthetic disguise (*Schein*) and a masking of true intentions behind the veil of illusion: Benjamin, *Illuminations*, p. 222. On this model, the aura ensures the autonomy of the

work of art by encasing it 'in a realm hermetically sealed off from the outer world and from the production relations of art': Andreas Huyssen, *After the Great Divide: Modernism, Mass Culture and Postmodernism* (London: Macmillan, 1986), p. 144.
23. See Pamela Clemit, *The Godwinian Novel: The Rational Fictions of Godwin, Brockden Brown, Mary Shelley* (Oxford: Clarendon Press, 1993), pp. 115–16.
24. Mann, *Mephisto*, p. 153.
25. Klaus Mann and Hermann Kesten (eds), *Heart of Europe: An Anthology of Creative Writing in Europe, 1920–1940* (New York: Fischer, 1943), p. xxv.
26. Mann, *Mephisto*, p. 97.
27. Ibid., p. 249.
28. Mann, *The Turning Point*, p. x.
29. Ibid., p. 3.
30. Ibid., p. ix.
31. See Benjamin's essay 'On the Concept of History' ('Über den Begriff der Geschichte', written in 1940), *Die Neue Rundschau*, 61 (1950), 560–70 and Arendt's collection *Between Past and Future* (Harmondsworth: Penguin, 1961).
32. Ibid., p. ix.
33. Ibid., p. 9.
34. Ibid., p. 5.
35. Ibid., p. 5.
36. Ibid., p. 4.
37. Ibid., p. 8, p. 39.
38. Thomas's patriotic conservatism declined rapidly after 1922 with the emergence of what he saw as the barbarism of extremist national groups and the assassination of the Republican Foreign Minister of the Weimar Republic, Walter Rathenau. For an interesting early review of *Reflections of an Unpolitical Man* (also translated as *Reflections of a Stranger to Politics*) see Genevieve Maury, 'Germany and Democracy', *Living Age*, 16 July 1921, 142–8 (originally in the Swiss political and literary monthly *La Revue de Genève*, February 1921).
39. W. H. Auden, 'To a Writer on His Birthday' (1935), *The English Auden*, ed. Edward Mendelson (London: Faber & Faber, 1977), p. 157.
40. Thomas Mann, *The Letters of Thomas Mann*, trans. Richard and Clara Winston (Harmondsworth: Penguin, 1970), p. 132.
41. Martin Travers, *Thomas Mann* (New York: St Martin's Press, 1992), p. 77.
42. Thomas Mann, *Mario and the Magician and Other Stories*, trans. H. T. Lowe-Porter (Harmondsworth: Penguin, 1975), p. 123.
43. Ibid., p. 138; p. 135.
44. Ibid., p. 145.
45. Both Martin Travers and Alan Bance characterise Cipolla as a 'demonic artist', reinforcing the equation of art and magic; see Alan Bance, *Mann the Magician, or The Good Versus the Interesting* (Southampton: University of Southampton, 1987), p. 17.
46. Walter Benjamin, 'Hitler's Diminished Masculinity' (1934), in Walter Benjamin, *Selected Writings, Volume 2, 1927–1934*, ed. Michael W. Jennings, trans. Rodney Livingstone (Cambridge, MA: Belknap Press, 1999), p. 792.

47. Thomas Mann, *Briefe I* (Frankfurt: S. Fischer, 1961), p. 315.
48. Mann, *Mephisto*, p. 11; p. 179; p. 203.
49. Ibid., p. 90.
50. Elizabeth Houston, 'Appropriations of Shakespeare in Nazi Germany', unpublished dissertation (University of Leicester, 2000), p. 11. Klaus's comments in the journal *Das Wort* in 1937 are useful on this subject. He claims: 'I left Germany ... because if I'd remained in "freedom," I would have had to suffocate in the air of the Third Reich'; quoted by Shelley Frisch in the introduction to the 1984 translation of *The Turning Point* (London: Oswald Wolff, 1984), p. 7.
51. Reich-Ranicki, *Thomas Mann and His Family*, p. 157, p. 156.
52. Herman Hesse, *Steppenwolf* (Harmondsworth: Penguin, 1965), p. 6.
53. Klaus's political realism is more in line with his father's later position, an example of which is evident in a BBC Radio broadcast in June 1952, 'The Artist and Society', in which Thomas claimed that 'behind the word "society" the political stands hidden ... It is very badly hidden behind it, because the artist as critic of society is already made political, is already the politicising artist – or, in a word: the moralising artist.'
54. Siegfried Kracauer, *From Caligari to Hitler: A Psychological History of the German Film* (Princeton, NJ: Princeton University Press, 1947), p. 30.
55. Marshall Berman, *All That Is Solid Melts Into Air* (London: Verso, 1983), p. 37.
56. Ibid., p. 40.
57. Ibid., p. 43; p. 171.
58. Ian Watt, *Myths of Modern Individualism: Faust, Don Quixote, Don Juan and Robinson Crusoe* (Cambridge: Cambridge University Press, 1997), pp. 204–5.
59. Christopher Marlowe, *The Tragical History of the Life and Death of Dr. Faustus*, ed. John Jump (London: Methuen, 1981), p. 14.
60. Ibid., p. 87; p. 76.
61. Mann, *Mephisto*, p. 72; p. 109.
62. Ibid., p. 78.
63. Ibid., p.105; p.112; p.105.
64. Ibid., p. 123.
65. Ibid., p. 52; p. 108. In Hamburg, Höfgen is described as doing 'good work' but it is his wish to transcend morality and to 'join the ranks of the great' that leads to his downfall: see p. 184.
66. The 'propaganda of disgust' is a phrase developed in the three-part Channel 4 series 'The Anatomy of Disgust' broadcast in the UK in August 2000.
67. Mann, *Mephisto*, pp. 178–9.
68. Ibid., p. 180.
69. Ibid., p.189. The prime minister declares 'isn't there a bit of him in us all? I mean, hidden in every real German isn't there a bit of Mephistopheles, a bit of the rascal and the ruffian?'; p. 189.
70. Ibid., pp. 225–6, p. 254.
71. Ibid., p. 243.
72. Ibid., p. 263.
73. Benjamin, *Understanding Brecht*, p. 100.

Conclusion: liberating the fear of modernity

1. Thomas Hardy, *Jude the Obscure* (Harmondsworth: Penguin, 1986), p. 56.
2. Ibid., p. 57.
3. Ibid., p. 71.
4. Ibid., p. 71.
5. Franz Kafka, *The Diaries of Franz Kafka 1910–1923*, ed. Max Brod (Harmondsworth: Penguin, 1972), p. 330.
6. For a post-Marxist consideration of this lowering of 'ontological pretensions' see Ernesto Laclau, 'Politics and the Limits of Modernity', in Andrew Ross (ed.), *Universal Abandon* (Edinburgh University Press, 1988), pp. 63–82 and Laclau's and Chantal Mouffe's *Hegemony and Socialist Strategy: Towards a Radical Democratic Politics* (London: Verso, 1988).
7. One interesting example of the fear and renunciation of freedom is found at the end of Saul Bellow's Second World War novel *Dangling Man* (1944).
8. Zygmunt Bauman, *Postmodernity: Chance or Menace?* (Lancaster: Centre for the Study of Cultural Values, 1991), p. 2.
9. Alasdair MacIntyre, *After Virtue: A Study in Moral Theory*, 2nd edn (London: Duckworth, 1985), p. 250.
10. Stanley Cavell, *Conditions Handsome and Unhandsome* (Chicago, IL: Chicago University Press, 1990), p. 31.
11. Richard Bernstein, *The New Constellation: The Ethical-Political Horizons of Modernity/Postmodernity* (Cambridge: Polity Press, 1991), p. 74.
12. Robert Musil, *The Man Without Qualities*, Volume 1 (London: Minerva, 1995), p. 49.
13. Kafka, *The Diaries of Franz Kafka*, p. 330.
14. Zygmunt Bauman, *Life in Fragments* (Oxford: Basil Blackwell, 1995), p. 18; p. 12.
15. Ibid., p. 42.
16. Ibid., p. 36.
17. Bauman, *Postmodernity: Chance or Menace?*, p. 5.
18. Jürgen Habermas, 'Modernity – An Incomplete Project', in Hal Foster (ed.), *Postmodern Culture* (London: Pluto Press, 1985), p. 12.
19. William Corlett, *Community Without Unity* (Durham, NC: Duke University Press, 1993), p. 3.
20. Habermas, 'Modernity – An Incomplete Project', p. 137.
21. See Peter Osborne, *The Politics of Time* (London: Verso, 1995), pp. 1–29 and Robert Eaglestone, *Ethical Criticism* (Edinburgh: Edinburgh University Press, 1998), pp. 175–7.
22. A phrase taken from the title of Page Stegner's book on Vladimir Nabokov: Page Stegner, *Escape Into Aesthetics* (London: Eyre & Spottiswoode, 1987).
23. Saul Bellow, 'The Writer as Moralist', *Atlantic Monthly*, 211 (March 1963), 58. Henry Roth made a more radical statement about the moral condition of America in 1966: 'I don't believe that American society, taking it by and large, deserves to exist, morally; and if it doesn't morally it doesn't deserve to exist in any other way': Henry Roth, *Shifting Landscape* (London: Weidenfeld & Nicolson, 1995), p. 129.
24. Myra N. Love, *Christa Wolf: Literature and the Conscience of History* (Berlin: Peter Lang, 1991), p. 67.

25. Christa Wolf, *Cassandra: A Novel and Four Essays*, trans. Jan Van Heurck (London: Virago, 1984), pp. 106–7.
26. Christa Wolf, *The Writer's Dimension: Selected Essays* (London: Virago, 1993), p. 53.
27. Love, *Christa Wolf: Literature and the Conscience of History*, p. 35.
28. Paul Auster, *New York Trilogy* (London: Faber & Faber, 1988), p. 78.
29. See, for example, Peter Brooker, *New York Fictions* (London: Longman, 1996), pp. 155–9 and Kenneth Millard, *Contemporary American Fiction* (Oxford: Oxford University Press, 2000), pp. 180–5.
30. Auster, *The Red Notebook and Other Writings* (London: Faber & Faber, 1995), p. 109.
31. Auster, *New York Trilogy*, p. 8.
32. Ibid., p. 72; p. 76.
33. Auster, *The Red Notebook*, p. 109.
34. Auster, *New York Trilogy*, p. 3.
35. Ibid., p. 56.
36. Auster, *Leviathan* (London: Faber & Faber, 1993), p. 98.
37. Ibid., p. 117.
38. Auster, *Ground Work: Selected Poems and Essays 1970–1979* (London: Faber & Faber, 1990), p. 134.
39. Auster, *New York Trilogy*, p. 251.
40. Michel Foucault, *The History of Sexuality, Volume 1: An Introduction*, trans. Robert Hurley (Harmondsworth: Penguin, 1981), p. 90; Foucualt, 'The Eye of Power', in Colin Gordon (ed.), *Power/Knowledge: Selected Interviews and Other Writings* (London: Harvester, 1980), p. 156.
41. Foucault, *The History of Sexuality, Volume 2: The Use of Pleasure* (Harmondsworth: Penguin, 1992), p. 25.
42. Foucault, 'On the Genealogy of Ethics', in Paul Rabinow (ed.), *Ethics: Subjectivity and Truth*, trans. Robert Hurley (London: Allen Lane, 1997), p. 256.
43. Francis Fukuyama, *The Great Disruption: Human Nature and the Reconstitution of Social Order* (London: Profile, 1999), p. 251; p. 254.
44. Ibid., p. 255.
45. Bauman, *Postmodernity: Chance or Menace?*, p. 15.
46. Naomi Klein, *No Logo* (London: HarperCollins, 2000), p. xviii.
47. Ibid., p. xviii. See Shaya Mercer's documentary *Trade Off* (US, 2000) for vivid footage of the Seattle demonstrations.
48. Ibid., p. 5.
49. Ibid., pp. 445–6.
50. Adrienne Rich, 'Compulsory Heterosexuality and Lesbian Existence' (1980), reprinted in *Adrienne Rich's Poetry and Prose*, eds Barbara Charlesworth Gelpi and Albert Gelpi (New York: Norton, 1993), pp. 203–24.
51. MacIntyre, *After Virtue*, p. 6.
52. Stuart Hall, 'New Ethnicities' (1989), in David Morley and Kuan-Hsing Chen (eds), *Stuart Hall: Critical Dialogues in Cultural Studies* (London: Routledge, 1996), p. 443.
53. An example of the corporate ownership of art is embodied in the 'Sensation' Exhibition, first shown at the Royal Academy, London in 1997, sponsored by the public relations and media mogul Charles Saatchi.

54. Colin Rhodes, *Outsider Art: Spontaneous Alternatives* (London: Thames & Hudson, 2000), p. 22.
55. Wolf, *The Writer's Dimension*, p. 54.

Bibliography

Adamson, Jane *et al.* (eds), *Renegotiating Ethics in Literature, Philosophy, and Theory* (Cambridge: Cambridge University Press, 1998).
Addelson, Kathryn Pyne, *Moral Passages: Towards a Collectivist Moral Theory* (New York: Routledge, 1994).
Adorno, Theodor, *Minima Moralia: Reflections from Damaged Life*, trans. E. F. N. Jephcott (London: Verso, 1984).
Adorno, Theodor and Max Horkheimer, *Dialectic of Enlightenment* (London: Verso, 1979).
Anderson, Mark, (ed.), *Reading Kafka: Prague, Politics and the Fin de Siècle* (New York: Schocken Books, 1989).
—— *Kafka's Clothes: Ornament and Aestheticism in the Habsburg Fin de Siècle* (Oxford: Clarendon Press, 1992).
Appignanesi, Lisa, *Femininity and the Creative Imagination: A Study of Henry James, Robert Musil and Marcel Proust* (London: Vision Press, 1973).
Aragon, Louis, 'A Man', *Little Review*, 9:4 (Autumn/Winter 1923–24), 18.
—— *Paris Peasant*, trans. Simon Watson Taylor (London: Jonathan Cape, 1971).
—— *The Libertine*, trans. Jo Levy (London: John Calder, 1993).
—— *Treatise on Style*, trans. Alyson Waters (Lincoln, NB: University of Nebraska Press, 1991).
Archer-Straw, Petrine, *Negrophilia* (London: Thames & Hudson, 2000).
Arendt, Hannah, *Between Past and Future* (Harmondsworth: Penguin, 1993).
Armstrong, Tim, *Modernism, Technology and the Body: A Cultural Study* (Cambridge: Cambridge University Press, 1998).
Artaud, Antonin, *Artaud Anthology*, ed. Jack Hirschman, 2nd edn (San Francisco, CA: City Lights, 1965).
Auden, W. H., *The English Auden: Poems, Essays and Dramatic Writings, 1927–1939*, ed. Edward Mendelson (London: Faber & Faber, 1977).
Auerbach, Erich, *Mimesis: The Representation of Reality in Western Fiction* (Princeton, NJ: Princeton University Press, 1953).
Auster, Paul, *The Invention of Solitude* (London: Faber & Faber, 1988).
—— *The New York Trilogy* (London: Faber & Faber, 1988).
—— *Ground Work: Selected Poems and Essays 1970–1979* (London: Faber & Faber, 1990).
—— *Leviathan* (London: Faber & Faber, 1993).
—— *The Red Notebook and Other Writings* (London: Faber & Faber, 1995).
Awkward, Michael (ed.), *New Essays on* Their Eyes Were Watching God (Cambridge: Cambridge University Press, 1990).
Ball, Hugo, *Flight Out of Time: A Dada Diary*, ed. John Elderfield, trans. Ann Raimes (Berkeley, CA: University of California Press, 1996).
Bammer, Angelika, *Displacements: Cultural Identities in Question* (Bloomington, W: Indiana University Press, 1995).
Bance, Alan, *Mann the Magician, or The Good Versus the Interesting*, published lecture (Southampton: University of Southampton, 1987).

Bangerter, Lowell, *Robert Musil* (New York: Continuum, 1988).
Barker, Paul (ed.), *Arts in Society* (London: Fontana, 1977).
Baudelaire, Charles, *Selected Writings on Art and Literature*, trans. P. E. Charvet (Harmondsworth: Penguin, 1992).
Bauman, Zygmunt, *Postmodernity: Chance or Menace?*, published lecture (Lancaster: Centre for the Study of Cultural Values, 1991).
—— *Life In Fragments* (Oxford: Basil Blackwell, 1995).
Becker, Lucille, *Louis Aragon* (New York: Twayne, 1971).
Bederman, Gail, *Manliness and Civilization* (Chicago, IL: University of Chicago Press, 1995).
Bell, Michael Davitt, *The Problem of American Realism: Studies in the Cultural History of a Literary Idea* (Chicago, IL: University of Chicago Press, 1993).
Bellow, Saul, 'The Writer as Moralist', *Atlantic Monthly*, 211 (March 1963), 58–62.
Benhabib, Seyla, *Situating the Self: Gender, Community and Postmodernism in Contemporary Ethics* (Cambridge: Polity Press, 1992).
Benjamin, Walter, *Illuminations*, ed. Hannah Arendt, trans. Harry Zohn (London: Fontana, 1973).
—— *Understanding Brecht*, trans. Anna Bostock (London: NLB, 1977).
—— *One Way Street and Other Writings*, ed. Susan Sontag, trans. Edmund Jephcott and Kingsley Shorter (London: Verso, 1992).
—— *Selected Writings, Volume 2, 1927–1934*, ed. Michael W. Jennings, trans. Rodney Livingstone (Cambridge, MA: Belknap Press, 1999).
Bentley, Eric (ed.), *The Theory of the Modern Stage* (Harmondsworth: Penguin, 1990).
Bergson, Henri, *Laughter*, trans. Fred Rothwell (London: Macmillan, 1911).
Berman, Marshall, *All That Is Solid Melts Into Air* (London: Verso, 1983).
Bernstein, Richard, *The New Constellation: The Ethical-Political Horizons of Modernity/Postmodernity* (Cambridge: Polity Press, 1991).
Berry, Ellen, *Curved Thought and Textual Wandering: Gertrude Stein's Postmodernism* (Ann Arbor, MI: University of Michigan Press, 1992).
Bersani, Leo, *Marcel Proust: The Fictions of Life and Art* (New York: Oxford University Press, 1965).
—— *Balzac to Beckett: Center and Circumference in French Fiction* (New York: Oxford University Press, 1970).
Bloom, Harold *Anxiety of Influence: A Theory of Poetry* (London: Oxford University Press, 1973).
Bloom, Harold (ed.), *Franz Kafka's* Metamorphosis (New York: Chelsea House, 1988).
Boa, Elizabeth, *Kakfa: Gender, Class and Race in the Letters and Fictions* (Oxford: Clarendon Press, 1996).
Boulby, Mark, *Herman Hesse: His Mind and Art* (Ithaca, NY: Cornell University Press, 1967).
Bourne, Randolph, *The Radical Will*, ed. Olaf Hansen (New York: Urizen, 1977).
Bradbury, Malcolm, *Dangerous Pilgrimages: Trans-Atlantic Mythologies and the Novel* (Harmondsworth: Penguin, 1996).
Brandon, Ruth, *Surreal Lives: The Surrealists 1917–1945* (London: Macmillan, 1999).
Brecht, Bertolt, *Brecht on Theatre: The Development of an Aesthetic*, ed. and trans.

John Willett (London: Eyre Methuen, 1964).
Brennan, Teresa and Martin Jay, *Vision in Context: Historical and Contemporary Perspectives on Sight* (London: Routledge, 1996).
Breton, André, *Nadja*, trans. Richard Howard (New York: Grove Press, 1960).
—— *Manifestoes of Surrealism*, trans. Richard Seaver and Helen R. Lane (Ann Arbor, MI: University of Michigan Press, 1972).
—— *Mad Love*, trans. Mary Ann Caws (Lincoln, NB: University of Nebraska Press, 1987).
—— *Communicating Vessels*, trans. Mary Ann Caws and Geoffrey T. Haris (Lincoln, NB: University of Nebraska Press, 1990).
—— *Earthlight*, trans. Bill Zavatsky and Zack Rogow (Toronto: Coach House Press, 1993).
Breton, André and Paul Eluard, *The Immaculate Conception*, trans. John Graham (London: Atlas Press, 1990).
Broch, Hermann, *The Death of Virgil*, trans. Jean Starr Untermeyer (New York: Vintage, 1995).
Brodersen, Momme, *Walter Benjamin: A Biography*, trans. Malcolm R. Green and Ingrida Ligers (London: Verso, 1996).
Brombert, Victor, *The Intellectual Hero: Studies in the French Novel, 1880–1955* (London: Faber & Faber, 1961).
Brooker, Peter (ed.), *Modernism/Postmodernism* (London: Longman, 1992).
—— *New York Fictions: Modernity, Postmodernism, The New Modern* (London: Longman, 1996).
Brown, Milton, *The Story of the Armory Show* (New York: Abbeville, 1988).
Buci-Glucksmann, Christine, *Baroque Reason: The Aesthetics of Modernity*, trans. Patrick Camiller (London: Sage, 1994).
Burgin, Victor, *In/Different Spaces: Place and Memory in Visual Culture* (Berkeley, CA: University of California Press, 1996).
Burwell, Rose, *Hemingway: The Postwar Years and the Posthumous Novels* (Cambridge: Cambridge University Press, 1996).
Butler, Christopher, *Early Modernism: Literature, Music and Painting in Europe 1900–1916* (Oxford: Clarendon Press, 1994).
Butler, Judith, *The Psychic Life of Power: Theories of Subjection* (Stanford, CA: Stanford University Press, 1997).
Cannon, Kelly, *Henry James and Masculinity: The Men at the Margins* (London: Macmillan, 1994).
Cartmell, Deborah *et al.* (eds), *Classics in Film and Fiction* (London: Pluto Press, 2000).
Cavell, Stanley, *This New Yet Unapproachable America* (Albuquerque, NM: Living Batch, 1989).
—— *Conditions Handsome and Unhandsome: The Constitution of Emersonian Perfectionism* (Chicago, IL: University of Chicago Press, 1990).
—— *The Senses of Walden: An Expanded Edition* (Chicago, IL: University of Chicago Press, 1992).
Caws, Mary Ann *et al.* (eds), *Surrealism and Women* (Cambridge, MA: MIT Press, 1991).
Chamberlain, J. Edward and Sander Gilman (eds), *Degeneration: The Dark Side of Progress* (New York: Columbia University Press, 1986).
Chambers, Iain, *Migrancy, Culture, Identity* (London: Routledge, 1994).

Chase, Richard, *The American Novel and its Tradition* (New York: Doubleday, 1957).
Chassegeut-Smirgel, Janine, *Creativity and Perversion* (New York: Norton, 1984).
Chernyshevsky, Nikolai, *What Is To Be Done?*, trans. Cathy Porther (London: Virago, 1982).
Ciatri, Pietro, *Kafka* (London: Secker & Warburg, 1990).
Clayton, Jack, *Saul Bellow: In Defense of Man*, 2nd edn (Bloomington, IN: Indiana University Press, 1979).
Clemit, Pamela, *The Godwinian Novel: The Rational Fictions of Godwin, Brockden Brown, Mary Shelley* (Oxford: Clarendon Press, 1993).
Cohen, Margaret, *Profane Illumination: Walter Benjamin and the Paris of Surrealist Revolution* (Berkeley, CA: University of California Press, 1993).
Conrad, Joseph, *Heart of Darkness* (Harmondsworth: Penguin, 1986).
—— *The Secret Agent* (Harmondsworth: Penguin, 1986).
Conroy, Mark, *Modernism and Authority: Strategies of Legitimation in Flaubert and Conrad* (Baltimore, MD: John Hopkins University Press, 1985).
Copjec, Joan (ed.), *Radical Evil* (London: Verso, 1996).
Copjec, Joan and Michael Sorkin (eds), *Giving Ground: The Politics of Propinquity* (London: Verso, 1999).
Corlett, William, *Community Without Unity* (Durham, NC: Duke University Press, 1993).
Cowley, Malcolm (ed.), *The Portable Hemingway* (New York: Viking, 1944).
—— *Exile's Return: A Literary Odyssey of the 1920s* (New York: Penguin, 1994).
Crane, Stephen, *The Works of Stephen Crane*, Volume 5, *Tales of Adventure* (Charlottesville, VA: University Press of Virginia, 1970).
Critchley, Simon, *The Ethics of Deconstruction* (Oxford: Basil Blackwell, 1992).
Crunden, Robert, *American Salons: Encounters With European Modernism, 1885–1917* (New York: Oxford University Press, 1993).
Davies, Philip John (ed.), *Representing and Imagining America* (Keele: Keele University Press, 1996).
De Botton, Alain, *The Consolations of Philosophy* (London: Hamish Hamilton, 2000).
DeKoven, Marianne, *A Different Language: Gertrude Stein's Experimental Writing* (Madison, WI: University of Wisconsin Press, 1983).
Dellamora, Richard, *Masculine Desire: The Sexual Politics of Victorian Aestheticism* (Chapel Hill, NC: University of North Carolina Press, 1990).
Derrida, Jacques, *Of Grammatology*, trans. Gayatri Chakravorty Spivak (Baltimore, MD: Johns Hopkins University Press, 1970).
Dews, Peter, *The Limits of Disenchantment: Essays on Contemporary Continental Philosophy* (London: Verso, 1995).
Dickstein, Morris (ed.), *The Revival of Pragmatism: New Essays on Social Thought, Law, and Culture* (Durham, NC: Duke University Press, 1998).
Dollimore, Jonathan, *Sexual Dissidence: Augustine to Wilde, Freud to Foucault* (Oxford: Clarendon Press, 1991).
—— *Death, Desire and Loss in Western Culture* (Harmondsworth: Penguin, 1998).
Donaldson, Scott, *By Force of Will: The Life and Art of Hemingway* (New York: Viking, 1977).
—— (ed.), *The Cambridge Companion to Hemingway* (Cambridge: Cambridge University Press, 1996).

Dostoevsky, Fyodor, *The Idiot*, trans. David Magarshack (Harmondsworth: Penguin, 1955).
—— *Notes From Underground/The Double*, trans. Jessie Coulson (Harmondsworth: Penguin, 1972).
—— *Selected Letters of Fyodor Dostoyevsky*, eds Joseph Frank and David Goldstein, trans. Andrew MacAndrew (New Brunswick, NJ: Rutgers University Press, 1989).
Douglas, Ann, *The Feminization of American Culture* (New York: Macmillan, 1996).
—— *Terrible Honesty: Mongrel Manhattan in the 1920s* (London: Macmillan, 1997).
Dubnick, Randa, *The Structure of Obscurity: Gertrude Stein's Language and Cubism* (Urbana, IL: University of Illinois Press, 1984).
Eaglestone, Robert, *Ethical Criticism: Reading After Levinas* (Edinburgh: Edinburgh University Press, 1997).
Eliot, George, *Middlemarch* (Harmondsworth: Penguin, 1985).
Eliot, T. S., *Collected Poems, 1909–1962* (London: Faber & Faber, 1963).
Ellman, Maud, *The Poetics of Impersonality: T. S. Eliot and Ezra Pound* (Brighton: Harvester, 1987).
Ellman, Richard, *James Joyce* (Oxford: Oxford University Press, 1983).
Eluard, Paul, 'Poetry's Evidence', *This Quarter*, 5:1 (1932), 146.
Emerson, Ralph Waldo, *Essays and Lectures* (New York: Library of America, 1983).
Faulkner, William, *The Sound and the Fury*, ed. David Minter (New York: Norton, 1987).
—— *The Sound and the Fury* (London: Picador, 1989).
Felski, Rita, *The Gender of Modernity* (Cambridge, MA: Harvard University Press, 1995).
Ferraro, Thomas, *Ethnic Passages* (Chicago: University of Chicago Press, 1993).
Fiedler, Leslie, *Waiting for the End* (New York: Stein & Day, 1964).
Flaubert, Gustave, *Three Tales*, trans. A. J. Krailsheimer (Oxford: Oxford University Press, 1999).
Foster, Dennis, *Sublime Enjoyment: On the Perverse Motive in American Literature* (Cambridge: Cambridge University Press, 1997).
Foster, Hal (ed.), *Vision and Visuality* (Seattle, WA: Bay Press, 1988).
—— *Compulsive Beauty* (Cambridge, MA: MIT Press, 1995).
Foucault, Michel, *Power/Knowledge: Selected Interviews and Other Writings*, ed. Colin Gordon (London: Harvester, 1980).
—— *The History of Sexuality, Volume 1: An Introduction*, trans. Robert Hurley (Harmondsworth: Penguin, 1981).
—— *The History of Sexuality, Volume 2: The Use of Pleasure*, trans. Robert Hurley (Harmondsworth: Penguin, 1992).
—— *Ethics: Subjectivity and Truth*, ed. Paul Rabinow, trans. Robert Hurley (London: Allen Lane, 1997).
Fowler, Doreen and Ann J. Abadie (eds), *Faulkner and the Southern Renaissance* (Jackson, MI: University of Mississippi Press, 1982).
Freedman, Jonathan, *The Cambridge Companion to Henry James* (Cambridge: Cambridge University Press, 1998).
Freud, Sigmund, *The Standard Edition of the Complete Psychological Works of Sigmund Freud*, eds James Strachey and Anna Freud (London: Hogarth, 1964).

Freud, Sigmund, *Jokes and Their Relation to the Unconscious*, trans. James Strachey (Harmondsworth: Penguin, 1976).
Fukuyama, Francis, *The Great Disruption: Human Nature and the Reconstitution of Social Order* (London: Profile, 1999).
Fuss, Diana, *Essentially Speaking: Feminism, Nature and Difference* (New York: Routledge, 1989).
Galvin, Mary E., *Queer Poetics: Five Modernist Women Writers* (Westport, CT: Greenwood Press, 1999).
Gambrell, Alice, *Women Intellectuals, Modernism, and Difference: Transatlantic Culture, 1919–1945* (Cambridge: Cambridge University Press, 1997).
Garb, Tamar, *Modernity and Modernism* (New Haven, CT: Yale University Press, 1994).
Gates, Henry Louis, Jr. and Nellie Y. McKay (eds), *The Norton Anthology of African-American Literature* (New York: Norton, 1997).
Gay, Peter, *Weimar Culture: The Outsider as Insider* (Harmondsworth: Penguin, 1974).
Gee, J. A. and J. P. Sturm (eds), *Letters of Joseph Conrad to Marguerite Poradowska, 1890–1920* (London: Oxford University Press, 1940).
Gerth, H. H. and C. Wright Mills (eds), *From Max Weber: Essays in Sociology*, trans. H. H. Gerth and C. Wright Mills (London: Routledge, 1991).
Gibson, Andrew, *Postmodernity, Ethics and the Novel: From Leavis to Levinas* (London: Routledge, 1999).
Gibson, Ian, *The Assassination of Federico García Lorca* (Harmondsworth: Penguin, 1983).
Gide, André, *L'immoraliste* (Paris: Folio, 1902).
—— *The Immoralist*, trans. Dorothy Bussy (Harmondsworth: Penguin, 1960).
—— *The Counterfeiters*, trans. Dorothy Bussy (Harmondsworth: Penguin, 1996).
Gilbert, Sandra and Susan Gubar (eds), *The Female Imagination and the Modernist Aesthetic* (London: Gordon & Breach, 1986).
Gilman, Sander, *Pathology and Difference: Stereotypes of Sexuality, Race and Madness* (Ithaca, NY: Cornell University Press, 1985).
—— *Disease and Representation: Images of Illness from Madness to AIDS* (Ithaca, NY: Cornell University Press, 1985).
—— *Franz Kafka, the Jewish Patient* (New York: Routledge, 1995).
Gilroy, Paul, *The Black Atlantic* (London: Verso, 1993).
Goethe, Johann Wolfgang von, *Faust*, ed. Cyrus Hamlin, trans. Walter Arndt (New York: Norton, 1976).
Goldman, Harvey, *Max Weber and Thomas Mann: Calling and the Shaping of the Self* (Berkeley, CA: University of California Press, 1988).
Gordon, William, *The Mind and Art of Henry Miller* (London: Jonathan Cape, 1968).
Gould, Michael, *Surrealism and the Cinema* (New York: Barnes & Co, 1976).
Gourmont, Remy de, *The Angels of Perversity*, trans. Francis Amery (Cambridge: Dedalus, 1992).
Gray, Ronald, *Franz Kafka* (Cambridge: Cambridge University Press, 1973).
Greene, Robert, *Just Words: Moralism and Metalanguage in Twentieth-Century French Fiction* (University Park, PA: Pennsylvania State University Press, 1993).
Griffin, Peter, *Less Than a Treason: Hemingway in Paris* (New York: Oxford University Press, 1990).

Griffith, John, *Joseph Conrad and the Anthropological Dilemma: 'Bewildered Traveller'* (Oxford: Clarendon Press, 1995).
Grimm, Reinhold *et al.* (eds), *From Kafka and Dada to Brecht and Beyond* (Madison, WI: University of Wisconsin Press, 1982).
Grosz, Elizabeth, *Sexual Subversions: Three French Feminists* (London: Allen & Unwin, 1989).
Guerard, Albert, *André Gide* (Cambridge, MA: Harvard University Press, 1951; 2nd edn 1969).
Gurko, Leo, *Ernest Hemingway and the Pursuit of Heroism* (New York: Crowell, 1958).
Habermas, Jürgen, *The Theory of Communicative Action, Volume 1: Reason and Rationalization of Society*, trans. T. McCarthy (Cambridge: Polity Press, 1984).
—— 'Modernity – An Incomplete Project', in Hal Foster (ed.), *Postmodern Culture* (London: Pluto Press, 1985), pp. 3–15.
Hall, Stuart, *Critical Dialogues in Cultural Studies*, ed. David Morley and Kuan-Hsing Chen (London: Routledge, 1996).
Halliwell, Martin, *Romantic Science and the Experience of Self: Transatlantic Crosscurrents from William James to Oliver Sacks* (London: Ashgate, 1999).
Hampson, Robert, '"If You Read Lombroso": Conrad and Criminal Anthropology', *The Ugo Mursia Memorial Lectures*, ed. Mario Curreli (Milan: Mursia International, 1988), pp. 317–35.
Hamsun, Knut, *Hunger*, trans. Duncan McLean (Edinburgh: Rebel Inc., 1999).
Hansen, Arlen J., *Expatriate Paris: A Cultural and Literary Guide to Paris of the 1920s* (New York: Little, Brown, 1990).
Hardin, James (ed.), *Reflection and Action: Essays on the Bildungsroman* (Columbia, SC: University of South Carolina Press, 1991).
Hardy, Thomas, *A Pair of Blue Eyes* (London: Macmillan, 1975).
—— *Tess of the D'Urbervilles* (Harmondsworth: Penguin, 1978).
—— *Jude the Obscure* (Harmondsworth: Penguin, 1986).
Harper, Phillip Brian, *Framing the Margins: The Social Logic of Postmodern Culture* (New York: Oxford University Press, 1994).
Harvey, David, *The Conditions of Postmodernity* (Oxford: Basil Blackwell, 1991).
Hawes, James, *Nietzsche and the End of Freedom* (Frankfurt: Peter Lang, 1993).
Hayman, Ronald, *Thomas Mann: A Biography* (New York: Scribners, 1995).
Heilbut, Anthony, *Thomas Mann: Eros and Literature* (London: Macmillan, 1996).
—— *Exiled in Paradise: German Refugee Artists and Intellectuals in America: From the 1930s to the Present* (Berkeley, CA: University of California Press, 1997).
Hemingway, Ernest, *A Farewell to Arms* (New York: Scribner's, 1929).
—— *The Torrents of Spring* (London: Grafton, 1984).
—— *The Sun Also Rises* (New York: Scribner's, 1986).
—— *The Essential Hemingway* (London: Arrow, 1993).
—— *A Moveable Feast* (New York: Scribner's, 1994).
Henricksen, Bruce, *Nomadic Voices: Conrad and the Subject of Narrative* (Urbana, IL: University of Illinois Press, 1992).
Herr, Cheryl, *Joyce's Anatomy of Culture* (Urbana, IL: University of Illinois Press, 1986).
Hesse, Herman, *Steppenwolf*, trans. Basil Creighton (Harmondsworth: Penguin, 1965).

Hickman, Hannah, *Robert Musil and the Culture of Vienna* (London: Croom Helm, 1984).
Hoffman, Gerhard and Alfred Hornung (eds), *Ethics and Aesthetics: The Moral Turn of Postmodernism* (Heidelberg: Universitätsverlag C. Winter, 1996).
Horak, Jan-Christopher (ed.), *Lovers of Cinema: The First American Film Avant-Garde, 1919–1945* (Madison, WI: University of Wisconsin Press, 1995).
Houston, Elizabeth, 'Appropriations of Shakespeare in Nazi Germany', unpublished dissertation (University of Leicester, 2000).
Howells, William Dean, *W. D. Howells As Critic*, ed. E. H. Cady (London: Routledge & Kegan Paul, 1973).
Hubert, Renée, *Surrealism and the Book* (Berkeley, CA: University of California Press, 1988).
Huelsenbeck, Richard, *Memoirs of a Dada Drummer*, ed. Hans J. Kleinschmidt, trans. Joachim Neugroschel (Berkeley, CA: University of California Press, 1991).
Hunter, Allan, *Joseph Conrad and the Ethics of Darwinism* (London: Croom Helm, 1983).
Hurston, Zora Neale, *Their Eyes Were Watching God* (London: Virago, 1986).
—— *Mules and Men* (New York: HarperCollins, 1990).
—— *Go Gator and the Muddy Water*, ed. Pamela Bordelon (New York: Norton, 1999).
Hutcheon, Linda, *The Politics of Postmodernism* (London: Routledge, 1989).
Huysmans, Joris-Karl, *Against Nature*, trans. Robert Baldick (Harmondsworth: Penguin, 1959).
Huyssen, Andreas, *After the Great Divide: Modernism, Mass Culture and Postmodernism* (London: Macmillan, 1986).
—— *Twilight Memories* (London: Routledge, 1995).
Huyssen, Andreas and David Bathrick (eds), *Modernity and the Text: Revisions of German Modernism* (New York: Columbia University Press, 1989).
Ignatieff, Michael, *Virtual War: Kosovo and Beyond* (London: Chatto & Windus, 2000).
Ingram, Allan (ed.), *Joseph Conrad: Selected Literary Criticism and 'The Shadow-Line'* (London: Methuen, 1986).
Ionesco, Eugène, *Rhinoceros/The Chairs/The Lesson* (Harmondsworth: Penguin, 1962).
—— *Notes and Counternotes* (London: John Calder, 1964).
Irigaray, Luce, *This Sex Which Is Not One*, trans. Catherine Porter (Ithaca, NY: Cornell University Press, 1985).
—— *Elemental Passions*, trans. Joanne Collie and Judith Still (London: Athlone, 1992).
—— *An Ethics of Sexual Difference*, trans. Carolyn Burke and Gillian C. Gill (London: Athlone, 1993).
—— *Je, Tu, Nous: Towards a Cultural Difference*, trans. Alison Martin (New York: Routledge, 1993).
Iser, Wolfgang, *The Implied Reader* (Baltimore, MD: Johns Hopkins University Press, 1974).
—— 'The Reading Process: A Phenomenological Approach', in David Lodge (ed.), *Modern Criticism and Theory* (London: Longman, 1988), pp. 212–28.
Jacobs, Robert G., 'Comrade Ossipon's Favourite Saint: Lombroso and Conrad', *Nineteenth Century Fiction*, 23 (1969), 74–84.

James, Henry, *The Portrait of a Lady* (Harmondsworth: Penguin, 1986).
—— *The Critical Muse: Selected Literary Criticism*, ed. Roger Gard (Harmondsworth: Penguin, 1987).
—— *The American Scene*, ed. John Sears (Harmondsworth: Penguin, 1994).
—— *The Bostonians* (Oxford: Oxford University Press, 1998).
James, William, *The Principles of Psychology*, 2 volumes (New York: Dover, 1950).
—— *Talks to Teachers* (Cambridge, MA: Harvard University Press, 1983).
Jameson, Fredric, *Marxism and Form: Twentieth-Century Dialectic Theories of Literature* (London: Verso, 1972).
Janouch, Gustav, *Conversations With Kafka*, 2nd edn, trans. Goronwy Rees (New York: New Directions, 1971).
Jay, Mike and Michael Neve (eds), *1900: A Fin-de-siècle Reader* (Harmondsworth: Penguin, 2000).
Jehlen, Myra, *Class and Character in Faulkner's South* (New York: Columbia University Press, 1976).
Jelavich, Peter, *Munich and Theatrical Modernism: Politics, Playwriting, and Performance 1890–1914* (Cambridge, MA: Harvard University Press, 1985).
Johnson, David, *Federico García Lorca* (Bath: Absolute Press, 1998).
Jordan, June, 'On Richard Wright and Zora Neale Hurston: Notes Toward a Balancing of Love and Hatred', *Black World* (August 1974).
Joyce, James, *Ulysses* (Harmondsworth: Penguin, 1986).
—— *A Portrait of the Artist as a Young Man* (Harmondsworth: Penguin, 1992).
Kaes, Anton, *From Hitler to Heimat: The Return of History as Film* (Cambridge, MA: Harvard University Press, 1989).
Kafka, Franz, *The Diaries of Franz Kafka 1910–1923*, ed. Max Brod, trans. Joseph Kresh and Martin Greenberg (Harmondsworth: Penguin, 1972).
—— *America*, trans. Edwin Muir (London: Minerva, 1992).
—— *Letters to Felice*, ed. James Stern and Jurgen Born, trans. James Stern and Elisabeth Duckworth (London: Minerva, 1992).
—— *The Castle*, trans. Willa and Edwin Muir (London: Minerva, 1993).
Karl, Frederick, *Franz Kafka: Representative Man* (New York: Ticknor & Fields, 1991).
Kennedy, Liam, *Susan Sontag: Mind as Passion* (Manchester: Manchester University Press, 1995).
Kenner, Hugh, *Dublin's Joyce* (London: Chatto & Windus, 1955).
Kern, Stephen, *The Culture of Time and Space, 1880–1918* (Cambridge, MA: Harvard University Press, 1983).
Kersnowski, Frank L. and Alice Hughes (eds), *Conversations with Henry Miller* (Jackson, MS: University Press of Mississippi, 1994).
King, Richard H., *A Southern Renaissance: The Cultural Awakening of the American South, 1930–1955* (New York: Oxford University Press, 1980).
Klein, Marcus, *Foreigners: The Making of American Literature, 1900–1940* (Chicago, IL: University of Chicago Press, 1981).
Klein, Naomi, *No Logo* (London: HarperCollins, 2000).
Kolocotroni, Vassiliki *et al.* (eds), *Modernism: An Anthology of Sources and Documents* (Edinburgh: Edinburgh University Press, 1998).
Kontje, Todd, *The German Bildungsroman: History of a National Genre* (Columbia, SC: Cambden House, 1993).

Kracauer, Siegfried, *From Caligari to Hitler: A Psychological History of the German Film* (Princeton, NJ: Princeton University Press, 1947).
Krauss, Rosalind E., *The Originality of the Avant-Garde and Other Modernist Myths* (Cambridge, MA: MIT Press, 1986).
Kristeva, Julia, *Powers of Horror: An Essay on Abjection*, trans. Leon S. Roudiez (New York: Columbia University Press, 1982).
—— *Strangers to Ourselves*, trans. Leon S. Roudiez (New York: Columbia University Press, 1991).
—— *Time and Sense: Proust and the Experience of Literature* (New York: Columbia University Press, 1996).
Kuenzli, Rudolf E. (ed.), *Dada and Surrealist Film* (Cambridge, MA: MIT Press, 1996).
Laidlaw, G. Norman, *Elysian Encounter: Diderot and Gide* (New York: Syracuse University Press, 1963).
Lauretis, Teresa de, *Technologies of Gender* (Santa Cruz, CA: University of California Press, 1987).
Lears, T. J. Jackson, *No Place of Grace: Antimodernism and the Transformation of American Culture, 1880–1920* (Chicago, IL: University of Chicago Press, 1994).
Leavis, F. R., *The Common Pursuit* (Harmondsworth: Penguin, 1962).
—— *The Great Tradition* (Harmondsworth: Penguin, 1993).
Levin, David Michael (ed.), *Modernity and the Hegemony of Vision* (Berkeley, CA: University of California Press, 1993).
Levinas, Emmanuel, *The Levinas Reader*, ed. Seán Hand (Oxford: Basil Blackwell, 1989).
Lewis, Helena, *Dada Turns Red: The Politics of Surrealism* (Edinburgh: Edinburgh University Press, 1990).
Lifton, Robert Jay, *The Protean Self: Human Resilience in an Age of Fragmentation* (New York: Basic Books, 1993).
Lombroso, Cesare, *Man of Genius* (London: Walter Scott, 1891).
—— 'Atavism and Evolution', *Contemporary Review*, 68 (1895), 42–9.
Lombroso Ferrero, Gina, *Criminal Man* (New York: Putnam's, 1911).
London, John, *The Unknown Federico García Lorca*, trans. John London (London: Atlas, 1996).
Lorca, Federico García, *Selected Letters*, ed. and trans. David Gershator (London: Marion Boyars, 1984).
—— *Poet in New York*, ed. Christopher Maurer, trans. Greg Simon and Stephen F. White (Harmondsworth: Penguin, 1990).
—— *Selected Poems*, ed. and trans. Merryn Williams (Newcastle: Bloodaxe, 1992).
Love, Myra N., *Christa Wolf: Literature and the Conscience of History* (Berlin: Peter Lang, 1991).
Luft, David, *Robert Musil and the Crisis of European Culture 1880–1942* (Berkeley, CA: University of California Press, 1990).
Lukács, Georg, *The Meaning of Contemporary Realism* (London: Merlin, 1963).
Lyotard, Jean-François, *The Inhuman*, trans. Geoffrey Bennington and Rachel Bowlby (Cambridge: Polity Press, 1991).
McGinn, Colin, *Ethics, Evil, and Fiction* (Oxford: Clarendon Press, 1997).
MacIntyre, Alasdair, *After Virtue: A Study in Moral Theory*, 2nd edn (London: Duckworth, 1985).

Mallarmé, Stéphane, *Mallarmé: Selected Prose Poems, Essays and Letters*, trans. Bradford Cook (Baltimore, MD: Johns Hopkins University Press, 1956).
Mangan, J. A. and James Walvin (eds), *Manliness and Morality: Middle-Class Masculinity in Britain and America, 1800–1940* (Manchester: Manchester University Press, 1987).
Mann, Erika and Klaus Mann, *The Other Germany* (New York: Modern Age, 1940).
Mann, Klaus, *The Turning Point: Thirty-Five Years in this Century: The Autobiography of Klaus Mann* (London: Oswald Wolff, 1984).
—— *The Turning Point: The Autobiography of Klaus Mann* (London: Serpent's Tail, 1987).
—— *Mephisto*, trans. Robin Smith (Harmondsworth: Penguin, 1995).
Mann, Klaus and Hermann Kesten (eds), *Heart of Europe: An Anthology of Creative Writing in Europe, 1920–1940* (New York: L. B. Fischer, 1943).
Mann, Thomas, *Confessions of Felix Krull, Confidence Man*, trans. Denver Lindley (Harmondsworth: Penguin, 1958).
—— *The Magic Mountain*, trans. H. T. Lowe Porter (Harmondsworth: Penguin, 1960).
—— *Briefe I* (Frankfurt: S. Fischer, 1961).
—— *The Letters of Thomas Mann*, trans. Richard and Clara Winston (Harmondsworth: Penguin, 1975).
—— *Mario and the Magician and Other Stories*, trans. H. T. Lowe-Porter (Harmondsworth: Penguin, 1975).
—— *Der Tod in Venedig und andere Erzählungen* (Frankfurt: Fischer, 1990).
—— *Death in Venice and Other Stories*, trans. David Luke (London: Minerva, 1996).
Mannheim, Michael, *The Cambridge Companion to Eugene O'Neill* (Cambridge: Cambridge University Press, 1998).
Marchand, Ernest, *Frank Norris: A Study* (Stanford, CA: Stanford University Press, 1942).
Marlowe, Christopher, *The Tragical History of the Life and Death of Dr. Faustus*, ed. John Jump (London: Methuen, 1981).
Matthews, J. H., *Surrealism and the Novel* (Ann Arbor, MI: University of Michigan Press, 1966).
May, Henry F., *The End of American Innocence: A Study of the First Years of Our Own Time, 1912–1917* (New York: Knopf, 1959).
Melling, Philip H., 'Samples of Horizon: Picaresque Patterns in the Thirties', in Stephen W. Baskerville and Ralph Miller (eds), *Nothing Else to Fear: New Perspectives on America in the Thirties* (Manchester: Manchester University Press, 1985), pp. 104–31.
Meriwether, James B. and Michael Millgate (eds), *Lion in the Garden: Interviews with William Faulkner* (New York: Random House, 1968).
Midgley, David, *Writing Weimar: Critical Realism in German Literature, 1918–1933* (Oxford: Oxford University Press, 2000).
Miles, David, 'The Picaro's Journey to the Confessional: The Changing Image of the Hero in the German Bildungsroman', *PMLA*, 89 (1974), 980–92.
Millard, Kenneth, *Contemporary American Fiction* (Oxford: Oxford University Press, 2000).
Miller, Henry, 'Encounter with Rank', *Journal of the Otto Rank Association*, 1:1

(Fall 1966), 57–65.
—— *The Henry Miller Reader*, ed. Lawrence Durrell (New York: New Directions, 1969).
—— *Tropic of Cancer* (London: Flamingo, 1993).
—— *Tropic of Capricorn* (London: Flamingo, 1993).
Miller, J. Hillis, *The Ethics of Reading* (New York: Columbia University Press, 1987).
Millett, Kate, *Sexual Politics* (London: Virago, 1977).
Minden, Michael (ed.), *Thomas Mann* (London: Longman, 1995).
Minter, David, *A Cultural History of the American Novel: Henry James to William Faulkner* (Cambridge: Cambridge University Press, 1996).
Mirzoeff, Nikolas, *An Introduction to Visual Culture* (London: Routledge, 1999).
Monas, Sidney, 'Across the Threshold: *The Idiot* as a Petersburg Tale', in Malcolm Jones and Garth Terry (eds), *New Essays on Dostoyevsky* (Cambridge: Cambridge University Press, 1983), pp. 67–93.
Moran, Joe, *Star Authors: Literary Celebrity in America* (London: Pluto, 2000).
Morley, David and Kuan-Hsing Chen (eds), *Stuart Hall: Critical Dialogues in Cultural Studies* (London: Routledge, 1996).
Motherwell, Robert (ed.), *The Dada Painters and Poets: An Anthology* (New York: George Wittenborn, 1951).
Mühr, Alfred, *Mephisto ohne Maske: Gustaf Gründgens Legende und Wahrheit* (Munich: Langen Müller, 1981).
Musil, Robert, *The Man Without Qualities*, 3 volumes, trans. Eithne Wilkins and Ernest Kaiser (London: Minerva, 1995).
—— *Posthumous Papers of a Living Author*, trans. Peter Wortsman (Harmondsworth: Penguin, 1995).
Naipaul, V. S., *A Bend in the River* (London: André Deutsch, 1979).
Newton, Adam Zachary, *Narrative Ethics* (Cambridge, MA: Harvard University Press, 1997).
—— *Facing Black and Jew: Literature as Public Space in Twentieth-Century America* (Cambridge: Cambridge University Press, 1999).
Nicholls, Peter, *Modernisms* (London: Macmillan, 1995).
Nietzsche, Friedrich, *Twilight of the Idols/The Anti-Christ*, trans. R. J. Hollingdale (Harmondsworth: Penguin, 1990).
—— *Human, All Too Human*, trans. Marion Faber and Stephen Lehmann (Harmondsworth: Penguin, 1994).
Nin, Anaïs, *The Journals of Anaïs Nin, Volume 1: 1931–1934*, ed. Gunther Stuhlmann (London: Peter Owen, 1970).
—— *Anaïs Nin Reader*, ed. Philip K. Jason (Chicago: Swallow, 1973).
—— *Henry and June*, ed. Rupert Pole (Harmondsworth: Penguin, 1990).
—— *A Woman Speaks* (Harmondsworth: Penguin, 1992).
Nordau, Max, *Degeneration* (Lincoln, NB: University of Nebraska Press, 1993).
Norris, Frank, *The Literary Criticism of Frank Norris*, ed. Donald Pizer (Austin, TX: University of Texas Press, 1964).
—— *The Octopus* (Harmondsworth: Penguin, 1994).
—— *McTeague*, 2nd edn, ed. Donald Pizer (New York: Norton, 1997).
Norris, Margot, *Joyce's Web: The Social Unraveling of Modernism* (Austin: University of Texas Press, 1992).
Nussbaum, Martha, *The Therapy of Desire: Theory and the Practice of Hellenistic*

Ethics (Princeton, NJ: Princeton University Press, 1994).
Oliver, Kelly, *Reading Kristeva: Unravelling the Double-Bind* (Bloomington, IN: Indiana University Press, 1993).
Oppenheimer, Helen, *Lorca: The Drawings* (London: Herbert Press, 1986).
Osborne, Peter, *The Politics of Time: Modernity and the Avant-Garde* (London: Verso, 1995).
Painter, George D., *Marcel Proust: A Biography* (London: Pimlico, 1996).
Pater, Walter, *The Renaissance* (Oxford: Oxford University Press, 1986).
Patterson, Michael, *The Revolution in German Theatre 1900–1930* (London: Routledge, 1981).
Payne, Philip, *Robert Musil's 'The Man Without Qualities': A Critical Study* (Cambridge: Cambridge University Press, 1988).
Perry, Ralph Barton, *The Thought and Character of William James*, 2 volumes (Boston, MA: Little, Brown, 1935).
Peters, Frederick, *Robert Musil, Master of the Hovering Life* (New York: Columbia University Press, 1978).
Pizer, Donald (ed.), *The Cambridge Companion to American Realism and Naturalism* (Cambridge: Cambridge University Press, 1995).
—— *American Expatriate Writing and the Paris Moment: Modernism and Place* (Baton Rouge, LA: Louisiana State University Press, 1996).
Poe, Edgar Allan, *Selected Tales*, ed. Julian Symons (Oxford: Oxford University Press, 1980).
Polizzotti, Mark, *Revolution of the Mind: The Life of André Breton* (London: Bloomsbury, 1995).
Pollard, Patrick, *André Gide: Homosexual Moralist* (New Haven, CT: Yale University Press, 1991).
Porter, Roy (ed.), *Rewriting the Self: Histories from the Renaissance to the Present* (London: Routledge, 1997).
Posnock, Ross, 'Henry James, Veblen and Adorno: The Crisis of the Modern Self', *Journal of American Studies*, 21:1 (April 1987), 31–54.
Predmore, Richard L., *Lorca's New York Poetry: Social Injustice, Dark Love, Lost Faith* (Durham, NC: Duke University Press, 1980).
Proust, Marcel, *Against Sainte-Beuve and Other Essays*, trans. John Sturrock (Harmondsworth: Penguin, 1994).
—— *On Reading* (Harmondsworth: Penguin, 1994).
Purdy, Dwight H., '*The Secret Agent*: Under Edwardian Eyes', *Conradian*, 16:2 (1992), 1–17.
Pykett, Lyn (ed.), *Reading* Fin de Siècle *Fictions* (London: Longman, 1996).
Raabe, Paul (ed.), *The Era of German Expressionism* (Woodstock, NY: The Overlook Press, 1985).
Raymond, Marcel, *From Baudelaire to Surrealism* (Paris: José Corti, 1985).
Reich-Ranicki, Marcel, *Thomas Mann and His Family*, trans. Ralph Manheim (London: Collins, 1989).
Remy, Michel, *Surrealism in Britain* (London: Ashgate, 1999).
Rentschler, Eric (ed.), *German Film and Literature: Adaptations and Transformations* (New York: Methuen, 1986).
Rhodes, Colin, *Outsider Art: Spontaneous Alternatives* (London: Thames & Hudson, 2000).
Rich, Adrienne, *Adrienne Rich's Poetry and Prose*, eds Barbara Charlesworth Gelpi

and Albert Gelpi (New York: Norton, 1993).
Richie, Alexandra, *Faust's Metropolis: A History of Berlin* (London: HarperCollins, 1998).
Richter, Hans, *Dada: Art and Anti-Art* (London: Thames & Hudson, 1997).
Ridge, G. R., *The Hero in French Decadent Literature* (Atlanta, GA: University of Georgia Press, 1959).
Roberts, John W., *From Trickster to Badman: The Black Folk Hero in Slavery and Freedom* (Philadelphia, PA: University of Pennsylvania Press, 1989).
Robertson, Ritchie, *Kafka: Judaism, Politics and Literature* (Oxford: Clarendon Press, 1985).
Rorty, Richard, *Contingency, Irony and Solidarity* (Cambridge: Cambridge University Press, 1989).
Rosario, Vernon A., *The Erotic Imagination: French Histories of Perversity* (New York: Oxford University Press, 1997).
Ross, Andrew (ed.), *Universal Abandon?: The Politics of Postmodernism* (Edinburgh: Edinburgh University Press, 1988).
Roth, Henry, *Call It Sleep* (Harmondsworth: Penguin, 1977).
—— *Shifting Landscape* (London: Weidenfeld & Nicolson, 1995).
Roughley, Alan, *James Joyce and Critical Theory: An Introduction* (London: Harvester, 1991).
Ruddick, Lisa, *Reading Gertrude Stein: Body, Text, Gnosis* (Ithaca, NY: Cornell University Press, 1990).
Ruoff, A. LaVonne Brown and Jerry W. Ward (eds), *Redefining American Literary History* (New York: The Modern Language Association of America, 1990).
Rushdie, Salman, *Imaginary Homelands: Essays and Criticism 1981–1991* (London: Granta, 1991).
Ruskin, John, *Unto This Last and Other Writings*, ed. Clive Wilmer (London: Penguin, 1985).
Russell, Alison, 'Deconstructing *The New York Trilogy*: Paul Auster's Anti-Detective Fiction', *Critique*, 31:2 (Winter 1990), 71–84.
Ruthven, K. K., 'The Savage God: Conrad and Lawrence', *Critical Quarterly*, 10 (1968), 39–54.
Said, Edward, *The World, the Text and the Critic* (Cambridge, MA: Harvard University Press, 1983).
Sardar, Ziauddin, *Postmodernism and the Other: The New Imperialism of Western Culture* (London: Pluto Press, 1998).
Satzinger, Christa, *The French Influence on Oscar Wilde's* The Portrait of Dorian Gray *and* Salome (Lewiston, NY: Mellen, 1994).
Saunders, Barbara, *Contemporary German Autobiography: Literary Approaches to the Problem of Identity* (London: University of London, 1985).
Saveson, John, 'Conrad, *Blackwood's* and Lombroso', *Conradiana*, 6:1 (1974), 57–62.
Schnitzler, Arthur, *Dream Story*, trans. J. M. Q. Davies (Harmondsworth: Penguin, 1999).
Shattuck, Roger, *The Banquet Years: The Origins of the Avant-Garde in France, 1885 to World War I* (London: Cape, 1969).
Smail, David, *Illusion and Reality: The Meaning of Anxiety* (London: Dent, 1984).
Smith, Jeanne Rosier, *Writing Tricksters: Mythic Gambols in American Ethnic Literature* (Berkeley, CA: University of California Press, 1997).

Smith, Stan, *A Sadly Contracted Hero: The Comic Self in Post-War American Fiction* (London: British Association of American Studies, 1981).
Sontag, Susan, *Against Interpretation* (New York: Farrar, Straus & Giroux, 1982).
—— *Illness as Metaphor/AIDS and its Metaphors* (Harmondsworth: Penguin, 1991).
Spangenberg, Eberhard, *Karriere eines Romans: Mephisto, Klaus Mann and Gustaf Gründgens* (Munich: Ellermann, 1982).
Spector, Jack J., *Surrealist Art and Writing, 1919/39* (Cambridge: Cambridge University Press, 1997).
Spilka, Mark, *Dickens and Kafka: A Mutual Interpretation* (London: Dobson, 1963).
—— *Hemingway's Quarrel With Androgyny* (Lincoln, NB: University Nebraska Press, 1990).
Spittles, Brian, *Joseph Conrad* (London: Macmillan, 1992).
Sprinker, Michael (ed.), *Edward Said: A Critical Reader* (Oxford: Basil Blackwell, 1992).
Stainton, Leslie, *Lorca: A Dream of Life* (London: Bloomsbury, 1998).
Stearns, Harold, *America and the Young Intellectual* (Westport, CT: Greenwood Press, 1921).
Stedman, T. L. (ed.), *Twentieth Century Practice: An International Encyclopædia of Modern Medical Science*, volume 12 (London: Sampson Low, Marston, 1897).
Stein, Gertrude, *The Autobiography of Alice B. Toklas* (Harmondsworth: Penguin, 1966).
—— *Writing and Lectures (1911–1945)*, ed. Peter Meyerowitz (London: Peter Owen, 1967).
—— *Three Lives* (Harmondsworth: Penguin, 1990).
—— *A Stein Reader*, ed. Ulla E. Dydo (Evanston, IL: Northwestern University Press, 1993).
Stern, J. P., *The Heart of Europe: Essays on Literature and Ideology* (Oxford: Basil Blackwell, 1992).
Symons, Arthur, *Selected Writings*, ed. Roger Holdsworth (Manchester: Carcanet, 1989).
Talbot, Eugene S., *Degeneracy: Its Causes, Signs and Results* (London: Walter Scott, 1898).
Tashjian, Dickran, *A Boatload of Madmen: Surrealism and the American Avant-Garde, 1920–1950* (New York: Thames & Hudson, 1995).
Taylor, Charles, *The Ethics of Authenticity* (Cambridge, MA: Harvard University Press, 1991).
Timms, Edward, *Karl Kraus, Apocalyptic Saint: Culture and Catastrophe in Habsburg Vienna* (New Haven, CT: Yale University Press, 1986).
Townsend, Kim, *Manhood at Harvard: William James and Others* (Cambridge, MA: Harvard University Press, 1996).
Travers, Martin, *Thomas Mann* (New York: St Martin's Press, 1992).
Tzara, Tristan, *Seven Dada Manifestos and Lampisteries*, trans. Barbara Wright (London: John Calder, 1977).
Walcutt, Charles, *American Literary Naturalism: A Divided Stream* (Minneapolis, MN: University of Minnesota Press, 1956).
Walker, David H. (ed.), *André Gide* (London: Longman, 1996).
Walker, Jayne, *The Making of a Modernist: Gertrude Stein from* Three Lives *to* Tender Buttons (Amherst, MA: University of Massachusetts Press, 1984).

Watson, Steven, *Strange Bedfellows: The First American Avant-Garde* (New York: Abbeville, 1991).
Watt, Ian, *Myths of Modern Individualism: Faust, Don Quixote, Don Juan and Robinson Crusoe* (Cambridge: Cambridge University Press, 1997).
Watts, C. T. (ed.), *Letters to R. B. Cunninghame Graham* (Cambridge: Cambridge University Press, 1969).
Waugh, Patricia, *Practising Postmodernism/Reading Modernism* (London: Edward Arnold, 1992).
Weinstein, Norman, *Gertrude Stein and the Literature of Modern Consciousness* (New York: Ungar, 1970).
Wellek, René, 'Literary Criticism and Philosophy', *Scrutiny*, 5: 4 (1937), 375–83.
Wharton, Edith, 'Visibility in Fiction', *Life and Letters*, 2:11 (April 1929), 263–72.
—— *Ethan Frome*, eds Kristin O. Lauer and Cynthia Griffin Wolff (New York: Norton, 1995).
—— *The Uncollected Critical Writings*, ed. Frederick Wegener (Princeton, NJ: Princeton University Press, 1996).
Wickes, George (ed.), *Henry Miller and James Laughlin: Selected Letters* (London: Constable, 1996).
Wilde, Oscar, *The Picture of Dorian Gray* (Harmondsworth: Penguin, 1985).
—— *De Profundis and Other Writings* (Harmondsworth: Penguin, 1986).
—— *The Letters of Oscar Wilde*, (ed.) Rupert Hart-Davis (Oxford: Oxford University Press, 1989).
—— *The Complete Works* (London: HarperCollins, 1994).
Willett, John, *The New Sobriety 1917–1933: Art and Politics in the Weimar Period* (London: Thames & Hudson, 1987).
—— *The Theatre of the Weimar Republic* (New York: Holmes & Meier, 1988).
Williams, Raymond, *The English Novel from Dickens to Lawrence* (London: Chatto & Windus, 1970).
Wineapple, Brenda, *Sister Brother: Gertrude and Leo Stein* (London: Bloomsbury, 1996).
Winston, Richard and Clara Winston (eds), *The Letters of Thomas Mann*, trans. Richard and Clara Winston (Harmondsworth: Penguin, 1975).
Wirth-Nesher, Hana, *City Codes: Reading the Modern Urban Novel* (Cambridge: Cambridge University Press, 1996).
—— (ed.), *New Essays on* Call It Sleep (Cambridge: Cambridge University Press, 1996).
Wolf, Christa, *The Quest for Christa T.*, trans. Christopher Middleton (London: Virago, 1970).
—— *Cassandra: A Novel and Four Essays*, trans. Jan Van Heurck (London: Virago, 1984).
—— *The Writer's Dimension: Selected Essays*, ed. Alexander Stephan, trans. Jan Van Heurck (London: Virago, 1993).
Wollaeger, Mark, *Joseph Conrad and the Fictions of Skepticism* (Stanford, CA: Stanford University Press, 1990).
Wyatt, David (ed.), *New Essays on* The Grapes of Wrath (Cambridge: Cambridge University Press, 1990).
Wysling, Hans (ed.), *Letters of Heinrich and Thomas Mann 1900–1949*, trans. Don Reneau (Berkeley, CA: University of California Press, 1998).

Young, Alan, *Dada and After: Extremist Modernism and English Literature* (Manchester: Manchester University Press, 1981).

Ziarek, Ewa, *The Rhetoric of Failure* (New York: State University of New York Press, 1996).

Zola, Émile, *Thérèse Raquin*, trans. Andrew Rothwell (Oxford: Oxford University Press, 1992).

Zurbrugg, Nicholas, *The Parameters of Postmodernism* (London: Routledge, 1993).

—— *Critical Vices: The Myths of Postmodern Theory* (Amsterdam: G + B Arts, 2000).

Index

abjection 9, 41, 53–78, 190, 193, 195
Adams, Henry 115, 117
Addelson, Kathryn Pyne 3, 210
Adorno, Theodor 11, 18, 199, 210
Amsterdam 180, 238
Anderson, Mark 146, 150, 229
Antin, Mary 147
Aragon, Louis 71, 79, 84–7, 220–1
  The Libertine 85–6
  'A Man' 85–7
  Paris Peasant 86
  Treatise on Style 85
Arendt, Hannah 22, 24–5, 78, 185, 211, 234, 235
Arensberg, Walter 111
Arnold, Matthew 33
Arp, Hans 72
Artaud, Antonin 61, 132, 217
Auden, W. H. 7, 157, 187, 235
Auerbach, Erich 88, 221
Austen, Jane 23
Auster, Paul 10, 200, 203–6, 208, 238
  The Invention of Solitude 203
  Leviathan 203–4
  Mr Vertigo 203
  New York Trilogy 203–4
avant-garde *see* Dadaism *and* Surrealism

Bakunin, Mikhail 86
Ball, Hugo 72–3, 75, 77, 218
Balzac, Honoré de 11, 45
Barnes, Djuna 111
Barthes, Roland 221
Baudelaire, Charles 8, 11, 31–6, 39, 48, 52–3, 70, 77, 86, 210, 212, 213, 216
  Les Fleurs du mal 34, 36, 42
  'The Painter of Modern Life' 11
Bauman, Zygmunt 10, 23–4, 197–9, 207, 210, 212, 237, 238

Beckett, Samuel 16, 75, 157
Bederman, Gail 115, 224
Beer, Gillian 134, 227
Bellow, Saul 200, 237
  Dangling Man 237
Benjamin, Walter 10, 65, 76, 79–80, 84, 182–5, 188, 194–5, 217–18, 219, 234–6
Bentham, Jeremy 13
Bergson, Henri 81, 104, 168, 232
Berlin 74, 180–1, 191, 233
Berman, Marshall 191, 236
Bernstein, Richard 197, 237
Bildungsroman 127, 158, 167, 183, 190, 197
Boulby, Mark 231
Bourne, Randolph 116–9, 224
Bradbury, Malcolm 111, 223, 224
Brecht, Bertolt 10, 157, 179, 282–4, 194, 233, 234
Breton, André 9, 70, 79–87, 111, 118, 123, 148, 218–20
  Communicating Vessels 82–4
  The Immaculate Conception 84
  Mad Love 82–4, 86
  Nadja 82–3, 86
Broch, Hermann 192
Brod, Max 148, 152, 229
Brooker, Peter 136
Buñuel, Luis 148
Burgin, Victor 134, 227
Burrows, Stuart 55, 216
Burwell, Rose 126, 226

Camus, Albert 157, 159
  The Outsider 157
Cannon, Kelly 113, 223
Carlyle, Thomas 33, 162
Cavell, Stanley 23, 25–6, 197, 211, 212, 237
Caws, Mary Ann 220–1
Cela, Camilo José 157, 230
  The Family of Pascal Duarte 230

Céline, Louis-Ferdinand   61
Cézanne, Paul   113, 121
Chambers, Iain   112, 117, 223
Charvet, P. E.   33, 212
Chase, Richard   39, 214
Chekhov, Anton   14, 164
Chernyshevsky, Nikolai   13–14, 75
Chicago   40–1, 113, 142
Chopin, Kate   122
Clayton, Jack   14, 211
Clifford, James   133, 227
Conan Doyle, Arthur   38
Conrad, Joseph   9, 23, 89–102, 104, 161, 164, 176, 221–3
   Heart of Darkness   90, 93–4, 161
   The Secret Agent   9, 89–102, 104, 107, 164
Cooper, James Fenimore   146, 169
Copjec, Joan   160, 230
Corlett, William   199, 237
Cowley, Malcolm   113, 125, 224, 225, 226
Crane, Stephen   40, 44, 214
   'The Open Boat'   44
Critchley, Simon   23, 211
Cullen, Countee   111

Dadaism   2, 8, 69–81, 84, 87, 96, 120, 122, 125, 129, 200, 218
Dalí, Salvador   138
Darwinism   11, 29, 42, 92, 94, 115, 134
de Botton, Alain   4, 210
decadence   7–8, 29–40, 48–70, 73, 76, 78
deconstruction   24–5
Defoe, Daniel   158
degeneration   30, 93–5, 99–101, 103
DeKoven, Marianne   122, 225
de Man, Paul   25
Derrida, Jacques   25
Desnos, Robert   82
Dickens, Charles   11, 45, 89, 229
Disraeli, Benjamin   91
dissidence   53, 160, 180, 213
Dobrolyubov, Nikolai   13
Doctorow, E. L.   200
   The Book of Daniel   200
Dodge, Mabel   111

Dollimore, Jonathan   35, 37–8, 53, 64, 213, 217
Dos Passos, John   49, 116, 157, 171
   Manhattan Transfer   49
   U.S.A.   171
Dostoevsky, Fyodor   13–16, 20, 25, 61, 75, 82, 90, 92, 95, 99, 136, 161–2, 197, 210–11
   The Devils   92
   The Idiot   15, 92, 161
   Notes from Underground   13–16, 20, 136, 162, 197
Douglas, Ann   114, 223, 224
Douglas, Mary   57
Dreiser, Theodore   40, 120
Duchamp, Marcel   76

Eaglestone, Roger   23, 211, 237
Eisenstein, Sergei   78
Eliot, George   23, 32, 88, 221
   Middlemarch   88
Eliot, T. S.   3, 7, 14, 23, 48, 94, 140, 147, 164, 174, 192
   'The Love Song of J. Alfred Prufrock'   48
   The Waste Land   136, 140, 174
Eluard, Paul   74, 81, 86, 220
Emerson, Ralph Waldo   112, 134, 162, 227
Enlightenment   12, 18, 137
ethics (versus morality)   3, 18, 24, 198
Erdrich, Louise   208
evil   7, 43–4, 160–2, 166, 177, 181, 190
exile   137, 151, 176, 180, 191, 193
expatriation   7, 9, 113, 123, 125, 127, 132, 137, 167, 170, 177, 200
Expressionism   18, 190

Farrell, James T.   158
Faulkner, William   9, 46, 69, 89–90, 97, 102–7, 111, 157, 170, 223
   As I Lay Dying   170
   The Sound and the Fury   9, 89–90, 97, 102–7
Felski, Rita   119, 225
Fiedler, Leslie   137, 227

Fitzgerald, F. Scott 69, 114, 126
  'Babylon Revisited' 114
Flaubert, Gustave 34, 45, 120–1
  Madame Bovary 34, 42
  Three Tales 120
Foucault, Michel 10, 53, 84, 205–7, 216, 217, 238
Franklin, Benjamin 12, 32, 146
French feminism 7, 9, 113, 117
Freud, Sigmund 136, 168, 216, 232
Fukuyama, Francis 206, 208, 238
Fuller, Margaret 117

Galsworthy, John 91–2
Gambrell, Alice 112, 124, 223, 225
Garvey, Marcus 145
Gaskell, Elizabeth 89
Gibson, Andrew 90, 94, 221, 222
Gide, André 8, 49–65, 77–8, 83–4, 129, 185, 215–17, 233
  The Counterfeiters 50
  The Immoralist 8, 49–65, 129, 167
  Strait is the Gate 50
  The Vatican Cellars 78
Gilman, Charlotte Perkins 117, 122
Gilman, Sander 222
Gilroy, Paul 113
Goebbels, Josef 180, 183, 189
Goethe, Johann Wolfgang von 50, 181, 191, 193–4, 215
  Elective Affinities 50
  Faust (Part I), 181, 191, 193–4
Gold, Michael 174
  Jews Without Money 174
Goldman, Emma 72
Göring, Hermann 181, 183, 189, 193–4
Gorky, Maxim 136
Gründgens, Gustaf 181, 189, 234
Guerard, Albert 49–50, 215, 216

Habermas, Jürgen 10, 17–18, 82, 199, 202, 206, 237
Hall, Stuart 209, 238
Hamburg 180, 236
Hamsum, Knut 136
  Hunger 136
Hansen, Arlen 113, 224

Hardy, Thomas 1–2, 21, 46, 196–8, 210, 237
  Jude the Obscure 196–8
  A Pair of Blue Eyes 210
  Tess of the D'Urbervilles 1–4, 21, 196–7
Harvey, David 70, 218
Hašek, Jaroslav 157
Hawthorne, Nathaniel 40, 112
Heilbut, Anthony 50, 215
Hemingway, Ernest 9, 111–14, 116–17, 119, 123–7, 129, 132, 147, 214–16
  The Garden of Eden 126
  A Moveable Feast 224
  The Sun Also Rises 113–14, 117, 123–7
  Torrents of Spring 127
Hesse, Herman 10, 157, 159, 162, 166–9, 172, 175, 190, 204, 231–2
  Demian 231
  The Glass Bead Game 231
  Narziss and Goldmund 231
  Steppenwolf 159, 162, 166–9, 172–3, 176–7, 190, 231, 233
Hillis Miller, J. 23–6, 46, 211, 215
Hitler, Adolf 179, 186, 188, 194
Hoffman, E. T. A. 190
Holitscher, Arthur 146
homoeroticism 2, 51, 56, 83
Horkheimer, Max 11, 18, 210
Houston, Elizabeth 189, 236
Howells, William Dean 11, 40–1, 116, 170, 214
Huelsenbeck, Richard 71–8, 179, 218–19
Hughes, Langston 111, 143, 171, 179
Hunter, Allan 96, 222
Hurston, Zora Neale 3, 10, 157, 159, 170–5, 179, 232
  'Characteristics of Negro Expression' 172
  Go Gator and Muddy the Water 171
  'How It Feels To Be Coloured Me' 172, 174
  Mules and Men 171–2
  Tell My Horse 171

Hurston, Zora Neale – *continued*
  Their Eyes Were Watching God
    159, 171–5, 177
Hutcheon, Linda 95, 222
Huysmans, Joris Karl 2, 8, 29, 31,
    35–7, 48, 57, 70, 212, 213, 214
  Against Nature 8, 29, 35–8, 42
Huyssen, Andreas 235

Ibsen, Henrik 179
idiocy 9, 89, 92–107
Ignatieff, Michael 4–6, 26, 204,
    210
Impressionism 33, 121, 138
Ionesco, Eugene 20–2, 25, 75, 159,
    211
  Rhinoceros 20–2, 159
Irigaray, Luce 9, 113, 117–20, 122,
    126, 131–2, 202, 224–7
Iser, Wolfgang 104, 168, 223, 232

James, Henry 7, 23, 32, 40–1, 45,
    48, 88–90, 112, 115, 212, 224
  The Ambassadors 112
  The American 147
  'The Beast in the Jungle' 48
  The Bostonians 115
  The Golden Bowl 88
James, William 25, 113, 115, 121,
    133–6, 138, 141, 145, 161–2,
    225, 227
Jameson, Fredric 19, 211
Janco, Marcel 72
Jannings, Emil 190
Jay, Mike 4, 210
Jehlen, Myra 102, 223
Johnson, Samuel 12
Johnston, David 143, 228
Jordan, June 172, 232
Joyce, James 2, 4, 14, 19, 47, 49, 65,
    69, 82, 111, 136, 157, 164, 174,
    192, 206, 210
  Dubliners 47
  *A Portrait of the Artist as a Young
    Man* 4, 49
  Ulysses 4, 164, 174, 176
Jung, Carl 136, 166

Kaes, Anton 233

Kafka, Franz 9, 61, 75, 111, 136–7,
    146–52, 159, 161, 175, 186,
    197–8, 201, 203, 229–30, 237
  America 9, 136–7, 146–53, 159,
    203
  'Metamorphosis' 77, 149
  The Trial 149, 161
Kant, Immanuel 17, 19, 25, 34, 77,
    134, 160–1, 227
Karl, Frederick 148
Kern, Stephen 11, 210
Kerr, Walter 21
King, Richard H. 223
Klein, Melanie 105, 223
Klein, Naomi 10, 206–8, 238
Kracauer, Siegfried 190, 236
Kraus, Karl 163, 230–1
Kristeva, Julia 8, 51, 54–5, 57–61,
    63–5, 215–17
Kuenzli, Rudolf 87
Kundera, Milan 200

Lacan, Jacques 58–9, 80, 123
Laidlaw, G. Norman 52, 216
Lang, Fritz (M) 181
Laughlin, James 128
Lawrence, D. H. 23, 94
Leavis, F. R. 22–4, 212
Lehan, Richard 30, 212
Levinas, Emmanuel 146, 229, 233
Lewis, Helena 74, 219
Locke, Alain 171
Lombroso, Cesare 89, 92–8, 101,
    164
London 91, 94–5, 101, 111
Lorca, Federico García 9, 111,
    136–48, 152, 227–30
  'A Poet in New York' 141, 145
  Poet in New York 136–47, 152
  'Thoughts on Modern Art' 138
Love, Myra 201–2, 237
Löwy, Michael 146, 149, 229
Luft, Friedrich 181
Lukács, Georg 17–19, 70, 197, 211
Lynch, Carlos Morla 139

Mallarmé, Stéphane 70–1, 77, 218
Mann, Erika 181, 186–7, 234
Mann, Heinrich 182, 234

Mann, Heinrich – *continued*
  Small Town Tyrant/The Blue Angel 182
Mann, Klaus 10, 157, 179–95, 223–6
  Anya and Esther 181
  Mephisto 10, 137, 179–84, 186–95
  The Turning Point 181, 185, 193
Mann, Thomas 2, 3, 8, 10, 18, 49–65, 77, 83, 92, 157, 159–61, 180, 184, 186–9, 194, 201, 204, 215–7, 230, 232, 235–6
  Confessions of Felix Krull, Confidence Man 50, 159–61, 164, 232
  Death in Venice 8, 49–65, 182–3
  'Mario and the Magician' 10, 180, 184, 187–8
  The Magic Mountain 56, 188
  'Tonio Kröger' 51
Mansfield, June 131–2
Marinetti, Filippo 73, 179
Marlowe, Christopher 191–2, 236
Matisse, Henri 113
May, Henry 116, 224
May, Karl 146
McCabe, Colin 16, 211
McCarthy, Joseph 200
McGinn, Colin 5, 18, 26, 39, 210, 211, 212, 214
McIntyre, Alasdair 197, 208, 238
Melling, Philip 159, 170, 230, 232
Melville, Herman 40, 112
Mill, John Stuart 13
Miller, Arthur 200
  The Crucible 200
Miller, Henry 9, 111, 113, 117, 119, 127–32, 157, 159, 224, 226
  Tropic of Cancer 113–14, 128–30, 159
  Tropic of Capricorn 129
Millett, Kate 129, 226
Miró, Joan 138
Mizejewski, Linda 122, 225
modernisation (defined) 10–11
modernism (defined) 12
modernity (defined) 11–12
morality (versus ethics) 3, 18, 24, 198
  amorality 7, 70, 71, 169, 184
  demoralisation 31, 35, 37, 39–40, 44–5, 47, 62, 64–5, 82, 197
  immorality 7, 30, 42, 45, 55, 63, 72, 74, 125
  moral agency 203–7
  moralism 8, 12, 41
  moral law 30, 162, 198
  moral value 1, 3, 19, 24, 77, 83, 174, 209
  universal morality 4–5, 115
Monet, Claude 138
Moran, Joe 125, 226
Motherwell, Robert 70, 74, 122, 218–9, 225, 233
Moureau, Gustave 36
Mukherjee, Bharati 208
Murnau, F. W. (*Faust*) 190, 194
Musil, Robert 3, 10, 17, 18, 136, 157, 159, 161–6, 172, 175, 181, 197–8, 210, 211, 230–1, 234, 237
  The Man Without Qualities 3, 17, 159, 162–6, 169, 172–4, 177, 197–8
  Young Törless 163
Mussolini, Benito 179
Müthel, Lother 181

Nabokov, Vladimir 16, 237
Nagel, James 126, 226
Naipaul, V. S. 161, 230
  A Bend in the River 161
Napolean Bonaparte 93
naturalism 7–8, 29–31, 29–49, 54, 72, 90, 103, 120–1, 179, 185, 197
Nazism 180–4, 186, 188, 193–4, 233
Neve, Michael 4, 210
Newton, Adam Zachary 175, 177, 233
New York City 9, 71–2, 111–12, 116, 136–53, 171, 229
Nicholls, Peter 7, 16, 72, 210, 211, 218
Nietzsche, Friedrich 37, 50, 55, 75–7, 128, 134–6, 166, 219
Nin, Anaïs 9, 111, 113–14, 117, 127, 130–2, 164, 179, 226–7
  The Journals, Volume 1 130–2
  Henry and June 131

Nin, Anaïs – *continued*
  The Novel of the Future 226
Nordau, Max 30, 212
Norris, Frank 8, 30, 31, 40–5, 48, 72, 103, 120, 165, 197, 214
  McTeague 30, 41–5, 48, 54, 103–4, 120–1, 165, 197
  The Octopus 41
  The Pit 41
  'The Responsibilities of the Novelist' 41
  'Zola as a Romantic Writer' 40

O'Neill, Eugene 179, 233
Ophüls, Max (*Liebelei*) 181, 233
Oppenheimer, Helen 142, 228
Osborne, Peter 70, 74, 185, 199, 218, 237

Pamplona 124
Paris 9, 12, 36–7, 42, 72, 74, 79, 111–14, 119–20, 122–32, 137, 191, 224, 229
Pater, Walter 33, 69, 76, 81, 217, 219
perverse, the 8, 31, 30–9, 44, 48, 132
Picabia, Francis 72
picaresque 7, 10, 50, 128, 158–78, 180, 203, 230
Picasso, Pablo 113, 121, 38
Pizer, Donald 41–2, 128, 132, 212, 214, 224, 226
Plato 63
Poe, Edgar Allan 8, 31–4, 36, 38, 86, 190, 203, 212–3
  'The Imp of the Perverse' 31, 36
  The Narrative of Arthur Gordon Pym 36
  'The Poetic Principle' 32
Poradowska, Marguerite 93
postmodernism 10, 19, 201, 204, 206
Pound, Ezra 3, 111, 147
pragmatism 25, 162
primitivism 94, 115, 120–7, 143
Proust, Marcel 2, 8, 31, 33–5, 39, 48, 61, 69, 105, 185, 213, 215
  'John Ruskin' 33
  'On Reading' 33–5

psychoanalysis 7, 58, 81, 105
Purdy, Dwight 221

Rank, Otto 127, 131, 164
realism 1, 16, 29, 32, 40–2, 45, 88–9, 157–8, 168
Reich-Ranicki, Marcel 181, 189–90, 234, 236
Reinhardt, Max 186
Reiss, Curt 189
Remy, Michel 82, 220
Renoir, Pierre Auguste 138
Rhodes, Colin 209, 239
Ricard, Samuel 206
Rich, Adrienne 208, 238
Richie, Alexandra 233
Richter, Hans 73, 219
Romanticism 8, 9, 30, 40–2, 47, 57, 60, 70, 78, 80–1, 102, 107, 118, 128, 133–4, 141, 162, 169
Roosevelt, Theodore 114–15, 119, 129
Rorty, Richard 134–6, 227
Roth, Henry 10, 147, 157, 159, 170–1, 174–7, 233, 237
  Call It Sleep 147, 159, 171, 174–8, 233
  'If We Have Bacon' 233
Rousseau, Jean-Jacques 90
Royce, Josiah 116
Rushdie, Salman 208
Ruskin, John 33–4, 177, 213
Rye, Stellan (*Student of Prague*) 190

Said, Edward 137, 227
Sand, George 32
Sandburg, Carl 142, 228
San Francisco 30, 41–2, 48
Saussure, Ferdinand de 97
Schlüsselroman 180, 182
Schnitzler, Arthur 49
  Dream Story 49
Schopenhauer, Arthur 160–1, 166
Schwitters, Kurt 73, 218
Scott, Walter 18, 103
Seymour-Smith, Martin 92
Shakespeare, William 1
Simmel, Georg 139

Sollier, Paul   221
Sontag, Susan   57, 83, 216, 217, 219, 220
Soupault, Philippe   79
Spangenberg, Eberhard   234
Spilka, Mark   126, 226
Spittles, Brian   91, 221
Stearns, Harold   225–6
Stein, Gertrude   2, 19, 71, 104, 111–13, 116–17, 120–3, 126–7, 130, 132, 147, 157, 218, 224–6
  The Autobiography of Alice B. Toklas   122
  'Composition as Explanation'   122
  'Geography'   113, 118
  'Identity: A Poem'   123
  The Making of Americans   121
  'Tender Buttons'   117, 121–3
  Three Lives   120–2, 130
Stein, Leo   116
Steinbeck, John   157, 161, 170, 175
  The Grapes of Wrath   170
  In Dubious Battle   170
  Of Mice and Men   161
Stevenson, Randall   16, 211
Stieglitz, Alfred   71–2, 111, 116, 224
Strindberg, August   179
Surrealism   8, 62, 69–71, 79–87, 148, 175
Symbolism   69–71, 75, 77, 82, 87–8, 175
Symons, Arthur   69, 218
Szabó, István (*Mephisto*)   194–5

Tabbert, Christa   201
Talbot, Eugene S.   222
Taylor, Frederick   146
Thoreau, Henry David   25
Tolstoy, Leo   18
Townsend, Kim   114, 224
trickery   2, 9, 50, 157, 161–2, 178, 180, 182, 188
trickster, the   164–5, 171–3, 183
Trilling, Lionel   47–8, 215
Tschink, Cajetan   183
Turgenev, Ivan   32
Turner, Frederick Jackson   114
Turner, Joseph   33

Twain, Mark   112, 169
  The Adventures of Huckleberry Finn   158
  The Innocents Abroad   147
Tzara, Tristan   70–9, 96, 218–19

Venice   55–7, 59, 62
Vienna   162–3

Watt, Ian   191, 236
Waugh, Patricia   94, 222
Weber, Max   17–18
Wegener, Paul   190
Weinstein, Norman   123, 225
Wellek, René   23, 212
Welles, Orson (*Citizen Kane*)   179
Wells, H. G.   90
West, Nathanael   158, 170
Wharton, Edith   8, 31, 45–8, 72, 124, 214, 215
  The Age of Innocence   45
  Ethan Frome   45–8, 54, 121, 124
  'Fiction and Criticism'   45
  Summer   46
  'Visibility in Fiction'   45
Whibley, Charles   38, 213
Whistler, James   112
Whitman, Walt   141
Wilde, Oscar   8, 29, 31, 35, 37–9, 48, 54, 64, 190, 212, 213
  'The Decay of Lying'   37
  The Picture of Dorian Gray   8, 29–30, 38–9, 160, 190
Williams, Raymond   89, 221
Wolf, Christa   10, 200–4, 206, 208–9, 238–9
  Cassandra   201–2
  Divided Heaven   201
  The Quest for Christa T.   200–2
  'The Reader and the Writer'   202
  What Remains   202
Wood, Michael   2, 4, 210
Woolf, Michael   128, 226
Woolf, Virginia   88, 105, 122, 157, 179, 227
  To the Lighthouse   136
Wordsworth, William   90
Wright, Richard   170
Wyatt, David   232

Young, Alan 218

Ziarek, Ewa 23, 211

Zola, Émile 30–1, 42, 85, 103, 214
   Thérèse Raquin 30, 42, 85
Zurbrugg, Nicholas 74, 219
Zurich 73–4